Their bicycles powered by Gremlin magic, Rolf and Rita hurtled faster than a racing car straight for the giant rocket, with white security cars trailing along behind them, sirens blaring distantly. Between them and the launch stand were hundreds of people sitting in the press stands.

"How can we get around them?" he asked Baneen.

"Not around, over," puffed the little gremlin, hanging on to the bicycle's handlebars. "Up and away!"

The bicycles soared into the air over a startled group of photographers, who jumped and knocked over each others' tripods. They bounced down on the apron of ground between the viewing stand and the canal of water, about two hundred yards across, that ran by the launch stand. "Up and over!" shouted Baneen. The two bicycles soared up like gliders and rose over the canal.

Rolf closed his eyes. He didn't mind flying in a plane, but in a bicycle . . . ! He felt his bike touch down again, but on something that wasn't quite solid ground. Opening his eyes, Rolf saw that they were pedaling up a wire, with Rita's bike right in front of him. Like circus acrobats, they raced up the steeply angled wire.

Pushing down a lump in his throat, Rolf shouted ahead to Rita, "This is the escape wire—the astronauts use this to slide down from the spacecraft in an emergency."

Rita half-turned to look at him over her shoulder. "I know. Isn't it fun?" She was grinning broadly.

Fun! Rolf felt paralyzed as they raced up the slim strand of wire, and she thought it was fun. *She's got more faith in gremlin magic than I have!*

—from *Gremlins Go Home*

HOUR OF THE
GREMLINS

GORDON R. DICKSON
BEN BOVA

HOUR OF THE GREMLINS

This is a work of fiction. All the characters and events portrayed in this book are fictional, and any resemblance to real people or incidents is purely coincidental.

Gremlins Go Home © 1974 by St. Martin's Press, 1983 by Ben Bova & Gordon R. Dickson; *Hour of the Horde* © 1970 by Gordon R. Dickson; *Wolfling* © 1968 by Gordon R. Dickson.

A Baen Books Original Omnibus

Baen Publishing Enterprises
P.O. Box 1403
Riverdale, NY 10471
www.baen.com

ISBN: 0-7434-8826-1

Cover art by Csanad Novak

First paperback printing, May 2004

Library of Congress Cataloging-in-Publication Number
2002028314

Distributed by Simon & Schuster
1230 Avenue of the Americas
New York, NY 10020

Production by Windhaven Press, Auburn, NH
Printed in the United States of America

Contents

GREMLINS GO HOME

-1-

It was a week before the Mars launch.

THE launch, everybody was calling it around Cape Kennedy.

Big deal! thought Rolf Gunnarson as he opened the garage door. The door slipped out of his hands and rattled noisily up on its tracks, slamming against the end of the tracks with a loud *thump!* For a moment Rolf winced, thinking the noise would wake his baby sister, then he set his jaw. Let it!

Rolf squeezed past his father's white official NASA car to get to his old three-speed bicycle. *So, I don't need a ten-speed, do I?* he muttered to himself. *He's just too busy with his space shot to listen to me. I really need that bike to get back and forth to the Wildlife Refuge. But he doesn't care about the ecology, the Refuge, or anything—except being Launch Director for this Mars flight!*

His face set in an unhappy scowl, Rolf wheeled the three-speed out of the garage and through the half-dozen cars parked along the driveway. Out on the street a big TV truck was parked. Inside the house

3

the TV men were laying cables and setting up lights
and cameras. They were going to interview his father.
THE launch was only a few days away.

"You'd think he was one of them—one of the
astronauts going to Mars," Rolf said to Shep, who
was lying in the shade of the orange tree in the
Gunnarsons' front yard. Shep looked like a ball of
brown and white wool with a red tongue hanging
out.

It was as hot a day as Florida can produce in August.
The sun blazed out of a brilliant blue sky that was
flecked here and there with gleaming white, puffy
clouds. But Rolf couldn't hang around the house any
longer. First it was his father telling him, "Not now,
Rolf! Can't you see I'm busy? After THE launch we'll
talk about it." Then it was the TV crew bustling around
the house, saying, "Hey kid, wouldya mind gettin' outta
the way?"

Rolf whistled for Shep to come along, and started
pedaling for the Merritt Island National Wildlife Refuge. He had been going to stay home from it today.
But now . . .

"I should've brought some lemonade or something,"
he told himself as he pumped along the street, passing the neat little houses with their lawns and flowering bushes and trees.

For a moment he thought about going back, but
then he shook his head. *Maybe I'll never go back,* he
thought grimly, as he turned off the street and headed
for the Old Courtney Pike.

He rode for several miles in silence, with Shep
scampering along beside him. Hot as it was, the speed
of his travel put a breeze in his face and set his
unbuttoned shirt flapping loosely behind him, so that
he felt the air slipping over his bare chest, blowing
out the armholes of his sleeves, like his own personal

air conditioner. *Just like the astronauts,* he thought, picturing in his mind how they must feel inside their air-conditioned space suits.

Riding the bike felt good—even in the heat. Not that any kind of heat could bother Rolf, really. He was used to it. Just like old Shep, looking as woolly as any other English sheepdog anywhere in the world, trotting along beside the bicycle with his red tongue hanging out. Anybody who didn't know better would think Shep was ready to melt. But Rolf knew the sheepdog could keep up with him like this all day. They were both Floridians born and bred. Shep would guess they were headed toward the Wildlife Refuge, a place he liked as well as Rolf did.

Most people didn't even realize that the Refuge existed. All they cared about, like Rolf's dad, was the Space Center part of Cape Kennedy. Actually, the Refuge was almost 85,000 acres in size. That was about ninety-nine percent of all the land the Space Agency owned on the Cape. The launching Center took up the remaining one percent. The Refuge was a haven for birds. Officially there were 224 different species of birds visiting there regularly—although Rolf himself had checked off 284 species last year. And there were the permanent residents, too; tough wild pigs, snakes, bald eagles and even alligators. A good place to get away to, when things at home got to the point where you wanted to kick holes in the wall.

Right now, however, the desire to kick holes in the wall was diminishing in him. As usual, the exercise of the ride and the prospect of getting back to the Refuge were working their good influence on him. Now that he was beginning to feel better, Rolf admitted to himself that it was not really things like not having a ten-speed bike that were bothering him. It was . . . he could not seem to say what it was. Sometimes, when he was away from home, like this, he would make up his mind not to let things get to him when he went home again. But they always did. Or at least, since this summer started, they always did. Remembering the past weeks, Rolf scowled again. Summer vacation was supposed to be something you looked forward to. But nothing seemed to have gone right this year—from his slipping off the diving board and hurting his leg, right up until now. First there had been that accident, then the upset of the house after his baby sister was born. Now THE launch . . .

Busy thinking, he reached the edge of the Refuge almost before he knew it. But then, suddenly, the road was in among the acres of wild land, and he looked around himself feeling good. Most people might have seen nothing much to enjoy. There were only sandy little hillocks covered with coarse grass and scrubby brush, in all directions, with an occasional bigger tree pushing crookedly higher against the glittering sky. But to Rolf it was a remarkable and fascinating place, busy with plant, bird and animal life, all of which were particular friends of his. From the wild sow with her four piglets right now trotting along in plain sight beside the road he was riding, to a brown hen pelican, nesting in a secret pool he knew of, far out among the brush—and who already had lost one of her three eggs because of the thinness of its shell, due to DDT—they were individuals with whom he was concerned.

The sow led her family off back into the brush, and a little farther on Rolf turned his bike from the concrete highway onto the asphalt road that led down in the direction of the Playalinda Beach part of the Refuge. Then, a short distance down the asphalt, he cut off the road entirely and bumped along on one of the old foot trails that wound through the Preserve.

Officially, no one was supposed to be here, right now. That was why he had not planned to come today. Playalinda Beach was officially closed when there was a rocket on the pad at LC-39, as the Mars rocket stood right now.

But who cared? All that the Beach's being closed meant was that nobody else would be around. *And who wants anybody else around?* Rolf asked himself. *It's good to be alone. Nobody here except me and Shep.*

Shep?

Rolf suddenly realized that Shep was no longer trotting beside his bike. By itself that wasn't so odd, since the trail was too narrow in spots to let the bike and the dog go side by side. But in that case, Shep should be right behind him. Rolf glanced back, squinting against the glaring sunshine.

Shep was behind him, all right. But a long way behind. The sheepdog was sitting at the last bend of the trail they had passed, some fifty yards behind Rolf, gazing at him disapprovingly. Rolf braked the bike and stopped. He put his feet down on the sandy ground and half turned around.

"Come on!" yelled. "Shep! Come on!"

Shep didn't move. But he barked—which complicated matters.

Shep wasn't like other dogs, in a number of ways. One of these was the way he barked. He had a gruff voice, to begin with, but there was more to it than that. When most dogs bark they seem to be saying, "Hey, glad to see you!" or "Look out! Warning! Stand back!"

Shep's bark was more like the shout of an angry old gentlemen telling someone to mind his manners. "About time you got here," Shep would seem to say. Or, "Stop that nonsense immediately."

"Rrarhf!" said Shep now. It was exactly as if he had snapped, "Get back here at once!"

"Shep," said Rolf slowly, "I'm in no mood for that today. Do you hear me?"

"Huroof!" said Shep.

"What's wrong with you, anyway?"

"Rharf! Rharf rharuff!"

"Listen, I'm going down this trail whether you like it or not."

"Rruff!"

"Then I'll go by myself!"

"Rrarhr!"

"Suit yourself," said Rolf, turning around and getting the bike started again. "Just go on and suit yourself!"

He rode off. After a few minutes, and a couple of bends of the trail, he caught a flicker of movement out of the corner of his eye and glanced down to see Shep once more pacing beside him.

"Mrrmp," muttered Shep darkly, deep in his woolly throat. But he kept moving alongside the bike. Rolf felt a small twinge of guilt.

"I do things you want to do sometimes, don't I?" Rolf demanded.

Shep was silent now. He trotted along with his black nose in the air. Rolf shrugged and gave up. Shep's reluctance to go down the trail was making Rolf all the more curious to see where it led. He must have been down this trail before, because he had roamed all over the trails in the Playalinda Beach area at one time or another. But just now he couldn't remember when, or which way this particular trail led.

They were mounting a small rise to a sandy top. Nothing could be seen beyond the top of the rise except the hot blue sky. Under Rolf's hard-pumping legs, the bicycle mounted to the crest and then pitched steeply down into a long dip.

Never saw this spot before! Rolf thought.

And it was just as the bike nosed downward that

Shep reached up, clamped his teeth firmly on the ragged edge of the cut-off jeans just above Rolf's knee, and dug all four paws solidly into the ground, putting on the brakes.

It was Rolf's weak leg, the one he had hurt at the pool. The bike skidded wildly, crosswise off the path and started to fall over. Even so, it shouldn't have fallen all the way, since Rolf was an experienced rider. He stuck out his leg to prop up the bike and stop the fall.

But his foot slipped on the sandy soil, his leg buckled, the bike fell, and Rolf went tumbling down the rest of the slope to the bottom of the dip.

"Shep!" he yelled—or tried to yell. Oddly, his voice came out as a small squeak. Furious, Rolf tried to sit up, but he didn't make it even halfway. The dip around him seemed to fill up with a pearly white mist. It was impossible for him to see anything an arm's length away. His head buzzed with a wild dizziness that made it feel as though he were spinning madly.

Rolf collapsed back onto the sand and everything blanked out.

-2-

Rolf gradually drifted back to consciousness.

The hot brilliance of the sun made everything seem red through his closed eyelids. Slowly, the buzz in his head eased off, and in its place he could hear two voices arguing. One voice was very deep-toned and very British in accent. The other was a high-pitched, very Irish tenor.

" . . . beastly fellows!" the deep voice was snorting.

"Ah, there you go again now," retorted the Irish-sounding voice. "Don't you know there's no one speaks like that, these days? Indeed, it's exactly like Dr. Watson with Sherlock Holmes, you sound, and out of a hundred years ago."

"Well you *are* beastly fellows," growled the other voice. "Pack of blackguards! Besides, what d'you mean—talk like a hundred years ago? Speak like any well-brought-up individual of good breeding, if I say it myself."

"That you don't," said the Irish voice, teasingly, "as I've no doubt you well know. It's an entirely artificial way of speech you've got there, copied out of th' late movies you've been watchin' on the TV . . . *yikes!*"

The deep voice growled again, but this time it was a real growl.

"Now, now—no need to be hasty," cried the Irish voice, suddenly seeming to come from a position higher up. "Indeed, no offense meant. None whatsoever, Mr. Sheperton."

Rolf cracked an eyelid open to see what was going on. And immediately wished he hadn't.

He saw Shep, with bared teeth and curled upper lip, staring up at a small bush. Floating slightly above the bush, in midair, was an impossible little man no more than a foot tall, with large pointed ears and big white eyebrows, like wings. He was dressed in a close-fitting, long-sleeved green jacket and tight green pants that ended in small black boots with pointed, curled toes.

And Shep was talking? "TV? Blasted impertinence! Talk the way I do because I am what I am. What if it's a bit old-fashioned? No harm in that."

"None whatsoever, Mr. Sheperton. None at all!" said the little man, still floating above the bush. "It's a darling way of speaking you have, indeed it is, when all's said and done. And if they speak the same way in old movies on the TV, now, why sure it must be that they're trying to catch the proper grand manner of speech belonging to gentlemen such as yourself."

Shep backed off from the bush. His lip uncurled.

Rolf closed his eyes again. It couldn't be—what he thought he was seeing and hearing. Shep talking like a human being and a little man in green answering him? He must have hit his head on a rock when he fell off the bike. . . . There, the voices had stopped. No doubt when he opened his eyes again he would see no one but good old Shep whining like an ordinary dog and trying to lick his face.

But—

"Let's put it out of mind then," said the Irish voice, quite clearly. "Sure and we've much more important matters to discuss, haven't we now?"

Rolf opened both eyes this time. The little man was floating down to the ground at the foot of the bush. Shep had seated himself on his haunches.

"If you mean the boy," Shep said gruffly, "there's nothing for us to discuss. He's my ward, you know. I'll not have him associating with blackguards, will-o-the-wisps—*or* gremlins. And it's a gremlin that you are, in spite of your green suit and green accent. . . . Speaking of the way *I* talk, how about you?"

"Now Mr. Sheperton, now," said the gremlin, or whatever he was, soothingly. "Let's not dig up old bones to pick. . . ."

"Don't know why not," muttered Shep—or Mr. Sheperton, as the gremlin called him. "Many a happy hour I've spent digging . . ."

"I meant only that there's no need for us to argue further on the matter of speech," said the gremlin. "It's the boy we should be talking about. A fine lad—"

"Naturally. Educated him myself," said Mr. Sheperton.

"And indeed it shows. Indeed it does," said the gremlin hastily. "But the point is, the lad's been troubled—there's no denying that."

"Life's not a bed of roses," gruffed Mr. Sheperton. "Have to take the rough with the smooth."

"To be sure. But why take the rough at all, if you may go smooth all the way 'round?"

"Builds character, that's why!" snapped Mr. Sheperton. "See here—whatever you call yourself nowadays—"

"Baneen," said the gremlin.

"See here, Baneen. These are human matters. You

keep your gremlin nose out of them!" Mr. Sheperton
went on. "The boy's had a rough summer. All this interest
of his in wild animals made him feel different from his
friends to begin with. Then, when he tried to get social
again, early this summer, he had the bad luck to crack
his leg going off a diving board—showing off, of course,
but what's the harm in that—and had to spend several
weeks in a cast. Mother busy with an infant sister. Father
all tied up with his work. Left him feeling all on his own,
just when he got all involved in this ecology business and
wanted to start doing something with his life. Very well.
He'll work his way through his problems one way or
another, and I'll thank you not to interfere."

"*You'll* thank me?" piped Baneen, skipping sideways
a few steps before Mr. Sheperton's nose, dancelike
on the curled toes of his boots. "Thank me, will you,
now? And if I'm not to interfere, what is it yourself
is doing?"

"I'm one of the family," growled Mr. Sheperton. "All
the difference in the world."

"Ah, indeed? Indeed? And does that give you the
right to keep the boy from even considering all the fine
help I could be offering?" Rolf's eyes opened wider at
this. "Why, a touch, merely a touch of gremlin magic,
and he'll find the answer to all his problems and dreams
at once. All that in return for just a wee bit of help,
hardly the liftin' of his littlest finger . . ."

Mr. Sheperton growled and got to all four legs.
Baneen leaped backwards a half step and then started
to rise right off the ground. But they were both frozen in their places by a sudden roaring voice:

"BANEEN! AND WHAT ARE YOU UP TO NOW,
ME SLIPPERY LITTLE MAN?" Another gremlin
stepped from behind a bush. "What's going on here?"
he demanded "And who are you, dog?"

"Sheperton. Mr. Sheperton," replied Shep, coldly.

Baneen glided back to the ground and touched down lightly. "Ah there, Lugh, darling," Baneen said, keeping one eye on Shep. "Sure and all, the grim beast would have killed me five times over if it'd not been for your mighty self coming to my rescue. . . ."

"Rescue is it? That depends on what it is that you've been up to," snapped the second gremlin. "Now answer me quick, or I'll be putting you under a spell in a damp cellar for five thousand years—and well, you know I can do it! That or anything else I've a mind to!"

Lying there watching them, Rolf believed the newcomer wholeheartedly. There was something about this gremlin named Lugh that was extremely convincing, although at the same time it was puzzling. Because in an odd way, Lugh seemed to be many times larger and more threatening than he actually was. Rolf squinted at him, wondering if the fall from his bike hadn't done something to his head, after all.

Plainly to view, Lugh was another gremlin like Baneen. Well, not exactly like Baneen. Lugh was half again as tall, wide-shouldered and burly. But it wasn't this alone that made him so impressive—and he *was* impressive indeed.

Somehow, although Rolf's eyes insisted that Lugh was no more than a foot and a half tall, some inner sense saw it differently. Lugh somehow gave the impression of being the size of a professional football player, massive, heavy-jawed, hard-fisted and more than a match for anything on two legs or four.

"Did you hear me, little man?" roared Lugh now, waving a fist under Baneen's nose. "Speak up, or it's down with you to the toads and mushrooms for five thousand years!"

"Whush now," said Baneen, with a slight quaver in his voice. "It's a terrible temper you have, indeed it is. And me only trying to do a bit of good for man, gremlin and beast alike. Ah, the hard misunderstandings that have been the lot of my life! The misunderstandings of those for whom I wished to do the poor best that I could . . ."

"Talk!" said Lugh fiercely.

"And aren't I, after doing that very thing, this moment?" Baneen said quickly. "As my tongue was just now saying, here was I in talk with Mr. Sheperton. . . ."

"Mr. Sheperton?" Lugh blinked, then turned to look at the dog. "Oh yes—Sheperton."

"*Mr.* Sheperton, if you don't mind!" Shep growled dangerously.

"Now, now, let's not be having a misunderstanding," said Baneen hastily, stepping between the sheepdog and Lugh. "Mr. Sheperton it is, indeed—so named by the family of the lad when they brought him home as a wee pup, nearly six long years ago."

Rolf blinked. Slowly, out of far back in his mind, swam up a memory of the day when his father had brought the dog into their house. It was true—the first name they had given to the fuzzy, wobbly-legged puppy stumbling over the kitchen floor had been "Mr. Sheperton." The name had been given because there was something pompous about the plump waddling puppy, even then. Of course, the original name was soon forgotten and shortened to "Shep."

"—and may I present now," Baneen was going on, "himself, Lugh of the Long Hand, Prince of all Gremlins on this chill and watery planet of yours, second to none but His Royal Majesty the King of Gremla Itself—long may its bright clouds of dust blow against the sunset."

Baneen wound up this short speech by blowing his nose sentimentally.

Mr. Sheperton and Lugh grunted ungraciously at each other in acknowledgement of the introduction.

"Prince I am, and don't you forget it," said Lugh, shaking his fist once more at Baneen. "If there's to be any dealings with human beings, I'll be the one to do them. That's understood?"

"To be sure, to be sure," Baneen soothed. "How could you think I'd go and forget such a thing? I was only preparing the matter for your royal attention— it was nothing more than that I had in mind. Why, says I to myself, here's a boy with troubles that a small touch of gremlin magic can mend, a noble dog to be assisted in his wardship of his—"

"Assisted? Who said I needed assistance?" gruffed Mr. Sheperton.

"No one. No one at all, at all. It was only a figure of speech I was making," Baneen went on. "And here we are, exiles from the planet of our birth, the beautiful and dry Gremla, longing for a way to get back to its lovely, dusty caves. Why not put it all together, thought I, and with the noble Lugh of the Long Hand—the darling of all Gremla that was—to oversee, sure the end can be nothing but happiness for all concerned."

"Get to the point, Baneen-og," rumbled Lugh. "You're reaching an end to the tether of my patience."

"There's no more than a word to be said," Baneen answered quickly. "Here we are marooned these thousands of years on this watery planet where the best of gremlin magic can lift us no more than a dozen feet into the air. And over there—" Baneen pointed in the direction of LC-39, "—is a fine big rocket about to go all the way to Mars, next door to Gremla so it is, and here is a boy whose father's work is all with that very rocket—"

A bellow from Lugh stopped him. The large gremlin had glanced at Rolf when he was mentioned by

Baneen, and—too late—Rolf had realized that he was lying there propped up on his elbows, his eyes wide open.

"BY THE GREAT CAIRNGORM OF GREMLA ITSELF!" Lugh roared, striding wrathfully toward Rolf and seeming to grow more gigantic with each step. "You've sprinkled the lad over with Gremladust, Baneen—and that with no permission from anyone, least of all myself! He's been lying here with his eyes open all this time, seeing and hearing and *understanding* every word ourselves and the dog have spoken!"

- 3 -

"Lugh!" yelped Baneen. "You overgrown, great—"

Lugh spun around to face the smaller gremlin, and Baneen's tone changed abruptly, sweetly, "—man of wisdom that you are, now. Surely yourself has figured out that the lad must be able to talk with us and see us, if he's to be the means of aiding our poor friend O'Rigami in his and our time of need."

Lugh, who looked as if he had just been about to leap at Baneen, settled back, frowning, and stroked his chin whiskers.

"Oh?" he said thoughtfully. "O'Rigami, is it now?"

"Who else, and what else would it be? Ah, I see it's yourself has it all figured out already. Here we are, out of the goodness of our green gremlin hearts—"

Mr. Sheperton snorted.

"—the goodness of our hearts, I was saying," Baneen went on blandly, "about to help this lad in his troubles. What more likely, I can see you're thinking, than he'd wish to do us a small favor in return? Sure, and it'd be no more than a second's effort for a bright lad such as himself who's not

18

bothered by cold iron and all the hard things men put about to bar out the likes of us."

"Ah. Hmm . . ." Lugh turned back to scowl thoughtfully at Rolf.

"Come, Lugh!" cried Baneen. "Surely you've got a smile for the young man, after your fearsome looks of a moment ago."

"A . . . smile . . ." muttered Lugh. He made an effort to smile at Rolf. It was about as effective as if a bulldog had tried to simper.

Mr. Sheperton either cleared his throat or growled. It was hard to tell which. "'Ware the gremlin bearing promises," he muttered. "If the Trojans had listened to that advice, they'd have never let that horse inside their gates. . . ."

"Just a minute," Rolf said. He sat up and crossed his legs. He was feeling braver now than he had a few minutes before. Not because of Lugh's smile—a tiger would not have felt much braver after having been smiled at by Lugh—but because something Baneen had said was ringing in his ears. Baneen had hinted that there was something that he, Rolf, could do that not all the gremlins with their obviously magical powers, could do. Rolf wanted to learn just what it was.

"Go on, Baneen," he said. "The least I can do is listen."

"Said the fly to the spider," growled Mr. Sheperton.

"Now, now, it's no spider I am at all!" Baneen snapped. "A wee wisp of a gremlin, that's all, far from the golden sands and stinging winds of my native home, helpless on a stranger shore. And so are we all, young Rolf. Indeed, all the gremlins in exile on watery Earth now cast themselves on your mercy. Only you, Rolf Gunnarson, whose name shall ring down the halls of human and gremlin history (if you so choose) can change the course of fate for men and gremlins and bring us safely back to Gremla."

Rolf's ears grew uncomfortably warm. The little man's grandiloquent words were a bit hard to take. He did not appear to be deliberately making fun of Rolf, but Rolf had become sensitive these last couple of years to what people said to him.

"That's a lot for some stranger to be doing for you, isn't it?" Rolf asked. "After all, I never even heard of your Gremla. In fact, dressed the way you are and everything you two look to me more like—what's the word for them?—leprechauns."

"Well, well, no doubt we do. But what's the matter to that?" said Baneen. "What's in a name? Sure, and if some people want to call us leprechauns, there's no harm done."

"You mean you really are gremlins, but you were just being *called* leprechauns?" demanded Rolf. "But how come then you speak with an Irish accent?"

"Irish accent, indeed!" cried Baneen. "Why, it's a pure and natural gremlin accent you're hearing from hundreds of thousands of years before Ireland rose from the sea. Is it our fault now that the Irish, folk with the fine, musical ear that they have, happened to pick it up from us? In truth, there's no such thing as an Irish accent—it's a gremlin accent you're hearing from them and us alike."

"Likely story!" grumphed Mr. Sheperton. "Rolf—"

"Well, it doesn't matter," said Rolf, quickly before the dog could get started again. "Baneen, you were saying you need help? What is it? What could I do for you?"

"Ah, it's free us from this prison world, you can," Baneen answered. "Set us on our way to home. Oh, to see fair Gremla just once again before . . . before . . ."

He broke down and apparently was unable to go on.

"Why, the dissembling jackanapes!" sputtered Mr. Sheperton. "Rolf, don't be misled and befooled. Like all gremlins, he's immortal. He could spend the next million years here and still go back to his Gremla, fresh as a daisy."

"That's right, now!" said Baneen, weeping openly now and wiping his eyes with his bushy eyebrows. "Reproach me with it, that I'm not mortal. Does that mean that I've no feelings?"

"You hear that, Shep?" said Rolf, embarrassed.

"As long as we're speaking to each other," the dog replied, with great dignity, "I'd prefer that you addressed me by my proper name: Mr. Sheperton."

But Rolf was already saying, "Go on, Baneen. Pay no attention to him. What can I do for you? Anything reasonable I'll be glad to do. Do you need something special so you can get back to Gremla?"

"Well now," said Baneen, suddenly dry-eyed again. "It's a mere handful of something or other we're after needing. Indeed, I don't even know the names of the little things, myself. But I can take you to one who does. The Grand Engineer he is, for our return to Gremla. His name's O'Rigami."

"O'Rigami?" echoed Rolf. The sound of the name was oddly familiar.

"Indeed, that's his very self," Baneen said. "He's that busy a man he can't be coming here to meet you. But if you'll permit me to weave a wee bit of a spell so's you can enter our Gremlin Hollow . . ."

Baneen's fingers were already making strange fluttering passes in the air. Mr. Sheperton began something that might have been the growl of a warning, but it was cut off almost immediately.

Rolf found himself wrapped in a pale yellow glow, like a faintly luminous fog, and gently lifted to his feet by unseen hands. He walked—without consciously directing his feet—further down the path where he had fallen. The ground seemed to go down and down; the wind from the nearby ocean was absolutely still and silent. But all around him, just beyond the fringes of his fog-shrouded vision, Rolf could hear tiny buzzings and murmurings, and an occasionally high-pitched squeaky laugh.

Then the fog seemed to lift a bit, and he saw at his feet another gremlin. He was sitting cross-legged on the sand, head bent over his work. His hands were moving rapidly.

Rolf got down on his knees to see what the gremlin was doing. His tiny fingers were moving with furious speed. But as far as Rolf could see there was nothing in the gremlin's hands. Nothing at all.

The gremlin looked up and saw Rolf watching him. He bowed his head deeply. "Ah, sssooo!" he hissed.

Rolf blinked. This gremlin was as small as Baneen, and even slimmer. He wore a white smock over his green suit and his fingers were extraordinarily long, delicate and supple. They kept moving incredibly fast.

The fog was lifting even more, and beyond the busy gremlin Rolf could see dozens of others swarming about an object that looked—no, it couldn't be. But it was. A kite. A huge paper kite.

Something was happening to Rolf's sense of vision, as far as its real size went. Rolf's eyes and his mind were battling over how large the kite really was. To his eyes, it looked like a regular kite, the kind Rolf himself flew at the beach, but Rolf's mind kept insisting that the kite was as big as a jet airliner. And indeed, there seemed to be room enough on it for hundreds of gremlins. Maybe thousands. Or even more.

He shook his head, as if to clear it.

"Wercome to my modest assembry center," said the white-smocked gremlin.

"Eh . . . hello," Rolf stammered. "You're a gremlin too?"

"Of course! Born and bred on Gremra five-point-three thousands of centuries ago. That is, Earth centuries, of course. The year of Gremra is much different from your own."

"Oh . . . yeah." Rolf felt a bit dazed. "But . . . it's just that—uh—you don't seem to talk with the right accent. . . ."

"*Hai!*" The little gremlin jumped to his feet. "My humbre accent is that of true gremrin attempting to speak your ranguage."

"It sounds Japanese."

"Not so! Honorable Japanese race have acquired accent from gremrins riving amongst them."

"But . . ." Rolf was getting totally confused. "I thought gremlins all talked with an Irish accent, and the Irish . . ."

"Beg to differ . . ."

There was a sudden pop—about as loud as the pop of a cork from a toy gun—and Baneen suddenly appeared beside them.

"Now, now, Rolf me bucko! This is no time to be bothering with trifles of tongue and tone. There's too much to be done!"

Rolf blinked at him.

"Rolf Gunnarson," Baneen went on, without even taking a breath, "may I introduce you to the Great Grand Engineer of All Gremla in Exile—O'Rigami."

O'Rigami hissed and bowed.

Rolf found himself bowing too, even though he was still sitting on his heels on the sand floor of the Gremlin Hollow.

"A small token of my esteem," O'Rigami said gently.

His right hand flickered out. For one astonished moment, Rolf could have sworn that the hand and the arm to which it was attached stretched several feet across the sand to where the other gremlins were working on the kite. Within an eyeblink, O'Rigami's hand and arm had returned to normal, but now there was a small square of paper in front of him.

The square of paper seemed to disappear as O'Rigami's amazing fingers quickly folded it into the shape of a beautiful, tiny swan with outstretched wings. The gremlin held it out in his palm, and the miniature paper swan suddenly fluttered its wings and took off. It flew in a circle around Rolf's head before coming down to land with the lightest of touches on his shoulder.

"A memento in honor of our meeting," O'Rigami said, bowing again.

"That's the neatest thing I ever saw!" Rolf said. He picked the swan from his shoulder and held it in his palm. But it wouldn't fly again; it simply sat there, lovely but unmoving. "How'd you do it?"

"Now that's a question would take too long to answer," said Baneen, at his elbow. "But it's a great and wonderful art, so it is."

O'Rigami lifted a hand modestly. "Merely the apprication of sound techniques of construction," he said, "together with the proper magic formuras."

"It's O'Rigami," said Baneen to Rolf, "who is in charge of constructing the craft which will carry us all safely back to Gremla—with the help of your rocket, of course."

Rolf turned to stare at the gremlin workmen again. "It looks like a kite. . . ."

"And what else would it be, indeed!" said Baneen. "One of the wondrous, great space-going kites of mighty Gremla, such as have explored the very depths

of the universe, sailing before the proud winds of
Gremlin magic in free space unhampered by any nasty
dampness. In such a kite, that very one there, will we
return to Gremla—that is, if all goes well—attached
to your rocket."

He coughed self-consciously.

"But it's pretty big—I mean," Rolf tried to think
of some way of putting it that wouldn't hurt their
feelings. "I don't think something that size can be
attached to the Mars rocket without making it fly
crooked—I mean, even if the launch crew didn't see
it attached to the rocket."

"Of course, now, they won't be seeing it," said Baneen
severely. "It'll be invisible. And as for size, that's no problem either. Haven't we O'Rigami himself here to fold it
so cleverly it'll seem to be no larger than your hand?"

"Fold?" Rolf stared from Baneen to O'Rigami, who
once again politely hissed and bowed. Suddenly Rolf's
mind made the connection it had been trying to make
ever since he had heard Baneen first pronounce the
other gremlin's name. "O'Rigami? Of course! Origami—
I knew I'd heard about it in school! It's the Japanese
art of folding paper. You mean he's learned this Japanese way of folding things so well that he . . ."

O'Rigami shut his eyes and turned his head away.

"Now, now, now!" cried Baneen, each word a note
higher than the one before it. "Watch your tongue, lad,
before you stumble upon an insult and break everything! Is it likely that a gremlin would be needing to
learn anything from humans like yourself, who've
merely been around for fifty thousand years or so? And
O'Rigami himself a respectable half-million in age and
more? It was the humans learned a wee bit of the
noble art from O'Rigami, himself, to be sure—not the
other way around. Indeed, isn't it named after him?"

"Well . . ." said Rolf slowly.

"And is it at all a human name it bears? When did you hear the likes of that from the Japanese islands? *O'Rigami*—why its ring is as pure Gremlin as that of the name of Lugh or Baneen."

"Ummm . . ."

"Tush and tush! Of course not," said Baneen. "Let's say no more on the subject. Indeed, it would be a proud human who'd dare to pretend to the beginnings of a skill like that of O'Rigami."

Baneen hooked a finger in the lowest buttonhole of Rolf's shirt and led him aside. The gremlin lowered his voice, almost whispering in Rolf's ear.

"A word to the wise—I'd watch your tongue, lad. There's nothing our Grand Engineer can't fold if he wishes. Rub him the wrong way and no telling what he'll do. How would you like Cape Kennedy folded into a flower pot? Or yourself into a postage stamp?"

Rolf's eyes widened. But before he could think of an answer, there was a shimmer in the air beside Baneen and the figure of a female gremlin with a pert, but sad, face and dressed in flowing green robes with a band of black around her left arm, took shape beside them.

"Ah, zair you are, Baneen," she said, in a soft, melancholy voice. "Sorrow and loneliness 'ave overwhelm me, waiteeng for you."

"Er—to be sure, to be sure," said Baneen. She tucked his right arm in hers and leaned against him. He looked uncomfortable. "But it's that terrible busy I've been, here, trying to work out a way to aid O'Rigami with the help of this lad, here—a human, you notice."

"I noteeced," said the female gremlin, now smiling sadly up at Rolf. "Ow are you, 'uman? I 'ope you 'ave not lost too many loved ones to ze Terror?"

"His name's Rolf," said Baneen. "La Demoiselle

here, lad, is a countess of fair Gremla. Naturally, the recent Revolution has awakened the deepest sympathies of her blue-green gremlin blood on behalf of those unfortunates of noble extraction—"

"Ah, deeply, deeply," sighed the Countess. "Seventeen times I 'ave cause ze blade of ze guillotine to stick wiz my gremleenish arts. In ozzer ways, also I 'ave also been useful. But 'ow little can any one person do? I am like ze Scarlet Pimpernel, zat noble Englishman—"

"Hear, hear," gruffed Shep behind them, obviously deeply moved.

"Ah, you too 'ave felt for these unfortunate ones, 'ave you, dog?" inquired La Demoiselle, turning to speak to Shep. Rolf took advantage of the opportunity to whisper puzzledly to Baneen.

"Is that the French Revolution she's talking about?" the boy asked. "I thought that all happened a couple of hundred years ago."

"It did," whispered back Baneen, producing a small green handkerchief and mopping his brow. "But the gremlinish feelings of such as the Countess, once awakened, do not go back to sleep easily. Let that be a lesson to you, lad—well, I must be going—"

"Ah, no you don't, naughtee one!" said La Demoiselle, turning back to snatch with both hands at Baneen as he faded out completely. "Oh! 'E 'as gone! Forgeeve me, M'sieu Rolf, but I mus' go find heem."

She vanished in her turn.

Rolf looked around him, but saw no one but Shep and O'Rigami nearby to explain matters to him.

"But what do you gremlins want me to do?" he asked O'Rigami.

"Ah, sooo," said O'Rigami, smiling widely. "Need some speciar suppries such as transistors. . . ." He pulled an almost invisibly small scrap of paper from a pocket in his white smock. But the paper grew strangely into a long strip as it touched Rolf's hand. A list of items was neatly hand-printed on it.

"Transistors and other necessary components," O'Rigami said. "If you wirr be so kind as to obtain them . . ."

"But wait a minute," said Rolf. "Why can't you get these things for yourselves?"

Baneen reappeared, alone, with a faint *pop*.

"Cold iron," said Baneen, simply. "Sure, and the places where the things are kept are full all round with iron this, and iron that. It would be like yourself having to fetch something you badly wanted out of the very center of a fiery furnace."

"All right, then," said Rolf, who had been thinking. "But why should I get them for you?"

"Indeed! Indeed!" exploded Shep. "The very idea, trying to put the boy to work for your blackguardly purposes! Naturally, he's not the sort to fetch and carry for a pack of gremlin scalawags! That's the spirit, lad. Tell them!"

"That's not what I meant," said Rolf. "What I meant—"

"Why now, you were only wondering what shape our gremlin gratitude would take, were you not?" cried Baneen. "To be sure, would we be accepting a favor and thinking of giving nothing in return? No, no, lad—what we have for you is no less than the Great Wish, itself. The same unlimited one wish given to any human clever enough to steal—ah, that is, return the Grand Corkscrew of Gremla, that symbol of kingship itself, should such as a human chance to find it after it had been lost. One wish—for whatever your heart desires!"

There was a sudden silent explosion in the background of Rolf's mind. All at once he had an image of his father and a lot of other people staring at him in awe after he had just announced that he would clean up all the pollution in the world with one snap of his fingers—and had just done it. But Shep was already growling back at the gremlin.

"What!" Shep was snorting. "He scorns your base attempt at bribery! Do you suppose a lad like this would think for a moment—"

"Just a minute, Shep," said Rolf hastily. "Baneen, could you make the world free of pollution—I mean, clean up all the pollution and make the environment safe forever, if I helped you?"

"The promise of a Baneen upon it, the moment our kite is safely headed for beautiful Gremla!"

"Do my ears deceive me?" demanded Shep. "Rolf, boy, think before you—"

"Indeed and indeed, the word of a Baneen, himself!" shot out Baneen quickly. "Ah, it's a bargain, then, and may the memory of it be warm in your heart for years to come. Now, off with you and gain the transistories, or whatever they're called, by tomorrow noon—"

"Just a second," said Rolf. "Where am I supposed to get them?"

"Is this," Shep was asking the sky, in a tragic voice, "the youngster I've stuck with through thick and thin? The boy I've raised like one of my own—"

"Now, Rolf me lad," said Baneen, briskly, "surely you know as well as anyone of a certain store not ten blocks from your very home, that has transistories and all such radio things and devices piled like coals in a coalshop, within its walls?"

"Oh," said Rolf. "Sure. But—wait another minute. These things may be expensive; and my bank account—"

"Rolf, Rolf," cried Baneen. "Did you think us the sort to ask for the use of the life savings of such a friend as yourself? Ah, never! Not a penny will any of these transistories cost your pocket. Just have yourself at the store this night about ten o'clock and we'll make it quite simple for you to slip inside and steal each and every one of them!"

- 4 -

Rolf looked nervously down the dark, deserted street. The whole town seemed to be asleep, and the only lights anywhere were the few street lamps glowing along the main avenue. One of the lamps was planted squarely in front of the hardware store.

"A black deed," muttered Mr. Sheperton. "Breaking into the hardware store to steal things for the gremlins. I thought I had brought you up better than that."

Rolf *shushed* him.

"You don't understand. Be quiet."

"Be quiet? I certainly will not be quiet!" Mr. Sheperton snapped back, but in a growly whisper. "Got half a mind to set up a howl that would bring on the police. If only the moon were full . . ."

Still standing uncertainly in the shadows of the Rocket City movie theater's lobby, Rolf felt his nerves jangling. Shep was right. Stealing was no way to go. But if a little theft now would make the future right and safe again for the brown pelican and all the rest of the world's creatures that were being threatened

31

with destruction through pollution of one kind or another, certainly the end ought to justify the means?

"You were quiet enough at home tonight," he said to Shep. "Why didn't you say anything then?"

"Nothing for me to say," the dog replied. "Did you want *me* to cook dinner for you?"

Rolf's father had been out, as usual. The countdown for the Mars launch was too important for him to come home for dinner. His mother had been busy with the baby again, and when Rolf came home from Playalinda Beach he found that he had to fix his own dinner. He had opened a can of spaghetti and another of beef stew and eaten them both cold. Shep got his regular dogfood and half the beef stew.

Then Rolf had watched television for a while, fidgeting in the family room while his dinner made a cold lump inside him. He waited until it was late enough to slip out of the house. Rita Amaro had called to ask when his father would be on the TV news, and Rolf had hung up on her as quickly as he could.

Now, with everyone else asleep, Rolf still felt fidgety as he watched the empty street.

"If it's the police you're worried about," said Mr. Sheperton coldly, "I'm sure the gremlins will be keeping them busy on other things. They can cause all the mischief in the world whenever they choose to."

Rolf brightened a little. "Baneen said he'd help us. . . ."

"Us?" Mr. Sheperton's ears actually stood on end for an instant. "Not us, young man. You. You're the one who's decided on a life of crime."

"Aw, come on. It's only a few transistors."

"For a start."

Rolf didn't feel like arguing. He looked up and down the street once more. "Why'd they have to put that street lamp right in front of the hardware store?"

And just at the moment, that particular lamp suddenly dimmed, sputtered, and went completely dark. The hardware store's big front windows were swallowed by darkness.

"Baneen!" Rolf felt like shouting for joy. "He's helping us after all! Just like he said he would."

"Trust a gremlin to help you—to get into trouble," muttered Mr. Sheperton darkly.

But Rolf wasn't listening. He swiftly crossed the street and, keeping to the shadows along the building walls as much as possible, he hurried down the street toward the hardware store. Shep padded along behind him, his claws making tiny clicking sounds on the pavement. There were no other sounds. The night was as quiet as it was dark.

They slipped into the entryway of the hardware store. It was set in between two big plate-glass display windows. It was wonderfully dark in there. So dark, in fact, that Rolf couldn't see the door very well at all. *How can I pick the lock if I can't see the keyhole?* he wondered.

"Have you thought about the store's burglar alarm?" asked Mr. Sheperton.

"Huh? Burglar alarm?" Rolf touched the door handle in the darkness. . . .

And the door swung open!

Rolf felt it move, swing inward, and almost lost his balance. He lurched forward, trying to avoid falling, and suddenly found himself inside the hardware store.

"It wasn't locked! They forgot to lock up!"

"More likely another sample of gremlin magic, I'd say," Mr. Sheperton grumbled. "They'll help you all they can . . . as long as you're doing what they want. What they're really doing, of course, is helping you to become as tricky and thieving as they are themselves."

"Aw, come on Shep. . . ."

The dog growled.

"Uh, Mr. Sheperton. All we have to do is find the right transistors and a little bit of wire. The store'll never miss what we take."

"But this is only the first step, Rolf. The gremlins won't let you stop at this. Once you've started working for them, once you've allowed them to bewitch you with their promises, you'll be hooked. They'll always promise more than they give, and they'll ask you to do bigger, riskier, more rascally tasks for them. In the end, they'll have everything they want, and you'll be behind bars. Or worse. I remember the case of one man, a young violinist . . ."

Rolf shook his head. "Never mind. I've got to find what we need."

He took the folded piece of paper from his shirt pocket and tried to read O'Rigami's careful printing. It was too dark to see much, but somehow the paper seemed to be much longer than it had been when he first took it.

"Better not show a light this close to the windows," Rolf said, more to himself than Mr. Sheperton.

So he made his way slowly down the store's main aisle, going by feel and memory more than sight. After a few bumps, he ducked behind the big counter where the cash register was. Squatting down on his heels, Rolf took his penlight from his pants pocket and clicked it on.

O'Rigami's list did indeed look a lot longer than he had remembered it. The green letters shimmered as the tiny light shone on them, and Rolf blinked in astonishment as three new items wrote themselves in at the bottom of the list.

Taking a big breath, like a man about to plunge off a high diving board, Rolf got to his feet and started hunting through the store's bins and drawers for the items O'Rigami needed.

It took a long time. Rolf had to work in the dark, risking the penlight only in quick flashes to read the labels on the storage bins and the boxes lined up on the shelves. And the gremlins' list seemed to grow longer every time he looked at it.

Slowly a tiny pile of transistors, connectors, wire, and other items—including a green felt-tip pen, of all things—grew on the top of the back counter, next to the cash register.

Rolf was putting two more transistors on the counter. They were as tiny as fleas. Mr. Sheperton growled, "Stand still!"

Rolf froze.

The dog seemed to be sniffing the air. Then he said, "Keep your light off and get behind the counter. Quickly!"

No sooner had Rolf ducked behind it than a beam of light swept across the store. Peeking around the side of the counter, Rolf could see that a police car had nosed up to the curb and its headlights were shining right into the windows and door.

The door! Rolf felt his nerves jolting with electricity as he remembered that the door was unlocked. *What can I do? Maybe the back door . . .*

A policeman was already out of the car and heading for the door. Rolf didn't dare move; he couldn't even breathe. The officer walked slowly toward the unlocked door, glanced up at the still-dark street lamp, reached out and tried the door.

It stayed shut. He pushed on it, rattled it a few times, then turned back toward the car.

"It's okay," Rolf heard his muffled calling to the other policeman in the car. "Locked up tight. Better call the utility company and tell 'em they've got a bum light here."

"Not now!" his partner yelled back. "The radio's

going nuts. All the burglar alarms in the shopping center across town have gone off at once. We've gotta get there and find out what's going on."

The policeman jumped into the car. Before he could shut the door, his partner had put the car into reverse and backed away from the curb. They swung down the street with their red gumball light flashing.

Darkness returned to the hardware store. Slowly, Rolf stood up. His legs ached with nervous cramps. He was shivering and drenched with a cold sweat.

Mr. Sheperton got up too, and leaned his forepaws on the counter top. He huffed at the scattered pile of electronics components. "Quite a scare for a measly ten dollars worth of trinkets."

Rolf looked at the pile. Mr. Sheperton was right. All the junk on the table wouldn't cost much more than ten dollars.

He suddenly patted the dog's floppy-eared, furry head. "Come on Sh . . . Mr. Sheperton. Let's get out of here."

"And leave your booty?"

"We'll get it tomorrow morning. Legally. After the bank opens and I can raid my savings account. I didn't realize these things would be so cheap."

Sure enough, when Rolf tried the front door it was unlocked again. And as he and Mr. Sheperton trotted down the street toward home, the street lamp in front of the store turned on brightly.

Breakfast was about the only time that Rolf ever saw his father anymore. Tom Gunnarson had never been a loud, jovial man. But these days he was uptight, wound up, and hardly said a word to anyone as Mrs. Gunnarson put bowls of cereal on the table for her two men.

"How's the countdown going, Dad?" Rolf asked.

"Huh?" Tom Gunnarson seemed deep in private thought. He looked up at his son. "Oh, the countdown. Fine, right on schedule. Everything's working just right. No hitches at all. No gremlins anywhere."

Rolf nearly choked on a spoonful of cereal.

"G . . . gremlins?" he coughed.

"Mythical creatures," Mr. Gunnarson explained absently. "Whenever something goes wrong with a piece of machinery, the technicians say that gremlins have gotten into it. Gremlins get blamed for anything that goes wrong—they're supposed to be full of mischief. No such thing as gremlins, actually, of course."

Swallowing hard, Rolf stayed silent.

"No," his father went on, thoughtfully. "The countdown's been remarkably free of gremlins. Everything's going so smoothly that it's kind of spooky. Which reminds me—I may have a happy surprise for all of us, to announce to you in a day or two."

"If it's all going so smoothly, why can't you spend more time at home, then?" Rolf blurted.

"Rolf!" his mother snapped. "Don't be fresh. You know your father would be home if he could be. The launch . . ."

But Tom Gunnarson put a lean, strong hand on his wife's arm. "Actually, Rolf," he said, "it wasn't the launch itself that kept me busy last night." His voice sounded slightly blurred, tired. "We had a long session with the security people. . . ."

"Security?" Rolf squeaked. His heart gave a thump inside him.

"Yes. Somebody's been sneaking boatloads of tourists into the cleared area around Playalinda Beach. That's not really very dangerous right now, but the security people are getting very upset about it. That area has to be cleared before we can launch, and if some thieving boat captain is taking advantage of the tourists and holds up our launch . . ." Rolf's father clenched his fist tightly enough to bend metal. Fortunately he wasn't holding his spoon at that moment.

They finished breakfast in silence. Almost. The baby began crying as Rolf spooned the last of his milk-softened cereal flakes. Mrs. Gunnarson got up quickly and headed for the nursery. *Used to be my playroom,* Rolf couldn't help reminding himself.

His father got up a moment later. "See you later, son."

"Okay, Dad."

Tom Gunnarson called to his wife from the front door. She called back from the nursery, told him to try to get home early enough for a good night's rest. Then he was gone. Rolf sat in the kitchen. *Alone,* he thought, *again.* He pushed his chair back from the table and, without a word to his mother, went out the back door.

He was getting his bike out of the garage, when Rita came up. She was just Rolf's age—in fact, they had grown up together, but now she looked to him like a stranger.

"Hi," she said.

"Hi," he answered, busy rolling his bike out.

"Say, he was neat on television, last night," she said.

"Who?" he grunted, without looking at her.

"Your dad!" she looked surprised. "Didn't you watch him on TV last night? We saw him on the later news. And they had the same thing on again this morning, on the network show. Everybody in the country must have seen him this morning."

"Big deal," said Rolf.

"What d'you mean—big deal?" She stared at him.

"Big deal," he insisted. "You know what's important in the world today? Ecology, that's what. But you think you'd see anyone on the tube because he's doing work

in ecology? But anybody connected with a space
launch—that's neeaat." He drawled out the last word,
sarcastically.

"Rolf, you—" She almost exploded. He looked at her,
then. Rita Amaro was a happy girl, always smiling, her
teeth flashing brightly against the dark tan of her skin.
Rolf had decided secretly, last term in school after they
had more or less gotten out of touch with each other,
that she really was a pretty girl. When she grew up,
she'd probably be beautiful enough to be a movie star
or a stewardess, or something like that—and forget she
had ever known anyone like him. Right now she looked
ready to lose her temper. But she did not.

"He's your *father,* Rolf!" she said. "I'd think you'd
be proud. Man, you're weird!"

"He doesn't know anything about ecology," muttered
Rolf. "What's more, he doesn't care. He's just an
engineer."

She opened her mouth and this time he did brace
himself for an explosion, but instead, she closed her
mouth again.

"Rolf," she said, almost gently. "You're . . . I don't
know what—"

"Weird," Rolf got up on his bike and pushed off.
"That's what I am. Weird. And my father's famous. Big
deal!"

He left her standing in the driveway, looking after
him as if she was still half-mad, half-something to which
he could not put a name.

Shep appeared from somewhere as Rolf pedaled
down the street toward the center of town, and
raced alongside the bike. The morning sun wasn't too
high yet; the day was still cool. A good breeze was
blowing. Rolf wanted to get to the hardware store
just as they were opening up. But he had to stop
at the bank first.

There was a big cherrypicker crane standing in front of the hardware store, and the hard-hatted electrician up in the cab was yelling down to his assistant on the truck:

"I tell ya I can't find nothin' wrong with it! Whoever called in and said this lamp was out must've been kiddin'!"

"It was the cops called in," his helper yelled back.

The electrician shook his head. "Half the burglar alarms in town on the fritz and what're the fuzz doin'? Sendin' in phony complaints about street lamps!"

Rolf tried not to grin as he leaned his bike against the store front and walked in. Shep settled down on his belly beside the bike.

The pile of material was still on the back counter, beside the cash register. One of the young salesboys had just spotted it, and was standing there looking puzzled.

Rolf hurried back to him. "Uh, that's my stuff," he said. "I was in here yesterday just as they were closing up, and I didn't have enough money to buy all that stuff, so I asked the man to leave it there so I could pick it up this morning."

The salesboy frowned. He looked at the pile of electronic components, then at Rolf, then at the pile again.

"I was here last night, and I helped clean up after we closed shop. I don't remember . . ." Then, with a shrug, he said, "Well, whatever. I'll ring it up for you."

It came to exactly $13.13, which didn't leave much in Rolf's savings account.

Shaking his head unhappily at the thought of how long it had taken him to save that money, Rolf stashed the paper bag on his bike's rattrap and pushed on for Playalinda Beach.

"Come on, Shep," he called. "I want to see what they're going to do with this stuff."

-5-

As he pedaled out toward the Playalinda Beach area and the Gremlin Hollow, Rolf heard Shep mumbling under his breath while the dog trotted alongside the bike.

"What's the matter now?" Rolf asked.

"Your manners," answered Mr. Sheperton. "An absolute disgrace. The way you treated that girl . . ."

"Who? Rita?"

"You know very well that I mean Rita. You were shockingly rude to her."

Rolf felt a twinge of guilt, but he said nothing. With a shake of his head, he said, "Ahh . . . who cares?"

"You should," Mr. Sheperton replied. "And you do, I know. You can't hide your feelings from me, Rolf. You like her very much. She's the one you were showing off for when you took that fall off the high board—"

Rolf's bad leg ached suddenly at the memory of it. "I wasn't showing off!" he growled. But both he and the dog knew he didn't mean it.

Mr. Sheperton kept grumbling as Rolf pedaled along the highway.

"Uh, Shep—I mean, Mr. Sheperton," Rolf said after a few minutes of hard pumping up a small rise in the road. "Don't say anything to the gremlins about me and Rita, will you? They don't have to know that she was even around when I hurt my leg."

Shep snorted. "It's a bit late to keep the matter secret, with that trickster Baneen riding around on your handlebars all this time."

"Baneen? Handlebars?" Rolf blinked.

Something like a small noiseless explosion popped in front of him and Baneen was suddenly smiling up at him. Just as Shep had said, the gremlin was perched on the right handlebar of Rolf's bike.

"Well, well, well, well!" cried Baneen cheerfully. "And a beautiful day it is, to be sure. Ah now, and why would you be wanting to keep the fact of your friendship with such a fine young lady a secret, lad?"

"Never mind," snapped Rolf, recovering from his surprise. "What about you? Where did you come from? And how come you're here, anyway?"

"Why it's pure chance, pure chance—and just a mite of worry mixed in," said Baneen. "We gremlins having the second sight and all, it was a bit of a blow to me when I chanced to look in on you this morning and found you hadn't got the wee things we asked you to pick up for us. Ah, what will we do now, poor, helpless gremlins that we are—I asked myself? Lugh must hear of this, I said; and I went to find him. But before I did indeed find him, I changed my mind. It's a terrible thing, the wrath of mighty Lugh—"

"Poor, helpless gremlin that he is, of course," sneered Shep.

"Ah, don't be twisting my words now, don't," said Baneen. "I thought of the wrath of Lugh and I thought of the lad, here, and I thought it would do no harm to speak to Rolf first. So I made a small spell in a twinkling to bring me to you—and here now, I find you have the little things after all."

"That's right," said Rolf. "They're on the back of my bike, there."

"So indeed I see," said Baneen, casting a bright inquisitive glance past Rolf's elbow to the brown paper bag pinned in the bike's rattrap. He switched his gaze to the scrub grass and bushes beside the road. "You can turn off here, lad."

"Here?" Rolf asked, surprised. He looked and saw a trail he didn't recognize snaking away through the brush.

"It's a bit of a shortcut we've fixed up to our Hollow," said Baneen.

Rolf turned down the trail, which turned and twisted in strange ways. In seconds, it seemed, he was completely out of sight of the road they had just left.

"How far—" he started to ask.

"Not far, not far at all!" said the gremlin. "In just a second now, we'll be there. Once again it's yourself who'll be setting eyes on the high mysteries and secret workings of us gremlin-folk, that none but you know about. And it's certain sure that I am that none but you does know; because a fine lad such as yourself wouldn't have told anybody about us, would you now?" His voice and eyes suddenly seemed sharpened all together. "Not even that fine young lady you were talking with less than an hour ago?"

"Rita? Why would I—" Rolf broke off suddenly, stopping his bike and putting his feet down on the sandy soil. For they had come suddenly upon the lip of the Gremlin Hollow. Down below, he could see hordes of gremlins hard at work stretching out the large kite-shape of O'Rigami's. The Grand Engineer stood patiently off to one side, watching the work. Further away, Lugh was busily directing still more gremlins who carried, dragged, and tugged strangely shaped chests and boxes across the sand. A few gremlins were floating a foot or so off the ground, guiding green-colored crates that floated alongside them.

Everything in the Hollow was noise and bustle, a thousand tiny voices chattering and screeching at once. And, as usual, the gremlin magic was playing tricks with Rolf's vision. The kite once again looked as big as a jetliner, while the Hollow itself seemed no more than thirty or forty feet across.

Rolf started to pick up the sentence where he had left it, but before he could get out another word, Shep set up a furious barking.

"What's that? Stop! Stop immediately, do you hear me! Turn that thing round and get it out of here. . . ."

Rolf and Baneen turned together to look, because Shep was facing away from the Hollow, in the direction of the beach.

"Great Gremla protect us!" yelped Baneen. "It's a monster, headed right this way to destroy us all!"

"It's a bulldozer," Rolf yelled.

The machine was indeed roaring in their direction. It topped the rise that separated the Hollow from sight of the beach, and bore straight down toward the Hollow itself.

"Hey, it's going to tear up the kite!" Rolf cried.

"Stop! Stop, I say!" barked Mr. Sheperton.

But the bulldozer came right on.

"It's no good! It's no good!" cried Baneen, hopping madly on Rolf's handlebars. "Sure and we're all invisible here within the magic wards about this place. We're going to be scooped up like peas on a spade and drowned in the sand!"

- 6 -

The bulldozer roared and clattered like an angry demon with a hide of yellow steel. Instead of breathing fire, though, it puffed dirty black smoke into the clear sky.

It bore straight down on the Gremlin Hollow, pushing a huge pile of sand ahead of it on its wide ugly blade. Gremlins were dashing everywhere, screaming in terror and rage. O'Rigami was madly trying to fold up his kite before the 'dozer's treads ground it to shreds. Baneen huffed and puffed and made wild motions with his magical hands. The bulldozer didn't even slow down, although the driver sneezed once.

Rolf saw the great machine boring straight at him, like a moving mountain of sand threatening to bury him.

Mr. Sheperton barked furiously. Baneen fluttered up into the air, screeching, "It's no good, no good at all! He can't see us or hear us!"

And then Lugh's giant voice roared out, "WHAT IN THE NAME OF THE DUSTY SKIES OF GREMLA IS GOING ON HERE?"

Before anyone could utter another word, Lugh looked up at the approaching bulldozer.

His brows pulled down into a terrible scowl. His cheeks puffed out and his nostrils flared dangerously.

"A great ugly mechanical monster, is it? Well, we'll just see about that."

The bulldozer had just reached the edge of the Hollow, still pushing sand ahead of it. Some of the sand was already spilling into the Hollow and pouring over some of the gremlins who were shrieking and scattering every which way. O'Rigami's hands were flying faster than the eye could follow, folding up the precious kite. Rolf stood straddling his bike, with Baneen floating up at about his eye level and Mr. Sheperton growling and tense beside him.

Lugh thrust out his jaw and eyed the machine angrily. Fists planted dangerously on his hips, he strode off to one side of the oncoming monster, fury and vengeance in every stiff-legged, four-inch-long step.

"What's he going to do?" Rolf wondered.

"Not . . ." Baneen started, then pressed both his fists into his mouth and stared at Lugh, goggle-eyed. He zipped downward and touched his feet to the sandy ground.

Lugh thrust out his right arm and pointed at the yellow bulldozer. His voice became mighty and terrible:

"MAY THE GREAT AND THUNDEROUS CURSE OF GREMLA FALL UPON YOUR HEAD!"

Baneen fainted.

Mr. Sheperton snorted, almost like a sneeze.

Rolf hiccupped.

And the bulldozer slowed. Its roar became a rumble, then a squeak. The smoke-belching exhaust stack seemed to tremble, then shot a sheet of blue flame fifty feet into the sky. Both treads of the bulldozer snapped, and all the wheels fell off.

The driver yelled something wild and leaped from his seat as if his pants were on fire. He dived headfirst into the sand. The bulldozer's engine dissolved in a huge cloud of smoke. The metal sides of the machine fell away and turned to rust as they hit the ground. The whole machine seemed to crumble, like a balloon when the air goes out of it.

In less than a minute there was nothing left except a badly frightened driver and a mess of steaming, rusting machinery that was fast disappearing into the sand.

Lugh nodded his head once, the way a man does when he knows he's finished a task and done it well.

"Be that a lesson to all of you," he said firmly, "gremlin, man and beast alike. Lugh of the Long Hand is not to be pushed about."

Rolf simply stared. The bulldozer was completely gone now, hardly even a wisp of steam left to mark where it once stood. The driver was sitting on the sand, looking as if he didn't believe any of this, even though he had seen it. He was a young man, Rolf saw, with long black hair and a sun-bronzed skin. He kept shaking his head and staring at the spot where the bulldozer had been.

While Rolf watched, Baneen stirred himself and climbed weakly to his feet, using Rolf's leg for support. "I was afraid Lugh would invoke the Great Curse. It's a wonder it didn't bury us all with its terrible magic."

Another man was running up to the bulldozer driver. He was older, black skin shining with perspiration where his shirt was open and showing his chest.

"Hey, Charlie, what did you stop for? Where's the 'dozer?"

Charlie extended a shaking arm and pointed. "It . . . it was right there. . . ." His voice was trembling.

"Was?" The black man took a quick look around. "Where is it now?"

"Gone. Dissolved. Fell apart and rusted away—just like that." Charlie tried to snap his fingers, but it didn't work.

The black man stooped down and picked up a tiny fragment of rusted yellow-painted metal. "Rusted out?" His voice had suddenly gone high-pitched with shock. "A whole 'dozer don't rust out, not all at once."

"Thi-this one did!"

Charlie stared at his partner, then reached down and yanked him up onto his feet. "Come on, friend. You been out in the sun too long. We better get out of here before the ranger patrol flies past."

As the two men disappeared back over the rise, Lugh bellowed to the other gremlins, "Well, what are you standing there for, with your mouths hanging open? Back to work, all of you, before I turn you into toadstools."

Gremlins seemed to sprout out of the sand everywhere and hustled about busily. O'Rigami began to unfold his kite once more, just as calmly as if nothing had ever disturbed him.

"Lugh, me princely protector," Baneen called out, "You wouldn't be wanting that great heap of sand to stay there, would you now?"

"Well said. Get rid of it, trickster. And the beast's tracks, too."

Baneen smiled happily and danced a small circle around himself. "Ah yes, we wouldn't want them that near us, again, would we? Even to cover their own tracks."

Rolf looked up and saw the pile of sand growing dim and shimmering in the heat from the blazing sun. Before he could blink three times, the little mountain had completely disappeared. And so had the tracks of the bulldozer's caterpillar treads.

"Won't they wonder how their tracks vanished?" Rolf asked.

"Ah, no, lad," Baneen answered lightly. "Men never question their good luck. It's only the bad luck they wonder about."

"Maybe you ought to leave the tracks, though," said Rolf. "So I've got something to show to the authorities when I report this."

"Report? Report, lad? Sure, and there's nothing to report," said Baneen, hastily. "Their murderous machine's nothing but a pile of rust now, and the villains themselves have gone. Or, indeed, maybe they were no villains at all, but a couple of humans from the ranger station down the beach a ways, just doing their jobs."

Mr. Sheperton growled, swinging his head about so that he and Baneen stood nose to nose, almost touching.

"Why were they so anxious to get away before the next patrol plane came over, then, might I ask?"

"That's right," said Rolf.

"Hmm, they did say something like that, didn't they?" Baneen cocked his head to one side, as if thinking. "Scalawags! To think they'd push sand into our Hollow, our one little wee spot on the whole face of this vast and watery . . . But come, come, there's wisdom in letting well enough alone. They're gone now."

"But you can't let them get away with doing something like that, here in the very heart of the Wildlife Preserve," said Rolf. "I've just got to report them. What if they come back?"

"Ah, now, they won't be back at all, at all," said Baneen.

"How do you know?" Rolf demanded.

"Well, it's my gremlinish second sight tells me. Indeed—" Baneen closed his eyes and touched his nose thoughtfully with the tip of one green finger. "I

see the Hollow here . . . and the beach . . .
tomorrow . . . and the next day. . . ." He opened his
eyes. "No sign of the rascals or another such fearful mechanical monster. You can rest easy, lad, and
not trouble yourself further."

"Why," demanded Rolf, "are you so set against me
reporting them?"

"Yes," rumbled Mr. Sheperton. "Answer that, will
you? You're not telling everything you know. No more
gremlin trickery, Baneen. Who are these men, and what
are they up to?"

"And what makes you think I'd know?" Baneen said.

"I *know* you know," the dog answered.

"Do you now?"

"Yes I do."

"Hmp! These English and their superior airs."

Mr. Sheperton growled, low and menacing. Baneen
danced away from him and skipped behind Rolf.

"Well now . . . I'm not saying that there's anything
I know for certain. But—well, sure and it'll do no
harm to show you something."

Baneen trotted out toward the far edge of the
Hollow, and Rolf followed him up the slope, across a
couple of sandy little hillocks, and out toward the
beach.

Padding along beside Rolf, Mr. Sheperton grumbled,
"That little green rascal knows far more than he's told
us."

"But," Rolf said, squinting against the glare of the
dazzling sun that beat off the white sand, "If he really
knew what was going on, would he have let the
bulldozer get so close to nearly burying the Hollow?"

Mr. Sheperton seemed to shake his head. "There's
no telling what a gremlin will do—except that it will
be bad for any humans nearby."

Rolf turned to stare at Baneen, just ahead. The boy

could hear the hissing boom of the surf now, and felt the tangy salt breeze on his face. He started to run up toward where Baneen was, but the gremlin turned and put a finger to his lips, waving at Rolf to get down.

Bursting with curiosity, Rolf crawled on his stomach up to the top of the dune. Laid flat out, he peered through the grass. Mr. Sheperton lay beside him, panting wetly in his ear.

At first glance, the beach looked perfectly ordinary. But then Rolf saw that someone had dug a narrow channel into the beach, and put a sort of bridge over it. The bridge was covered with a thin layer of sand. The surf was breaking far out in the water, at least a hundred yards before the channel.

"Somebody's built a breakwater out there, like an underwater sandbar," Rolf said.

"Yes," agreed Mr. Sheperton. "And a place to bring in a boat and hide it under that sand bridge."

"Camouflage."

The putt-putting of an engine made Rolf turn his head toward the right. A boat was puffing through the sea, heading straight for the disguised channel. As the three of them watched, the boat came in and two grimy looking sailors in tattered shirts and shorts leaped from its deck and tied it securely to the posts that held up the bridge.

"They're the villains that sent the mechanical beast at us," Mr. Sheperton muttered. "They wanted more sand to cover their bridge and dump into their breakwater."

Another man appeared on the ship's deck. He was chunky and fat-faced. He wore a blue jacket and white slacks, and even had a perky little captain's hat perched on his head. He squealed orders at the two sailors, who were now back on the boat, sweating and struggling with heavy boxes.

"Come on, come on," the captain piped at them in a nasty nasal, high-pitched voice. "I want all the telescopes and binoculars stored away here so we can use all our space to carry people on the day of the launch. Move it, move it!"

"So that's it," Mr. Sheperton said. "He's the one that your father was worrying about. Bringing in tourists to watch the launch from here on the beach."

"There must be more to it than that, though," said Rolf. "They wouldn't go to that much trouble for a boatload of tourists two or three times a year."

"Quite right! How about that, you gremlin?" Mr. Sheperton demanded of Baneen.

"Ah well," said Baneen uncomfortably, "sure and the one in the sailor hat there does bring in people with guns to hunt and fish, now and then."

Rolf felt suddenly sick—in his mind's eye he saw images of the brown pelican and the young piglets, bloody and slaughtered.

"But this is a Preserve!" he said, fiercely. "It's the one little piece of the environment around here that's protected! And you say I shouldn't report someone like that?"

"But we've never let them harm the wee beasts and birds," said Baneen, hastily. "Not since we've been here has one of his hunters gained a single prey—"

"That doesn't make any difference!" said Rolf. "I don't care what you've been doing. I'm reporting this man and his crew."

"No lad, you can't!" said Baneen. "Listen to me, now. We mustn't have police and rangers and suchlike stamping up and down the beach here and tramping all over our Hollow."

"I'm sorry," said Rolf. "But this is one thing I just have to do."

"But you'll listen to me for a moment before doing it, won't you?" pleaded Baneen. "Wait, Rolf, just a second whilst I bring you one who can plead our desperate case better than myself. . . ."

"Don't listen to him, boy," growled Mr. Sheperton.

"I don't see how they've managed to avoid being seen, anyway, before this," said Rolf. "You ought to be able to see that oil slick and boat smoke from a ranger plane pretty easily."

He turned to look suspiciously at Baneen.

"Now, now!" cried the gremlin. "It was just the slightest touch of magic we've used in their favor, to be sure—just enough to keep them from being seen. Nothing invisible, mind you. Just a wee distraction or two to make the patrol rangers look the other way as they fly past the noise and dirt. But just a minute. Wait right here—"

He disappeared with a popping noise.

"Let's not wait for him, Shep—Mr. Sheperton, I mean," said Rolf.

"Quite right!" rumbled Mr. Sheperton. "Enough of the blackguard's lies and evasions—"

Baneen popped back into existence, pulling along with him another gremlin—also wearing green, it was true, but with a long, sad, greenish blue cloak around his shoulders, long dark hair hanging down under his hat, and a violin case under his arm.

"Rolf, let me—" puffed Baneen, breathlessly, "introduce that grand—gremlin musician— O'Kkane Baro."

The other gremlin took his hat off his head and swept it before him as he bowed gracefully. He had a handsome, if tragic, face.

"Glorious to acquaint you!" he cried, in a rich, full voice, "Glorious! If my heart was not breaking, I would dance with joy. But who dances in a world like this? I ask you!"

He sat down mournfully in the sand, laying the violin case aside. Rolf stared at him.

"Hist!" whispered Mr. Sheperton in his ear. "Don't let this rascal fool you, either. He's a gypsy gremlin. Do you know what Hokkane Baro means, in the Romany tongue?"

"Ah, but the heart of our poor friend is indeed breaking," said Baneen sorrowfully. "All these thousands of years that he has lived, now, only in the hope of seeing Gremla again—"

"Ah, Gremla, my sunshine, my beautiful!" exclaimed O'Kkane Baro resonantly, covering his eyes with one hand. "Never to see you again. Never . . . never!"

"Hokkane Baro means," whispered Mr. Sheperton severely, "the *big trick,* a con game they used to play on gullible peasants."

Rolf nodded. He had no doubt that Mr. Sheperton was right. But O'Kkane Baro's unhappiness was so convincing he began to feel a twinge of guilt in spite of himself.

"You'll see it," he said to the dark-haired gremlin. "Don't worry."

"Ah, but will he?" said Baneen. "Now that you're determined and all to report what you've seen. Sure, and it's only a matter of minutes after the authorities come prowling around here that our magic will be spoiled and our last chance at Gremla lost for good."

"Ah . . ." said O'Kkane Baro, unshielding his eyes. "But, why should we weep?" he spread his arms. "Let us laugh . . . ha, ha!" Rolf thought he had never heard such mournful laughter in his life.

"Yes, laugh!" cried O'Kkane Baro, rising to his feet. "Laugh, dance, be gay—sing! Music!"

He clapped his hands; at the sound, the lid of his

violin case opened and a gremlin-sized violin floated out
and up into the air. A gremlin-sized bow floated after
it and poised itself over the strings.

"Play, gypsy!" commanded O'Kkane Baro, stamping
his foot on the sand. The violin began to play, a wild,
thrilling air. "Weep, gypsy—" The violin switched suddenly to wailing chords. Tears began to run down
O'Kkane Baro's cheeks.

"Gremla . . . lovely Gremla . . . nevermore shall we
set eyes upon thee . . ." he sobbed.

The music was overwhelming. Baneen was also
crying. Tears were running as well out of Mr.
Sheperton's nose and Rolf was blinking desperately to
keep from joining them in tears.

"Wait . . ." begged Rolf. "Wait. . . ."

"Why wait?" keened Baneen. "All is over. And just
because someone could not go two days before
reporting some scoundrels. Ah, the whole gremlin
race, robbed of its last, last chance! Didn't I say we'd
see none of the animals or birds would come to
harm? But did that soften the hard heart of someone I need not name? No—"

"Wait!" gulped Rolf. "All right. Two days. I can wait
two days—but stop that violin!"

"Ah yes, stop the instrument, O'Kkane Baro!" sobbed
Baneen. "It's myself can barely stand the sorrow of it,
either."

Weeping, O'Kkane Baro waved at the violin, which
stopped playing and packed itself, with its bow, back
into its case. In the silence, a high-pitched voice, the
voice of the boat captain came clearly to their ears.

" . . . there! Right over the ridge there. Don't just
stand there, get over after them! You heard the music
coming from there until just a second ago!"

Rolf leaped to his feet and stared over the crest
of the dune. The two sailors they had seen, the boat

captain right behind them, were coming toward the dune. They all shouted when they saw Rolf.

"They spotted me!" Rolf cried. "What'll we do now?"

"Try an old gremlin trick, lad," advised the voice of Baneen behind him. *"Run!"*

-7-

Rolf took a fast look at the two burly sailors climbing the dune towa·d him. He started running down the other side of the dune, but the loose sand slowed him down.

He glanced over his shoulder and saw that the sailors had topped the rise and weren't far behind him. And they were gaining fast.

Baneen was dithering around, running in excited circles, waving his hands helplessly.

And Mr. Sheperton?

Rolf heard the dog barking furiously, the way he barked at automobiles that went down their home street too fast. Turning slightly, Rolf saw Mr. Sheperton charging at the two sailors, his bared teeth looking ferocious, even in his fuzzy mop of a head.

The sailors backed off for a moment. Mr. Sheperton surprised them, maybe even scared them. Then one of them pulled something long and menacing from his belt. Rolf couldn't tell whether it was a knife or a club.

"Shep . . . no!"

But Mr. Sheperton wasn't backing away. As long as Rolf was in danger, and he himself was conscious, the dog would attack the sailors.

"Baneen . . . do something!"

Suddenly Mr. Sheperton's open mouth started to spout foam. His barking began to sound more like gargling.

The sailor with the club, or whatever it was, went round-eyed.

"Mad dog!" he yelled. Spinning around, he raced back toward the safety of the boat. His friend went with him.

Mr. Sheperton raced after them, nipping at their heels, until they got to the top of the dune. Then he stood his ground and barked at them several more times. Rolf knew what Mr. Sheperton was saying:

"And don't come back! Blackguards! Cowards!"

Satisfied that everything was in proper shape, Mr. Sheperton trotted back down the sandy hill to Rolf and Baneen. Only then did Rolf realize that if the dog was really foaming at the mouth, it meant he was seriously ill.

"Shep . . . are you . . . ?"

"I don't know how many times it will be necessary to tell you," the dog said, a bit cross and out of wind, "that my name is Mr. Sheperton. And you, Baneen, if you don't mind, would you kindly remove this ridiculous shaving lather you've put on my face? Tastes of lime. Ugh."

"Ah, for such a grand hero as yourself, Mr. Sheperton, it was hardly necessary for me to do anything at all." Baneen wiggled his fingers and the foam instantly dried into crystal flakes that were carried away by the wind.

And suddenly Rolf dropped to his knees and hugged

the shaggy old dog. "Shep, Shep . . . I thought you were sick."

For once, Mr. Sheperton didn't correct the boy. He sat there and let Rolf hold him. His tail even wagged once or twice. Sounding rather embarrassed, he said at last, "Well, harumph . . . I suppose we'd better get away from here before those rascals work up the nerve to come back."

On the way back to the Hollow, Baneen kept talking about O'Rigami's space kite and how wonderful it would be to return to Gremla.

"And the most wonderful part of it all," the gremlin said, dancing lightly over the sand, "is that yourself will be in complete charge of the entire launching of the great, powerful rocket. The most important man of all, that'll be you, Rolf me bucko. Er. . . once you've attached the kite to the rocket properly, of course."

Rolf nodded. But inwardly he was wondering how he could possibly get to his father's rocket and attach the kite, even if O'Rigami made it invisible. Gremlin magic wasn't going to be enough for *that* job.

Mr. Sheperton stayed strangely quiet as they approached the Hollow. Rolf could see gremlins scurrying about, busy with a thousand unguessable tasks. Lugh stood in the middle, as usual, in a small mound of sand, pointing here, shouting there, his tiny bulldog's face red with scowling, his chin whiskers bristling.

Rolf picked up his bike and said farewell to Baneen. The gremlin, jigging happily, reminded him:

"Don't be forgetting tomorrow, now. Tomorrow O'Rigami will have the grand kite finished, and tomorrow night you'll be helping us to attach it properly to the rocket. Ah, Gremla, land of me youth! Soon we'll be back enjoying your dusty delights."

"Sure," Rolf said as he got on the bike. "Tomorrow."

He pedaled up and away from the Gremlin Hollow and got back on the road that led to the highway. But when he thought of the men with the boat and his own promise not to report them, he was conscious of an ugly, hollow feeling inside him.

Rolf's father wasn't home for dinner again that night. After helping his mother clean up the kitchen, Rolf went outside for a walk. The sun was low in the southwest, the breeze already had a bite of evening's coolness.

Mr. Sheperton came padding up to him, but Rolf said. "No, Shep. Stay. I want to think, not argue."

The dog muttered something about calling people by their proper names, as he trotted stiffly back toward the house.

Rolf walked out on the narrow sidewalk that fronted the lawn, and headed down the street slowly. "How deep am I getting myself into this?" he whispered to himself. "It all seems so crazy. For one thing, suppose something goes wrong when I'm helping the gremlins and I get caught?"

There was only one tree in this part of town worth climbing, a sturdy old live oak that had been growing for maybe fifty years before the houses had been built and the streets put in. Miraculously, it had escaped the bulldozers and builder, probably because it looked too big and tough to knock over easily.

The tree happened to be right next to the Amaros' old two-story house, close to Rita's window. Rolf hesitated in the dark at the foot of the tree, remembering all the times he had climbed up there for secret talks with her, back when they both had been real young kids. But now he needed to talk to her again, and the tree looked as climbable as ever.

He climbed up easily, but found that he'd gotten too big to crawl out on the limb that practically brushed her window. And the window was closed, because the house had recently been air conditioned.

Can't use our old signal, Rolf knew, remembering the way he'd whistle like a bobolink. *How can I call her?*

While he sat there hunched up on the big branch near the tree trunk, Rita opened the window. Over her shoulder she called, "Okay, Momma. I've got my window open. Tell me when the air conditioner is working again, and I'll shut it."

Rolf thought he could hear Baneen giggling in the shadows of the tree.

"Hey, Rita!" he whispered.

She jerked back a little in surprise. "Rolf? What are you doing there?"

"I wanted to talk with you."

She smiled, and it looked better than moonlight to Rolf. "Just the way we used to," she said. "Wait a minute."

She ducked inside for a moment, then crawled out on the window ledge.

"Hey, no . . . the branch can't hold . . ."

But Rita already had one bluejeaned leg on the branch. "I'm not as heavy as you are."

Or as careful, Rolf thought. But she crawled out on the branch. It dipped and swayed under her weight, but Rita calmly shinnied up until she was sitting safely next to Rolf.

"We haven't done this in ages," she said happily.

"Yeah," Rolf nodded. It *was* fun. Almost, it took him back two years, to before he had started going out to the Preserve, alone.

More seriously, Rita said, "I was beginning to think you didn't like me anymore. You've stayed away so much lately. . . . I'm sorry I said you were weird."

Rolf had forgotten that. "Oh, that's okay."

"You really have been acting strange. You know?"

"I guess so. . . ." He didn't know where to begin, how to tell her.

For a moment they just sat there, bare feet dangling in the cool evening air.

"Rita?" Rolf said. "Listen. There is uh . . . something I need your help for."

"Sure Rolf. What is it?"

"Your father's still on the night shift, isn't he?"

"Yes." Then she added proudly, "He's been promoted to sergeant. He's got a whole shift of guards under him now."

"But he's still working right at the launch pad, isn't he?"

"Yes."

Hesitating for a moment more, Rolf finally decided to take the plunge. "Look . . . I need to get up close to the rocket. Up onto the top platform of the checkout tower. Tomorrow night."

"Tomorrow night?" Rita's voice sounded shocked. In the darkness it was difficult to make out the expression on her face. "But that's the night before the launch! Nobody's allowed . . ."

Slowly, and as carefully as he could, Rolf explained to Rita about the gremlins and how they wanted to use the Mars rocket to help the return to Gremla.

He was earnestly explaining about O'Rigami and the space kite when Rita began laughing. He stared at her, and she laughed so hard he had to put out a hand to keep her from falling off the branch. Her shoulders were pumping up and down, and she put a hand over her mouth to keep from making so much noise that her parents would catch them. "Mmpff, mmppffff," came the sound from behind her hand.

"Hey, it's not funny," Rolf said.

"Oh, Rolf," she gasped. "When you want to put somebody on, you sure can do it. . . ." She started giggling again.

"'Tis no joke, me lovely maid." It was Baneen's voice, coming from right behind Rolf's ear.

Rolf turned his head slightly and saw that the gremlin was perched on his shoulder. Strangely, he felt no weight on the shoulder at all. Then, looking back at Rita, he could see that her eyes had gone white and round. Her laughter was stopped. Her mouth was open, and her eyes were enormous.

"Allow me the grand pleasure of being introduced to this charming young lady," Baneen said.

Still holding Rita by one arm, Rolf said, "This is Baneen—one of the gremlins. Baneen, this is Rita Amaro."

"Charmed, I'm certain," said Baneen, and he took his little green cap off, making a low sweeping bow to the girl.

Rita recovered her voice. "You . . . you're real!"

"As real as your beautiful brown eyes, Rita me girl. And as happy as your darling laughter. But all the gremlins on this vast dreary world would be sadder than a mud toad's croak if it weren't for this fine, brave lad here."

"Aw, come on, Baneen," Rolf said.

"You . . . you really want Rolf to attach this . . . kite thing . . . to the Mars rocket?"

"Exactly!" Baneen smiled at her. "What a clever lass she is! Sure, and you've caught on right away, my dear."

"I'll be in charge of the final countdown," Rolf said. "I'll have to delay the launch six minutes from its scheduled liftoff time. Right, Baneen?"

"That's what O'Rigami figures—although frankly I've no head for numbers and I can't be sure if six minutes is the right amount. But what difference, six minutes or sixty? The rocket won't go until *you* give the word, Rolf, me bucko."

Rita seemed aghast. "Rolf, you could foul up the whole launching!"

"Ah, no," Baneen assured her. "Just a wee delay and a slight detour. No problem at all."

She shook her head. "This could be really serious."

"I'm going to do it," Rolf said quietly. It was on the tip of his tongue to tell her about the Great Wish the gremlins had promised him. Then he remembered that she had always admired his father—who obviously had no concern for ecology.

"There's nothing to it, I tell you," Baneen repeated. "Why, with gremlin magic at work, we could put everyone in the launch center to sleep for a fortnight—ah, but we don't want to do that, desperate though we are."

"They've got to get off our planet and back to Gremla," said Rolf. "And I'm going to help them."

"I don't understand why. . . ."

"Well, lass, you see now, it's Lugh—big, blustering oaf that he is. A terrible-tempered gremlin. Terrible temper." Baneen shuddered. "He's a gremlin prince, you know. But our king, Hamrod the Heartless, was always playing tricks on Lugh. Loved to see the great burly Lugh of the Long Hand turn red with frustration and anger. So it was that Lugh stole the Great Corkscrew of Gremla, took himself and his entire household—all of us—and in one great magic huff-and-puff brought us all to Earth, these thousands of years ago."

Rolf and Rita listened, fascinated.

"Well, once safely here on this awful watery planet, Lugh found out two things. One, there were plenty of oafish humans about, to serve as the butt of *his* jokes.

No longer was Lugh at the mercy of Hamrod; now he had humans at his mercy. The tables were turned, so to speak.

"But the second thing he found out that here on this watery place, gremlin magic is pitifully weak—water ruins magic, don't you know—so our tricks amount to mere pranks. Watered down, they are."

"Like wiping out a bulldozer?" Rolf asked.

"Aye, the Great Curse. Pitiful, wasn't it? Why, on safe, dusty Gremla when the Great Curse is invoked, forty comets explode and the stars dance for a month. But here . . ." Baneen's voice dropped to a melancholy whisper, "well, about all we can do is play little pranks. Stopping clocks and making machines behave poorly, suchlike. Not even Lugh's great magic can get all of us at once more than ten feet off the ground. That's why we need your mighty rocket to help us get back to Gremla."

Rita asked, "But why does Lugh want to return to Gremla if your king is so nasty to him?"

"Ah, there's the nub of it all," Baneen said, dabbing at the corner of one eye with his eyebrow. "A clever girl you are, Miss Rita. You see, underneath all of Lugh's bad temper and bluster, beats a heart of fairy gold. He knows how miserable all we gremlins have been here on dripping old Earth, and he's willing to sacrifice himself to save all of us. I doubt that we could last another few hundred years here on Earth, with all this water about. Doubt it strongly, that I do."

"I don't know . . ." Rita said uncertainly.

"Ah, but I do know what Lugh will do if he can't get human help for our return to Gremla," Baneen said, with a shudder in his voice. "It'll be terrible. He'll use every grain of gremlin magic to make life as miserable as possible for you humans. Many's the time I've heard him mutter," and Baneen's voice took on some of the deep roughness of Lugh's, "If we can't use that rocket to get us back to Gremla, the humans will never get to use it to take themselves to Mars."

It was Rolf's turn to be shocked. "You never told me that! You mean if we don't help you . . ."

"Lugh will keep the rocket from flying off," Baneen finished for him. "And it's himself has got the power to do it. That great rocket will just sit there and grow moss on it before Lugh lets it go."

- 8 -

"I wish you'd stay close to home today," Mrs. Gunnarson said to Rolf as he ate breakfast. His father hadn't come home at all. He was staying at the Space Center for the final thirty-six hours of countdown.

"Aw, Mom," Rolf said, between spoonfuls of cereal, "There's nothing to do around here. All the other guys'll bug me about Dad being on TV and being Launch Director. . . ."

His mother looked at him penetratingly.

"Is that what they do?" she asked. " 'Bug' you?"

Rolf stared down at the cereal.

"You don't know what it's like, when your father's . . ." he muttered, letting the sentence trail off.

"You really should learn to get along with the other boys," she said. "For that matter, you should learn to get along better with your father."

"He doesn't need me," mumbled Rolf under his breath to the cereal.

"What?"

"Nothing." Rolf pushed away from the kitchen table

and then got up. "I'm going down to the Wildlife Preserve. Can you fix me a couple of sandwiches?"

"Just a moment," said his mother. He stood still, unwillingly. "Your father is worn out right now with his work—just as I'm worn out with the baby. But you're big enough to take a little of the family responsibility on your own shoulders, for a short while anyway. The launch will be over soon and your father did say he might have a pleasant surprise for us all then. Surely you can take care of a few things, including yourself, until that time comes."

"Well, sure," growled Rolf.

"All right, then. You can begin by making your own sandwiches and clean up the breakfast table." With that, Mrs. Gunnarson walked out of the kitchen.

Rolf cleared the table and put the dishes in the washer. Then he made up four sandwiches, took a plastic bottle of orange juice, and stuffed them all into the little knapsack on the back of his bike's seat. He whistled for Mr. Sheperton and pedaled down the street to Rita's house. She was already sitting on the shady porch in front of the old house.

"Want to meet Lugh?" Rolf asked her, straddling his bike at the base of the front steps.

Rita's eyes widened. "Could I?"

"Sure."

She leaped off her chair and ran into the house. In two minutes flat she was out again, holding a little lunchkit in one hand.

Together they biked down toward Playalinda Beach, with Mr. Sheperton gallumphing alongside them and the sea breeze pushing fluffy white clouds across the bright blue sky. It was like old times, before the launch and the gremlins made Rolf's life so complicated.

Except that Mr. Sheperton didn't say a word to

Rolf all the way down toward the beach. He didn't even bark. And he stayed alongside Rita's bike, on the side away from Rolf.

He's sore at me, Rolf realized.

"That time you hurt your leg diving off the high board," Rita called to him, raising her voice enough to be heard over the whistling wind, "why did you try that dive? You'd never been off the high board before."

Rolf shrugged. "I had to show people. The other guys were calling me chicken . . ."

"No they weren't," Rita said. "I was there and I heard them. There was a lot of horsing around going on, but nobody called you chicken."

He could feel his face getting red. "Well—I guess I was getting sore at them for showing off in front of you girls. I didn't want to be left out. They were always calling me the runt and bugging me. And you were watching them, and I didn't want you to think I was chicken. . . ."

"Oh, Rolf," she said, shaking her head. "Boys are so silly. Why would I think you're chicken? I've known you all my life; I know you're not chicken. A little silly sometimes, maybe . . ."

She laughed, and Rolf found that he was laughing with her.

"I guess I just wanted you to think that I was as big as any of the guys. As important as any of them."

Her face grew serious again. "Is that why you're helping the gremlins? So that they'll help you feel important?"

"Yeah . . . no . . ." Rolf felt confused. "Aw, I don't know. I'm not even sure how I got into this."

Baneen did not meet them before they got to the Hollow, as usual. In fact they came into the very Hollow itself before any sort of attention was paid

them by the gremlins. When they reached the lip of
the hollow they saw why. All work seemed to be at
a standstill, with all the gremlins watching one corner of the Hollow that seemed to be obscured by a
cloud of green smoke. Curious, Rolf went toward the
smoke, with Rita and Mr. Sheperton behind him, and
as he got close, he heard voices coming from it.
Specifically, he heard Baneen's voice, on a high sar-
castic note.

" . . . Ah, round is it, indeed? A round universe?"
Baneen was saying. "And what happens to magic when
you're on the underside of it, may I ask now? It's all
upside-down is it? And all the spells backward?"

"Not so!" hissed the voice of O'Rigami—and Rolf
with Rita and Mr. Sheperton pushed through the green
smoke to find a clear space within which O'Rigami and
Baneen were confronting each other, with perhaps six
feet of distance between them. "Being round, all praces
on universe identicar. Sperrs arways the same!"

"Ah, dear me, and do you really believe such
nonsense?" demanded Baneen, still sarcastically. "It's
a fever you must be having, for certain. I've noticed
you're not looking yourself, nowadays—"

As he spoke, he passed his hands one over the other
and O'Rigami turned from his normal gremlin green
color to a bright reddish brown plaid in color.

"Am in perfect shape and coror!" snapped O'Rigami,
turning sharply back to green. His fingers twinkled and
a piece of paper which had appeared from nowhere
suddenly took on the shape of a miniature garden
fountain. "Also happen to understand more of universe
than others who might stirr be too ignorant—"

The fountain suddenly spouted a fine stream of
water which arched up through the air forward and
curved down again abruptly to splatter Baneen gen-
erously behind his pointed gremlin ears.

Baneen yelped and dodged. Suddenly he turned into a crocodile which charged at O'Rigami, jaws agape, drinking up the water from the fountain as it came.

O'Rigami's flying fingers abruptly fashioned a Spanish bullfighter's cape with which he executed perfectly that pass with the cape known as a veronica. Completely fooled by the cape, the crocodile thundered past, discovered itself facing nothing, and whirled about. But O'Rigami had already folded a complete stony medieval castle about himself and was hidden in it.

The crocodile turned abruptly into a gopher, which leaped forward and began to tunnel into the earth out of sight and toward the castle. The castle arose on two thin green legs and scurried aside. It unfolded and disappeared suddenly, revealing O'Rigami, whose flying fingers wove a fisherman's net in the air where the castle had originally been.

The gopher popped up through the earth where the castle been. The net fell about it in folds, entangling it. And abruptly the gopher turned back into Baneen, trapped in the netting.

"Help!" cried the little gremlin. "Help. O'Rigami, help now! Turn me loose!"

"Onry," said O'Rigami, sternly, "on condition you wirr not insist any more on this nonsense about the universe being frat!"

"I promise. Indeed, I promise!" cried Baneen. "Word of Baneen!"

"No, you don't!" said O'Rigami. "This is fourteen thousand, five hundred and ereventh time you've brought up same argument. I don't want to argue it with you ever again. Give me your gremrinish word— or you stay in that net for the next million years!"

"Ah, no!" begged Baneen. "Not that! O'Rigami, friend of me youth—"

"Your gremrinish word, or there you stay!" said O'Rigami implacably, folding his arms.

Baneen sighed and drooped inside the net.

"All right," he said, sulkily. "My gremlinish word—I'll agree the universe is round from now on!"

O'Rigami waved his hands and the net vanished. Baneen climbed to his feet and brushed himself off. But his face was sulky.

"Ah," he said, "but it's a terrible thing, it is, for one true gremlin to require the Unbreakable Promise from another. Bad dreams to your cruel mind, O'Rigami, and may your conscience prick you that did such to an old friend—"

Just then he became aware of Rolf and the others watching, and his sulky look was transformed into a smile.

"But here's the lad and the lass as well, to say nothing of Mr. Sheperton!" Baneen exclaimed. "Welcome to our humble abode, fairest of lasses. It's pleased we are that you've come to visit with us."

Rita's eyes sparkled like a child's on Christmas morning. "How did you know I was coming here? I mean, you weren't surprised to see me at all, were you?"

"Of course not. Gremlins can foresee the future, you know—er, only on special occasions, such as this one, that is. And only up to a limited point, don't you know."

"Foresee the future?" Rita asked. "Can you . . ."

"Ah, but it's not my chatter you've come for, is it?" Baneen said. "You've come to meet our masterful and baleful leader, Lugh of the Long Hand, Prince of the Royal House of Gremla."

Rita laughed, delighted. "He knows everything!"

But Rolf, somehow, was feeling much less than happy. Baneen led Rita into the misty-aired Hollow and Rolf fell into step behind them.

Mr. Sheperton, walking beside Rolf, muttered, "Trust

a gremlin to flatter a human straight out of his—or her—senses." But he seemed to be saying it more to himself than to Rolf.

Baneen was saying, as they went through the Hollow, "Lugh's not here at the present moment. He's out watching those scalawag poachers in their great oily boat."

"They're back again?" Rolf asked.

"Sure enough. That squeaky-voiced captain and his two ugly sailors have brought a few businessmen with them this time. He's showing them what a grand view they're going to have of the launch. And promising them roast wild duck for their dinners! Lugh's there at the beach, protecting them from being spotted by the rangers. And boiling in his own juices if I know Lugh the Terrible-Tempered."

"Hmph," said Mr. Sheperton.

"So I'd be advising you," Baneen continued, "to be careful of not being seen by the poachers. And be even more careful of not triggering the wrath of Lugh. He'll be in a foul mood, no doubt. Making magic on a continuous basis for several hours is a terrible strain, especially next to all that water, you know."

Lugh did look terribly strained when they saw him. And angrier than ever. He was standing atop a high dune that overlooked the beach, his cheeks puffed out, his face red, his fists clenched at his sides. From time to time, as a breeze puffed in from the sea, he would actually float off the sand a few inches, like a balloon, and then settle down again slowly.

Baneen called to him when they got near enough. "Lugh, me magic-making marvel, I've brought you some visitors to help pass away the morning."

Turning, Lugh gruffed, "Visitors, is it? I'll thank you, tricky one, to watch those smelly, water-crawling spalpeens for a while."

"Nothing could please me more, Lugh darling," Baneen said happily, "than to give you a bit of rest from your mighty labors. I'll take care of the scalawags for you."

And Baneen planted himself on the dune's crest, puffed out his cheeks, squeezed his fists until the knuckles went chartreuse, and put on a glowering scowl just like Lugh's.

"Ahhh . . ." said Lugh. "I feel better already. You'll be the lass Baneen told me of. You've come to help this lad here?"

"Well," Rita said, sitting on the sand, "I suppose so. . . ."

"Hah. And a good thing it is that you have. It's almost time for us to leave this foulsome planet, and we'll be needing all the help we can muster."

"It's not a foulsome planet!" Rita snapped. "It's a beautiful planet."

Lugh glared at her. "Is it now? Well, maybe once it was, when we first came here, but not today. Not when you've got ugly ones like those down in the boat dirtying up the very air we breathe with their smelly engines and oily garbage."

"Well, you're helping them!" Rita said. "You're protecting them. Why don't you use some of your gremlin magic to chase them away?"

Rolf watched her, goggle-eyed. Any minute now, he knew, Lugh was going to explode and turn her into a tree stump. He reached out for Rita's arm.

But Lugh's answer was strangely soft, quiet, even sad. "Ah, lass, but it's not our world. It belongs to you humans—it's the world you made for yourselves, in a manner of speaking. Once we thought that we might help you, if you had the will to handle matters right—but it turned out to be of no use, no use at all."

He stalked away, moodily.

"What does he mean?" Rita demanded of Baneen.

The little gremlin shook his head, but without taking his eyes off the men he was supposed to be watching.

"It's a sad tale, indeed," he said. "And a specially sad tale in the part of it that concerns Lugh, himself. It was his idea, you see, to disguise the Great Corkscrew and use it as a test to find one human who cared more for others than himself. And when no such human could be found, it was Lugh that took it the hardest of us all—though never a sign would he show of how he felt."

"No such human could be found?" Rolf echoed. "Surely there've been lots of humans who cared more for others than themselves?"

"Oh, indeed, there have been—but it was for other *humans* they cared. Never yet has a human been found who cares more for other *creatures* than he or she does for himself or herself."

"But how would a corkscrew show the difference—" Rita began.

"Ah, but it's not just any corkscrew!" said Baneen, swiftly. "It's the Great Corkscrew of Gremla, that symbol of Gremlin kingship that belonged to Hamrod the Heartless and which Lugh himself stole away from the king when he brought us here—to pay Hamrod back for all his pranks and tricks upon Lugh, himself. You see, in olden days—so far back that your world of Earth was still a steaming mudball, cooling down into a planet—the Great Corkscrew was a test of Gremlin kingship. Only one wielding more power and magic than any other gremlin could pull it from its case. He who could withdraw the Corkscrew was rightwise king of all Gremla. Every thousand years or so, whoever was our Gremlin king must pull forth the Corkscrew to prove his right to rule."

Baneen paused and sighed heavily.

"If at that time he could not pull it out," he went on, "then all other gremlins who wished to try had their chance—until one succeeded and gained the throne. Ah, but the sad year came, and the sad month and the sad day—the then king of Gremla not having been able to pull out the corkscrew—when every other gremlin on Gremla had tried as well, and none had been able."

"None?" said Rolf. "One of them must have had a little stronger magic than any of the rest. It just had to be."

Baneen shook his head.

"No, lad," he said. "It's clear you don't understand the strange and marvelous principles of magic. It's not how strong your magic is, but how much of it you have. The greater your soul, the more magic you can carry. And over the centuries, unbeknownst to ourselves, our gremlin souls had become smaller and smaller, so that even the largest soul among us could not hold enough magic to let its owner pull the Great Corkscrew from its case."

"But," said Rita, "if nobody could pull the Great Corkscrew out, what happened to the kingship?"

Baneen shrugged.

"Indeed, what could happen?" he said. "Since no one could pull the Corkscrew forth, it fell into disuse as a test of king-worthiness. The then king stayed on the throne, and those who came after him were smaller and smaller of soul until at the end, Hamrod the Heartless was rumored to have none at all—and sure his actions seemed to testify to that. But still it was said, that secretly Hamrod would go and pull at the Corkscrew now and then to try and prove himself rightful king. It was to deprive him of that hope of kingship-proof that Lugh stole the Corkscrew away and brought it here."

"What's all this about using the thing as a test, then?" growled Mr. Sheperton. "If no one could pull it out, what was the use of it?"

"Ah, but it was only no *gremlin* who could pull it out!" said Baneen. "That did not mean there was no human about with a soul large enough to free it. Indeed, Lugh's conscience had been troubling him for some time then about our gremlin rights on this world of yours and whether it had not become our world—a second Gremla, as it were—just by our being here so long. He decided that we would change our age-old custom of keeping to ourselves, and follow humans, if only humans could prove themselves worthy of being followed. So, to find out if such proof was possible, he set up a legend and a place, and disguised the Corkscrew itself so that no one could guess its origin, and then waited for what would happen."

"What did happen?" asked Rolf.

"Do you need to ask, Rolf?" demanded Mr. Sheperton. "Isn't it clear the rascal's trying to make us believe that the celebrated sword in the stone of Arthurian legend was no other than his gremlin Corkscrew?"

"And so it was," Baneen nodded.

"Stuff and nonsense!" snorted Mr. Sheperton. "Corkscrew indeed! It was a sword!"

"But—" said Rolf. "King Arthur pulled the sword out of the stone and was crowned king of England because of it—"

"So he did and was. But it was only with gremlin aid he was able to pull the blade forth—though little he suspected that, himself," said Baneen. "It happened that by the time young Arthur got his chance to try pulling loose the sword nearly everyone in England who stood a likelihood of being accepted king, if he did pull it forth, had tried and failed. Now, Arthur was very great of soul—

but not quite great enough by the width of a dragonfly's wing, as all we gremlins know. So it happened that a number of us went and pleaded with Lugh, and Lugh consented to our getting invisibly within the stone to push, while Arthur pulled—and so the sword came forth."

"Hurrah!" cheered Mr. Sheperton.

"Ah, but if you remember, it all turned out sadly," said Baneen. "Arthur prospered for a while, and brought justice to his kingdom. But you remember how his reign ended—the knights of the Round Table all divided against themselves, with Lancelot on one side and Arthur on the other, so that everything fell back to savagery and barbarism again."

There was a moment's silence.

"I'd like to try pulling that Corkscrew out," said Rolf, thoughtfully.

Baneen had been doing all this talking while keeping his eye on the boat and his fists clenched at his sides. In the process he had gradually drifted upward off the ground. He reached down now with one hand to make a brief pass in the air before Rolf. There was a shimmer and something took shape. It was not easy to see it clearly, but it was something like a massive bone handle attached to something metallic that was wrapped and sheathed in light.

"Try it, indeed, lad," said Baneen, heavily. "It can do no harm—though no good, either."

Rolf hesitated a second, then took hold of the handle with both hands and pulled. He strained, but the handle did not move.

"You see?" said Baneen wistfully. He waved his hand and the Great Corkscrew faded once more from sight. "Had you been able to pull it forth, you could have called on the House of Lugh of the Long Hand, and on Lugh himself, for any single thing you wished—for so did Lugh swear, giving his gremlinish word, back before Arthur was crowned king. But as you see, you cannot do it—no human nor gremlin can, these days. And that was why, when Arthur failed, Lugh determined that there was no hope for us in humans, and we must all return to Gremla. So we are, indeed, now, as you know—*Gremla save me!*"

The last words came out in a yelp; and from beyond the dune they suddenly heard several men's voices yelling at once. Rolf looked up at Baneen and saw the little gremlin now floating nearly a dozen feet off the ground, drifting like a soap bubble in the breeze, his tiny arms folded across his chest, his face still scowling mightily.

"What? What's all this?" barked Mr. Sheperton.

The yelling voices were coming from the boat. In the distance, the voice of Lugh bellowed, "Baneen, you wart-toad, get down there!" Rolf sprinted up to the top of the dune. He flattened out on his belly and motioned to Rita to do the same. She did, right beside him, and they both peered carefully through the tall grass.

The poachers' boat was a mess. A tall geyser of water was sprouting amidships, and the engine in the stern was boiling off a huge cloud of smoke. The sailors were scampering around the deck, plainly not knowing what to do first.

The captain was screeching, "She's sinking! She's sinking!"

Two men in business suits and sunglasses were looking pale and frightened. They were up at the prow of the boat, their mouths open.

"Help!" came Baneen's voice from high above, as suddenly the geyser of water shifted its angle until it began dousing the businessmen. They spluttered noisily and waved their arms, trying to ward off the liquid showering down on them.

"I said *get down*!" Lugh roared. He was back on the scene now, looking up at Baneen.

Baneen made some twisting motions, paddling his feet in midair. He cried out helplessly: "By the Sacred Stone of Gremla, I've used up so much magic on those scalawags that I can't get down again!"

Lugh's face looked like a thundercloud. "Let the spalpeen hang there 'til sundown, then," he muttered. And he stalked off, heading back for the Gremlin Hollow.

Rolf lay there in the sand, turning to watch the furious activity in the boat, which was still leaking and smoking. Then he looked up at Baneen again.

The little gremlin seemed genuinely frightened. "Lugh, me darling, don't leave me here, please! The wind's shifting . . . see, I'm blowing out to sea. You wouldn't have me land in a watery grave would you, Lugh, oh most handsome and powerful of gremlins . . . would you, Lugh . . . would you?" Baneen's voice got higher with each word. And sure enough, he was starting to drift toward the crest of the sand dune, heading toward the ocean.

Lugh stopped and looked back up at Baneen. "A watery grave it is for you, trickster. You've gotten yourself into this predicament with your tricks; now see if you can get yourself out. I'll not help you."

"Water's bad for gremlins," Rolf said to Rita.

"It could be very bad for Baneen if he falls into the ocean," Mr. Sheperton admitted grudgingly. "Gremlins are immortal, of course, but still—"

"Look," Rolf pointed. "He's drifting over this way. Maybe we can grab him when he comes up to the top of the dune."

"The people from the boat will see us," Mr. Sheperton said.

"They've got enough troubles right now," Rolf

answered quickly, glancing at the still-frantic action on the boat. "They won't be looking this way. And besides, we can't just let Baneen float away without trying to help."

Mr. Sheperton gazed for a long moment at Baneen's flailing form, floating slowly toward them. "He's too high," the dog said with a shake of his shaggy head. "I can't jump that high."

Rita nodded. "I'm afraid he's right, Rolf. We can't reach him, even from the crest of the dune."

Rolf could feel his face settle into a stubborn frown. "Oh, yeah? Well, we're not going to sit here and let him go out to sea without at least trying to help."

He got to his feet and walked slowly down toward the bottom of the dune. About halfway down, Rolf looked up, checked Baneen's position, then started trotting along the dune's slope to get exactly under the gremlin. He waited a few moments, letting Baneen drift closer to the top of the dune.

Then Rolf started running. He sprinted up the slope of the dune, toward the crest, stride, stride, each stride longer than the one before it. Baneen was already at the crest and starting to drift past when Rolf hit the top and leaped!

His outstretched fingers wrapped around one of Baneen's feet. Rolf hit the sand with a thud and sprawled over on his face, with the yowling, yelping Baneen safely in one hand.

"What's that?" yelled the man in the suit.

Rolf had landed on the seaward side of the dune. Mr. Sheperton dashed out and picked up Baneen in his teeth, while Rita came over to help Rolf to his feet.

"It's that kid and the dog again!" the captain squeaked. "After them, and this time I want them brought back here!"

All five of them, the two drenched businessmen, the two grimy sailors, and the captain scrambled out of the boat and toward Rolf and his friends.

Rolf started back for the dune's crest, holding Rita by one arm. But at the top, he saw Lugh, standing there with his legs straddled wide and his arms folded against his chest.

"You're a brave lad," Lugh said sternly. "Don't worry about those spalpeens."

Lugh gave a fierce glance, then pointed one finger at the advancing five men. *"May the Wrath of Gremla strike your heads."*

Rolf turned to watch.

Immediately, a rain of bottles, cigarette butts, beer cans, wadded-up paper, plastic cups, a thousand and one items fell out of the empty air onto the heads of the approaching men. They yelled and screamed, flung their arms over their heads, tripped and sprawled on the sand as bottle after bottle, can after can, ashtrays, paper plates, a cloudburst of junk fell upon them.

Lugh smiled grimly. "They've been tossing those things out of their nasty boat for weeks, they have. And I've been saving it all for them."

Rolf stared, amazed, as the five men staggered and limped back under the safety of their camouflaged bridge. The trash kept pouring down on them until they were all under protection. Magically, none of the trash littered the beach. It was all clean.

Rolf's last glimpse of the men, as he and Rita went over behind the sand dune's shoulder, showed him all five of them cowering under the bridge, trembling and wide-eyed. Even the captain was stained with dirt and sweat, and his beautiful jacket was covered with sand.

As they walked back to the Gremlin Hollow, with

Lugh several paces ahead of the rest, Baneen began to prance around as spryly as ever.

"Ah, you saved me, lad. Saved me from a fate worse than death . . . water." The little gremlin shuddered.

"It was awfully brave of you," Rita agreed.

Rolf fluttered his hands in embarrassment.

"And such a leap!" Baneen went on. "Like an Olympian the boy jumped. And here I thought you had a bad leg, me bucko. Could it be all healed now?"

Rolf had forgotten about his bad leg. "Yeah . . ." he said, feeling a strange glow inside. "I guess it *is* all healed."

"Ah, you see?" Baneen said, turning to Mr. Sheperton. "The lad's dealings with gremlins hasn't been all that bad for him, now has it? We cured his leg without half trying."

Mr. Sheperton huffed, "Typical gremlin chicanery. Don't take credit, Baneen, for Rolf's good health. His leg mended on its own. He just hadn't tested it until today. You had nothing to do with the healing of it."

"Perhaps, perhaps. But the lad still *thought* his leg was weak, until I arranged to show him otherwise."

"You arranged?" Rolf said, thunderstruck.

"Ah, well, it was really nothing . . . nothing at all," said the little gremlin, carelessly. "And it did my heart good to see those scalawags running about in the sinking boat. Let's talk of more interesting things—"

"No, you don't!" barked Mr. Sheperton. "We've had enough of your sneaky gremlin hint-and-slip-away. Let's have the matter straight, for once. Rolf, Baneen was only having fun at the expense of the people in the boat. There was never a thought in that tiny brain of his about your leg until after it was all over. Don't let him try to pretend otherwise."

"Oh, to be sure, and it's the grand, wise dog you

are, to be saying what was in my mind and what was not!" cried Baneen. "Had enough of our gremlin ways, you say—and did it ever cross your mind we'd have become a bit tired of your grump, grump, grumping doggish ways, all the time? Sure it's more than green flesh and blood can take, your everlasting criticism and belittling of our gremlin doings and all things gremlinish!"

"Wait a minute," said Rolf hastily. Neither Baneen nor the dog, however, were listening.

"Want to have it out, do you?" Mr. Sheperton snarled. "Come on, then! Called a spade a spade ever since I was a pup—I'll call a gremlin a gremlin to my dying day. If you don't like it—" He bared his teeth.

Baneen shot up in the air out of the dog's reach and hung there, vibrating with indignation.

"You and your great fangs!" he cried. "Thinking you can get away with anything. But beware, dog—we gremlins are not unprotected. Push me but one small push more, and I'll call forth a dragon to crunch and munch and slay you!"

"Hah!" snorted Mr. Sheperton. "Call forth a dragon, indeed! Enough of your rascally tall tales!"

"'Tis no tall tale!" shouted Baneen, almost dancing in the air with rage. "As you may find out to your cost, unless you mend your ways!"

"Come, come! A dragon? What sort of fool do you take me for? If you've got a dragon, let's see it!"

"Woe to you, if I call him forth!"

"Woe me not, gremlin! I said, produce this dragon or admit you've not got him."

"You'll rue that word, Mr. Sheperton—"

"Just as I thought!" snorted the dog disgustedly. "There's no such thing as a dragon around you gremlins."

"No such—!" screeched Baneen.

"That's what I said."

"No DRAGON?"

"None!"

"Dog, it's too far you've gone this day—"

"Wait. Wait—" said Rolf, hastily. "Look, there's no need for the two of you to get all geared up about this. Baneen, why don't you just give Mr. Sheperton your gremlinish word the dragon exists. Then—"

"Gremlinish word?" Baneen swallowed suddenly and looked unhappy. "Guk—"

"AND WHAT'S ALL THIS ABOUT GREMLINISH WORDS?" thundered a familiar voice. Lugh stalked into the midst of them.

"Ah . . . Lugh, darling, are you sure you heard the lad just right, now?" stammered Baneen. "Was it really the word grem—"

"I heard what I heard, and well you know I heard it," scowled Lugh. "What's all this talk about the Unbreakable Promise—and by humans and dogs, at that?"

"Not about to have my intelligence insulted!" huffed Mr. Sheperton. "Your green friend here was just threatening me with a dragon."

"And I," said Rolf, still trying to pour oil on the troubled waters, "just suggested that Baneen give Mr. Sheperton his . . . er . . . gremlinish word that the dragon existed, and let that settle the matter."

Lugh's scowl grew even blacker.

"Where did you hear about the gremlinish word, boy?" he demanded.

"Why, just the other time I was here," said Rolf, "Baneen and O'Rigami were having a little argument about the shape of the universe—"

"So!" Lugh swung on Baneen, fixing him with a fiery eye. The smaller gremlin slid apologetically down out of the air to the ground. "You let slip that there's a promise no gremlin can ever break, did you, me noisy chatterer? And now you've let your tongue run away with you about our gremlin dragon? Very well, we'll let this be a lesson to you. You've threatened the dog with the dragon. Now, produce it!"

"Ah, sure, and so much isn't needful, surely—" began Baneen.

"PRODUCE IT!"

"Wait!" Rolf swallowed hard. "You mean there really is—" He put his arms protectively around Mr. Sheperton's neck. "You're not going to sic any dragon on my dog—"

"Let it come," snarled Mr. Sheperton, raking the ground with his forepaws. "By St. George, I'll meet the creature tooth to tooth and nail to nail!"

"Shep, be quiet, won't you?" said Rolf desperately. "Lugh—" Lugh was standing with his arms folded, staring at Baneen, who was unhappily making passes in the air with his hands. Around the Hollow, all the other gremlins had fallen silent and were standing, watching. A puff of red smoke billowed up between Baneen's hands, and the little gremlin jumped back.

Rolf shoved himself hastily in front of Mr. Sheperton, facing the smoke.

"Wait!" he cried. "If anything happens to Shep I won't lift a hand to help you get your kite—"

"Too late," said Lugh, grimly.

The red smoke thinned—revealing not a large and fearsome creature with scales and fiery breath, but a small round table with a green tablecloth and a small white structure, something like a bird house, sitting in the middle of it.

"What?" said Rolf, staring at it.

"Baneen!" snapped Lugh commandingly. Baneen gulped and turned toward the little house.

"Mighty dragon of mighty Gremla!" he piped. "Come forth! Come forth and slay!"

From the dark doorway of the birdhouse came a small puff of smoke, then nothing for a few seconds, then another puff of smoke. Finally a third puff of smoke appeared with a tiny flicker of yellow flame in the midst of it.

"*Come forth,* dragon!" cried Baneen, in a high, desperate voice. "We command you!"

A tiny green dragon-head poked itself out of the opening, looked around, sighed heavily and withdrew. There was a metallic rattling sound inside the bird house, another sigh, and a small voice squeaked thinly. "Slay! Slay!"

The dragon came dancing out of the bird house on to the table, a minuscule sword in each of its front paws.

"Slay! Slay!" it cried, making threatening gestures all around with the swords and puffing out small round puffs of smoke with an occasional flicker of flame in them. "Slay! Slay . . . slay . . . sl . . ."

The dragon began to pant. The flame disappeared entirely and the puffs of smoke themselves grew thin. The swords it held began to droop.

" . . . Slay . . ." the dragon wheezed. It looked appealingly at Baneen. "Slay . . . how much . . . longer? I'm . . . slay . . . not as young as I . . . slay . . . used to be, you know. . . ."

"Enough!" said Lugh abruptly with a wave of his hand. "Back into your house and rest easy. The word of Lugh of the Long Hand is that you won't be called on for at least another ten thousand years."

"Huff . . . thank you . . . sir . . ." panted the dragon. It withdrew into its house; and house, table and all, disappeared in another puff of green smoke.

"Back to work, all the rest of you." The other gremlins returned to their activities.

"Let that settle the matter, then!" snapped Lugh.

Lugh stalked off. Rolf, Rita, and Mr. Sheperton were left facing a crestfallen Baneen.

"Well, well," grumped the dog in a curiously apologetic tone of voice. "Didn't mean to put you on the spot, Baneen, old man. Didn't really believe you had a dragon. Apologies, I'm sure."

"Ah, now, and that's kind of you, Mr. Sheperton," said Baneen, sadly. "But that great monster Lugh had the right of it. It was me own fault for threatening you with the poor creature. Sure, and my tongue clean ran away with me."

"Say no more," gruffed Mr. Sheperton.

"But it was a full-sized dragon, once, indeed it was," said Baneen, looking appealingly at the dog and the two humans alike. "Back on bright and dusty Gremla. The personal dragon of the House of Lugh, full twenty cubits in height and forty-six cubits long. However, it was necessary to shrink it down a bit in order to bring it to this Earth of yours; and as I've mentioned before—the watery place that it is here, not even Lugh could grow the creature back to its proper size again—not that we'd have wanted to risk letting it run around loose and maybe get killed off, like all your native dragons were, back in the days of the knights. Ah, it's cruel they were to the native dragons, your iron ancestors, murdering them on sight; and all in the name of honor and glory."

Baneen sighed heavily. Rolf found himself sighing right along with the small gremlin. A few dragons, still alive, could have made modern life much more interesting.

-9-

"What was it Baneen and the other gremlin—" began Rita as they were cycling home.

"O'Rigami," said Rolf. "He's the Grand Engineer."

"Oh?" Rita said. "What were he and Baneen talking to you about just before we left?"

"The blueprints," said Rolf, still deep in his own thoughts. "I don't know why they can't steal their own blueprints instead of leaving it up to me for everything."

"They want you to steal a blueprint?" cried Rita. "A blueprint of what?"

"Of the spacecraft's life-support system," Rolf answered. "I told them I couldn't. Even if I could get into Dad's office and even if the blueprints were there for me to find, I wouldn't recognize which one was the right one even if I saw it. I'm going to get them a poster, instead."

"A poster?"

"Sure," Rolf glanced at her as he pedaled. "You remember that wall-poster I got out at the Cape Kennedy Visitor's Center last May? The one with the chart on the back of what the spacecraft controls look like."

"But that's not the same thing as a blueprint," Rita said.

"I know, but for gremlins it doesn't make much difference, I guess." Rolf thought back to the way O'Rigami had explained it all to him. "It's only necessary for O'Rigami to touch the Speciar Virtue—"

"The what?" asked Rita.

"The Speciar Virtue . . ."

"You sound like you've got a Japanese accent."

"It's a gremlin accent," said Rolf, gloomily. "One of them, anyway. I meant the Spe*cial* Virtue of an object. O'Rigami says that all he needs to do is touch the Special Virtue of the spacecraft to the Magical Device—the space kite, that is. I'm just hoping that there's the right Special Virtue in my poster." He shook his head. "Gremlin magic doesn't work the way our science does."

Rita said, "I don't understand it."

"Neither do I," admitted Rolf. "Anyway, I hope the poster works as well as the blueprints for O'Rigami. But that's the easy part. It's getting up on the launch tower that worries me. I've got to do that tonight."

Mr. Sheperton, who had been trotting along between the two bikes, muttered, "Tomfoolery, all this gremlin nonsense."

Rolf frowned at the dog, then looked back at Rita. "That's why you've got to help me."

"Me?"

"Well," said Rolf. "I can't get into the Space Center and up to the launch tower all by myself. Your dad checks the men on the gates every night. If you went there because you wanted to talk to him, I was thinking maybe you could keep his attention while I sneaked in—"

"Rolf!" Rita was clearly upset. "I couldn't do that."

"Then we're done for."

"Not we. *You,*" said Rita, a little coldly.

"I mean all of us, the gremlins, the space program, everything."

Rita stared at him again. He could feel her eyes searching through him as he pedaled straight down the road, toward the setting sun.

"Why do you say the space program and . . . everything?" she asked at last.

"Because," he said, looking at her again, "I think Lugh can really keep the rocket from going up, if he wants to. Dad's always talking about the millions of parts in every rocket and how each one has to work just right. If Lugh can stop just a few of them, important ones, from working, nothing would happen. Or the whole rocket might blow up!"

"He wouldn't do that! Would he?"

Rolf shrugged. "He's got some temper. I saw him demolish a bulldozer—zowie! Just like that."

Rita nodded her head. "If the rocket doesn't go up—or blows up—that would cause trouble for the whole space program, all right."

"You know it," said Rolf.

"I . . . well, what good is it going to do, your getting up in the launch tower?"

"I've got to attach the kite onto the spacecraft," Rolf said.

Rita said nothing for a long moment.

"I don't know . . ." she said. "Why did you start out helping them, in the first place?"

She stared penetratingly at him. He rode along for a few seconds, scowling at the road.

"Baneen told me I could have a Great Wish—the same sort of thing I guess you get if you pull their Corkscrew out of its case. I asked them to clean up all the pollution and make the ecology safe and he gave me the word of Baneen they would, just as soon as I'd helped them."

"Did you ask for his gremlinish word?" Rita asked. Rolf shook his head.

"I didn't know about gremlinish words then," he said. "I suppose I should have."

"You'd better now."

"I guess. Only . . ." he hesitated. "You know, the more I think of it, the more I think the gremlins just can't do it. Maybe I should have suspected when Baneen agreed just like that."

"Can't do it?" She was watching him as they rode along.

"Not really," he growled. "How can they? Cleaning up all the pollution in the world is too big a job, for one thing. And even if they could clean it up, how could they protect the environment from now on without staying on the job to protect it? In fact, if they could do all that, how come they haven't done it before on their own?"

He shook his head.

"No," he said, "the more I think of it, the only way anything that big can be done would be with all humans and all gremlins working together."

"Then that's what you want to ask for," said Rita.

"How can I?" he said. "I can't make them promise to stay here as the price for my helping them get away. They can't do both things at the same time."

"Rolf," she said suddenly and energetically, "you don't make any sense at all! If this is the way you feel, how come you're helping them leave at all?"

He shrugged.

"I guess . . ." he said, slowly, "I guess it's because I suppose they've got a right to go home—just like the animals here in the Preserve have got a right to live without being hunted and the brown pelicans have got a right not to have the shells of their eggs weakened by DDT pollution."

They rode along in silence for a little while.

"It's all right," said Rita after a while. "I'll help you."

Rolf lifted his head.

"Great," he said.

"Terrible!" groused Mr. Sheperton.

At seven-thirty that night, Rolf and Shep, stood just outside the Gate Number Twelve of the Space Center. Rolf straddled his bike as Baneen floated a few feet off the ground beside him. They were all invisible—even Rolf's bike.

" . . . and what I don't see," Rolf was saying to Baneen, "is why you can't keep me invisible once I'm past the gate. If you'd just go in with me."

"Lad, lad," said Baneen sadly, "sure, and how am I to explain to you the terrible mysteries and such of gremlin magic, the same which has taken millions of years for gremlins to develop and you'd want an answer to every question about it that comes to mind!"

"Terrible . . ." muttered Shep, trailing off to something too low to be understood.

"As a matter of fact," said Baneen, "there's a metal cable underneath the road at the gate, with enough iron to keep a gremlin out. For a gremlin to cross cold iron is sort of like a human getting an electric shock. It's terribly hurtful."

"You could go around the gate," said Rolf.

"Well, now, there's bits and things of iron—or steel, if you will have it—all over the Space Center, no telling when a gremlin might run into it; and it's all most uncomfortable. Which is why, eager as we all are to see the fair, cloudless skies of Gremla, once more, it's been decided we wait safely in our Hollow until launch time and then magic ourselves directly to the safety of the space kite you'll have fixed to the rocket by then. . . ."

He broke off abruptly. Rita had just come riding down the road out of the darkness into the lights of the gate and dismounted to speak to the gate guard.

"Hi, Tom." Her voice came clearly to their ears from less than thirty feet away. "Has my dad been by yet?"

"Not yet, Rita," the guard said. "What is it?"

"Oh, nothing—I just wanted to ask him about having one of my girl friends stay over next weekend. Her folks are going out of town. . . ." Rita chattered on.

"What a fine lass she is, to be sure," said Baneen, fondly.

"Indeed she is!" snapped Shep. "No thanks to corrupting gremlin influences!"

"Now, is that a nice thing to say—" Baneen broke off again. A white Space Center security car was wheeling up to the inside of the gate. It stopped and Rita's father got out.

"Rita!" he said. "What are you doing here?"

He walked over to the gate, toward the guard and his daughter.

"Dad, Mom said to ask you," Rita said, energetically. "You know Ginny Magruder? Well, her folks are going over to New Orleans for three days, for a wedding of her cousin, and Ginny doesn't want to go, because it'll be nothing but older people and she doesn't like those cousins, anyway. So I said, why not come and spend the weekend with me; and she was really happy—you should have seen her. So, she said she'd have to ask her own folks, and she did and they said yes—"

"Off you go, lad!" hissed Baneen. "Now, whilst they're both still listening to her. The dog and I will meet you back here in an hour and a half."

"Don't know why I couldn't—" Shep began to grumble.

"No. Stay," said Rolf. He did not want to worry about anyone but himself on a trip like this. He hopped on his bike; and then remembered something.

He turned to Baneen.

"I don't have the space kite yet—"

"Go, lad! Go!" whispered Baneen, giving his bike a shove, that—light as it was—started the wheels rolling, so that Rolf's feet went automatically to the pedals.

"Look in your hip pocket when you get to the rocket!" he heard Baneen whisper behind him. Then he was past the gate and suddenly visible.

But the backs of both the guard and Rita's father were to him. Furiously, he began to pedal off down the road toward the tall, spotlighted shape of the distant rocket, illuminated according to custom, this night before the launch.

Gate Twelve was the closest of all the entrances to the Space Center to the launch pad of the rocket. But it was still several miles away; and it took Rolf some twenty minutes of hard pedaling to reach it. As he came close to the floodlighted area, he slowed down and finally stopped, just outside the lights that were making the pad and the rocket itself almost daylight-bright. He hid his bike in the brush just off the road and moved slowly up behind one of the lights in the darkest shadow behind it. Hidden in that shadow, he studied the launch area for evidence of guards.

There *had* to be guards, he thought—and there were. After some minutes of watching he located two of them: one, sitting in one of the white, security sedans and another making a regular round of the pad and the rocket, up along the top of the launch pad itself. As he watched, the security sedan started up and drove off, taking one of the guards away.

The other guard was now around the far side of the launch pad, as out of sight of Rolf, as Rolf was out of his sight. Rolf stepped forward into the light and began the long climb up the ramp that led to the launch pad.

It was too far up the ramp to run. Rolf went as fast as the slope would let him, however, and reached the top of the pad without being seen. Being his father's son, he had absorbed enough knowledge about launchings to find his way to the primary service elevator without trouble. The primary elevator was a cage of metal bars, close-set enough so as to shield out most of the light from the floodlights without. Rolf dared not turn on the ceiling light of the elevator, which he knew was there. He groped his way to the control panel in one wall, pressed the up button and the cage rose.

He rode the elevator to the transfer point—about seventy-five feet above the surface of the pad—then left it for the narrow walkway that took him across to the secondary elevator of the launching tower. This other elevator was a more open cage, and he was able to see the pad below him as he rose. As he looked down, he saw the foreshortened figure of the first guard come back up on the level surface of the pad and look around.

Rolf gulped, but there was not time to think about the guard now. He rode the elevator to its top level, got out and crossed another narrow catwalk that led him directly to the spacecraft itself, sitting on top of the three tall sections that were the fuel-laden stages of the rocket.

He reached the spacecraft and put a hand on its smooth metal side. It's beautiful, he thought. *Like a work of art.* Now for the gremlin space kite. He reached into his hip pocket.

For a moment he thought there was nothing there, and his breath stopped in his chest. Then he felt a small papery object, and he brought it out. In the light from below, he looked at it. It was the space kite, all right, but no bigger now than the paper swan O'Rigami had folded for him when he first met the gremlin Grand Engineer.

Hardly believing that this could in fact be the kite he had seen earlier, he reached up and pressed it against the outer skin of the spacecraft.

There was something like a soundless *poof*. The tiny shape began to swell with rapidly increasing speed. In a moment it was as big as Rolf's hand, as big as a basketball, as big as . . .

The panic that had erupted in Rolf as the object suddenly began to grow in size and conspicuousness, suddenly began to die down. For the first time he noticed that as the kite got bigger, it was also getting filmier and filmier, until he could begin to see right through it . . . indeed, until it finally faded away into invisibility. Rolf stood gazing at last at a spacecraft that looked as if it had nothing attached to it at all.

So that was the secret of the space kite! He might have known the gremlins would have figured out some way to keep their space vehicle from being noticed by the human astronauts that would be boarding the metal spacecraft in the morning. He turned without wasting any more time, and hurried back to the secondary elevator to start his ride down again.

He reached the changeover point and switched to the primary elevator. This slid him downward with the noiselessness of smoothly running electrical equipment; and he had all but forgotten about the guard when it reached bottom and the door opened automatically.

"Who's that?" called a voice from the pad just outside. "What's going on there?"

A second later the bright beam of a flashlight lanced through the open door of the elevator cage and there was the sound of running footsteps.

Rolf shrank back into a corner of the elevator, his heart thumping like the heart of a wild rabbit in a trap. If only he knew some gremlin magic—at least enough to make himself invisible. There was no way out but the open doorway of the elevator and the guard was coming straight for it. In a moment he would be discovered; and then . . .

The guard burst into the cage, actually running past Rolf.

"Who's here?" shouted the guard. "Who—"

He started to turn around. There was no chance to dodge past him without being seen. In desperation, Rolf stammered out the first thing he could think of.

"M-May the Great and Thunderous Curse of Gremla fall upon your head!" he stammered out loud.

"Wha—aaaCHOO!" exploded the guard, turning around. His flashlight wavered from floor to ceiling, out of control, as he burst into a series of gargantuan sneezes. "Who said . . . ACHooo! Ach—"

Rolf did not wait to answer him. Slipping past the blinded, sneezing man, he headed out across the pad, and down its slope toward his bicycle as the echos of body-racking sneezes floated after him through the floodlit night.

After that narrow escape, it was almost nothing to wait for a moment when the guard on Number Twelve Gate had his back turned, and slip past him into the open freedom of the Wildlife Preserve where Shep and Baneen were waiting with the invisibility that would shield him on the road home.

-10-

THE launch was set for ten a.m., Eastern Daylight Time. At seven-thirty that morning, as Rolf and Rita rode their bikes out toward the Preserve, with Mr. Sheperton tagging along beside them, the roads were already crowded with carloads of people who had driven in to watch the Mars rocket's liftoff.

In the Indian and Banana rivers, small boats were anchored for the same purpose. And several miles offshore in the deep ocean water, there were even a couple of large cruise ships whose passengers had come to watch the event.

"At least the poachers won't cause any trouble," Rolf shouted to Rita as they pedaled. "Their boat's still being repaired, thanks to Baneen."

"And how are we going to get into the Refuge?" Rita asked him. "There'll be police and security cars all over the place—it's closed up tight now."

Rolf didn't answer for a moment. He was busy shifting the rolled-up poster on the handlebars of his bike. The poster was too long to be carried safely on the rattrap behind him.

"Baneen's going to meet us halfway there and help us get there," he said at last.

"By making us invisible?" asked Rita.

With a shrug, Rolf answered, "I don't know. Gremlin magic is pretty strange. Sometimes it works fine, but just when you need it most—"

A gray sedan with official markings on its side nosed out of the traffic and started coming up toward them on the shoulder of the road. Rolf and Rita pulled their bikes aside. Rolf's heart was hammering with sudden memories of the night before. *Did the guard recognize me after all?* But the sedan went right past them; the two officers inside didn't even flick an eye at him.

With a loud "Whew!" Rolf started pedaling again.

"You know," Rita said, pulling up alongside him, "it's sort of too bad that the gremlins are going. They're kind of fun."

Rolf blinked at her. He had been thinking about something for a long time now, he realized. Just when it started to bother him, he wasn't sure. Possibly it was right after the trouble with the bulldozer out at the Hollow when both Lugh and Baneen had admitted that they didn't like people such as the boat captain who had been bringing people out to the Preserve illegally and polluting the environment. He couldn't put it into words, but something about the gremlins was nagging at him.

"You're right," he said to Rita. "I don't know if it's a good thing that they're going—"

"Good riddance to bad rubbish," Mr. Sheperton growled.

Rita still looked startled every time she heard Mr. Sheperton speak. She could accept the gremlins, but the dog's speaking always seemed to surprise her.

"Now listen Shep . . . er, Mr. Sheperton," Rolf said crossly. "I know Baneen and the others can't always be trusted to tell the exact truth, but even if they haven't been on Earth for millions of years or whatever it is, they've been around here for a long time. I wonder if maybe we don't need them?"

They were cycling past a car that had all its windows open as it inched along in the heavy traffic. A small boy's high-pitched voice piped, "He's talkin' to his doggy, Mommy. Look, he's talkin' to his doggy."

"Yes, dear," answered a woman's voice, absently. "Isn't that nice of him?"

"Need gremlins?" Rita asked as they continued along the jam-packed road. "But all they do is cause trouble. I thought they admitted that themselves."

"That's what Baneen says," Rolf admitted. "But I wonder how much of that is just showoff stuff—"

"Like diving off a high board?" Mr. Sheperton suggested drily.

"Man, can't you say anything pleasant anymore?" Rolf snapped.

"Gremlins can't be trusted," Mr. Sheperton insisted. "We need them like a flea needs flea powder. Look at what they've done to you: turned you into a thief, almost, and gotten you to sneak into the launch pad. Why, if you'd been caught—"

"Well I wasn't," said Rolf. "Not because you helped, either!"

Rita tried to nip the argument by getting back to the original subject. "If we need the gremlins the way you said we did, they must know about it, with their ability to see the future and all. So why are they leaving?"

"That's what I'd like to find out," said Rolf. "The *real* reason they're going. I've got the feeling that they've told me already, but in a very sneaky, roundabout, gremlinish sort of way. Some of the things that Lugh and Baneen had said . . . I can't seem to put my finger on exactly what it is. If I knew what it was that was really making them go, maybe I could talk them out of it."

"Talk a gremlin out of anything," muttered Mr. Sheperton, from beside Rolf's bike. "That's like talking the moon out of the sky. They're too much the experts at talking people into things, to be talked themselves. If you want to convince a gremlin of something, you've got to show him proof that is proof!"

Rolf just shook his head, feeling very confused.

"Ah, now, here we are, and a grand and lovely morning to you all," said Baneen's voice.

Rolf looked down and saw the gremlin perched on his handlebar again. This time he noticed that Baneen was sitting on the plastic handgrip of the handlebar, not on the steel itself.

"Fear not, lad," Baneen winked up at him. "None of the folks in their fume-making cars going by can see or hear me. Any more than they can hear Mr. Sheperton's grumpy old voice."

Shep growled at him.

"How long have you been there?" Rolf asked.

Baneen had turned to make horrible faces at the people in the cars they were passing. He waggled his big pointed ears, crossed his eyes, stretched out his mouth by pulling at its corners with his green fingers, and stuck out his tongue. No one noticed him at all, but several people began sneezing as they passed.

"How long have you been listening to us?" Rolf demanded.

"Why, I came as quickly as I could, overloaded as I am with duties, this glorious morn of our departure," said Baneen. "But it's true that I arrived just this moment past. Why do you ask, lad?"

"I just wondered," said Rolf.

"How are you going to get us past the patrols that are keeping people out of the Preserve?" Rita asked.

"Ah, surely that's no trouble at all," said Baneen smilingly. "Just turn in here. . . ."

They nosed their bikes off the shoulder of the road and onto the hard-packed sand. Mr. Sheperton followed them.

"And a tiny bit o' gremlin dust . . ." Baneen flung something invisible up out of his hand. The world seemed to turn into a milky white mist for a moment.

"And here we are!" Baneen said as the mist cleared.

They were indeed at the Gremlin Hollow, Rolf saw.

But things were different. For once, the hurry and scurry were missing. Little flickers and glimpses of gremlins moving about, as usual, but they seemed to be dragging along like deep-sea divers trudging on the bottom of the ocean. The glimpses Rolf caught of their small pointy faces showed them all to be wearing unusually sober, saddened expressions.

The only two completely visible were O'Rigami, who looked as imperturbable as ever, and Lugh, who stood scowling at things in general—even more blackly than usual.

Rolf got off his bike and handed the poster to O'Rigami. It was so big it nearly knocked the gremlin over.

"Ahh, many thanks," said O'Rigami, staggering slightly under the poster's weight. He bowed politely, then turned and gave the poster a flick of his hands. It floated out in midair, unrolled, and spread itself neatly on the sandy floor of the Hollow.

"Very fine," O'Rigami said. "Not precisery what we need, but crose enough."

He clapped his hands together.

"Gremrin weavers, front and center!"

There was a sort of semivisible scurry around and above the laid-out paper. Squinting at the scene, Rolf found it reminded him of how things look to someone driving through a fog—you sort of sense something is out there before you really see it.

It was impossible for any human eye to see exactly what was going on, but Rolf thought he could make out that something rather invisible was being put together on top of the poster as it lay face up. Something like the rippling of heat waves flowed across the poster from one end to the other, then slowly settled down and ceased.

"Excerrent!" said O'Rigami, to the almost-invisible gremlin workers. "Now, take firm grip."

There was evidently a good deal of effort involved in this part of the job, for a double line of gremlins flickered into visibility at both the top and bottom edges of the poster. Their tongues were clenched between their lime-colored teeth, feet planted wide, and their cheeks puffed out with effort as they clutched grimly onto something that was a good eight inches above the poster itself.

"Ready?" asked O'Rigami.

The half-visible little figures braced themselves. Suddenly, one of them at the far bottom corner of the poster lost his footing and fell. Like dominoes, the whole line along the bottom of the poster went down.

"Take care! Take care!" cried O'Rigami. "Take grip once more."

The line along the bottom of the poster formed up again.

"Now," shouted O'Rigami, "three times—as I count. Ready? *One!*"

Both lines of half-visible gremlins raised and lowered their arms. Something misty—a sheet of mistiness—formed between them, above the poster at the level where their hands were clenched.

"*Two!*" cried O'Rigami.

Their arms moved up and down again, accompanied by a chorus of tiny grunts and wheezes. Rolf suddenly realized that what they were doing was like what he and his friends used to do down at the beach, when they were shaking the sand off a blanket. Except that this "blanket" was a thin film of mistiness, and there was no sand on it.

"*Three!*" roared O'Rigami, jumping clear off the ground with his hands raised over his head.

The gremlins holding whatever-it-was flapped it once more, mightily, and fell over backward, becoming visible as they lay about looking exhausted. What they had held had also become completely visible now—it was like a thin blue veil of finest silk, shot with white. It floated downward and settled exactly on top of the poster.

O'Rigami hissed with satisfaction, stepping forward to the very edge of the veil-like object.

"Why," exclaimed Rita, "it *is* a blueprint!"

In fact, what lay on the ground now, although it seemed to be made out of exquisitely fine silk, looked exactly like a very complicated technical blueprint.

"Of course," O'Rigami said to Rita. "What did you expect, a beach branket?"

"But how could you get that from the poster?" Rolf asked, staring at the blueprint.

"Now, now, lad," said Baneen abruptly. "It's as simple as enchanting a princess. The poster was made up from designs of the actual spacecraft, was it not? And since the spacecraft itself was constructed from blueprints, must it not be that the form of the blueprints was living in the design of the spacecraft, and the form of the spacecraft was living in the design of the poster? Like equals like, as one of those Greek geometers used to say. Sure and it was only the skill of the gremlin weavers it took to extract the design and make it visible."

"Oh," said Rolf, his head buzzing.

He would have said more, but now O'Rigami had just produced a small bagful of the transistors and other little items Rolf had gotten from the hardware store.

"Now," said the Grand Engineer, "we add the connectors, correctry magicked, to the brueprint, thereby energizing it and—"

He tossed the handful of small electronics components into the air. They floated out over the blueprint, descended to it, and disappeared. All but one tiny piece of red wire, which stood at one end and scurried in circles about the blueprint. O'Rigami pointed a finger and stamped his foot, the wire hopped, scooted to its proper position, and vanished with a small *poof.*

"Connection is estabrished," continued O'Rigami. "Now we attach the activated brueprints to both the human spacecraft and the space kite."

He clapped his hands. The blueprint disappeared, leaving only the poster below it, untouched. O'Rigami turned to Lugh and bowed.

"Ready to board," he announced.

Lugh was scowling worse than ever. The look on his face would have stopped a charging bull elephant in full stride. The only good thing about it was that it did not seem to be directed at anyone in particular.

"Ready is it?" snarled Lugh. "All right then, what are the lot of you waiting for? Get on board and shake the garbage and asphalt of this miserable world from our gremlin boots!"

There was a sort of uneasy waveriness in the air of the Hollow and suddenly gremlins became visible, hundreds of them, thousands of them, all looking unhappy.

"What are you waiting for?" roared Lugh. "Did we or did we not give them their chance nearly two thousand years ago? BOARD!"

And like tiny lights going out all around Rolf, Mr. Sheperton and Rita, the hordes of gremlins began to disappear, leaving the Hollow empty with a strange and aching loneliness that Rolf could actually feel. It was a feeling such as he had never imagined before. Suddenly Lugh's last few words made sense to him, and he understood why the gremlins were really leaving Earth and why it was up to him to stop them.

"Wait!" he cried.

But all the gremlins in the Hollow were gone now except Lugh, O'Rigami and Baneen. Even as he shouted, O'Rigami gave the two humans and the dog a polite bow and disappeared. Lugh winked out almost the same instant, and Baneen thinned to transparency, flickering like a candle flame that was dying.

-11-

"Wait, Baneen!" Rolf shouted again, desperately.

For a second, it seemed that Baneen was almost gone. Then he grew solid again.

"Forgive me, lad," he said softly, "but I can't wait. It's time for us all to be going now, and they're waiting for me aboard the space kite. Farewell . . ."

A single tear ran down the side of his nose. He lifted a hand in a wave and began to fade again.

"Just a minute—please, Baneen—just a minute!" Rolf shouted. "Listen! I know why you're going! But you don't need to!"

"Farewell . . ." sang Baneen, mournfully. As he grew fainter and fainter he said, "A long farewell to Earth." His tone changed abruptly and he almost smiled as he added, "And, Rolf me boy, sorry to have tricked you into helping us. It was the only way we could get away, you know."

"That's not important," Rolf insisted. "What's important is—I know why you're going! And you don't need to!"

"Ah, yes. Too bad that—you know *what*?" Baneen flickered halfway back to solid visibility.

Rolf could hardly stand still, and Rita was eyeing him in astonishment. Mr. Sheperton was sitting on his haunches, mumbling something.

"I know why you gremlins are leaving, I tell you!" said Rolf desperately. "And you don't have to! Come back, Baneen. Listen to me for just a minute!"

Baneen flickered again, faded almost completely out, then grew more and more solid until he once more stood before them as real as themselves.

"Now lad, it's no use trying to trick a gremlin. Sure, we've known all the tricks ourselves since your ancestors were painting themselves blue and hiding in caves."

"It's not a trick!" Rolf said. "I really do know why you're going back to Gremla. I would have figured it out before, but you kept telling me how you had no use for Earth and how beautiful Gremla was. But you all really like it here on Earth, don't you?"

"Ah, what difference does it make? In less than a minute we'll be all aboard the space kite and ready for blastoff. Look—" Baneen pointed a tiny green finger. The mist of the Hollow seemed to be dissolving. Well, not exactly dissolving as much as shrinking, pulling itself together into one ball of milky whiteness that grew smaller and smaller as Rolf and the others watched it.

"You see?" Baneen said. "The magic gate is closing. I've got to get through it before it shrinks altogether and I'm stranded here while my brothers and sisters fly back to Gremla." He edged toward the shrinking sphere of whiteness.

Rolf grabbed at his skinny arm. "If you hated Earth so much, why didn't you leave centuries ago?"

Baneen looked distinctly uncomfortable. "Well, as I told you, lad, there's that dampness which keeps our magic from lifting us more than a wee distance above the ground. It's helpless we were, entirely, until you humans got the idea of building space rockets. . . ."

The milky white sphere was down to the size of a big beach ball.

"You gremlins had nothing to do with our inventing rockets?" Rolf demanded.

"Well now," said Baneen, squirming in Rolf's grip, "maybe we did give the idea a wee push here and there. What with Mr. Da Vinci, and those Chinese fellows, and Mr. Goddard later on—"

The sphere was down to the size of a basketball. Baneen pulled, trying to get away from Rolf.

"Wait," said Rolf. "Listen to me. It was all Lugh's doing, wasn't it? All of you had come to like it here, but Lugh wasn't going to have anything to do with humans unless they were perfect, would he? He tried to make humans live up to a test that gremlins themselves couldn't even pass, nowadays. And when they couldn't do it, he decided to take you all back to Gremla—but none of you really want to go, now. You're all *Earth* gremlins—look at you, so Irish-sounding anybody'd expect to see you start sprouting shamrocks! O'Rigami, Japanese to the core! O'Kkane Baro, who's probably more gypsy than gremlin, from the way he looks to me. And La Demoiselle, who's not only so French you can't believe it, but all wound up in a bit of Earth history that won't mean a thing back on Gremla. Don't tell me, all of the rest of you really want to leave Earth! It's just Lugh! Isn't it?"

"Y-yes . . ." stammered Baneen—and clapped a hand over his mouth immediately. "What am I saying? Miscalling my own Prince—but it's true. Indeed it's true. Lugh would have it that we mustn't associate with humans unless they were able to show themselves worthy of our association. Not but what most of us have done our wee best, here and there, when the opportunity came up, little tricks to nudge your people in the right direction. But little avail it was, what with Lugh giving you a mighty push to hurry up and develop your machines and your engines, and all the rest of it, until you had something that could fly us back to Gremla as secret passengers. But how could you know about Lugh, lad?"

"Because I was the same way," Rolf said. "I was doing exactly the same thing, this last year. My mother was all wrapped up in my baby sister, and my dad had to work night and day for this launch, but I blamed them both for not being able to give me all the time they used to. I was expecting them to be perfect where I was concerned, no matter what they had to deal with anyplace else. I finally realized what I was doing, by seeing Lugh do the same thing. He's never gotten over the way it used to be back on Gremla, and he wanted Earth to be Gremla all over again. But it isn't—and he's just got to live with it, the way I have to live with my own family."

He let go of Baneen's arm, but the gremlin merely stood now, staring at him.

"Glory be!" breathed Baneen. "If Lugh could hear you—perhaps he'd change his mind yet.

"But—" the little gremlin wrung his hands together, "he'd never stop now, not for any simple word—"

"I'll stop him!" barked Mr. Sheperton. "I'll stop the whole pack of them, see if I don't!"

With that, the dog leaped at the magic gate.

"No!" yelped Baneen.

But Mr. Sheperton dove right through and disappeared. And the gate shriveled and shrank like a popped balloon, right behind him. As soon as Mr. Sheperton's tail flicked out of sight, the milky white sphere disappeared altogether.

"He's ruined the gate!" Baneen cried. "And he'll ruin

the space kite on the other side!" Then Baneen's eyes really went wide with terror. "And how am I going to get aboard? HOW AM I GOING TO GET ABOARD?"

Rolf simply stood there, stunned. It was Rita who recovered her senses first.

"How much time do we have before the rocket takes off?" she asked.

That snapped Rolf back. He glanced at his wrist-watch. "Oh no!! There's only six minutes left!"

Baneen was scampering around, distraught, pulling his eyebrows down into his mouth and chewing on them, mumbling, "Hmlgghmmgrmll—"

Rolf grabbed him by the shoulder. "Baneen! Can you get us to the launch pad inside of six minutes?"

The gremlin shook himself. "Well I could . . . no, that wouldn't work. Or if—no, that's no good. . . ."

"Quick!" Rita said. "It's got to be right away!"

"There's only one way to do it," Baneen said, looking up at them. "But it means I'll have to go with you—and all that iron and steel—" He shuddered.

"We've got to!" Rolf insisted.

Baneen squared his shoulders. "You're right, lad. There's nothing else to do. Even though it may be the end of me, what matters one poor wee gremlin when—"

"Can it!" Rita shouted. "Let's get going!"

"Right!" cried Baneen. "Onto your bikes, you two." And he glided up and sat on Rolf's handlebar.

"The bikes?" Rita asked.

"We've only got five minutes," said Rolf.

"Trust me," said Baneen, with an almost saintly smile on his gremlin face.

It wasn't like any bike ride in the history of the world. The instant their feet touched the pedals, the bicycles took off like racing cars and went faster and faster. The bush and sand dunes went blurring past.

"There's the road now!" Baneen yelled over the howling wind. He was hanging onto the plastic handgrip of the handlebar with one tiny hand, and keeping his hat jammed on his head with the other. "Follow it in to the base!"

They were going at least seventy miles an hour, Rolf guessed—and straight toward the double line of cars that still jammed the road.

"We'll crash," cried Rolf, as he squeezed the handbrakes. But the brakes didn't slow the bike at all. He and Rita—with Baneen hanging on by one hand—hurtled directly at the traffic on the road.

-12-

For one instant it seemed they were going to smash right into the side of a big mobile home. Then the handlebars twitched by themselves, and suddenly both bikes were weaving in and out among the cars and trailers and campers, zooming along the road at fantastic speed, the wind screeching past so fast that Rolf could scarcely breathe.

Frantic drivers jammed on their brakes. Children and mothers sat staring, pop-eyed, as the two bikes roared past them at the speed of jet planes. Half the time Rolf simply closed his eyes as they scooted between cars, around trucks, and—he swore—*over* a busload of tourists from Dayton, Ohio.

Baneen had slipped off the handgrip and was flapping in the wind, hanging on with one hand and screaming madly.

"Ouch! Oh! All this—oof!—iron and steel! Ouch! Great Gremla protect me—ouch!"

Behind them the cars they passed set up a honking, like a mechanical chorus of angry machines. They zipped past a checkpoint, and the guard standing beside his gray sedan let the radio microphone drop from his hand as he stared at the two nearly supersonic bikes roaring by. His partner picked up the microphone and started babbling into it.

They passed the entrance to the Space Center so fast that the guards there were knocked down by the blast of wind. They scrambled to their feet and started yelling into their microphones:

"Two bicycles—must be doing five-hundred miles an hour—yeah, yeah, *bicycles*! No, I don't have sunstroke!"

Back at the Manned Launch Center, Rita's father shook his head at the hastily typed report that had just been handed to him. Security guards were bustling around the room he was in, other men and women were sitting at radio desks and working typewriters.

Mr. Amaro's eyes widened as he read the report. "Five-hundred miles an hour? Bicycles? Are they all going crazy out there?"

An excited voice came through one of the radio loudspeakers: "I can see 'em! They're a couple of kids— the bikes are goin' so fast they're just a blur. And they're headin' straight for the VAB!"

Mr. Amaro crumpled the typewritten sheet in his hand. "Crazy or not, nobody's getting into the Vehicle Assembly Building without a pass! Come on."

Meanwhile Rolf and Rita were zooming along, heading for the enormous, massive shape of the VAB, where the rockets are put together before they are taken out to their launch pads.

"Ouch! Oh! Will we never get there?" Baneen was groaning.

"Look!" Rita yelled over the howling wind. "Security cars coming!"

Rolf saw the white cars speeding toward them from both sides of the VAB. "We can't go around!" he shouted. "They've got both sides blocked!"

"Do something!" Rita yelled to Baneen.

"All right—owoo!" cried Baneen. "Straight up, then—ooch, ouch! The whole building's full of iron, isn't it?"

They hurtled directly at the straight solid wall of the VAB as if they were going to smash themselves against it. Rolf involuntarily closed his eyes, and the next thing he knew their bikes were racing straight *up* the wall, defying gravity and going as fast as ever.

Down at the base of the building, Mr. Amaro hopped out of his car before the driver had even brought it to a complete stop. He snapped his head back so fast that his uniform cap fell off.

"I don't believe it!" he muttered to himself. "I see it, but it's impossible!"

The two bikes went right up to the top of the wall and disappeared over the edge of the roof.

"It's like being on top of a mountain," Rolf yelled as they bounced onto the roof of the VAB. "This is the highest point in all Florida, I bet."

"It's nice being away from all those horns and the people yelling," Rita agreed.

But they only had a moment to enjoy the quiet and the view. With Baneen still *ouch*ing every inch of the way, they hurtled straight for the far edge of the roof.

Rolf felt his stomach drop away as his bike—and Rita's—raced right off the roof and did a "Wheelie" on the back wall of the VAB. They both sailed down the wall with only their rear wheels touching. Rolf squinted downward. There was nothing between his madly pedaling feet and the ground except hundreds of feet of very thin air.

"Don't look down!" he yelled to Rita, as his hands suddenly went clammy.

"Why not?" Rita hollered back. "It's fun! Man, is that a long way down!"

Rolf concentrated on keeping his teeth from chattering.

They got to the ground and scooted off again, just as a couple of security cars pulled around the corner of the building.

"Whew," said Baneen, pulling himself back up to a sitting position. "At least we're away from that nasty iron for a moment or two."

Rolf glanced at his wristwatch. Two minutes to go before liftoff.

They were heading straight for the giant rocket and its launch stand, with a half dozen white security cars trailing along behind them, sirens blaring distantly. But now Rolf saw that between them and the launch stand were more cars, and hundreds of people sitting in the press stands.

"How can we get around them?" he asked Baneen.

"Not around," puffed Baneen. "Over." Then the gremlin asked in a lower, sadder tone, "By the way, lad, that launching stand and the great tall tower—they're made of iron, aren't they?"

"Steel," said Rolf.

Baneen's eyes rolled up and the corners of his mouth dropped. "Ah, well—up and away!"

The bicycles soared into the air for a short distance, then bounced back to the ground. Another hop, longer this time, took them over a row of parked cars. Baneen winced and fidgeted. Then they bounded over a startled group of photographers, who jumped and shouted, and knocked over each others' tripods in their surprise.

Bouncing, they reached the press stands where the reporters and photographers were eagerly watching the final moments of countdown. They soared over the watchers, who yelled and ducked as the bikes cleared their heads by inches.

They bounced down on the apron of ground between the viewing stand and the canal of water that ran between the launch stand and the VAB.

"Water!" screeched Baneen. "Merciful Gremla!"

The canal was about two hundred yards across, and deep, as Rolf knew. And they were hurtling for it too fast to swerve aside.

"Up and over!" shouted Baneen, his voice quavering.

The two bicycles soared up like gliders and rose over the canal. Baneen put a hand over his eyes while he wailed, "Water . . . oo!"

Rolf also closed his eyes. He didn't mind flying in a plane, but in a bicycle . . . !

He felt his bike touch down again, but on something that wasn't quite solid ground. Opening his eyes, Rolf saw that they were pedaling up a wire, with Rita's bike right in front of him. Like circus acrobats, they raced up the steeply angled wire.

Pushing down a lump in his throat, Rolf shouted ahead to Rita, "This is the escape wire—the astronauts use this to slide down from the spacecraft in case something goes wrong right before the rocket ignites."

Rita half-turned in her seat to look at him over her shoulder. "I know. Isn't it fun?" She was grinning broadly.

Fun! Rolf felt paralyzed as they raced up the slim strand of wire, and she thought it was fun. *She's got more faith in gremlin magic than I have!*

Meanwhile, more than a dozen white security cars had pulled up to a screaming halt beside the launch pad.

Half a dozen guards ran over to Mr. Amaro's car. He jumped out and started shouting to them:

"Well, where are they? Have you seen them?"

"No, sir. Can't find them anywhere!" None of the men was looking high enough to see the two bicycles zooming up the escape wire. The bikes were just a blur anyway; they were going so fast.

"Well, spread out," Mr. Amaro ordered. "They must have sneaked in among the crowd someplace."

One of the guards, his face sweaty and worried-looking, asked, "Sir, should we ask Mission Control to put a hold on the countdown? Those kids might be anyplace—"

"No," Mr. Amaro said. "They've got awfully fast motorbikes, I'll admit. But they'd have to be able to fly to get across the canal and into the launch area itself. There's no chance of that."

"Right," the other guard agreed.

Up, up and up the two bikes raced while Baneen shuddered and moaned. "Iron and steel, iron and steel. Ooohhh."

Finally they thumped to a stop, and Rolf saw that they were now on the same platform he had come to the night before, in the elevator. The spacecraft was standing at one end of the platform, smooth and white. The space kite itself was hanging from the spacecraft's outer skin, looking tiny and barely visible—but at the same time, Rolf thought it looked big as a jetliner. He could see thousands of gremlins jostling around inside the kite, flickering in and out of visibility like a set of winking Christmas lights.

Somewhere a loudspeaker was saying, "Thirty seconds and counting. . . . The launch tower is now starting to roll away from the rocket vehicle and spacecraft."

And the tower was beginning a slow, grinding, growling motion.

"Lugh, ye great hulking heap of princely magic!"

Baneen cried out, hopping on the steel platform as if it were covered with hot coals. "Come . . . ooooh! . . . quick. There's grand news!"

"Twenty seconds and counting . . ."

Lugh appeared at the edge of the kite, as if he were standing on a wing of it. "What is it now, trickster? Are you staying with the humans, after all?"

"Listen—ouch!—quick, Lugh me darling. There's no need to leave Earth. None at all. For any of us!"

Before Lugh could reply, though, Rolf broke in, "Where's Shep—Mr. Sheperton?"

"Ten seconds, nine, . . ."

"The dog?" Lugh scowled. "Tried to rip our kite off the rocket, he did. I cooled him off. Down there!"

Lugh pointed, turned his back and walked off toward the edge of the platform. Rolf stared down in the direction the other had indicated and saw Mr. Sheperton paddling weakly in a large pond of water.

That's the water that feeds into the exhaust cooling sprays! Rolf realized. *In a few seconds the pumps will suck Shep down and then fire him right into the hot exhaust gases when the rocket takes off!*

"Nine, eight . . ."

"Stop the launch!" Rolf yelled. Desperately, he looked about him. Lugh still stood with his back turned. Then a glitter caught Rolf's eye. The Great Corkscrew of Gremla was taking form beside him. He glanced at it, and saw standing behind it O'Rigami, La Demoiselle, and O'Kkane Baro, along with other gremlins whose names he did not know. The voice of Baneen whispered in his ear.

"Pull it out, lad—quickly. We'll help!"

Already, O'Rigami and the others were disappearing into the glitter of the case of the Great Corkscrew. Frantically, Rolf took hold and pulled. There was a moment when nothing happened and then suddenly the Great Corkscrew slid easily from its case and the brilliant light flashing from it glittered all around. Lugh spun about.

"Stop the launch!" shouted Rolf, holding the Corkscrew aloft and waving it at the gremlin prince.

"Five . . . four . . ." boomed the loudspeaker. Lugh stood, staring.

Rolf could not wait any longer for Lugh to act. He threw the Corkscrew aside, and dived for the hook at the end of the escape wire. In an eyeblink he was sliding madly back *down* the wire, racing toward the ground and the water at the edge of the launch pad, nothing between him and a five-hundred-foot fall except the strength of his fingers as they clutched the hook of the handgrip.

The loudspeaker droned. "Two, one . . . zero . . ."

Rolf's feet touched the ground and he ran pell-mell to the edge of the tank and without an instant's hesitation, dived in. Mr. Sheperton was still struggling in the water as if some invisible force were binding his legs.

"Shep, Shep—I'm here! I'll save you!" Rolf yelled as he swam toward the dog.

"Too late . . ." gargled Mr. Sheperton, weakly, and his head sank beneath the surface of the water.

In the Launch Control room—a place filled with technicians and engineers sitting at row after row of control consoles—Mr. Gunnarson snapped a ballpoint pen in half and threw the pieces on the floor beside his desk.

"No ignition! The rockets didn't light off!"

A half dozen men huddled around him.

"Must be the firing sequencer."

"Or the main squib."

"Or a pump failure."

Mr. Gunnarson wanted to slam the desk with both his fists. Instead, he swallowed hard and said as calmly as he could.

"Are there any malfunction lights showing on the consoles?"

"No, everything's green."

He took a deep breath. "All right. Set the countdown sequencer back to T minus two minutes and go through it again. Maybe we've just got a loose connection. Tell the astronauts that we're recycling to T minus two—and counting!"

"Right!" The men scurried back to their consoles.

Mr. Amaro appeared at Mr. Gunnarson's elbow. "There's been some funny kind of disturbance around the pad—a couple of kids on motorcycles. . . ."

"Not now!" Mr. Gunnarson snapped. "We've got a bird loaded and ready to go. Like a live bomb out there!"

One instant Rolf was diving under the water to grab at Shep's sinking form, and the next instant he was standing in the middle of the Gremlin Hollow, dripping wet, with Shep beside him.

"What the—"

Shep shook himself, and a shower of water sprayed from his soaked fur. "Hey, wait, cut it out!" Rolf yelled, trying to protect himself with his hands.

He rubbed the water from his eyes and felt the hot Florida sun baking him dry. Then the air of the Hollow shimmered and Rita appeared, holding both their bicycles, looking rather surprised and troubled.

"Rolf, you're all right!"

"Yeah, sure . . . but . . ."

Suddenly the air about them was filled with fireflies, thousands of dancing lights that spun around their heads and settled to the ground. Wherever one of the sparkling lights touched down, it turned into a gremlin. And now the gremlins were laughing and dancing lightly, grabbing each other and whirling around, arm in arm. Baneen was dancing with La Demoiselle. O'Rigami was twirling with O'Kkane Baro.

Lugh appeared, and he was neither laughing nor dancing. Rolf had never seen the gremlin leader look more grim or more terrible. At the sight of their prince, the other gremlins stopped dancing and their laughter faded into silence.

"So!" said Lugh, looking up at Rolf and at the same time seeming to tower mountainously over him. "You'd trick a gremlin would you—you'd try to pull the wool over the eyes of Lugh of the Long Hand? Well, it's a short delay you'll find you'll have gained, in a moment—and a long time of sorrow to repent interfering with our departure! So, you bid me stop the launch by virtue of the Great Wish gained when you drew our Corkscrew from its case, did you? I suppose you'll not be shy about drawing the Corkscrew forth once more, just to show me while my eyes are on you, how the strength to do so is in you, and you alone?"

"I . . ."

"Ah, now, Lugh!" chattered Baneen, appearing beside Rolf with O'Rigami and the rest. "Sure, and it's a terrible hard thing to do, drawing the Great Corkscrew from its holding place. You wouldn't be requiring the lad to do it more than once, and that second time right on the heels of his first mighty effort. How much better to admit ourselves beaten—"

"SILENCE!" roared Lugh. Silence fell over the Hollow. "BOY, LET ME SEE YOU DRAW THE CORKSCREW FORTH!"

The Great Corkscrew, once more in its case, winked into existence in front of Rolf. Half-paralyzed by Lugh's voice, he reached out and took hold of it, pulling at it. And then, a strange thing began to happen . . .

In front of Rolf's eyes . . . in front of Lugh, himself . . . first Baneen, and then, one by one, O'Rigami, La Demoiselle, and O'Kkane Baro, along with other nameless gremlins, began once more to disappear into the glare and glitter of the case . . . and the Corkscrew once more came forth in Rolf's hand.

Lugh stared. For a second his jaw worked, but no sound came out. Then, incredulously, he spoke.

"What . . . what *is* this? MUTINY?"

Baneen and the others reappeared.

"Ah, Lugh, darling!" cried the little gremlin. "Sure, and we'd never go against your wishes, ordinarily. But it's fond of this world we are, to be sure, after all these thousands of years, and—"

"Silence!" thundered Lugh. "What kind of gremlins are you?"

"We are ze good gremlins!" cried La Demoiselle. "Eet ees because we are true gremlins zat we fight to stay on ze Earth!"

"FIGHT?" roared Lugh. "Well the lot of you know that it's myself alone—" he shook one knobby fist, "is more than a match for all of you put together. What, must I take you all up under my arm and carry you back to Gremla by force? If so be it, I will—"

He began to roll up his sleeves.

"Wait!" shouted Rolf. Lugh paused and looked at him. "Wait," Rolf said again, more quietly. "This is my fault, but somebody's got to tell you you're wrong—"

"Silence, human!" rumbled Lugh ominously, continuing to roll up his sleeves.

"I'm not going to be silent," said Rolf. "You're just like I was—"

Lugh paused in rolling his sleeves, and stared at Rolf in astonishment.

"I?" he said. "Lugh of the Long Hand, like a mere human-lad?"

"That's right," said Rolf, determined now to get the words said, no matter how Lugh would react to them. "I kept trying to make my parents be the way I wanted them, in spite of the fact that they had other responsibilities. And you've been trying to turn Earth into another Gremla—into Gremla all over again, with the drawing of the Great Corkscrew and someone being king, and all that—and now that it hasn't worked, you're going to run away, back to Gremla and Hamrod the Heartless. Even Hamrod's better than admitting you were wrong!"

Lugh's ears rotated slowly, twice.

"Do I hear what I think I hear?" he muttered. "A human, saying such to *me*?"

"It's time somebody said it to you!" Rolf shouted. "None of the other gremlins want to go back to Hamrod. They've come to love Earth—and so have you, only you won't admit it! If you'd admit it to yourself, you'd be willing to work with humans, even if none of them has a big enough soul to draw the Great Corkscrew from its case without help, any more than there's any gremlin who can. Can *you* pull the Great Corkscrew loose by yourself? Of course not! So what makes you the one to decide whether all the gremlins on Earth have to go back to Gremla?"

Lugh began to swell . . . his actual body began to enlarge until he seemed to be growing to twice his normal size. As for his aura, that large impression that hovered over him at all times, it grew and grew until it seemed as large as a mountain. He spoke—and his voice was so deep that it seemed to come from the bowels of the earth and shake the very Hollow around them like an earthquake.

"L I G H T N I N G!" said Lugh, in that awful voice.

Suddenly the sky was black with clouds over their heads. A roll of thunder rumbled, echoing the sound of Lugh's voice and a jagged spear of lightning shot down from the clouds and was caught, still jagged and so bright none of them could look at it, in Lugh's right hand.

He poised the shaft of lightning, aiming it toward Rolf.

"B O Y!" he said. "A D M I T Y O U L I E!"

Wincing away from the blinding glare of the lightning shaft burning in Lugh's hand, Rolf shook his head stubbornly.

"No!" he cried. "I'm right! You're the one who's wrong!"

For a moment there was a terrible hush in the Hollow. Lugh stood still. Then he lifted his arm.

Suddenly the lightning shaft flew from his hand back up to the clouds. The clouds themselves rolled up and disappeared. Bright sunshine poured down again on them all; and a great sigh of relief went up from thousands of gremlin throats.

"Ah, sure, your honor!" piped the voice of Baneen. "And wasn't it yourself said that if you could find a human who cared more for another creature than himself, you'd give that human the Great Wish? And haven't we here a lad who today risked everything, his own life included, for that of his faithful dog—and sure, if a dog's not a creature now, what is?"

Lugh stared fiercely at Baneen, and then at Rolf, and then off into the distance.

"Quick, lad!" whispered Baneen in Rolf's ear. "Make your wish—*now!*"

"I wish," said Rolf, rapidly, "that gremlins would work with humans from now on to clean up the world and keep it clean and safe!"

"There, Lugh, darling!" cried Baneen, dancing in front of the gremlin prince. "It was yourself heard his wish. Do you grant it, now?"

Lugh glared at Baneen and turned to glare again at Rolf.

"Harrumph!" he growled, deep in his throat. "*Rahumpf!* HAHR-rumphff . . . all right!"

He turned and stalked off. The gremlins in the Hollow burst into wild cheering.

Abruptly, the ground shook. The air vibrated as if some giant's breath were roaring across the world. And off in the distance, as wave after wave of thunder rolled across the Hollow, they all saw the Mars rocket lifting up, up, climbing straight into the cloudless blue sky on a tongue of sheer flame.

"A beautifur feat of engineering," Rolf heard O'Rigami say.

The Mars rocket climbed higher, the roar of its mighty engines diminished. It became a distant speck, then a bright, fast-moving star shining in the morning sky. Then it got so far away that none of them could see it any longer.

Rolf felt as if he wanted to cheer, but it was all too magnificent and overpowering for something as small as one human voice. But it really did not matter. The gremlins were all cheering, for him. Rita was trying to hug him. The gremlins nearby were trying to hug him. Mr. Sheperton was standing on his hind legs, trying to lick Rolf's face. It was all sort of a wonderful mess.

- 13 -

" . . . Crazy, the whole business," said Rolf's father, thoughtfully. "Absolutely crazy! On the other hand, does it matter? The bird got off all right, with only that short two-minute hold at the last minute—"

"What caused that?" asked Rolf's mother. "You didn't tell me."

"One of those one-in-a-million things," Rolf's father dismissed the hold with a wave of his hand. "A loose connection in the ignition wiring. When we recycled and tried again, the light was white and there was no evidence that it had ever been anything else. But I'm not talking about that. . . ."

Rolf fidgeted in his chair at the breakfast table. Rita, he knew, would be waiting at her place for him, by this time, but he dared not call attention to himself by leaving the table. His father, like most generally easygoing men, had one or two crotchets. One of them was that the whole family should be together at the breakfast table.

" . . . We never see each other the rest of the time," he was in the habit of saying. "The least we can do is sit down and have a decent breakfast together before the day starts."

All of which, of course, did not mean that Rolf could not leave the table—but he would bother his father by doing so, and his father's reaction, when bothered, was suddenly to start remembering all the questions he normally did not get around to asking Rolf, such as where he was all day yesterday, and why didn't he use his dependent's pass to watch the rocket launch, and what had he been doing lately anyway? Rolf could lose more time than he would just sitting and waiting for his father to remember it was time to go to the office.

" . . . Almost enough to make you believe in gremlins," his father was saying.

"Gremlins?" Rolf's mother asked, trying to get a spoonful of applesauce into the baby without half of it going on to the flowered bib around the baby's neck.

"Gremlins—imaginary little troublemakers that are always keeping things from working right," said Rolf's Dad with another wave. "Someone dreamed them up during World War II, I think. I didn't mean it seriously about believing in them. Not that there aren't all kinds of things . . ."

His mind wandered.

"What things, dear?" asked Rolf's mother, wiping the baby's chin with the bib.

"Well, that business the guards reported about some people on motorcycles running all over the place."

"Did they find them?" Rolf's mother asked. "The checkout girl in the supermarket was saying . . ."

Rolf's dad snorted. He sounded almost like Shep.

"I've heard the rumors!" he said. "Bicycles riding at a hundred ninety miles an hour up one side of the VAB and down the other? Bicycles bouncing all over the Press Stand? Ridiculous. Besides, if there was anyone actually involved in something like that, how would they have gotten out of the Space Center, with every security man and car on duty looking for them?

"Well, at least everything's A-okay with the spacecraft. The astronauts have been reporting that everything's working absolutely perfectly. No gremlins aboard the spacecraft!"

Rolf struggled to keep a straight face.

Mr. Gunnarson sneezed.

"Are you catching a cold?" demanded Rolf's mother, looking suddenly at him.

"No . . . no, I don't think so," said Rolf's father. "Just thinking about that sneezing fit everybody had out at the launch a minute or two after the hold was called. No one knows about that either. There's a notion that some unusual cloud of pollen blew in about that time. Well, there you are. Things all over the place not making sense—"

He gestured at the newspaper he had just laid down.

"Half a dozen U.S. senators opposed to the Wildlife Reclamation bill got caught in an elevator that stuck between floors and missed their chance to vote against the bill. It passed," he said. "Some boat owner who'd been sneaking people into the Playalinda Beach area to watch launches ran it up on the beach there and was stranded. Got caught. Claimed he was going into a canal a friend of his had made months before—only somebody had moved the canal. Nonsense! Actually, he'd missed the canal entrance by a good fifty yards. Must have been blind. Then, here, it says that it looks as if the Space Program's going to get a financial shot in the arm so that the Space Lab can get to work on wider-ranging studies of how to combat air pollution and topsoil erosion while surveying for more deposits of natural resources."

"Wasn't the Space Lab doing a lot of that sort of thing anyway?" Rolf's mother asked, lifting Rolf's baby sister out of her highchair.

"Of course. Amazing how few people seemed to know about it though," Rolf's dad answered. "Still, this is going to make that part of the work here a lot more important. Which reminds me—the surprise I mentioned I'd have for you after the launch. I've been asked if I want to shift into this new ecological study work."

"You?" said Rolf, staring at him.

"Yes. It's been a pet project of mine for some time. I didn't want to say anything to you both because I wasn't sure it could be pushed through. But it's all set now. I'd be Engineering Director for it," said Mr. Gunnarson, thoughtfully. "It means I'd have to go running off on trips to various parts of the world from time to time, but maybe we could tie some of those trips in with family vacations."

"Why, I think it's marvelous!" said Rolf's mother. "Why didn't you tell me until now?"

"Well, you were asleep when I came in at four a.m. after we got the launch wrapped up," said Rolf's father. "Besides, the only time this family ever gets together is at breakfast, and I thought we'd all talk about it together."

He looked at Rolf, who was staring back at him.

"What do you think, Rolf?" he asked. Rolf gulped.

"Cool!" he said, hastily, getting up from the table. "But I've got to go now. Rita's waiting for me."

"Rita. That's nice," said his mother. "I'm so glad to see you spending some time with your friends for a change."

"By the way, you didn't ask me for a dependent's pass to the launch," said Rolf's father. "Where were you yesterday?"

"Oh, just around," said Rolf, halfway out the door.

"And come to think of it," said his father, "weren't you asking about a ten-speed bike back there a week or so ago?"

"Uh . . . well," Rolf edged back toward the kitchen door. "I guess my old three-speed is fast enough, Dad. Really."

"But . . ."

"I've got to go!" Rolf slipped out the kitchen door and paused only briefly in the hall to grab a towel from the linen closet.

"Where are you going, dear?" called his mother.

"Swimming! Down at the pool!" Rolf shouted back, stepping out the back door. His bike was waiting there with his bathing suit already in the rattrap. He added the towel to it and climbed on. *Wait,* he thought, *until I tell Rita. . . .*

"I thought—" A shadow that was his dad's face spoke to him through the curtains of the half-open kitchen window, "you said you couldn't swim because your leg bothered you—"

"Oh, my leg's fine!" Rolf called back. "It's been fine for weeks. See you!"

He cycled off.

"That boy . . ." he heard his father beginning behind him; but the rest of the words were left behind. Rolf wheeled down the street in the morning sunlight; and for a second his father's words about the new job and family vacation came back to him. His father—of all people! He felt sharply uncomfortable for a second, thinking how he had misjudged his dad. Then, the uncomfortableness was washed away by the thought of the trips. It really would be cool zipping around the world. Wait until he told Rita, and the other kids at school. He would have to ask Baneen how to go about finding the local gremlins in other places, once he got there. He wondered if the dogs in Spain or Japan spoke Spanish or Japanese, or whether he would be able to understand them the way he was still able to understand Shep. . . .

No point in letting the fact that he could see gremlins and talk to animals go to waste.

HOUR OF THE HORDE

1

It had happened again. That primitive, unconquerable power in him that he could not seem to deny had reached out once more, savagely, down the muscles of his good arm and hand, to take over his painting.

Exhausted, Miles Vander threw the number four brush he held, now bloodily tipped with alizarine red, back into the pint fruit jar of muddy turpentine holding the other long, yellow-handled brushes. A feeling of dull exhaustion and frustration dropped on him like the doubled folds of some heavy blanket.

All at once he was aware again of his own starved-looking body, his bent shoulders, his uselessly hanging left arm that polio had crippled six years ago. The paralyzed hand was now tucked into his left pants' pocket, out of sight, and the loose sleeve of his white shirt, billowing about the wasted arm in the late sunlight of the warm spring afternoon, disguised for the moment its unnatural thinness. But he was suddenly, grimly, once more aware of it just the same.

For a few hours, caught up in his painting, he had forgotten both his crippling and the stubborn artistic search he had never stopped these last five years. Now emptied and worn-out, he stood with the aftertaste of one more failure, staring at his canvas, as the freshening breeze of the late afternoon blew the white shirt coldly about him, molding it to his cooling body.

The painting showed the scene before him—only, it did not. He stood on the parkway grass above the west bluff over the Mississippi River. Rippleless below him, between high rock walls narrowly footed with green park lawn, the three-hundred-yard width of the upper river flowed darkly blue, with picture-postcard calmness, beneath the white concrete of a freeway bridge bearing a glassed-in overhead walkway for students moving between the east and west campuses of the university.

These things made up the landscape he had been painting for three and a half hours. And he had set them all down on canvas—the tall gray-brown river bluffs, the grass-covered flats at the foot of the bluffs, even the white-paddle-wheeled steamboat that was the university's theater-on-the-river moored below the bridge. He gazed at them now, and at the large, heavily leaved old elm trees, the reddish-brown brick of the student union and the university hospital on top of the far bluff, and the blue, near-cloudless sky above them all.

These things lay, as they had lain all through the hours of his painting, bathed in the gentle sunlight of late May—making a warm, even comforting, scene. But this was not the way his brushes had reproduced them on canvas.

On the now wetly gleaming, color-laden three-by-four-foot square of cloth he had painted not what he faced, but that old savage animal instinct of man to which he could not seem to close his eyes—ever. Into the soft, living greens and blues and browns of the scene across the river had crept the icy bleakness of oil-based ultramarine blue hardened with gray. Into the soft yellow sunlight had come the smouldering fire of alizarine red, raising a sullen reddishness like the color of spilled blood.

The resulting painting showed the works of man, by which man was himself to be judged, grayed and brooding, stripped down, and hardened and stained with the bloody marks of savage guilts and primitive failures.

Miles felt exhausted, weak—even a little dizzy. He had emptied himself once more of his inner creative energy. But once more he had made—not the image of the world he wished to show, but only that image's other face; like the other side of a coin, its devil face. Wearily he began cleaning his brushes and packing his paints for the return to his room.

Midway across the glassed-in walkway above the freeway bridge he stopped to rest for a minute, propping his now-covered canvas and heavy paint box upon the railing that protected the glass side of the walkway. While he caught his breath, he stared down once more at the scene of his painting.

Back the way he had come was the top of the bluff on which he had set up his easel, and facing him now was the bluff's rugged, near-vertical face of gray limestone rock, roughened, cracked, and gullied by weather, standing above the lower strip of parkway greensward at its foot. As always, the sight of that bluff-face pumped new strength and purpose into him. What he had done once, he could do again. A little warmth woke in him again.

He had been defeated once more this afternoon, but not conquered, after all. Already, drawing strength from the sight of the gray-brown cliff face, the thoughts began to kindle of the next time he

would put brush to canvas. There was still time for
him to succeed. After all, if he was a failure, at least
he was a failure, so far, only in his own eyes.

His painting, even as it was, had won him the
unusual attention of his instructors at the university
school of art. It had also won him, now that he was
graduating, a grant which would let him spend the next
two years in Europe, moving about and painting as he
liked. Then free at last from academic distractions,
painting, painting, and continually painting, he would
finally win out over that savage, primitive bleakness of
viewpoint which seemed determined to express itself
in everything he did.

The slight dizziness from the long afternoon's effort
made him giddy again for a moment. He leaned against
the railing. But then he stiffened.

The day had darkened. He looked up swiftly at the
sun.

It was as if a heavy orange filter had been drawn
across its surface. Rolling, enormous and sullen, it
burned with a flaming redness just above the western
horizon, so dimmed that he could stare directly into
it without squinting. Moreover, as he looked down
again, unbelieving, he saw the landscape had also
changed. It was coated and darkened and shadowed,
now, by the all-pervading redness of the sunlight. The
color of alizarine red, which was the shade of his own
inner, primitive fury, seemed to have escaped from his
painting to stain the real landscape now—all earth and
sky and water—with the angry color of spilled blood.

-2-

Miles stood motionless.

A giant's hand seemed to close powerfully about his chest, squeezing the breath out of him. Not breathing, he stared at the changed sun and the red-washed landscape, and an old, old fear dating back to the polio attack—fear of his own traitorous body's finding some way to jail him a second time, before his work could be accomplished—woke inside him.

Grimly he forced himself to breathe and move. He leaned his upper thighs against the heavy shapes of his paint box and cloth-covered painting, pressing them hard against the railing to keep from falling. He rubbed his eyes viciously with the fingers of his good hand and for a painful moment blinked through watery tears at blurred surroundings. But when his gaze cleared again, the redness of sun and land was unchanged, and the fear began to grow into unreasoning anger, like a bubble of fire expanding under his breastbone.

His doctor at the university hospital had told him last month that he was working too hard. His landlady and even Marie Bourtel, who loved him and understood him better than anyone else, had pleaded with him to slow down. So, to be sensible, he had forced himself to get at least six hours' sleep a night these last two weeks—and *still* this false and untrustworthy body had failed him, after all.

With brutal fingers he rubbed his eyes once more. But the color of light and sun would not change. Furiously, helplessly, he looked around the walkway for a phone booth.

Probably, he thought, he should stop using his eyes immediately, so that they would not get any worse. He would phone his doctor. . . .

But the walkway bookstore, holding the only phone in the long passageway, was locked up behind glass doors because it was Sunday. Maybe he could get somebody to help him. . . .

Because it was Sunday, the walkway was all but deserted. But looking now, Miles saw three other figures near its far end. The nearest of them was a tall, thin, black-haired girl hugging an armful of books to her nearly breastless front. Beyond the girl were a squarely built, blue-suited older man who looked like one of the academic staff and a stocky, sweatered young man with the brown leather scabbard of a slide rule hanging at his belt. Miles started toward them, lugging his paints and canvas.

But then, suddenly, hope leaped faintly within him. For the other three were also staring around themselves with a dazed air. As he watched, they moved toward each other, like people under a huddling instinct in a time of danger. By the time he reached them they were close together and already talking.

"But it has to be something!" the girl was saying shakily, hugging her books to her as if they were a life belt and she afloat on a storm-tossed sea.

"I tell you, it's the end!" said the older man. He was

stiff and gray in the face, and he spoke with barely moving, gray lips, holding himself unnaturally erect. The reddened sunlight painted rough highlights on his bloodless face. "The end of the world. The sun's dying. . . ."

"Dying? Are you crazy?" shouted the sweatered young man with the slide rule. "It's dust in the atmosphere. A dust storm south and west of us maybe. Didn't you ever see a sunset—"

"If it's dust, why aren't things darker?" asked the girl. "Everything's clear as before, even the shadows. Only it's red, all red—"

"Dust! Dust, I tell you!" shouted the young man. "It's going to clear up any minute. Wait and see. . . ."

Miles said nothing. But the first leap of hope was expanding into a sense of relief that left him weak at the knees. It was not him then. The suddenly bloody color of the world was not just a subjective illusion caused by his own failing eyesight or exhausted mind, but the result of some natural accident of atmosphere or weather. With the sense of relief, his now-habitual distaste for wasting precious time in social talk woke in him once more. Quietly he turned away and left the other three still talking.

"I tell you," he heard the sweatered young man insisting as he moved off, "it'll have to clear up in a minute. It can't last. . . ."

But it did not clear up, as Miles continued on across the east campus toward his rooming house in the city beyond. On the way he passed other little knots of people glancing from time to time up at the red sun and talking tensely together. Now that his own first reaction to the sun change was over, he found a weary annoyance growing in him at the way they all were reacting.

To a painter, a change in the color values of the

daylight could be important. But what was it to them, these muttering, staring people? In any case, as the sweatered young man had said, it would be clearing up shortly.

Pushing the whole business out of his mind, Miles slogged on homeward, feeling the tiredness creeping up in him as the working excitement drained out of him, and his one good arm, for all its unusual development of muscle, began to weary with the labor of lugging canvas and paint box the half mile to his rooming house.

But the subject of the sun change was waiting for him even there. As he walked in the front door of his rooming house at last, he heard his landlady's television set sounding loudly from the living room of her ground-floor apartment.

"No explanation yet from our local weather bureau or the U.S. Meteorological Service. . . ." Miles heard, as he passed the open living-room door. Through it, he had a glimpse of Mrs. Arndahl, the landlady, sitting there with several of the other roomers, silently listening, "No unusual disturbances in the sun or in our own atmosphere have been identified so far, and the expert opinion believes such disturbances could not have taken place without. . . ."

There was a stiffness, an aura of alarm about those watching and listening to the set, that woke annoyance again in Miles. Everyone around him, it seemed, was determined to get worked up about this purely natural event. He stepped by quickly but quietly on the brown carpet before the open door and mounted the equally worn carpet of the stairs to the silence and peace of his own large second-floor room.

There he gratefully laid down at last his canvas and painting tools in their proper places. Then he flopped heavily, still dressed, back down on his narrow bed. The white glass curtain fluttered in the breeze from his half-open window. Weariness flooded through him.

It was a satisfying weariness, in spite of the failure of the afternoon's work—a deep exhaustion, not merely of body and mind, but of imagination and will as well, reflecting the effort he had put into the painting. But still . . . frustration stirred in him once more—that effort had still been nothing more than what was possible to any normal man. It had not been the creative explosion for which he searched.

For the possibility of that explosion was part of his own grim theory of art, the theory he had built up and lived with ever since that day when he had been painting at the foot of the west bluff, four years ago. According to the theory, there should be possible to an artist something much more than any painter had ever achieved up to now. Painting that would be the result of the heretofore normal creative outburst many times multiplied—into an overpassion.

To himself, more prosaically, he called this overpassion "going into overdrive," and it should be no more impossible than the reliably recorded displays of purely physical ability shown by humans under extreme emotional stress—in that phenomenon known as hysterical strength.

Hysterical strength, Miles knew, existed. Not merely because he had evidence of it, but also in the thick manila envelope of newspaper clippings he had collected over the last four years. Clippings like the one about the distraught mother who had lifted the thousands of pounds of her overturned car in order to pull her trapped baby from underneath the vehicle. Or the instance of the bedridden old man in his eighties who had literally run to safety, as cleverly as any slack-wire performer, across a hundred feet of telephone wire to a telephone pole to escape from the third floor of a burning apartment building.

He did not need these things to believe in hysterical strength, because he had expressed it. Himself.

And what the body could do, he told himself again now, wrapped in exhaustion on his bed, the creative spirit should be able to do as well. Someday yet he would tap it artistically—that creative overdrive. And when he did, he would at last tear himself free of that bitterness in him that saw old animal guilts and angers, all the primitive limitations of man—mirrored in everything he tried to reproduce on canvas.

When that moment came, he thought, dully and pleasantly now, sinking into drowsiness, a scene like the one he had painted today would show the future, the promise of Man—instead of a human past of bloody instinct and Stone Age violence underlying all that civilization had built.

The exhaustion lapping around him sucked him slowly down into sleep, like a foundering boat. He let himself sink, unresisting. It was an hour before he was due to meet Marie Bourtel off campus for dinner. Time enough for him to rest a few minutes before washing and dressing to go out. He lay, his thoughts flickering gradually into extinction. . . .

Sleep took him.

When he woke, Miles could not at first remember what time of day it was or why he had wakened. And then it came again—a pounding on his door and the voice of his landlady was calling through it to him.

"Miles! *Miles!*" Mrs. Arndahl's voice came thinly past the door, as if she were pushing it through the crack underneath the door. "Phone call for you! Miles, do you hear me?"

"It's all right. I'm awake," he called back. "I'll be there in a minute."

Groggily he swung his legs over the edge of the bed and sat upright. The single window of his room was a square of night blackness, with the shade not drawn above it. His eyes went to the large round face of the windup alarm clock that stood before the mirror on his dresser. The hands stood at five minutes to ten. He had been asleep at least four hours.

In the mirror his sleep-tousled dark hair, fallen down over his forehead, gave him a wild and savage look. He shoved the hair back and forced himself to his feet. He stumbled across the room, stepped out of the door, and walked numbly down the hall to the upstairs extension phone, which was lying out of its cradle. He picked it up.

"Miles!" It was the soft voice of Marie Bourtel. "Have you been there all this time?"

"Yes," he muttered, still too numb from sleep to wonder why she asked.

"I called a couple of times for you earlier, but Mrs. Arndahl said you hadn't come in yet. I finally had her check your room anyway." The usually calm, gentle voice he was used to hearing on the phone had an unusual edge to it. An edge of something like fear. "Didn't you remember you were going to meet me for dinner at the Lounge?"

"Lounge?" he echoed stupidly. He scrubbed his face with the back of his hand that held the phone, as if to rub memory back into his head. Then contrition flooded him. He remembered the plan to have dinner with Marie at six thirty at the Lounge, which was an off-campus restaurant on the east bank of the river. "Sorry, Marie—I guess I did it again. I was painting this afternoon, and I came back and lay down. I must've fallen asleep."

"Then you're all right." There was relief in Marie's voice for a second; then tension returned. "You don't know what's been happening?"

"Happening?"

"The sun's changed color! About five o'clock this afternoon—"

"Oh, that?" Miles rubbed the back of his hand again over his sleep-numbed face. "Yes, I saw it change. I'd just finished painting—what about it?"

"What about it?" Marie's voice held a sort of wonder. "Miles, *the sun's changed color*!"

"I know," said Miles a little impatiently. But then, rousing him from that first impatience to sudden near anger, came recognition of the relief in Marie's voice a few seconds before, when she had said: *"Then you're all right."*

Those remembered words jarred unpleasantly back to mind his own first few moments of alarm when he had seen the sun's changed color. He heard the edge in his own voice as he answered her.

"I know the sun's changed color! I said I saw it happen! What of it?"

"Miles—" Marie's voice broke off, oddly, as if she were uncertain of what to say to him. "Miles, I want to see you. If you've been asleep all this time you haven't had dinner yet, have you?"

"Well . . . no. I haven't." Miles was abruptly reminded of the emptiness inside him. Come to think of it, he had not eaten since breakfast, thirteen hours before.

"I'll meet you at the Lounge in ten minutes then," said Marie swiftly. "You can have some dinner, and we can talk. Ten minutes?"

"All right," he said, still somewhat numb with sleep.

"Good-bye, Miles."

"Good-bye."

He hung up.

Slowly waking up in the process, Miles went back to his room, washed his face, put on a fresh shirt and a sport coat, and left the rooming house for the half-mile walk back across the two campuses and their connecting walkway to the business section beyond the east campus. As he passed the landlady's living room, the door was still ajar, and from within he heard the voice of a television announcer, still talking about the change, and saw the backs of a number of people sitting and listening.

The irritation which Marie's concern for him had awakened in him expanded again to include these people. It was ridiculous, almost superstitious of them, to be stampeded into fear just because of what seemed to be a change—undoubtedly temporary, undoubtedly freakish—in the color of the sun.

"Latest reports over Honolulu say that the redness persists—" The TV announcer's voice was cut off sharply as Miles softly closed the front door of the house behind him. He headed up the darkened street under the towering, dark-leaved branches of the elms toward the footbridge and the east bank of the river where the Lounge was.

His walk across the campus and over the footbridge was like a walk though an evacuated city. There seemed to be nobody about. But once on the far side of the river, when he pushed open the door of the Lounge, he found the place crowded; only the crowd was all clustered at one end, around the television set at the front of the bar. Forty or fifty people, many of them students, were seated and standing there, packed closely together, listening in absolute silence to the same sort of news broadcast he had overheard as he was leaving his rooming house. He threaded his way through them and went back into the rear area where the high-backed wooden booths were; all of these were empty.

Miles took a corner booth in the back of the room. It was the booth he and Marie always took if it was available, and after a few moments their usual waitress, a girl named Joan, a part-time student in the English Department, came through the swinging doors from the kitchen, saw him, and came over to ask him what he wanted.

"Just coffee—two coffees, for now—" Miles remembered suddenly that Marie had said she had already eaten. "I guess just one dinner, come to think of it. Are there any hot beef sandwiches left?"

"Lots of them," said Joan. "Hardly anyone's been eating. They're all listening to television. We're listening, back in the kitchen. You know the weather people can't figure it out? The sun's actually changed. I mean, it isn't just something in our atmosphere—" She broke off in the face of Miles' silence. "I'll get your coffee."

She went off. She had scarcely brought two cups of coffee back and left again in search of Miles' sandwich when the sound of footsteps from the front of the Lounge made him look up. He saw Marie coming quickly down the aisle between the booths toward him.

She looked at him with the brown eyes that were now so dark and luminous they seemed to have doubled their size in her white face.

"Miles. . . ." She reached across the table to lay her hand on his arm. "Do you feel all right?"

"All right? Me?" He smiled at her, for clearly she needed reassurance. "I'm still a little dopey from sleep and I could stand some food. Outside of that, I'm fine. What's the matter with you?"

She looked at him strangely.

"Miles, you can't be that much out of touch with the rest of the world," she said. "You just *can't!*"

"Oh—" The word came out more harshly than he

had meant it to. "You mean this business about the sun changing color? Don't worry, it hasn't done any damage yet. And if it did, that's not my line of work. So why worry about it?"

The waitress came up with Miles' order and said hello to Marie.

"Isn't it terrible? It's still going on," she said to Marie. "We're all following the news, back in the kitchen. They're just beginning to see it from planes in the South Pacific now—and it's still red."

She went back to the kitchen.

"I'll tell you why you ought to worry," said Marie quietly and tensely, taking her hand from his arm and sitting back almost huddled in her corner of the booth. "Because it's something that affects the whole world, all the people in the world, and you're one of them."

Automatically he had picked up his fork and begun to eat. Now, at these words, he laid his fork down again. The wave of exhaustion inside him, the wave of anger first pricked to life by the alarm and concern of the people on campus he had passed on his way back to the rooming house, returned with force to wash his appetite away. The mashed potatoes and gravy he had just put into his mouth seemed to have no more taste than if they were made of flour and water and artificial coloring.

"The other two billion won't miss me if I stick to my own work," he said. "I've got more important things to worry about. I spent all day today painting the river bluffs and the freeway bridge. Do you want to know how it came out?"

"I can guess how it came out," answered Marie. She too was a student in the school of art at the university. Like Miles, she was graduating this spring. Unlike Miles, she had neither a grant for European study waiting for her nor the supporting belief of her instructors that she had the makings of a truly unusual artist in her. It did not help that Miles himself could see promise in her work. For even he could not bring himself to class that promise with what he himself was after in painting.

"Marie," an instructor had said bluntly to Miles one day in a burst of frankness, "is going to be good—possibly quite good—if she works hard at it. You're either going to be unmatchable or impossible."

Yet in spite of this, there were elements in Marie's work which were the equivalent of those very elements for which Miles searched in his own. Where he was stark, she was beautiful; where he was violent, she was gentle. Only, he wanted his equivalents of these things on a different level from that on which she had found hers.

"Well, it was the same thing all over again," said Miles. He picked up the fork once more and mechanically tried to force himself to eat. "The painting turned savage on me—as usual."

"Yes," answered Marie in a low voice, "and I know why."

He looked up sharply from his plate at her and found her eyes more brilliant upon him than ever.

"And this business about the sun proves it," she went on, more strongly. "I don't mean the change in color itself; I mean the way you're reacting to it—" She hesitated, then burst out with a rush. "I've never said this to you, Miles. But I always knew I'd have to say it someday, and now this thing's happened and the time's come! You aren't *ever* going to find the answer to what's bothering you about the way you paint. You never will because you won't look in the right direction. You'll look everywhere but there!"

"What do you mean?" He stared at her, the cooling hot beef sandwich now completely forgotten. "And what's this business of the sun got to do with it?"

"It's got everything to do with it," she said tightly, taking hold of her edge of the table with both hands, as if her grip on it were a grip on him, forcing him to stand still and listen to her. "Maybe this change in the color of the sun hasn't hurt anything yet—that's true. But it's frightened a world full of people! And *that* doesn't mean anything to you. Don't you understand me, Miles? The trouble with you is you've got to the point where something like this can happen, and a world full of people be frightened to death by it— and you don't react at all!"

He looked narrowly at her.

"You're telling me I'm too wound up in my painting?" he asked. "Is that it?"

"*No!*" Marie answered fiercely. "You're just not interested enough in the rest of life!"

"The rest of life?" he echoed. "Why, of course not! All the rest of life does for me is get between me and the painting—and I need every ounce of energy I can get for work. What's wrong with that?"

"You know what's wrong!" Marie started out of her corner and leaned across the table toward him. "You're too strong, Miles. You've got to the point where nothing frightens you anymore—and that's not natural. You're all one-sided, like that overdeveloped arm of yours and nothing on the other side—" Abruptly she began to cry, but silently, the tears streaming down her face, even while her voice went on, low and tight and controlled as before.

"Oh, I know that's a terrible thing to say!" she said. "I didn't want to say it to you, Miles. I didn't! But it's true. You're all one huge muscle in the part of you that's a painter, and there's nothing left in you on the human side at all. And *still* you're not satisfied. You keep on trying to make yourself even more one-sided, so that you can be a bloodless, camera-eyed observer!

Only, it can't be done—and it *shouldn't* be done! You can't go on in this way without destroying yourself. You'll turn yourself into a painting machine and still never get what you want, because it really isn't pictures on canvas you're after, Miles. It's people! It really is! Miles—"

Her words broke off and echoed away into the silence of the empty dining area at the back of the Lounge. Into that silence, from the bar at the front, came the unintelligible murmur of the announcer speaking from the television set and still relaying news, or the lack of it, about the sudden change of color of the sun. Miles sat without moving, staring at her. Finally, he found the words for which he was reaching.

"Is this what you called me up, and asked me to meet you here, to say?" he asked, at last.

"Yes!" answered Marie.

He still sat, staring at her. There was a hard, heavy feeling of loneliness and pain just above his breastbone. He had thought that at least there was one person in the universe who understood what he was trying to do. One person, anyway, who had some vision of that long road and that misty goal toward which he was reaching with every ounce of strength he had and every waking hour of his days. He had thought that Marie understood. Now it was plain she did not. She was, in the end, as blind as the rest of them.

If only she had understood, she would have realized that it was people he had been striving to get free of, right from the start. He had been trying to pull himself out of the quicksand of their bloody history and narrow lives, so that he would be able to see clearly, hear clearly, and work without their weight clinging to his mind and hampering the freedom of his mind's eye.

But Marie had evidently never seen this fact, any more than the rest.

He got to his feet, picked up his check and hers, and walked away from her to the cashier and out of the Lounge without another word.

Outside, still the streets were all but deserted. And through this desert cityscape, under a full moon made dusky by the reflection of reddened sunlight, he returned slowly to his rooming house.

3

In the night he woke suddenly for no apparent reason. He lay staring at the darkness of the ceiling above him and wondering what had wakened him at such an hour. The bedroom was hot and stuffy, and he had kicked off all his covers.

His pajama top was wet with perspiration. It clung like a clammy hand to his chest, and this, plus the thickness of the air, filled him with a strange sense of some lurking presence as of a crouching danger in the dark. He wondered whether Marie was sleeping peacefully or whether she had also wakened.

It was unnatural for the room to be so stuffy and hot. He got up and went to open the window, but it already stood wide open from the bottom, as high as it could be raised. Outside, the night air hung unmoving, as unnaturally warm and stuffy as the room air.

No breeze stirred. Below, silhouetted against the corner streetlight beyond, a tall, horizontal-armed oak towered over the lilac bushes and the small flowering crab tree in the dark rooming house yard. Bushes and trees alike stood like forms of poured concrete, all stiffly upright, darker than the night.

Distantly, thunder muttered. Miles looked up and out at the horizon above the trees, and the flicker of heat lightning jumped, racing across the arc of black sky in which no moon or stars were showing. The thunder came again, more loudly.

He stood watching as the lightning and thunder increased. Still no breath of air moved. The lightning flared along the distant edge of darkness like the cannon flashes of some titanic war of the gods, just out of sight over the horizon. The thunder grew. Now the heat lightning had given way to chain lightning, which stitched wild, jagged thrusts of brilliance across the sky.

The air sighed suddenly outside the window. It blew damply against him. The thunder roared. Suddenly the skies split with thunder directly above him, and a lightning flash left a searing afterimage of trees and bushes painted on his vision. The wind blasted, and suddenly there was a dry, hard pattering all around.

It was hail. At once, before he could move back and close the window, the full hailstorm was on him. In the wild lightning he saw the yard below full of dancing whiteness, saw the bushes bent over and even the ornamental flowering crab tree bent nearly to the earth.

Only the oak, he noticed, refused to bend. It stood towering as before. Its leaves lay over flat, and its branches swayed to the wind, but its trunk ignored the storm. It stood unyielding, upright, all but indifferent.

Hail was stinging Miles' face and arms. He pulled back from the window, closing it all but an inch or two. Even through that little space, the wind whistled icily into the room. He got back into bed, huddling the covers up around him.

Before he knew it, he was asleep once more.

"The Ship. . . ."

It seemed that those were almost the first words Miles encountered on going downstairs after waking the next morning. They were on the lips of his land-lady as he left for breakfast and his first class, and they echoed around him from everybody who was abroad in the red light of this early day as he crossed the campus. When he reached the room in which the seminar on Renaissance art was held, it seemed to be the only topic of conversation among the gradu-ate students there as well.

"Too big to land, anyway," Mike Jarosh, a short, bearded man who was one of the graduate history majors, was saying as Miles came in. "As big as the state of Rhode Island."

"They'll probably send down a smaller ship," somebody else put in.

"Maybe. Maybe not," Mike said. "Remember, the ship just appeared there, in orbit a thousand miles out. None of the telescopes watching the sun saw it coming, and it appeared right in front of the sun, right in front of their telescopes. If whoever's in the ship can do that, they may be able to send down people to the surface of the Earth here just by some way of transferring them suddenly from the ship to here—"

The professor in charge of the seminar, Wallace Hankins, a thin, stooped man, half-bald but with his remaining hair still as black as his eyebrows, came in the door just then, cutting off Mike in mid-sentence.

"Any news? Any broadcasts from the ship—" Mike was beginning to ask him, when Hankins cut him short.

"Yes, there's been some kind of message," Hankins said. "The United Nations Secretary-General just received it—the broadcasts don't say how or why. But that's all beside the point. It's plain there's no use trying to hold any kind of seminar under these conditions.

So we won't try it today. The rest of you go about your business—and, with luck, we'll meet again here next week at the same time under conditions more conducive to a discussion of Renaissance art."

The babble of excitement that broke out at this announcement, Miles thought, would have suited a group of grade-school children better than a dozen hardworking graduate students. The others hurried off as, more slowly, he put his own books back into the briefcase from which he had taken them while Mike Jarosh was talking. Hankins had stood aside to let the class members stampede past him out the open door. So it happened that, as Miles was leaving last, he came face to face with Hankins.

"I'm sorry to lose a day," said Miles honestly, stopping.

Hankins looked back at him, his round face under the high, hairless forehead more than a little sour.

"The Renaissance seems out of fashion at the moment," he said and, following Miles out through the door of the seminar room, closed it behind both of them.

Miles, briefcase in hand, headed back down the worn marble steps of the staircase inside the history building and out of the building back toward his rooming house. He was not quite sure what he should do with this unexpected gap in his daily schedule. Automatically, he thought of setting up his easel somewhere outside and trying to work—and then he remembered that outdoor painting would be all but impossible as long as the sun continued to be this color. Color values would be all off.

No sooner had he thought of this than he was intrigued by the notion of doing a painting under the red light, just so that he could see in what way the colors were off once the sun returned to normal.

He hurried on to the rooming house and went up the stairs to his room with enthusiasm beginning to burn inside him. But as he entered his room, his spirits took a sudden drop. The sight of the canvas he had painted yesterday afternoon, now drying in the corner, reminded him abruptly of Marie and the storm of the night before.

He was suddenly face to face with a strong sense of guilt and loss. No matter how wrong Marie had been last evening, two things remained unchanged. It was her concern for him that had made her say what she had and also, he had no one else in the world that was close to him.

He sat down heavily on the edge of his bed, newly made by Mrs. Arndahl. The strap springs creaked dolefully under his weight. He had been looking forward to the release and freedom of his year in Europe. The thought of loneliness had never occurred to him until now. But now he felt it come to him powerfully at the thought that he might easily lose Marie for good.

He got abruptly to his feet. He had been wrong in walking out like that. It had not been fair to expect her to understand what moved him in his wholehearted search without ever a word of explanation of that search. At least he could find her and make that explanation now. He owed her that much.

He got up, went over to open the top drawer of his dresser to take out a brown manila envelope. He put it into the inside pocket of his jacket and headed back out of the rooming house.

At this hour Marie was usually in the second-floor study room of the university library. But when he got there, he found the room deserted except for three or four stray figures looking dwarfed and foolish among the long tables and empty chairs. Marie was not one of them. He turned and left the library.

The most logical place to look next was the girls'
dormitory, in which Marie was a counselor.

He went there. It was on the other side of the
campus, a tall red-brick building with a row of glass
doors across the front of it. He went through one
of the doors into the lobby and asked for Marie at
the desk. The clerk buzzed Marie's room, and less
than a minute later Marie herself called down on
the house phone. Miles heard her voice with a sense
of relief.

"It's me," he said. "Can you come down?"

"I'll be right there," her voice answered. His heart
moved in him. It was the same soft, calm voice as ever.
He had expected any reaction but this, after he had
walked out on her the way he had the night before.

"You can wait in the lounge," the pointed-faced little
clerk said to him.

He had waited in that lounge many times before,
but when he went in now, like everything else, it
was different. Usually there were only four or five
vaguely impatient or irritated males seated in the
heavy armchairs and couches scattered decorously
about the room. Now nearly all the farther seats
were empty. The nearer ones had been drawn in
around the television set and were occupied by a
small crowd of girls. These listened to the
omnipresent television announcer in such uniform
silence that Miles had no difficulty overhearing what
the announcer was saying.

"Word has been received from reliable sources here
at the UN," the announcer was saying, "that the
message was not sent by any mechanical means from
the ship now in orbit about our world but was delivered in person by two of the passengers or crew from
the ship. The same source also provides the information that the two beings in question appear to be two

men with somewhat swarthy features, in every respect, including the suits they wear, as human as we are. Further word is expected shortly.

"Now some details about the ship, as the details have been gleaned by telescope from the surface of our world. The ship itself appears to be at least as large as was originally estimated. There seems to be no evidence of windows or entrances in its outer surface. Moreover, no sign has been seen of a small ship leaving it or of any means by which the two from the ship could have made the trip down to the UN buildings here in New York. No landing of any type of alien craft has been reported and no unusual visitors have been escorted to the building. . . ."

His voice droned on. Miles went to the opposite end of the room and sat down on a heavy green sofa pushed back against the wall. It was only a few minutes before Marie appeared in the entrance to the lounge. He got up swiftly and went to meet her.

"Miles—" she said as he came up to her.

"Can we get out of here?" he said. "Somewhere away from television sets and radios?"

"I'm on duty here at the dorm starting at one o'clock," she answered. "But we could go someplace and have an early lunch until then."

"Good," he said. "Let's go to someplace downtown that isn't overrun by people from the U."

They took the bus toward downtown Minneapolis. As the bus rolled across the freeway bridge, Miles gestured toward the window beside which Marie was sitting.

"Look," he said, indicating the rock wall below which he had stood painting the afternoon before. "You see the bluff there? Do you think you could climb it?"

Marie stared at the steep rise of rock.

"I guess so—if I had to," she said. She turned, frowning in puzzlement at him. "I don't think I'd like to. Why?"

"I'll tell you later, while we're having lunch," said Miles. "But look at it now—will you?—and just imagine yourself climbing it."

Marie looked back out of the window and kept her eyes on the bluff until the bus passed the point where that side of the river could be seen. Then she looked questioningly at Miles.

When he said nothing, however, she looked away, and neither of them said anything more until they left the bus downtown.

Miles, in fact, waited until they were actually inside the restaurant they had picked—a small, medium-priced eating place with no television set.

"About last night—" he began, after the waitress had given them menus and left.

Marie laid down her menu. She reached out across the table to put her hand on his.

"Never mind," she said. "It doesn't matter."

"But it does matter," he answered. He withdrew his hand, took the manila envelope out from the inside pocket of his jacket, and handed it to her. "There's something I want you to understand. That's why I had you look at that bluff on the way here. I should have told you about it a long time ago; but when I first met you, well, I just wasn't used to telling anyone about it, and later I liked to think you understood without being told. Then, when I found you didn't last night— that's why I blew up. Take a look in that envelope."

Looking strangely at him, Marie opened the envelope and poured out the sheaf of yellowing newspaper clippings on the white place mat. She looked through them while he waited. Then she looked back up at him, frowning.

"I guess I *don't* understand," she said.

"They're all instances of hysterical strength," Miles said. "Have you ever heard of that?"

"I think so," she said, still frowning. "But what's it all got to do with you?"

"It ties in with what I believe," he said. "A theory of mine about painting. About anything creative, actually . . ." And he told her about it. But when he was done, she still shook her head.

"I didn't know," she said. She shuffled the clippings with her fingers. "But, Miles, isn't it a pretty big guess on your part? These"—she shuffled the clippings, again looking down at them—"are hard enough to believe—"

"Will you believe me if *I* tell you something?" he interrupted.

"Of course!" Her head came up.

"All right then. Listen," he said, "before I met you, when I first had polio, I took up painting mainly to give myself an excuse to hide from people." He took a deep breath. "I couldn't get over the fact I was crippled, you see. I had a knack for art, but the painting and drawing were just an excuse that first year, after I'd been sick."

"Miles," she said gently, reaching out to put her hand on his again.

"But then, one day, something happened," he said. "I was outside painting—at the foot of the bluff I pointed out to you. And something clicked. Suddenly I was in it—*inside* the painting. I can't describe it. And I forgot everything around me."

He stopped and drew a deep breath.

"I shouldn't have done that," he said. "Because it just happened I was attracting a gallery. Some kids had come up to watch me painting. Kids not much younger than I was—and I guess after a while they must have started asking me questions. But I didn't even hear them. I was all wrapped up in what I was painting, for the first time—and it was like a miracle, like coming alive for the first time since I'd been sick."

In spite of himself, remembering, his hand curled into a fist under her fingers. She held tightly to the fist.

"When I didn't answer," he went on after a second, "they evidently began to think that I was embarrassed by being caught painting, and they began to jostle me and move my brushes. But I was still just barely conscious of them, and I was scared stiff at the thought of quitting work on that painting, even for a second. I had a feeling that if I quit, even for that long, I'd lose it—this *in*-ness I'd discovered. But finally, one of them grabbed up my paint box and ran off with it, and I had to come out of it."

"Oh, Miles!" said Marie, softly. Her fingertips soothed his hard-clenched fist.

"So I chased him—the one who'd taken it. And when I was just about to grab him, he dropped it. So I brought it back—and then I found out something. My canvas was gone."

"They took it?" said Marie. "Miles, they didn't!"

"I looked around," he went on, seeing not her across the table as much as the much-remembered scene in his mind's eye, "and finally, I spotted the one who'd taken it. He'd run off the other way from the one who took my paints and up around the road leading to the top of the bluff, and now he was running along the bluff overhead."

Miles stopped speaking. With an effort he pulled his inner gaze from the four-year-old memory and looked again at Marie.

"Marie," he said, "I wasn't thinking of anything but that painting. It seemed like life itself to me, just then, life I'd found again after thinking I'd lost it for good with polio. It seemed to me that I had to have that painting, no matter what happened. And I went and got it."

He hesitated.

"Marie," he said, "I climbed up that bluff and got in front of the kid who'd taken it. When he saw me coming, he threw it facedown on the grass and ran. When I picked it up, it was nothing but smears and streaks of paint with grass sticking all over it."

"Miles!" said Marie, her fingers tightening on his fist. "How terrible!"

"No," said Miles, "not terrible." He looked deeply into her brown eyes. "Wonderful. Marie, don't you understand! *I climbed up that cliff!*"

She stared back at him, baffled.

"I know, you said that," she said. "And you must have climbed awfully fast—"

"Yes, but that's not it!" said Miles. "Listen! I climbed up that cliff—and I had only one arm. Only one arm and one hand to climb with!"

She still stared, without understanding.

"Of course," she said. "That's right, you only had one arm—" She broke off suddenly, on a quick intake of breath.

"Yes. You see?" Miles heard his own voice, sounding almost triumphant. "Marie, a cliff like that can't be climbed by a one-handed man. You need to hold with one hand while you move the other to a fresh handhold, and so on. I came back there the next day and tried to see if I could climb it again. And I couldn't. I couldn't even get started. The only way I could possibly have done it would have been to balance on my feet alone while I changed handholds."

He nodded at the clippings on the place mat before her.

"To climb like that," he said, "I'd have needed the strength and speed written about in those news clippings."

She gazed at him, her face a little pale.

"You don't remember how you did it?" she asked at last.

He shook his head.

"It's all sort of a blur," he said. "I remember wanting to go up the cliff, and I remember climbing up it, somehow, very quickly and easily, and the next thing I knew, I was facing the kid with my painting." He stopped, but she said nothing. "You see why I lost my head with you last night? I thought you understood that what I was after was something that didn't leave any strength or time left over for the rest of the world. I thought you understood it without being told. It wasn't until after that I began to see how unfair I was being in expecting you to understand something like this without knowing what I'd been through and what I was after."

He pulled his hand out from under her now-quiet fingers and took her hand instead in his own grasp.

"But you understand now, don't you?" he asked. "You do, don't you?"

To his surprise she shivered suddenly, and her face grew even more pale.

"Marie!" he said. "Don't you understand—"

"Oh, I do. I understand. Of course, Miles." Her hand turned so that her fingers grasped his. "It's not that. It's just that knowing this now somehow makes it all that much worse."

"Worse?" He stared at her.

"I mean"—her voice trembled—"all this business about the sun and the ship and the two men, or whatever they are. I've had a feeling from the beginning that it all meant something terrible for us—for you and me. And now, somehow, your telling me this makes me even more afraid."

"What of?" he asked.

"I don't know." He could feel her shiver again, just barely feel it, but the shiver was there. "Something . . . something that's going to come between us—"

From across the room a sudden, measured voice interrupted her. Looking in that direction, Miles saw that two men had just entered the restaurant and sat down at a table against the farther wall. On the table one of them placed a portable radio, and even with the volume turned down, its voice carried across to the table where he sat with Marie. Anger exploded in him.

"I'll make them turn that thing down!" he said, starting to get to his feet. But Marie caught hold of his arm.

"No," she said. "Sit down. Please, sit down, Miles. Listen—"

"By television and radio," the radio was saying. "We now bring you the President of the United States, speaking to you directly from the East Room of the White House. . . ." The musical strains of "Hail to the Chief" followed closely upon the announcer's words. Marie got quickly to her feet.

"Miles, quickly," she said. "Let's find a television set."

"Marie—" he began harshly, with the backwash of his anger at the two men and the radio across the room in his voice. Then he saw the peculiar rigidity of her face, and a feeling of uneasiness washed in to drown the fury.

"All right," he said, getting to his feet in turn, "if you want to."

She hurried out of the restaurant, and he had to stretch his legs to keep up with her. Outside, in the sudden glare of red sunlight, she paused and looked, almost frantically, right and left.

"Where?" she asked. "Oh, where, Miles?"

"The nearest bar, I suppose," he said. Looking about himself, he spotted the neon sign of one, palely lit and violet-colored in the red sunlight, half a block down the street from them. "This way."

They went quickly down the half block and into the bar. Within, no one was moving—neither bartenders nor customers. They all were sitting or standing still as carvings, staring at the large television set set up high on a dark wooden shelf at the inner end of the bar. From that ledge, the lined, rectangular face of the President of the United States looked out. Miles heard the tail end of his sentence as they entered.

"For simultaneous announcement to all countries of the world," said the slow, pausing voice in the same heavy tones they had heard a dozen times before, speaking on smaller issues of the country and the world. "These two visitors also supplied us with a film strip to be used in conjunction with the announcement. First, here is a picture of our two friends from the civilization of worlds at the center of our galaxy."

The rectangular face disappeared, to be replaced by the still image of two men in what seemed to be gray business suits, standing before a window in some sort of lounge or reception room—probably a room in one of the UN buildings, Miles thought.

It was as the radio announcer had said earlier. There was nothing about the two to distinguish them from any other humans. Their noses were a little long, the skin of their faces a little dark, and there was a suspicion of a mongoloid fold above the eyes. Otherwise, they might have been encountered on the streets of any large city in the world, east or west, without the slightest suspicion that they had come from anywhere off the planet.

"These gentlemen," the Presidential voice went on slowly, "have explained to the representatives of the nations of our world that our galaxy, that galaxy of millions upon millions of stars, of which our sun is a minor star out near the edge"—the figures of the two men disappeared and were replaced by what looked like a glowing spiral of dust floating against a black background—"will shortly be facing attack by a roving intergalactic race which periodically preys upon those island universes like our galaxy which dot that inter-galactic space.

"Their civilization, which represents many worlds in many solar systems in toward the center of the galaxy, has taken the lead in forming a defensive military force which will attempt to meet these predators at the edge of our galaxy and turn them aside from their purpose. They inform us that if the predators are not turned aside, over ninety percent of the life on the inhabited worlds of our galaxy will be captured and literally processed for food to feed this nomadic and rapacious civilization. Indeed, it is the constant need to search for sustenance for their overwhelming numbers that keeps them always on the move between and through the galaxies, generation succeeding generation in rapacious conquest."

Suddenly the image of something like a white-furred weasel, with hands on its two upper limbs and standing erect on its two hind limbs, filled the television screen. Beside it was the gray outline of a man, and it could be seen that the creature came about shoulder-high on the outline.

"This," said the disembodied voice of the Chief Executive, "is a picture of what the predator looks like, according to our two visitors. The predator is born, lives, and dies within his ship or ships in space. His only concern is to survive—first as a race, then as an individual. His numbers are countless. Even the ships in which he lives will probably be numbered in the millions. He and his fellows will be prepared to sustain staggering losses if they can win their way into the feeding ground that is our galaxy. Here, by courtesy of our two visitors, is a picture of what the predator fleet will look like. Collectively, they're referred to in the records of our galaxy as the Silver Horde."

Once more the image in the television screen changed.

"This is one of their ships," said the President's voice.

A spindle-shaped craft of some highly polished metal appeared on the television screen. Beside it, the silhouette of a man had shrunk until it was approximately the size of a human being standing next to a double trailer truck.

"This is a scout ship, the smallest of their craft— holding a single family, usually consisting of three or four adults and perhaps as many young."

The image on the television set shrank almost to a dot, and beside it appeared a large circular craft nearly filling the screen.

"And this is the largest of their ships," said the President. "Inside, it should have much the appearance and population of a small city—up to several thousand individuals, adult and young, and at least one large manufacturing or tool-making unit required by the Horde for maintenance and warfare, as well as food-processing and storage units."

The voice of the Chief Executive lifted, on a note that signaled he was approaching the end of what he had to say.

"Our visitors have told us," he said, "that defense of the galaxy is a common duty. For our world to join in that defense is therefore a duty. What they require from us, however, is a contribution of a highly specialized nature." His voice hesitated and then went on more strongly. "They tell us that the weapons with which our galaxy's defensive force will meet the Horde are beyond the understanding of our science here on Earth. They tell us, however, that they are part physical, part nonphysical in nature. The number of fighting individuals we can contribute, therefore, to our galaxy's defense is limited by our relatively primitive state of awareness as far as these nonphysical forces are concerned. We can send only one man. This one individual—this one man who is best suited to be our representative by natural talent and abilities—has already been selected by our visitors. He will shortly be taken over by them, adjusted so as to make the best possible use of these talents, and then turned loose for a brief period to move about our world and absorb an identification with the rest of us. This process of absorbing an identification has been compared by our visitors to the process of charging a car battery, to exposing its plates to a steady input of electrical current. Once he has been so 'charged,' all of us on this world who have managed to contribute to the 'charging' will continue to have some sort of awareness in the backs of our minds of what he is going through up on the battle line, to which he will then be transported. And from this linkage he will draw the personal nonphysical strength with which he will operate his particular weapon when the encounter with the Horde occurs."

The President's face once more appeared on the television screen. He paused, and standing in the bar,

Miles felt the impact of the older man's eyes upon him—as, evidently, did everyone else in the room.

"That is all for now," said the President slowly. "As soon as we have more information, people of America and people of our world, it will be released to you. Meanwhile, in this trying and strange time into which we have suddenly been plunged by events, let me ask you all to go on with your lives in their ordinary fashion and show patience. As we approach what lies in store for us, what lies in store for us will become more plain to us all. God bless you, and good afternoon."

His face vanished from the screen. There was a moment of grayness; then the face of an announcer flickered on.

"The voice you have just heard," the announcer said smoothly, "was that of the President of the United States. . . ."

There was a slowly beginning, gradually increasing combination of sighs and rustles of movement within the bar as the people there came to life and action again. Miles turned to Marie and saw her standing white-faced, still staring at the television screen.

"Come on," said Miles. "Let's get out of here."

He had to take her by the arm before he could break the trance that held her. But when he touched her, she started and seemed to come awake. She turned obediently and followed him out once more into the red-lighted street.

In the street she leaned against him, as if the strength had gone out of her. He put his arm around her to steady her and looked anxiously about him. Two blocks down the street, a lone cab was coming toward them. Miles whistled, and the cab came on, angling into the curb to stop before them.

Miles bent down to open the rear door. As he did, he became conscious of the fact that besides the driver, there was a man in a blue suit in the front seat and another man sitting in the back seat. He checked, with the door half-open.

"It's all right," said the man in the back seat. "You're Miles Vander, aren't you? And this will be Miss Bourtel."

He reached into his inside suitcoat pocket and brought out a leather case, which he flipped open. Miles saw a card in a plastic case, with the man's picture and some lines of fine type underneath.

"Treasury Department," said the man. "You're to come with us, Mr. Vander. We'll drop Miss Bourtel off on the way."

Miles stared at him.

"Please get in," said the man in the front seat beside the driver, and the evenness of his tone made the words more a command than an invitation. "We were told we'd find you here. And there's no time to lose."

Within the circle of Miles' arm, Marie leaned even more heavily against him. Worry for her tightened Miles' chest.

"All right," he said abruptly. He helped Marie into the back seat of the taxi next to the man sitting there and then got in himself, closing the door behind him.

"We'd better go—" he was beginning, when the man in the front seat cut him short.

"That's all right. We've got our instructions on that, too," he said. He sat half turned in the front seat, with one elbow over the back to the seat so that he looked directly into Miles' face. "Look at her."

Alarmed, Miles looked sharply around again at Marie. She sat with her head against him, her eyes closed, unmoving, breathing deeply and slowly.

"Don't worry," said the man in the front seat. "She's only asleep. The aliens arranged it—the two from the ship—to get her through the business of seeing you picked up by us. We're to deliver her to the university hospital, where they'll take care of her for an hour or two, until she wakes. When she does wake up, she won't be alarmed about what's happened to you anymore."

Miles stared at him.

"What *is* all this?" Miles burst out.

"I don't blame you for not suspecting," the man in the front seat answered. The taxi was already pulling away from the curb and heading off down the street in the direction of the distant university. "We'll be taking you immediately to the airport, where a military airplane will fly you to Washington. You're the man that the two aliens from the spaceship—our two visitors from the center of the galaxy—have picked to be this world's representative, defending the galaxy against the Silver Horde, and everything we've done so far, like our finding you and Miss Bourtel's falling asleep, has been arranged by them."

4

The process by which Miles was whirled away after that to the university hospital, where they left Marie sleeping, to the airport, by jet to Washington, by blue civilian sedan there to a large building which he dimly recognized as the Pentagon, and within the Pentagon to a suite of rooms more resembling a hotel suite than anything else—all this passed like the successive shapes of some bad dream. And after all the rushing was over, after he had at last been settled in the suite of rooms, he discovered that he had nothing to do but wait.

The two men who had picked him up in Minneapolis and brought him here stayed with him through the dinner hour. After the dinner cart with its load of clinking empty plates and dirty silverware had been wheeled out again, the two men watched television, with its endless parade of announcers, throughout the evening—the sound turned low at Miles' request. Miles himself, after prowling restlessly around the room and asking a number of questions to which his guardians gave noncommittal answers, finally settled down with a pencil and some notepaper to while away his time making sketches of the other two.

He had become lost in this, to the point where he no longer noticed the murmur of the television or the passage of time, when there was a knock at his door and one of the guards got up to answer. A moment later Miles was conscious that the man had returned and was standing over him, waiting for him to look up from his sketching. Miles looked up.

"The President's here," said the guard.

Miles stared, then got hastily to his feet, putting his sketches aside. Beyond the guard, he saw the door to his suite standing open and a moment later heard the approach of feet down the polished surface of the corridor outside. These came closer and closer. A second later the man Miles had been watching on television earlier that day walked into the room.

In person, the Chief Executive was not as tall as he often appeared in pictures—no taller than Miles himself. Close up, however, he looked more youthful than he appeared in news photos and on television. He shook hands with Miles with a great deal of warmth, but it was something of the warmth of a tired and worried man who can only snatch a few moments from his day in which to be human and personal.

He put a hand on Miles' shoulder and walked him over to a window that looked out on a narrow strip of grass in what appeared to be a small artificial courtyard under some kind of skylight. The two men who had been with Miles and the others who had come with the Chief Executive quietly slipped out the door of the suite and left them alone.

"It's an honor . . ." said the President. He still stood with his hand on Miles' shoulder, and his voice was deep with the throatiness of age. "It's an honor to have an American be the one who was chosen. I wanted to tell you that myself."

"Thank you . . . Mr. President," Miles answered, stumbling a little over the unfamiliar words of the title. He burst out then in spite of the urgings of courtesy. "But I don't know why they'd want to pick me! Why me?"

The older man's hand patted his shoulder a little awkwardly, even a little bewilderedly.

"I don't know either," murmured the President. "None of us knows."

"But—" Miles hesitated, then plunged ahead. "We've only got their word for everything. How do we know it's true, what they say?"

Again the Presidential hand patted him sympathetically on the shoulder.

"We don't know," the older man said, looking out at the grass of the artificial courtyard. "That's the truth of the matter. We don't know. But that ship of theirs is something—incredible. It backs up their story. And after all, they only want—"

He broke off, looked at Miles, and smiled a little apologetically.

Miles felt a sudden coldness inside him.

"You mean," he said slowly, "you're ready to believe them because they want only one man? Because they want only me?"

"That's right," said the Chief Executive. He did not pat Miles on the shoulder now. He looked directly into Miles' eyes. "They've asked for nothing but one man. And they've shown us some evidence—shown us heads of state, that is—some physical evidence from the last time the Horde went through the galaxy millions of years ago. We've seen the dead body of one of the Horde—preserved, of course. We've seen samples of the weapons and tools of the Horde. Of course, these could have been fakes—made up just to show us. But, Miles—" He paused, still keeping Miles' eyes locked with his own. "The best guess we can make is that they're telling the truth."

Miles opened his mouth to speak, then closed it again, helplessly.

Finally, he got the words out.

"But," he said, "if they're lying. . . ."

The President straightened. Once more he put his hand on Miles' shoulder, in a curious touch—a touch like an accolade, as if he were knighting Miles.

"Of course," he said slowly, "if it should turn out to be that . . . your responsibility might turn out to be even greater than it is."

They stood facing each other. Suddenly Miles understood—just as in the same moment he understood that it was just this message that the other man had come personally to give him. It was clear, if unspoken, between them. Yet Miles felt a strange, angry need to bring the understanding out in the open. A need to make it plain the thing was there, like touching with his tongue, again and again, the exposed root of an aching tooth.

"You mean, if it turns out that they want to make me into something dangerous to people back here," he said, "you want me to do something about it, is that it?"

The President did not answer. He continued to look at Miles and hold Miles' shoulder as if he were pledging him to some special duty.

"You mean," said Miles again, more loudly, "that if it turns out that I'm being made into something dangerous to . . . the human race, I'm to destroy myself. Is that it?"

The President sighed, and his hand dropped from Miles' shoulder. He turned to look out at the grass in the courtyard.

"You're to follow your own judgment," he said to Miles.

A great loneliness descended upon Miles. A chilling loneliness. He had never felt so alone before. It seemed as if the President's words had lifted him up and transported him off, far off, from all humanity into an isolated watchtower, to a solitary sentry post far removed from all the rest of humanity. He too turned and looked out at the little strip of grass. Suddenly it looked greener and more beautiful than any such length of lawn he had ever gazed upon in his life. It seemed infinitely precious.

"Miles," he heard the older man say.

He lifted his head and turned to see the President facing him once more, with his hand outstretched.

"Good luck, Miles," said the President.

"Thank you." Miles took the hand automatically. They shook hands, and the Chief Executive turned and walked away across the room and out the door, leaving it open. The two Treasury agents who had picked up Miles originally came back in, shutting the door firmly behind them. They sat down again without a word near the TV set and turned it on. Miles heard its low murmur again in his ear.

Almost blindly, he himself turned and walked into one of the two bedrooms of the suite, closing the door behind him. He lay down on the bed on his back, staring at the white ceiling.

He woke suddenly—and only by his waking was he made aware of the fact that his drifting thoughts had dwindled into sleep. Standing over him, alongside the bed, were two figures that were vaguely familiar, although he could not remember ever having seen them before in his life. Slowly he remembered. They were the two figures, still business-suited, that had been shown on the television screen as he and Marie had watched the President's broadcast in the bar. Suddenly he understood. These were the two aliens from the monster ship that overhung Earth, under a sun that they had colored red to attract the attention of all the people on the world to the coming of that ship.

Reflex, the reflex that brings an animal out of sound sleep to its feet, brought Miles to his. He found himself standing almost between the two aliens. At close range their faces looked directly into his, no less human of feature or color or general appearance than they had looked before. But this close, it seemed to Miles that he felt an emanation from them—something too still, too composed to be human. And yet the eyes they fixed upon him were not unkind.

Only remote, as remote as the eyes of men on some high plateau looking down into a jungle of beasts.

"Miles," said the one on his left, who was slightly the shorter of the two. His voice was a steady baritone—calm, passionless, distant, without foreign accent. "Are you ready to come with us?"

Still fogged by sleep, still with his nerves wound wire-tight by the animal reflex that had jerked him up out of slumber, Miles snapped out what he might not have said without thinking, otherwise.

"Do I have a choice?"

The two looked steadily at him.

"Of course you have a choice," said the shorter of the two calmly. "You'd be no good, to your world or to us, unless you wanted to help us."

Miles began to laugh. It was harsh, reflexive laughter that burst from him almost without intention. It took him a few seconds to get it under control, but finally, he did.

"Want to?" he said—his real feelings bursting out

in spite of himself. "Of course I don't want to. Yesterday I had my own life, with its future all planned
out. Now the sun turns red, and it seems I have to
go to some impossible place and do some impossible
thing—instead of what I've been planning and working toward for five years! And you ask me if I *want*
to!"

He stared at them, checking just in time the bitter laughter that was threatening to rise inside his
throat again. They did not answer.

"Well?" he challenged. "Why should I want to?"

"To help your race live," answered the shorter one
emotionlessly. "That's the only reason that will work.
If you don't want that, then we've been wasting our
time here—and time is precious."

He stopped speaking and gazed at Miles. Now it was
Miles' turn to feel that they were waiting for him to
say something. But he did not know what to say.

"If you don't want to be your people's representative in the fight against the Horde," said the shorter
one, slowly and deliberately as if he were spelling
matters out for Miles, "you should tell us now, and we
will leave."

Miles stared at him.

"You mean"—Miles looked narrowly at him—"you
wouldn't choose somebody else?"

"There's no one else to choose," said the shorter one.
"No one, that is, who'd be worth our time to work with.
If you don't want to go, we'll leave."

"Wait," said Miles, as the two turned away. They
stopped and turned back again.

"I didn't say I wouldn't," said Miles. "It's just that
I don't understand anything about all this. Don't I have
a right to have it explained to me first?"

"Of course," answered the taller one unexpectedly.
"Ask us whatever you want to know."

"All right," said Miles. "What makes me so different from everybody else in the world, to make you pick me?"

"You have a capability for identification with all the other people in your world," answered the short one, "that is far greater than that of anyone else alive on that world at this present moment."

"Understand, we don't say," put in the taller one, "that at the present moment you've got this identification. We only mean that the capacity, the potential to have it, is in you. With our help that potential can be developed. You can step forward in this ability to a point your own race won't reach for many generations from now, under ordinary conditions."

"Your race's representative against the Horde has to have this identification," said the shorter one. "Because you're going to need to draw upon their sources of—" he hesitated, and then went on—"of something that they each possess so far only in tiny amounts. You must combine these tiny amounts in yourself, into something large enough so that you can effectively operate the type of weapon we will be giving you to use against the Horde."

He stopped speaking. For a moment Miles' mind churned with the information that had been given him. It sounded sensible—but he felt unexpectedly stubborn.

"How do I know this is all going to be for the benefit of human beings anyway?" he asked. "How do I know that it's not a case of our not being in danger at all—but your needing me and whatever this thing is that everybody has a little bit of just for your own purposes?"

Their faces did not change as they gazed at him.

"You'll have to trust us on that point," said the taller one quietly.

"Tell me one thing then," said Miles, challenging him. "Do you really look just like human beings?"

"No," said the smaller one, and the word seemed to echo and reecho in the room. "We put on this appearance the way you might put on a suit of clothes."

"I want to see you the way you actually are," said Miles.

"No," said the shorter one again. "You would not like what you saw if we showed you ourselves as we are."

"I don't care," said Miles. He frowned. "I'm an artist. I'm used to looking at things objectively. I'll make it a point not to let whatever you look like bother me."

"No," repeated the shorter one, still calmly. "You think you wouldn't let it bother you. But it would. And your emotional reaction to us would get in the way of your working with us against the Horde, whether or not you believe it now."

"Fine! I have to trust you!" said Miles grimly. "But you don't trust me!"

"Trust us or not," said the taller one. "If your world contributes a representative to the galaxy's defense, that will entitle it to whatever protection all our galaxy's defensive forces can give it. But your contribution is tiny. In the civilization from which we two come anyone, such as I or my friend here, can operate many weapons like the one you'll be given to handle. In short, one of our people has fighting abilities worth many times that of the total population of your world. So to us it's a small matter whether you join us or not. Your help counts—because the slightest additional bit of strength may be enough to swing the balance of power between the Horde and ourselves. But it is small to us, no matter how big it seems to you."

"In short," put in the smaller one, "to us you represent a fraction of a single individual defender like myself against the Horde. To yourself, you represent several billions of your people. The choice is up to you."

"If we're just one isolated little world, way out here," said Miles, with the uneasy suspicion that he was clutching at straws, "and not worth much, why should the Horde bother with us at all? If there are so many of you worth so much more in toward the center of the galaxy?"

"You have no understanding of the numbers and rapacity of the Horde," said the smaller one. "Suppose we show you a picture."

Instantly the room was gone from around Miles. He stood in the midst of dirt and rock—an eroded desert stretching to the horizon. Nowhere was there an intelligent creature, an animal—or even any sign of a bush, or tree, or plant. There was nothing—nothing but the raw surface of a world.

Suddenly he was back in the room again.

"That is what a world looks like after the Silver Horde has passed," said the shorter one. "That was a picture taken by those few who survived of the race that held the center of this galaxy before us, several million years ago. The Horde broke through then and processed everything organic for food. Its numbers are beyond your imagining. We could give you a figure, but it would have no real meaning for you."

"But," said Miles suddenly and sharply, "if the Horde came through the last time and cleaned off all the worlds like that which had life on them, how is it there are records like this?"

"We've never said that all of the galaxy's worlds would be ravaged by the Horde," said the taller one. "Some small percentage will escape by sheer chance. Even if we fight and lose, some of the ships that oppose them will escape, even from battle with the Horde. And these will begin to populate the galaxy again. So it was the last time, a million of your years ago, when the Horde came through. Those who lived here before us in the galaxy's center met them, as we will meet them, and fought them and lost. For a million years after that, the Horde fed its numbers on the living worlds of our galaxy until the pickings became so lean they were forced to move on. But as I say, some ships eluded them. Here and there a world was missed. After the Horde had passed, civilization began over again."

"And in the millions of years that have passed since," said the other, "even the ravaged worlds began to recover. Look at that same world again, the one we showed you. See it as it is today."

Once more Miles found himself standing in some other place than in the room at the Pentagon. Only, about him now were hills covered with a species of grass and a type of tall, twisted tree. Distantly, there were sounds as of small birds chittering, and something small and almost too fast for him to see scurried through the grasslike ground cover perhaps thirty feet from where he stood. Then, abruptly, he was back in the room again, facing the two aliens.

"All through the galaxy you will find worlds like that," said the shorter. "Their temperature and atmosphere and the rest of their physical makeup make them entirely inhabitable. But their flora and fauna are primitive, as if it had only been less than a billion years since they cooled from the whirlpool of coalescing stellar dusts and fragments that they were originally. But they are not that young. They've simply started over again, from the minute life of their oceans, since the Horde passed."

"Worlds like that will be available for settlement by your people if you survive the Horde," said the taller one.

"But even if I go, you say I may make no difference in stopping the Horde," said Miles. "And if I stay, our world may be one of those that the Horde somehow misses, anyway."

"This is perfectly true," said the smaller one. They both looked at him impassively. "But as I said earlier, our time is precious. You'll have to give us your answer now."

Miles turned and looked out the bedroom window, which also looked onto the small strip of grass of the interior courtyard. Beyond the strip of grass was a bare concrete wall. He looked at that and saw nothing on it—no mark, no shape. It was nothing but a featureless wall. Equally blank was the reaction he felt within him toward the rest of the world. In spite of what Marie had said, in spite of what these aliens seemed to think, it was not people that mattered to him—but painting.

And then, leaping out of nowhere as if to clutch at his throat and stop his breathing, came a sudden understanding. If his world were wiped out, if his race were destroyed, what would become of his painting?

Suddenly it pounced upon Miles, like a lion from the underbrush, the realization that it was not merely the continuance of his work that was at stake here, but the very possibility of that work's existing at all. If he should stay here and paint, refusing to go with these two, and then the Horde came by to wipe out his world, and his paintings with it, what good would any of his painting have done? He had no choice. He had to defend the unborn ghosts of his future canvases, even at the risk of never being able to paint them.

He turned sharply to the two aliens.

"All right," he said. "I'm with you."

"Very well," said the shorter one. Miles' acceptance had not altered the expressions of their faces or the tones of their voices, any more than anything else he had said or done.

"What do I do then?" asked Miles. "I suppose we go to your ship?"

"We are already in the ship," said the shorter one. "We've been in it ever since you agreed to join us."

Miles looked about him. The room was unchanged. Beyond the little window, the strip of lawn and the far wall of the interior courtyard was unchanged. He turned to see the two aliens moving out of the bedroom into the living room of the suite. He followed them and stopped short. The two Treasury agents were gone, and where there had been a door to the Pentagon corridor there was only wall now. The aliens waited while he stared about him.

"You see?" said the shorter one, after a moment.

"There's no door," Miles said stupidly.

"We don't use doors," said the aliens. "Soon, neither will you. This suite will be yours until we deliver you to the Battle Line. Now, if you'll come back into the bedroom, we will begin your development."

Once more they led the way back into the bedroom. They stopped by the bed.

"And now," said the shorter one, "please lie down on your back on the bed."

Miles did so.

"Please close your eyes."

Miles did so. He lay there with his eyes closed, waiting for further orders. Nothing happened. After what seemed only a second he opened them again. The two aliens were gone.

Outside the bedroom window, night darkness held the courtyard. Darkness was also in the bedroom and filling the aperture of the half-open door to the sitting room. In spite of the fact that he seemed merely to have closed his eyes for a moment, he had a confused impression that some large length of time had passed. An impulse came to him to get up and investigate the situation, but at the very moment that it came to him, it slipped away again. A heavy sort of languor crept over him, a soothing weariness, as if he were at the end of some long day of hard physical effort. He felt not only weary, but also comforted. Dimly, he was aware that some great change had taken place in him, but he was too much at ease on the bed, soaked and steeped in his weariness, to investigate now what had happened.

Above all, he felt wrapped in peace. A great silent song of comfort and reassurance seemed to be enfolding him, buoying him up—lifting him up, in fact, like the crest of a wave on an endlessly, peacefully rocking ocean. He mounted the crest and slid slowly down into the next trough. The darkness moved in on him. He gave himself up to the rocking comfort.

Slowly consciousness slipped away from him, and he felt himself falling into a deep but natural sleep.

When he woke a second time, it was once more daylight, or its equivalent, beyond the windows of his bedroom. Daylight—not red, as the daylight had been since the moment of his painting on the river, but cheerful yellow daylight—filled the interior courtyard via the skylight. He looked around the room and saw the two aliens standing side by side not far from the bed, watching him.

Slowly he became conscious of himself. He felt strangely different, strangely light and complete. So lacking in the normal little pressures and sensations was he that he glanced down to see if his body was still there.

It was. He lay on the bed, wrapped or dressed in some sort of metallically glinting silver clothing that fitted him closely, covering all but his hands and his face. His body had never felt this way before. Nor his mind, for that matter. His head was so clear, so free of drowsiness and dullness and all the little hangovers of human tiredness, that his thoughts seemed to sing within it. He looked again at the two aliens.

"You can get up now," said the smaller.

Miles sat up, swung his legs over the side of the bed, and rose to his feet. The sensation of his rising was indescribable. It was almost as if he floated to his feet without muscular effort. As he stood facing the two aliens, the feeling of lightness in his body persisted. He felt, although his feet were flat on the floor, as if he were standing on tiptoe, with no effort involved.

"What's happened to me?" he asked wonderingly.

"You are now completely healthy. That's all," said the taller alien. "Would you like to take a look at yourself?"

Miles nodded.

He had barely completed the nod when the wall behind the two aliens suddenly became a shimmering mirror surface. He saw himself reflected in it, standing beside the bed wrapped in his close-fitting silver clothes, and for a moment he did not recognize himself.

The man who stood imaged in the mirror was erect and straight-limbed and looked bigger—bigger all over in some strange way—than Miles had remembered his mirror image's ever looking before. But it was not this so much that caused Miles to catch his breath. There was something drastically different about him now. Something had happened. He stared at himself for a long moment without understanding, and then he saw it. And an icy feeling of excitement ran down his spine.

In the tight silver sleeve that enclosed it to the wrist, his left arm was as large and full-muscled as his right. And the hand that terminated it was in no way different from the healthy hand at the end of his right arm.

Miles stood staring at it. He could not believe what he saw. And then—he could believe it, but he was afraid that if he looked away from it for an instant, what he saw would evaporate into a dream. Or what he saw would go back to being the way it had been these last six years. But he continued to stand there, and his mirrored image did not change. Slowly, almost dazedly, he turned his eyes to the two aliens.

"My arm," he said.

"Of course," said the small alien.

Miles turned back to the mirror surface. Hesitantly he lifted his good right arm to feel the left hand and arm. They were solid and warm, alive and movable, under the fingertips of what had been his lone good hand. A bubble of joy and amazement began to swell within him. He turned once more to the aliens.

"You didn't tell me about this," he said. "You didn't tell me my arm would be fixed."

"It was of a piece with the rest," said the taller alien. "And we did not want you to commit yourself because of anything like a bribe."

Miles turned back to the mirror surface, feeling his left arm and marveling at it once more. The sensation in the arm as he moved it woke him to the sensations of the rest of his body. Looking at himself closely in the mirror surface now, he saw that he was heavier, more erect, in every way stronger and more vital than he had been before. In his mind he tried to find words to express how it was with him now, but the words would not come. He felt all in one piece—and he felt invisible. That was the closest he could come to it. There were no sensations of sublevel pains, weariness, or heaviness about him. He and his body were one, as—he could now remember—he had not felt since he had been very young. He turned back to the aliens.

"Thank you," he said.

"There is no need to thank us," said the shorter of the two aliens. "What we did to you we did as much for ourselves as for you. Now it's time for you to start to become charged with the identification sense of your fellow humans."

Miles stared at him with interest.

"Shall I lie down on the bed again?" Miles asked.

"No," said the taller alien. "This next is nothing we can do for you. You have to do it all yourself. You've been away from the surface of your world for two and a half days now. During that time the people of your world have been informed through all possible news media that soon you'll be back and moving about among them. They've been told, if they see you, not to speak to you or show any awareness of you. They're simply to let you wander among them and treasure up in their minds the sight of you."

"That's all I do?" demanded Miles.

"Not quite all," said the smaller of the two. "You have to open your inner consciousness to their sense of identification with you and what you'll be doing in their name. You must endeavor to feel toward them as they feel toward you. You must learn to consider them precious."

"But where do I go first? What should I do?" Miles asked.

"Simply—wander," the shorter alien said. "Do you know a poem called *The Rime of the Ancient Mariner?* Written by a man named Coleridge."

"I've read it," said Miles.

"Then perhaps you remember the lines with which the Ancient Mariner explains his moving about the Earth to tell his story," said the smaller one. There still was no perceptible emotion in his voice, but as he quoted the two lines that followed, it seemed that they rang with particular emphasis in Miles' mind and memory.

> . . . I pass, like night, from land to land;
> I have strange power of speech. . . .

"You will find," the smaller of the two aliens went on, "that it'll be with you as it was with the poem's Ancient Mariner. If you want to move from one place to another, you only need to think of the place you want to be, and you will be there. If you want to lift yourself into the air or fly like a bird, you can do it by thinking of it. You'll find that no lock will be able to keep you out of any place you want to enter. No wall will bar you. If you wish, you can walk through any barrier. The people of your world who can be reached by the news media have been warned to expect this. They have been told to expect you anywhere—even in their own homes. They have been asked to cooperate by ignoring you when you appear suddenly among them."

"What if they don't ignore me?" asked Miles. "Your asking them to do it doesn't guarantee they will."

"Those who don't ignore you," said the taller alien, "won't be offering you the necessary identification you are out to gather from as many of your race as possible. So remove yourself from the presence of anyone who does not cooperate, because you will be wasting your time. As far as any inimical actions are concerned, you'll find that while you can touch anything you like, you can't be touched or hurt by anything, unless you wish it—right up to and including your race's nuclear weapons. Nothing can hold you, and nothing can harm you."

He fell silent. Miles stood uncertainly for a moment.

"Well," he said at last. "Shall I go now, then, and start?"

"The sooner, the better," said the taller alien. "Simply think of the spot on the surface of the Earth where you want to be and you'll be there."

"And when shall I come back?" asked Miles.

"When you've gathered together an identification sense with enough of your fellow humans, you'll know it," said the shorter alien. "Simply decide then to come back here to the ship and you'll be here. Then we'll leave together for the defense line that's being set up outside the spiral arm of the galaxy to meet the Silver Horde."

"All right," said Miles slowly. He felt strange. It was as if everything that had happened to him had happened within a few moments. At the same time, he was surprised to feel that he was not overwhelmed by it all. Now, particularly since he was in this rebuilt, newly perfect body, all that the aliens said seemed entirely natural, and all that he had to do seemed entirely normal.

He wondered where on Earth it would be best to go to first. While he was still wondering, a stray impulse made him look once more into the mirror image of the wall. He saw himself there, and he could not help smiling at what be saw. He turned back to the aliens.

"I'm a new man, all right," he said to them.

For the first time since he had met them, Miles saw one of them shake his head. It was the shorter alien.

"No," said the shorter alien. Neither of them was smiling back. "You're not a *new* man. You're Everyman."

5

He had been puzzling over the point at which he wished to arrive first on his return to Earth, but at the last minute it proved to be no trouble whatsoever. Like the point of a compass needle drawn toward the magnetic north, he found himself suddenly on the steps of the dormitory where Marie lived. It was night about him. On the street running through the campus the streetlights were lit, and the headlights of cars flickered past through the high shrubbery that shielded the dormitory grounds from the street itself. On each side of the row of glass doors that gave entrance to the building, a tall lamp glowed yellowly. He walked up and through the doors into the lobby.

As he entered, he saw that the lounge beyond the desk was empty. He went to the desk itself. On duty was the same small girl with dark glasses and a pointed face who had been on duty the last time he had called here for Marie. She glanced at him for a second as he came in, then quickly glanced away again, down at her desk below the counter, where some textbooks and a notebook were spread out. She kept her eyes on the textbooks as he came up. He stopped at the counter and leaned over it.

"I know it must be late," he said. "But this is a sort of emergency. Would you ring Marie Bourtel's room for me, please?"

She did not answer, and she did not move. He saw her profile, just a couple of feet from him, bent rigidly above an open textbook. There was a faint shine on her forehead as of perspiration—and suddenly he realized that she was following directions. She was ignoring him, even to the point of not looking at him or replying to him when he spoke directly to her.

He sighed, a little heavily. All at once, he seemed to sense the quality of her fear. It came through to him like the faint rapid beating of a bird's heart, felt as the bird is held in the hand. It occurred to him that he could probably turn and go up the stairs to Marie's room. Then he had a better thought. He looked at the board of numbers that hung beyond the little clerk, with a hook beneath each number and keys on some of the hooks. Above each hook was a name. He sought out Marie's name, noted that the hook held no key, and looked for the number below the hook. Marie's room number jumped at him. It was forty-six. That would mean she was on the fourth floor. Now that he stopped to think of it, he remembered her mentioning she was on the fourth floor.

He concentrated on the hook and closed his eyes for a second. When he opened them, he stood in darkness in a small room. The blind on the single window was drawn nearly all the way. Below it the window had been raised a little, and the white curtains waved sleepily in the soft inrush of cool night air. The girls in the dormitory were normally assigned two to a room, but Marie, as a counselor, had a room to herself. Looking about, he saw her now, a still figure under the covers of the bed in one corner of the room.

He walked softly over toward her and looked down at her sleeping face. She slept on her side, her pale features in profile against the white pillow and her hair spread out behind them upon it. One hand was up on the pillow beside her face.

"Marie," he said softly.

She did not awaken. He repeated her name a little louder.

This time she stirred. Her hand drew back down under the covers, but her eyes did not open. He reached out one hand to the switch of the bedside lamp on the small table only a foot or so from her face. Then he changed his mind, and his hand drew back. To waken her to the sudden glare of the lamp seemed too much of a shock.

He looked over at the slight rectangle below the shade where the window was open. An inspiration came over him. He thought of the light, the pale light coming in through that opening, as gathering and strengthening in the room, and as he watched, it built up around them. Either that—or his eyes became accustomed to the dimness—he was not quite sure which.

"Marie," he said, bending over and murmuring directly into her ear.

She stirred again, and this time her eyes blinked and then sleepily opened. For a moment they stared at him without recognition, and then they flew wide.

Her head lifted, and her mouth opened. For a moment he thought that she had not recognized him after all: that she had taken him for some intruder and was about to scream. But before he could put his hand over her mouth, fearful eyes filled with the shadow of the darkened room.

"Miles . . ." she whispered on a long slow breath.

"Marie," he said. He bent over and kissed her. And her arms went up and around his neck, at first softly and then fiercely holding him. For a moment they clung together, and then he drew back, loosening her arms but holding her hands with his own hands as he sat down on the edge of the bed.

"Marie," he whispered. "Never mind what you've been hearing people on Earth should do. Talk to me."

"Yes, Miles," she said, and her mouth curved in a slow, oddly tender smile. "You came here to me," she said.

"I had to accept, Marie," he said. "I had to agree to do what they asked."

"I know," she murmured, looking at him through the dimness. "Oh, Miles! You came to me!"

"I had to see you first," Miles said, still holding her hands. "I wanted you to know all about it, before I"—he hesitated—"went ahead."

She lay looking at him in the faint but pervasive light from the slightly opened window which he had increased.

"What're you going to do now?" she asked him.

"I don't know," he said. "What I'm supposed to do, I guess. Roam around the world and see if I pick up some kind of charge from the people I meet and see."

Her hands tightened on his.

"How long will you do that?" she asked softly.

"I don't know," he answered. "The aliens said I'd know when I was ready. According to them, I don't think it's supposed to take too long. They kept talking about the fact that time was precious."

"Maybe you shouldn't be here talking with me then," she said, but her hands held as tightly to him as ever.

"Maybe not," he echoed. And strangely, once he had said it, the feeling of urgency began to grow inside him, as if somewhere within himself he contained the knowledge that time indeed was precious: the knowledge that he must not waste it, as he was wasting it now.

"I guess I've got to go," he said. He released his fingers from her grip, which held tightly for a second more and then let him go.

"But you'll come back?" she asked, as he stood up beside the bed. He saw her face, by the trick of the shadow in the room seeming to lie far below him instead of merely an arm's length away.

"I'll come back," he answered.

"I don't mean before you leave," she said quickly. "I mean afterward. You'll come back safely?"

"I'll come back safely, all right," he said. And with the words a strange, bright, animallike anger seemed to kindle inside him, a deep, white-hot atavistic fury, a determination that he would come back—in spite of anything.

He bent over and kissed her once more, then released the arms she had locked around his neck and stood erect again.

"Good-bye," he said and willed himself to be back once more on the sidewalk before the dormitory.

Instantly he was there.

He turned and walked off a little from the light of the entrance into the shadow of the Norway pines lining the driveway. He wondered what to do first. Where to go? With all the world to choose from, he found himself confused by the countless number of places he might visit. Finally, he threw it all from his mind and chose at random. He had never been to Japan. He thought of Tokyo.

Abruptly, he was there. It was bright morning. He stood on a crowded street, and passersby flowed about him as if he were a rock in a stream. The buildings were all Western-looking. The people he saw were all in Western dress. Only the rattle of their voices, sounding high-pitched and unfamiliar, gave a touch of strangeness to the scene. Then it was as if his mind had broken through a thin film like a soap bubble that enclosed him—and he found himself understanding what they were saying.

He stood listening and watching those who came by for any reaction to his appearance there, dressed in his strange silver suit. But although eyes glanced at him, they glanced away again. For a moment he was astonished that the response of the people in the world should be so strongly conditioned by the instructions of the aliens. And then something that came to him by the same route as his understanding of the Japanese words being spoken around him told him that it was as much politeness as anything else that was keeping the gaze of those about him from lingering on him. He began to walk down the street.

As he did, he began to lose his self-consciousness. The understanding and communication he seemed to be holding with the people about him, just below the level of consciousness, grew stronger as he passed among them. He was conscious of *feeling* their presence about him, as if some hidden radarlike eye was registering their presence over and above the impressions of sight and sound and smell that touched his senses. It was like something felt and something heard. As he opened himself to it, he felt it like a great, soft, sad roar of sound, a sort of voiceless music reflecting the character and the spirit of the people about him.

The flavor of that soundless sound, that inner feeling that flowed from them as a group, reached in and touched him deeply. And now that he devoted his attention to it, he began to distinguish—in a sense, to touch—individual threads in the pattern. Threads that were individual emotional responses or empathies—he did not know the right word for whatever they might be, but he felt them like living things under his fingers. Also, now that he had picked out these individual feelings, he could feel that from each one he touched in this manner he himself gained a little bit. From each one he learned something; he was in some way a little stronger.

So this was what it was like—the "charging" process that the aliens had mentioned.

On impulse, he switched to Peking. Here the people were dressed differently, and the streets were different in appearance—and the people did not ignore him but came crowding around him. But here, too, he encountered the feeling again. Again there was a totality that was different—a group difference, but within this, making it up as it were, were the individual characteristics from which he took something to add to himself.

But here the attention was all on him, and he was not gaining as much from those who surrounded him. Their hands reached out to him, and though their fingers slipped off him as if he were encased in glass, very little of the learning process came through to him from them. He closed his eyes and willed himself to another Chinese scene that he had seen once in a traveler's photograph.

When he opened his eyes, he stood on top of a huge block of stone—a miniature mountain several hundred feet high. About him were other miniature mountains, rising from a flat landscape, with peaceful small lakes and quiet, small green islands at their foot. It was like a giant's toyscape all about him. Below, moving in rows across a flooded rice field, he could see the bent backs of people at work. And from them and from all of the scene around and to the horizon came much more strongly the group feeling he had now encountered twice before. Here they were not aware of him, and

he felt himself drawing knowledge and strength from
them as the sun sucks up moisture from the surface
of a body of water.

But after a while he began to reach the limit of that
absorption. His mind took him to London, to a street
down which he had walked on a trip several years
before—a street entering Piccadilly Circus. It was
Regent Street, and the pale light of dawn was just
beginning to wash the faces of the buildings along its
curving length. There were few people about, but from
these he received strongly and clearly. Again, again,
again—always what he felt or tasted or heard within
him was different. But now he knew what he was
looking for, and from this point he began his pilgrimage
about this world of his birth.

He roamed it, his world, from a Spanish hillside to
a Yukon lumbering camp, from the mountains of
Mexico to the streets of Brasilia, to Cape Town, to the
African jungle, to Bokhara, to Moscow and the Rus-
sian steppes.

He walked down the streets of Helsinki. He drifted
in the thin air above the sharp mountains that divide
Genoa from Milan. He skimmed a few feet above
fishing craft in the blue harbors of the north Medi-
terranean shore. Daylight and dark, all the hours of
light and shade and weather and seasons flickered
about him, like the changing slides of scenes shown
on a screen by a slide projector. And gradually these
scenes blended together. Light and dark, north and
south, land and sea, winter and summer, yellow, black,
brown and white and red—all peoples, all places, and
all times wove themselves into a tapestry of feeling that
was the overfeeling of the people of Earth and of Earth
itself.

But by the time he had achieved this tapestry of
feeling some days had passed. He floated once more,

at last, above the point where the Mississippi and the Minnesota rivers joined and the twin cities of St. Paul and Minneapolis lay together. This had been his starting place. He was aware now for the first time that since his beginning—how many days ago?—he had not felt any need for food or drink or sleep. The only need he had felt was the need that had grown in him to know and understand the people he surveyed. Now it was almost done.

He had grown in knowledge in his traveling. He understood now what he had felt in a cruder sense when he had first realized that if the Horde destroyed the world, his paintings might as well never have been painted. He felt a strong thread now—not thread, cord, for it was woven of all the threads of feeling he had gathered from individuals about the Earth—connecting anything he did with the people of Earth.

In a sense, everything that was made or done by any member of the human race belonged to the race. This was something he had never understood before. But, he reminded himself now, Marie had known it—or at least she had sensed it and had tried to tell him that night of the day in which the sun had turned red.

It was Marie he wanted to see just once more before returning to the ship and whatever waited for him at the hands of the two Center Aliens.

It was night—as it had been when he had seen her last. Hanging in midair below a few scattered gray clouds, under a nearly full moon, and some three hundred feet above the meeting of the rivers and the green river bottom, he turned toward the buildings of the campus, which even at this distance were visible in the moonlight. He willed himself once more into Marie's room.

As before, it was late and she was asleep, one hand up on the pillow beside her face. He stepped to the bedside and stood looking down. He felt an impulse to speak to her. But something checked him.

He stood looking down at her in the night dimness of the room. Slowly he began to understand why he had checked. The tapestry, that woven cord of identification with all the people he had passed among in the last number of days, was something that did not allow him an individual connection with some single person anymore. As the shorter alien had said to him before he left the ship, he was not Miles Vander any longer—he was Everyman.

But if he came back alive, things would be different. He would be Miles Vander once more. And Marie would still be here.

His time was up. He looked away from Marie and, lifting his head, looked in his mind's eye out to the alien spaceship.

In that moment, he was there.

He stood in the living room of the suite that he had first entered in the Pentagon. The two aliens stood facing him.

"I'm ready now," he told them.

"That's good," answered the shorter one. "Because time is short."

He waved a hand at one wall of the room. Miles looked at it or through it—he was not sure which—and saw the sun, changing back as he watched from its red to a normal yellow color, and below it the Earth, blue under that yellow light. As he watched, the blue globe that was the Earth began to shrink. It shrank rapidly, dwindling into the blackness of star-filled space around it.

Abruptly, all space began to move. The lights of the stars lengthened and became streaks. They became fine bars of light extending in both directions.

"Where to now?" asked Miles.

"To our defense line, beyond the spiral arm of the galaxy," answered the shorter alien.

Even as he spoke, Miles felt a sudden sense of disorientation—a strange feeling as if, in less than no time at all, he had suddenly been wrenched apart, down to the component parts of his very atoms, and spread out over inconceivable distances, before being, in the same infinitesimal moment, reassembled at some far distant place.

"First shift," commented the taller alien. "At the best we can do there will be five more like that, with necessary time for calculation between."

It did indeed require five more such moments of disorientation called shifts to complete their journey. Miles came to understand that in that moment of disorientation the ship and all within it changed position across many light-years of distance. But having jumped suddenly in this manner from one point to another, it was forced to stop and recalculate, even though its calculators were awesome by human standards, for a matter of hours or days before it could establish its due position and figure the position toward which it would next shift. All in all, it took what Miles estimated to be something like a week and a half of interior time aboard the ship before they finally reached the defense line toward which they were heading.

They came out not at the line itself but some hours of cruising time away. This, Miles was given to understand by the shorter alien, was because of the safety factor required in the calculation of a shift. For a shift brought them only approximately to the destination they had figured, and to calculate without a margin of safety might mean coming out in the space occupied by some other solid body—with a resultant explosion that would have been to a nuclear explosion as a nuclear explosion is to that of a firecracker.

As it was, it took several hours of driving through curiously starless space before Miles began to pick out what seemed to be a star, a single star, far ahead of them.

As they grew close to this, however, it began to take on the disk shape and yellow color of a sun, like the sun of Earth.

"No," said the shorter alien, standing beside Miles in the large, almost featureless room with the large screen which seemed to be the pilot room of the aliens' ship. Miles looked at him. Miles was becoming used to having his thoughts answered as if he had spoken them aloud.

"It's not a real star," went on the smaller alien. "It's an artificial sun—a lamp we've set up here to light our Battle Line for us when we meet the Horde."

"Where's the defense line?" Miles asked.

"It ought to be in view in a few minutes," answered the shorter alien.

Miles turned to look at the other. In spite of the change that had taken place in him, and in spite of the fact they had been together aboard the ship now for some days, he had gotten no feeling of response from the two aliens. It was as if they were wrapped around, not merely with human appearances, but with some sort of emotional and mental protective device that kept him from feeling them the way he had felt the people of his own world, as individuals. It struck Miles now that from the first he had had no names for the two of them. They had simply been the taller and the shorter, in his mind, and whenever he had spoken to one, the one at whom he directed his words seemed instinctively to know he had the responsibility to answer.

"What are you people like, in there toward the center of the galaxy?" Miles asked now, looking down

at the other. "I don't think I ever asked you." The alien
did not turn his head but kept gazing into the screen
as he answered.

"There's nothing I can tell you," he said. "You are,
as I said, a barbarian by our standards. Even if I could
explain us to you, you wouldn't understand. Even if
you could understand what we're like, knowing it would
only frighten and disturb you."

A little anger stirred in Miles at this answer. But
he held it down.

"Don't tell me you know everything, you people?"
he asked.

"Not everything," answered the alien. "No. Of course
not."

"Then there's always the chance that you might be
mistaken about me, isn't there?" said Miles.

"No," said the alien flatly.

He did not offer any further explanation. Miles, to
keep his anger under control, made himself drop the
subject. He turned back to watching the screen. After
some minutes, during which the orb of the distant
sunlike lamp continued to swell until it was very nearly
the size of the sun as seen from Earth, he began to
catch sights of glints of reflected light forming a rough
bar across the lower part of the screen.

"Yes," said the alien beside him, once more answering his unspoken question. "You're beginning to see
part of the ships, the supply depots, and all else that
make up our defense line."

As they got even closer, the line began to reveal itself
as visible structures. But even then, Miles discovered,
the screen could not hold any large part of it in one
picture. With a perception he suddenly discovered he
now possessed, Miles estimated the line to stretch at
least as far as the distance from the solar system's sun
to its outermost planet.

They seemed to be moving in toward the thickest part of the line, and as they got close, Miles saw round ships very much like the one he was on. These floated in space, usually with a raftlike structure nearby, and were spaced at regular intervals across the screen.

Miles had assumed that they were fairly close by this time. But to his intense surprise they continued to drive onward at a good speed, and the ships continued to swell on the screen before him. It was some seconds before he realized that the ships they were approaching were truly titanic in size, as large in proportion to the ship he was on as the ship he was on would have been to a four-engine commercial jet of Miles' native Earth. These great ships were certainly no less than several thousand miles in diameter.

"If you want a word for them," the alien beside Miles answered his unspoken thought, "you might call them our dreadnought class of fighting vessels. Actually, they're not fighting vessels the way you'd think of them at all. They're only vehicles to carry a certain critical number of our own people, who will use their personal weapons on the Horde when the Horde gets within range. Without our people inside it, that ship you see is a simple shell of metal and not much more."

It was becoming clear to Miles that they were headed for one monster of a ship in particular. He assumed they would be transferring him into the larger ship and wondered what it would be like inside that enormous shell of metal. But instead of coming right up to the dreadnought, they slowed and stopped in space perhaps four or five miles from its surface. At first Miles did not understand this. Then, turning around, he discovered he was alone in the room. His wide-ranging awareness, developed during those last days on Earth, echoed back the information to him that he was now alone on this ship. Plainly, the two aliens had gone to the larger vessel to report or whatever their duty required them to do.

It was some minutes before either returned, and then only one came back. It was the taller of the two who finally materialized alone in the pilot room of the ship, where Miles was waiting, and Miles' awareness told him that the two of them were alone in the ship.

"I'll take you now to your position on the line," said the taller alien. As usual, he did nothing that Miles could see with his hands; but the unbroken surface of the dreadnought filling most of the screen began to slide off it at one side, and Miles knew that they were moving away from it and down the Battle Line toward its left end.

If the dreadnought had proved to be larger than Miles had ever imagined, the distance to the left end of the line from its middle turned out to be even longer than he had estimated. For several hours they slid at high speed past globe-shaped vessels of varying size, from the enormous bulk of the dreadnought down to the ships smaller than the one Miles was on. As they approached the far end of the line, the ships grew progressively smaller. Also, their shape changed. No longer were they all globular. Many of them were rod- or cigar-shaped.

"These are the ships," the taller alien explained to Miles, without being asked, "of those outlying races that prefer to fight in their own way and with the ships they have built themselves and with which they are familiar. Because they're effective, we let them do this. You, and those you'll be joining, will fight in ships and weapons we supply."

There was something chilling about this pronouncement. Miles had not grown close to either of the two Center Aliens, but if he had felt closer to one than another, it had been the shorter instead of the taller. The taller one had always seemed more remote and less approachable than the smaller alien. Now that remoteness came through to Miles with extra force. Miles felt as a speck of dust might feel, lectured by a mountain. He was not being given a choice—he was only being given orders.

In silence they moved on, until the ships dwindled to the point of being very small indeed, until, finally, the point was reached at which the ships, instead of hanging in space beside the raftlike structures which evidently held their supplies and material, were small enough to lie on those rafts. Still they went on, until they came at last to what seemed to be the end of the line.

Here, on a raft several times the size of a football field, lay a ship hardly bigger than a nuclear submarine of Earth. The larger ship holding Miles and the taller alien stopped perhaps half a mile from it.

"Now," said the taller alien—and without warning he and Miles were transported to the raft.

Miles found himself standing on a metal surface at the foot of a metal ladder leading up to an open doorway in the side of the ship. There was no visible shell about the raft to enclose a breathable atmosphere, yet he breathed. The doorway was dark, in contrast with the light outside from the distant sunlamp. Miles could not see what might be inside.

"This ship," said the taller alien quietly, "is the smallest of our scout ships. It is staffed by twenty-two individuals, each a representative of a world like your own. You will become the twenty-third—and last—individual to make up its crew. In the weeks to come, you, with the others, will learn to maneuver it and together use its weapon. Now follow me. I'll take you to join the rest of the crew."

The taller alien floated up the ladder. Miles, starting to float behind him, felt an unexpected spasm of stubbornness. Instead of levitating, he seized hold of the ladder and climbed it like an ordinary mortal.

As his head drew level with the entrance, he could see inside. The taller alien was waiting for him in what seemed to be a small room or hatchway with a further entrance beyond. Miles joined him, and the alien turned without a word to lead him through the interior hatchway into a large room furnished with chairs and tables of various sizes and dimensions. Miles walked after him into the light of the room—and stopped abruptly.

The room was full. On its furniture and around its walls stood and sat a variety of different-appearing beings. All were four-limbed, standing upright on the lower two and with handlike appendages at the end of their upper pair. They all were of roughly the same size and proportions and general shape. But there was tremendous variety.

No two had the same skin color. No two had the same facial appearance. All had roughly similar features, as far as possessing two eyes and a single nose and mouth was concerned. But from there on everything was different. Their appearance ranged from that of the completely innocuous to the completely ferocious— from one being who seemed as round and inoffensive as a toy bear to one who seemed a walking tiger, equipped with a pair of ripping teeth projecting from the upper jaw over his lower lip.

"Members of this ship," said the alien, stepping aside to let them all see Miles, "let me introduce you to your new fellow crew member, who on his own world is known as Miles Vander."

He spoke in a tongue which Miles had never heard

before but which Miles found he understood, as he had earlier understood all the various languages of Earth.

He turned back to face Miles.

"I'll leave you in their hands," he said in English. And disappeared.

Miles looked around him.

Those of his new fellow crew members who had been seated about the room were now getting to their feet and moving forward. Those who had been on their feet were also moving forward.

"Well," said Miles, speaking in the language he had just heard, "I'm glad to meet you all."

There was no response. They continued to close in on him, making a tight circle with no space between any of them. Now he sensed it—with all his new sensitivity. There was an atmosphere in the room of savagery and bloodlust, of anticipation and fury. They closed in silently like wolves about a stranger wolf, the one with the tiger-like features moving in directly before Miles and directly toward him.

The tigerlike being came on. Even when the others stopped, now locked in a tight ring around Miles, he came on until he stood only at arm's length from Miles. And then he stopped.

"My name is Chak'ha!" he said. He spoke the common language in a growling, throaty combination of sounds that no human vocal apparatus could have originated or imitated, but Miles understood him perfectly.

And even as he said it, Chak'ha launched himself, clawlike nails outstretched, tusks gleaming, at Miles' throat, and Miles went down under the attack.

6

As he fell backward with the being called Chak'ha on top of him, Miles felt panic, like a cold jagged knife, ripping upward through his belly toward his throat.

For a moment he froze, staring up at the toothed face snarling down into his own. Then, out of something deep within him came a counteracting mingled fear and fury, as primitive and brutal as the attack on him. Suddenly he was fighting back.

It was a simple, instinctive, animallike battle. They rolled on the metal deck together, fighting, scratching, biting, and digging at each other with every nail, tooth, or bony extremity that could be used as a weapon. For some seconds, for Miles, there was nothing but this. He had awakened into an instinctive rage out of simple fear for his life. But just as the rage had followed fear, now something beyond rage followed again.

It came over him like drunkenness. Suddenly he found that he did not care what Chak'ha was doing to him as long as he was able to continue what he was doing to Chak'ha. The adrenalized passion of destruction filled and intoxicated him.

In a second all those meanings which the activities of his upper mind had given his life until now were washed away in the brutal impulses from the older centers of his brain. His response to the light and shape and beauty that was art left him. His deep bond with the rest of the human race, which he had forged before being brought to this place, was forgotten. So was Marie. All that was left was the deep, primeval urge to tear and kill.

He had his hands now around the thick-skinned, leathery throat of Chak'ha, his thumbs digging in. Chak'ha's saber teeth and claws were slashing him wildly, but he felt no pain—he was only dimly aware of the blood running from his many wounds. *Die! Die!* his mind shouted at the alien as he tried to tighten his grip on the other's windpipe, wherever in that thick neck it might be. . . .

But Chak'ha was not dying. He was continuing to slash at Miles—and gradually Miles began to realize that his own grip was weakening. All at once he became aware that he was losing blood too fast. He was failing.

A cold inner wind blew suddenly across his hot passion for killing. It was not the alien who was in danger of dying—it was himself. Something deeper than panic moved in him, and suddenly he remembered all that, for a moment, he had forgotten: Marie, the paintings he had yet to do, the people of his Earth. His grip was slipping weakly from Chak'ha's neck now—*but he could not afford to die!*

Without warning, for the second time in his life, he went into a state of hysterical strength.

Suddenly the tiger-faced alien was a toy in his hands. Chak'ha had already pulled loose from Miles' grip on his throat and half turned away. But Miles caught him again now easily. Miles turned him, slid one arm under

Chak'ha's right armpit and the other under the alien's left armpit, then clasped his hands together behind the other's neck and pressed. Chak'ha's neck bent like a straw-filled tube of leather, and there came from it a creaking sound.

Abruptly, a strange gray fog seemed to fold itself about the mind and body of Miles. Dimly, he was aware that it was nothing his opponent had done. Nor was it anything that had been done by any of those standing in a tight circle around him and his enemy. It was something that seemed to come from the ship itself or from something beyond the ship.

Unexpectedly, the fires of his hysteria were smothered. His muscles lost their strength. He was aware of his arms falling limply away, his fingers loosening and losing their grasp together behind Chak'ha's neck. Like a man under heavy sedation, he rolled off the back of his opponent and lay lost in the gray fog.

He was vaguely aware of the fact that Chak'ha, beside him, was also lying limply, wrapped in the same helpless condition. Above and around him, Miles was vaguely conscious of the circle of onlookers breaking up and drifting away. He saw a couple of them pick up the lax form of Chak'ha and carry it off. Alien hands also grasped him by the shoulders and legs and lifted him.

He felt himself being carried—where or to what, he was indifferent. He saw the ceiling of a corridor swaying above him; he saw the upper part of a doorway and then the ceiling of a smaller room. He felt himself thrown onto what seemed to be a soft surface, the soft undersurface of a niche in the wall that could be a bunk or a bed. Then he was left alone, and he slept.

When he awoke at last, it was a gradual awakening. He felt that he had been asleep for some time that was not a short time. At first he felt nothing; then he became gradually conscious of his stiffness and the soreness that encompassed his whole body.

He still lay on the bunk on which he had been thrown. He lifted his head now to look at himself. Nothing, he could see, had been done for him. On the other hand the deep bites and scratches—in fact, all the injuries he had taken in his battle with Chak'ha— were already scabbed over and healing. He felt weak, but aside from this, and aside from the aches, which were no worse than those after a hard game of football as he remembered it from his junior high school days, he felt as good as ever.

He turned his head. Across the width of the small room from him, on another bunk, was the tiger-faced alien. Chak'ha was also awake and looking back at him. The other's two tusks glinted in the illumination from the lighting panel overhead, while the rest of the heavy body lay still half-hidden in the shadow of the bunk. It was impossible to read Chak'ha's expression, but even with the weakness and the aches, Miles felt gathering once more within him the white heat of that lustful joy of killing he had experienced during the fight.

He grinned at Chak'ha challengingly. But the other dropped his own gaze, and abruptly Miles understood, partly through the sensitivity to the emotions of others that had been given him with his new body by the Center Aliens, but partly also through some likeness between him and Chak'ha that had nothing to do with the Center Aliens at all, that he had conquered at least this one of his fellow crewmen.

"Do you jump everybody who comes aboard here for the first time?" asked Miles.

Chak'ha lifted his gaze and answered. "No more," he said. "This boat is full now. You were the last. Now I'm last."

There was something odd about the meaning of the word of their strange common shipboard language which Chak'ha had used to give the meaning of "last"— something almost like a pun, a double meaning. It was as if Chak'ha said "last" but at the same time also gave it the meaning of "least." It was a subtle but undeniable connotation that Miles could not quite pin down, for the odd reason that he found he knew this strange language too well. He spoke it and translated it into English in his head at the same time. But he was not able to compare his translation with the actual sounds that he heard and that his own tongue and lips and throat made, for the reason that the knowledge that the Center Aliens had given him of this tongue was way down within him in the level of automatic verbal habit. He could no more hear with an unprejudiced ear the strange words he spoke than a man can hear with analytical detachment the accent with which he speaks his native tongue.

He shook his head a little and dropped the question of the double meaning.

"What do we do now, then?" he asked Chak'ha.

"Do?" answered Chak'ha. "Nothing. What's there to do?"

He dropped back on the bed and rolled over on his back, staring at the ceiling of his bunk.

There was a lifelessness, an air of defeat, to Chak'ha's answer. Puzzled but curious, Miles made an effort to get up. Wincing, he managed to get his legs over the edge of the bed and rise to his feet. He was stiff and sore but, he decided, certainly able with a little bit of willpower to make himself get around. He walked stiffly out of the small room and into the corridor outside.

Another member of the crew was passing. It was a round, bearlike alien. Miles stiffened, ready for anything up to and including physical attack. But the rotund alien merely gave him the briefest and most incurious of glances and walked on. Miles turned to stare after him, then followed. Now would be as good a time as any to explore this vessel to which he had been assigned.

It was exactly that, in the next hour, which he did. Gradually he examined the vessel's interior from stem to stern. He also counted the rest of the members of the crew. Including himself, there seemed to be twenty-three, each one curiously different from the others.

But even more curious than these differences was the ship itself. Astonishingly, it seemed to have no power plant at all—beyond what might lie concealed in the small space below the console of the control panel in the bow room of the ship. Beyond this control room, which was set up for no more than three individuals to work in at one time, there were crew quarters, rooms with from one to as many as four bunks in them, the number of bunks seeming to vary without reason or purpose from room to room. There was the lounge, which he had first entered, taking up the large middle part of the ship and furnished with a number of different items of what he took to be furniture or recreational devices—among them, he was half-amused, half-embarrassed to see, was a very earthly overstuffed chair with a small, round coffee table alongside it.

Within the rest of the hollow cigar shape of the ship Miles discovered twenty of what looked like gun emplacements, ten on each side of the vessel.

In each one of these was what seemed to be a weapon, consisting of a gunner's seat joined to a heavy mechanism on a swivel. Handgrips flanked the mechanism on the side facing the gunner's seat, and on the far side there projected toward a bubble-shaped transparency what Miles at first took to be the equivalent of a gun barrel. But on closer examination, he found that it was not a hollow cylinder as any gun barrel with which he was familiar should be. It was a solid rod of metal, in the end of which he could discover not even the pinhole end of a passage for whatever force the weapon expelled.

Moreover, thought Miles, if the solid rods were indeed the equivalent of rifle barrels, whatever force they projected must pass harmlessly through the transparent bubble before them. And if this was the case, why could not the Horde defend itself simply by using an equivalent of the transparent material as armor around its own ships?

There were too many questions for him to answer by himself. He needed help. So far the only one who had spoken to him at all had been Chak'ha. He turned back toward the room in which the tiger-faced alien lay on his bunk, but a feeling of wariness stopped him. Chak'ha was going no place. There would be ample time to ask him questions later. Perhaps, thought Miles, caution placing a hand on his shoulder, it would be to his advantage to see what he could deduce on his own before exposing his ignorance—even to the one other crew member he had conquered.

He went back to the lounge and sat down in the overstuffed chair he had noticed there earlier. The minute he seated himself the small coffee table beside him chimed softly, and silently, from nowhere that he could see, a cup of coffee materialized, black and steaming, sitting on a saucer in the center of the table.

Miles was not hungry. It came back to him forcefully now that he had not been hungry—had not in fact wanted any food at all—since the Center Aliens had first altered and improved him. But as the coffee cup appeared, he became conscious that at the back of his mind, as a sort of counterpoint to his bodily stiffness and soreness, he had been thinking about coffee out of habitual reflex. Curious now, he tested the table once more by thinking about a slice of apple pie. It, too, appeared on the table, beside the cup of coffee and with a fork on the plate that held it.

But when he picked the fork up to taste it, a globe of grayness, an opaqueness, formed abruptly about him. Suddenly he was unable to see anyone else in the room. A little alarmed, he put the fork down on the coffee table, and the opaqueness immediately cleared. He picked up the coffee cup, and once more the barrier to sight surrounded him.

With that, he understood.

He was to be given privacy while he ate. Either that, or his crewmates were to be protected from the sight of his eating. More likely, thought Miles, it was the latter.

He ate the pie and drank the coffee. As soon as they were emptied, the utensils which had held the pie and coffee disappeared from the coffee table. The opaqueness cleared from about Miles' chair, and he sat back to observe his crewmates as they passed through or rested in the lounge.

Within the next three or four hours, as he watched, fully three-quarters of the twenty-two other individuals he had counted aboard this ship passed before his eyes. Occasionally there were gray blurs in other parts of the room, as other crew members indulged in whatever eating or other habits were native to them. Outside of these occurrences, however, no one that Miles watched appeared to have anything particular to do or to be engaged in any particular job or function. And this observation was reinforced by a general air of idleness, of indifference, even of hopelessness, that seemed to hang about the ship and its crew as a whole.

There was curiously little communication among the crew members Miles watched. They moved about singly, as individuals, and at no time during the three or four hours he watched did he see two of them engage in anything lengthy enough to be called a conversation. On the other hand, there was a curious pattern of behavior that seemed to hold them all. It was a pattern that Miles at first *felt,* with that same new sensitivity to the emotions of others that had been wakened in him by the Center Aliens. He felt it without being able to trace it to any specific actions or lack of actions. Then, gradually, he began to interpret what he sensed.

Briefly put, it seemed that each individual aboard had certain other individuals whom he ignored. And to all individuals that he did not ignore, he deferred. Furthermore, he in turn was ignored by all the individuals to whom he deferred.

As, Miles suddenly realized, the bearlike alien had ignored him, after one brief glance, when they had met in the corridor earlier.

It dawned on Miles that everyone except Chak'ha had ignored him since he had entered this ship—and in particular had ignored him during his exploratory tour of the vessel just now before coming to the lounge.

With that, the answer came plainly to him. There was evidently a pecking order aboard, a social system in which each member of the crew was deferential to those above him and contemptuous of those beneath. There were no equals on the ship then. Obviously, the way you moved up in rank was to fight your way up— as he had fought and beaten Chak'ha, thereby making Chak'ha last and least. For in such a system a newcomer like Miles himself, entering the ship as someone without his position in the order established, would be challenged first by the lowest member of the pecking order.

So now with his victory over Chak'ha, he was second from the bottom in that order, thought Miles. Why—the remembered, inviting white passion of battle glowed suddenly again to life inside him—all he needed to do to improve his situation on this ship was to fight his way up through the ranks. There could be no danger of losing his life in the process, since evidently the Center Aliens who had built the vessel had made provision against such killing.

Anyone, then, with the guts to take the necessary punishment could challenge anyone else aboard with impunity. Chak'ha, after all, for all his saber teeth, would not have been too difficult to handle if his attack had not come without warning. Obviously, the tigerish alien knew nothing of wrestling, or he would have shown the knowledge during the fighting before Miles had clamped the full nelson on him and caused the fight to be stopped.

None of the other aliens aboard whom Miles had seen—except perhaps the bearlike one—looked like an impossibly powerful or dangerous opponent. Of course, now that Miles had learned that they were not allowed to kill or cripple one another, he could probably not count on another explosion of hysterical strength to help him win, as it had with Chak'ha.

But on the other hand, with a little study of his opponents and a plan of attack—above all, making sure that he was the one who did the attacking, without warning. . . .

An emotional reaction set in suddenly, like a cold and heavy wave of seawater taking him in the face and leaving him gasping. Miles sat stiffly, shocked at his own thoughts.

Could this be he, Miles, sitting here and eagerly measuring the other occupants of the lounge with a careful eye to see how vulnerable they might be to his own teeth, nails, and muscles?

Disgust and anger with himself welled up inside him. So this was all it had been worth, all those years of his painting and theorizing and working? Nothing more than something he could forget in a minute, once he was given a new, strong, two-armed body to play at fighting with, under rules that guaranteed he could not be badly hurt or killed?

What had happened to him?

For that matter, what had happened to the purpose for which he had been brought here? Had he been physically rebuilt, charged with the hopes of a world of people, and shipped out here to the edge of the intergalactic dark just so that he could come to this ship and roll on the deck fighting with equally charged members of other races like his own?

If so, there was something the Center Aliens had not told him—something suspicious and potentially rotten about this whole business of the Silver Horde and the Battle Line.

But whatever it was, beginning now, he was going to make it his business to find it out. Meanwhile, he told himself grimly, he would not be tricked again into losing his emotional perspective.

He would remember that inside this superbly healthy and unkillable body with two strong arms was still the mind and identity of the thin, tense, one-armed human named Miles Vander. Miles Vander, who had a people to save and paintings to paint. He would remember he was not here to fight Chak'has. He was here to fight the Silver Horde, if the Silver Horde honestly existed, not to struggle for some position in a physical pecking order aboard this one small ship.

Perhaps the Center Aliens were not to blame, and it was just that the other racial representatives aboard had not been able to remember that. Perhaps, isolated and waiting here, they had done their best to keep in mind the original purpose that had brought them here and had still failed, giving in at last to the boredom and loneliness of their situation, surrounded by strangers of races other than their own.

He, however, would not be breaking like that. Now that he had been awakened to the danger, he felt the old, inflexible determination that had become part of him back on Earth hardening like spring steel inside him.

He would never break, because he was not like his fellow alien crew members on this ship—not like anyone else in the universe. He was Miles Vander, who had a special personal memory of loneliness and years of striving to make sure he would not give in.

7

The tiger-faced head of Chak'ha rolled upon the bunk—rolled away from the gaze of Miles. Clearly Chak'ha did not want to talk about it.

Miles had come back to the room of the ship in which he had awakened. Chak'ha was still there, lying on his bunk. But when Miles had started to question him about the pecking order, the combats, and the relationship of all this to the coming of the Silver Horde, he had felt unhappiness rising from the lax body of the alien like a cloud of sickness.

"There's just nothing to do," Chak'ha said, looking away from him now, looking at the blank inner wall of his bunk. "There's just nothing else to do."

"Nothing to do but fight with each other?" Miles demanded. "No training to be done? No practicing with our weapons? No practicing with the ship itself? What kind of fighting ship is this?"

"It isn't a fighting ship," said Chak'ha to the wall. "It's the *Fighting Rowboat.*"

"The *Fighting Rowboat?*"

"That's what we all call her," muttered Chak'ha.

Miles stared at him. In their common shipboard language, the name Chak'ha had just given the ship was a bitter sneer at the vessel and all those aboard her. The name connoted not only worthlessness, but puffed-up, bragging worthlessness—as if someone whose duty it was to fight should be nicknamed the Ferocious Mouse. Chak'ha remained with his face turned away, offering no further explanation.

"Look at me!" ordered Miles. Slowly, reluctantly, the tiger mask turned back to confront him.

"What do you mean, this isn't a fighting ship?" demanded Miles.

"I mean what I say," said Chak'ha stubbornly. "This ship will never fight anything—let alone the Silver Horde."

"How do you know?"

"Everybody knows," said Chak'ha with a sullen air of hopelessness. "Everybody on the ship knows. We began to know it when we found out they didn't care what happened to us or what we did here."

"Who didn't care? The Center Aliens?" said Miles.

"Them. All the others in this Battle Line," said Chak'ha. "It's plain they don't care. It became plain to the first few of us who arrived here. Wait. You'll see. You'll find out that it makes no difference to them what happens to us—except that we aren't allowed to kill each other when we fight. You saw how you and I were stopped."

"Well, if we aren't here to fight the Silver Horde, what are we here for?" said Miles harshly.

"Who knows?" replied Chak'ha gloomily. "I suppose the Center Aliens know, but they're not likely to tell us."

"Nobody—no one aboard this ship knows?" demanded Miles.

Chak'ha, without moving upon his bunk, gave the

impression of shrugging to Miles' emotion-sensitive perceptions.

"Maybe some of the higher-up ones here know," he said. "Maybe Eff"—the name was a sound like the letter *f* prolonged and ending in a sharp whistle—"who's second. Or Luhon, who can beat anybody aboard. Maybe somebody like that knows. I don't."

"Which one's Luhon?" demanded Miles. "I'll ask him."

Chak'ha's head rolled on the bunk, negatively.

"He won't tell you."

"Never mind that," said Miles. "Tell me which one he is."

"He's thin and quick and gray-skinned," said Chak'ha in a lifeless voice, "and his external ears are pointed."

Without a further word, Miles turned and went out of the room. He reentered the lounge and studied its occupants, but none of them fitted the description Chak'ha had given him. He turned and went back through the ship, searching through the other crew quarters—at least those rooms of which the doors were not closed. Still he met nobody fitting the description he had been given. Finally, he turned and went forward. There, alone in the bow control room, he saw a slight, gray-skinned, furless individual with ears that would have fitted well on a pixie or elf out of Earth's legends. Whoever he was, if he was Luhon, he looked like a light-bodied, harmless being to have outfought everybody else aboard the ship. Miles studied him for a second, watching him from the doorway of the control room. The other was playing with the keys on a control console. He ignored Miles, as all aboard had ignored him, and Miles was able to notice how smoothly and swiftly the fingers of the other moved. For all his apparent slightness of limb, he must have muscle if he topped the pecking order, Miles concluded, and if suppleness and his ordinary speed of movement were any index, it might be that his speed was really remarkable. It was hard to believe that this slim creature sitting before him could be at the head of the social system aboard the ship. Still, Miles reminded himself, for all his ferocious appearance, Chak'ha had turned out to be least of them all. Appearances plainly were no index to the dangerousness of his fellow crew members.

Miles went forward into the room until he stood just behind the other individual, who appeared to be checking out the console of the control board before him. Glancing at that control board now, Miles was surprised, for a fleeting second, to discover that he understood its controls as well as he understood the common language they spoke aboard the ship. Then he swung his attention back to his reason for coming here.

"Are you Luhon?" he demanded.

The other neither turned nor moved. Instead, he went on with his movements, ignoring Miles as if Miles were nowhere in existence, let alone less than three feet behind him.

"I said," repeated Miles, slowly and distinctly, "are you Luhon? If you are, I want to talk to you."

The other continued to work with his controls, apparently deaf and blind to the presence of Miles in the same room with him.

"I don't want to fight with you," said Miles evenly, keeping the white flare of his newly discovered battle lust and fury carefully under control. "I only want some information from you—information I think I have a right to have. I only want to know whether it's true that this ship will never go into battle against the Silver Horde and, if that's true, why the Center Aliens brought us all here together after all. If you don't know the answer to either of those things, you don't have to speak. All you have to do is shake your head."

Luhon's head did not move. He went on with what he was doing.

Miles waited as the seconds fled away into minutes.

"*Will you answer me?*" he said at last, clenching his teeth on the anger building inside of him.

Luhon made no response.

Suddenly the inner fury broke loose in Miles. It boiled up whitely inside him. His arm muscles tensed and jerked with the impulse to reach out, grab the other by the shoulders, spin him around, and choke an answer out of him.

Luhon still continued what he was doing, unperturbed. But just in time, Miles noticed the pointed right ear twitch and flick backward in Miles' direction.

Caution clamped suddenly again on Miles. Apparently he was not as ignored as he had thought. Evidently Luhon was not only aware of him, but confident enough of his own physical superiority to stay with his back turned to Miles—practically inviting Miles to attack first. Such confidence, coupled with the fact that Luhon was acknowledged by Chak'ha to be first in the pecking order among the twenty-three members of the crew, rang a sudden warning in Miles.

The time might come, thought Miles, when he might want to have it out with Luhon. But not yet—not, at least, until he had seen more of the other, particularly in action, and discovered the source of Luhon's power and victory over his fellow crew members.

Miles turned and went out of the control room. He went back through the ship, out through the open hatch and down the steps onto the open platform on which the ship lay. He needed to think, and in order to think clearly, he needed to get completely away from the apparent puzzle of the ship, with its twenty-three representatives of twenty-three races apparently brought here for no purpose but to quarrel and to fight with one another.

He explored the platform. It was a flat structure—like a raft in the blackness of the surrounding space, harshly and metallically revealed by the unmoving, unchanging glare of the artificial sun that the Center Aliens had apparently set up to illuminate the Battle Line. From where Miles stood on the platform that artificial sun was larger than, but not as yellow as, the sun of Earth. It had a white, fluorescent glare, which his eyes could not endure to look at directly for more than a fraction of a second. The shadows this light cast on the surface of the raft were as hard and sharp and black as those cast by rocks on an airless moon. Miles walked around the platform and discovered a sort of shed, which he entered. Inside were twenty-three strange machines and stores of what appeared to be—judging by the fact that one of them was a pile of earthly foodstuffs—special rations for each of the various crew members aboard the ship. Miles went on through the shed and out a door at the far end. Behind the shed he saw, lying in a metal cradle, a smaller craft which looked like a miniature version of their ship. It was apparently some sort of courier boat, with two seats inside it.

Inspiration woke in him. He went hastily up to the ship, slid open the door in its side, and climbed in, closing the door behind him. Seating himself in one of the seats, he examined the control board of the small vessel.

As he had suspected, the controls here were immediately as understandable to him as the controls at which Luhon had been working in the larger ship had been.

The white anger, still surging below the conscious level in him, erupted suddenly in a flare of new determination.

He would get an answer—one way or another.

He touched the controls of the ship before him with hands as sure as if they had practiced for years. The little ship floated upward from its cradle, turned slowly in the blue-white glare of the artificial sun, and headed up the Battle Line.

For a few seconds it seemed rather to hang in space than to move. But then, without any physical feeling of acceleration, it apparently began to move faster and faster. The nearer ships of the line swelled up on the vision screen before him and fled past it, one by one. There was no sensation of any change in the rate of speed with which it moved, but Miles began to perceive that this small ship went quickly while between the anchored vessels, then slowed down for a few miles on either side of each ship's location while passing, then took up again its between-ship velocity. A feeling of exhilaration began to warm and glow within Miles. At his fingertips, the little ship moved as if it were an extension of his own physical being. He felt as if its speed were his speed; its power, his power; its sureness of response, his own.

Now he was already past the area of smaller, intermediate, and odd-shaped alien ships and approaching the first of the large globe-shaped ships of the Center Aliens. He could see the first of them now, far ahead of him at full magnification on the battle screen built into the console on which his fingers rested—

Without warning, there was someone alongside him in the other seat of the two-man ship. Miles turned his head and looked.

It was one of the Center Aliens. He was so like the two who had brought Miles from Earth, in the stillness of his pseudohuman features, that for a moment Miles thought one of his old acquaintances had rejoined him. But then he felt the stranger-quality in this particular Center Alien—as he had felt emotional differences in Chak'ha and Luhon and others of his own crew. This Center Alien said nothing; but his hands rested on the other console, which was a duplicate of the control console before Miles, and the little ship turned and headed back the way it had come.

For a second Miles stared. Then his own fingers leaped to the controls before him. But there was no response from the ship. It was as if his console had gone dead and only the one in front of the Center Alien controlled the ship.

"What're you doing?" snapped Miles, turning to the other. "I want to talk to somebody—somebody in authority!"

"Talk to me," answered the Center Alien. There was no inflection to his words, but Miles felt an indifference in the alien as remote and icy as contempt. The other continued to drive the two-man vessel back the way it had come, without looking at Miles.

"I was told our ship isn't ever going to fight the Silver Horde!" said Miles. "Is that true?"

"Quite true," answered the Center Alien.

"Then why bring me out here in the first place?" demanded Miles. "Why bring any of us on the *Fighting Rowboat?*"

"It's true that individually, and even collectively, you add little directly to our general Battle Line strength," answered the Center Alien. "All of you together amount to less than one of the least of my own people in that respect. But there is more than the direct addition of strength to be considered. Besides his own personal powers, which vary widely from individual to individual, each one in the Battle Line has a function in which all are equal. That is to act as a resonator, or amplifier, of the group strength and as a channel through which that strength may be directed at the enemy. There is what you might call a feedback effect—from the group to the individual and back again—where the psychic force is concerned."

"Feedback?" Miles stared at him. "Psychic force?"

"The weapons aboard your ship, and aboard all our ships," said the Center Alien, as their small two-man ship continued to slide past the odd-shaped vessels of the Center Aliens' outer allies, "have a dual function. They bring to bear against enemy ships not only a physical, but what I call a *psychic* force. 'Psychic' is not the correct word, but it is the closest I can come to a word in your understanding. The physical element of these weapons is effective enough— it can rip open any Horde ship that comes within effective range. But it is the weapons' ability to project our general psychic strength against the invaders on which our whole strategy of defense is based."

Miles frowned.

"Why?" he asked.

"Because the strategy of the Horde's attack is based, by contrast, on the overwhelming numbers of its ships and people," said the alien. "The Horde counts on being able to pay any price required by a battle, just as long as for every dozen or hundred or thousand of its own ships which are lost, it accomplishes the destruction of at least one opposing ship."

"A thousand for one?" Miles looked narrowly at the other.

"At least that high," replied the Center Alien emotionlessly. "The basic belief of the Horde is that it can afford the losses in ships that any enemy force can inflict on it and still have enough of its own ships left to conquer. But there is, we hope, a point at which even the Horde will refuse to pay the price of conquest. And it is this point we hope to reach with the aid of a psychic force."

Miles frowned again. The words of the Center Alien sounded as if they should make sense to him, but at the same time their real meaning seemed to skitter away from his understanding like a dried leaf before a November wind.

"The psychic force can kill then?" he asked.

"No." The Center Alien spoke the short negative word briefly. "The psychic force is no more than that same strength of identification you absorbed from those individuals of your home world who felt for you before you left. Ask yourself if that feeling inside you can kill. Identification implies empathy, and an empathic response cannot be used to destroy, being creative in nature. Creation and destruction are antithetical within the same process, just as synthesis and analysis cannot proceed by the same process at the same time—or, in terms possibly more familiar to you, you cannot drive one of your home world's automobiles in forward and reverse gear off the same motor at the same time. Even if it were possible to do this from an engineering standpoint, the two attempts at motion in opposite directions would cancel each other out into motionlessness—a nonexistence of motion. So with any attempt to kill using the psychic force."

"Then I don't follow you," said Miles grimly.

"I am explaining," said the Center Alien, "why our weapons have a physical as well as psychical element. The psychic force cannot kill—but it can control, to the extent of dominating the individual by the group will or the will of the lesser group by the greater. So we will use it against the Horde. With sufficient outflow of psychic power, we hope to hold paralyzed all the invaders who come within range of our weapons while our weapons destroy them."

He paused. Miles nodded slowly.

"I see," said Miles thoughtfully.

"Yes," said the Center Alien, "you see. By this means we hope, not to conquer the Horde—for that is impossible—but to convince them that we can slaughter them almost at will, while remaining very nearly invulnerable to their weapons, and so make them pay such a heavy price in lost ships for each ship of ours they manage to destroy that they will turn away toward some other galaxy that may be less strongly defended against them."

"If the psychic force is that effective," said Miles harshly, "why can't we on the *Fighting Rowboat* be with you when you hit the Horde with your own ships?"

"Because the psychic force is not, in fact, that effective," said the alien. "Each use of it requires an expenditure of energy by each of the individuals making use of it. As long as they do not become weary, these individuals may not only use their own innate psychic force, but also may draw on our general pool of strength and channel it through themselves to make them many times as effective as they would be alone. But the energy of no one, not even us of the Center, is inexhaustible, and you twenty-three would become exhausted very much more quickly than we. Exhausted, an individual loses contact with the general pool of strength. In such a case you would face the Horde with only your own feeble psychic powers and physical weapons, and your ship's destruction by the Horde would follow almost immediately."

"What of it?" demanded Miles. "It's our necks we're risking—"

"They are not yours alone," interrupted the alien.

"You refuse to understand. As contributors of original psychic force your twenty-three are nothing—less than the weakest of one of my own race, all of you combined. So that if we lost you, we would lose less than one effective individual unit like myself in terms of original force. But as resonators and amplifiers, you are individually equal to all other individuals in the Battle Line. So that in losing you in that respect, we would be losing the equivalent of twenty-three units."

He paused.

"Do you see now," he said, "why we prefer to keep you back out of the battle and safe, where we can draw on you for resonated strength, without risking your almost certain loss if you joined us in the fighting?"

Again he paused. But Miles said nothing.

"You are unhappy about this," said the Center Alien. "That is because you are still a victim of those primitive emotions which we of the Center long ago amputated from our own egos so that we would continue the intellectual development that has made us what we have become. Because you have such emotions, you assume that we have them also and that our decisions about you are colored by emotion. But they are not. Here in this Battle Line, you are just as a group of chimpanzees would be back on your native world armed with high-powered rifles. The fact that the chimpanzee can be rote-trained to hold the rifle and pull its trigger does not mean it can be trusted with the weapon in the sense that a human soldier could be trusted to carry, maintain, and use his gun effectively against an enemy. That is why, when we actually join battle with the Horde—and whether we do or not will depend on whether our Center computational matrix calculates that we have a chance for victory if we do join battle—the actual fighting contact will be made by us of the Center and some few of the older, more advanced races on whom we can rely. It is simple logic that dictates this, as it dictates that you be held out of the fight and safe."

Miles stared ahead into the vision screen of the small craft. In that screen now, he saw the distant, fast-swelling shape of the platform on which the *Fighting Rowboat* rested.

"The numbers of the Horde," said the Center Alien, "are literally beyond your imagination. Equally beyond you are the questions and factors involved in the function of this Battle Line, which would not exist here and now if it were not for us of the Center. Face the fact that these things are too great for your mind to grapple with, and resign yourself to your situation."

They were almost on the platform now. The Center Alien said no more but brought the little ship in for a landing in its cradle. As it touched down, he disappeared from the seat beside Miles. Wrapped in his own bitter thoughts, Miles slowly opened the door on his side of the craft and climbed out. He went back into the main ship.

But this time he avoided both the control room and the lounge. Instead, he went down the connecting corridors until he came to the first of the weapons, standing isolated and alone with its empty transparent bubble that faced outward into the blackness of intergalactic space. For a long moment he stood looking at it, and now his mind, alerted by what the Center Alien had said, saw with the same sort of knowledge that had told him about the control consoles of both ships that these weapons had been neglected and ignored.

It was not that they were rusted or decayed. There was no sign of dust or cobwebs on them. But with that feeling part of his mind which had become so sensitive lately, Miles felt the coldness of long disuse that hung like a fog about the weapon before him. Feeling it now, he began to understand at least part of what the Center Alien had been trying to tell him. Psychic force must pulse through this device before him if it were to help destroy the Horde. But he also now recognized something that the Center Alien had not bothered to tell him. If this weapon were to be operated in battle, a certain amount of the psychic force of whatever individual operated it would necessarily have to be used up first merely to warm it up in a psychic sense, before it would fire. *That* was the penalty of the long disuse with which the twenty-three aboard this ship had treated it. It confirmed the indifference, amounting to contempt, of the Center Alien as he had explained his superiority over Miles on the way back here.

It did more. It explained the self-contempt in which the twenty-three held themselves. Their undeniable, unavoidable knowledge of their own inferiority and uselessness compared to the power and wisdom of the Center Aliens—in fact, to everyone else in this Battle Line. It would be that knowledge and self-contempt which had driven them to set up the pecking order, so that all but the weakest of them would have at least one other individual to whom they could feel superior.

Miles became aware that his jaw muscles were aching. He had clenched them some time since. He forced himself to relax them. Inside him, his understanding of the situation here was complete at last, carved on his mind like letters in stone.

What use was it to them—to himself and the human race—to be physically saved from extermination if the price of that saving was to face the fact that their greatest accomplishments and dreams were less than line drawings on a cave wall and that in the eyes of the race which dominated the galaxy, men were no more than ape-men scratching themselves mindlessly as they lolled in the sun?

The Center Alien had advised him to resign himself to the situation. Miles laughed harshly. Wise and powerful the Center Aliens might be, but here was proof that their wisdom and knowledge was not all-perfect.

If nothing else, they had underestimated humans—and Miles himself. Powered by that same capacity for emotion that this advanced people had despised and discarded, Miles knew that he was no more capable of resignation than an eagle is of forgetting he has wings. There was no point in his trying resignation.

Therefore, he would not. The old, familiar, grim determination that had kept him at his painting formed within him again now, but with a new purpose. Deeply, he realized now that he was not afraid of the Silver Horde or daunted by the Center Aliens. He was not about to obey the latter blindly, as if they were but one more superior member of a larger pecking order.

He would make up his own mind about what he would do. And that meant that in spite of both Horde and Center Aliens, the *Fighting Rowboat* would take its place in the battle—when the time came. Yes, the *Fighting Rowboat* would fight—if he had to take her out alone against the Silver Horde, she would fight.

8

"Tell me his name again," said Miles.

"His name is Vouhroi," replied Chak'ha.

They were seated together in the ship's lounge. Miles had made Chak'ha bring his own chair and table unit over close beside Miles' own. Now, unlike all the others aboard the ship, they sat in the lounge together in conversation, as they had for nearly two weeks now. Chak'ha had resisted this closeness at first, but Miles had forced it. Then, in the end, the tiger-faced alien had yielded and accepted what was almost a friendship. In fact, he had become more dependent on it than was Miles, so that he followed Miles about and stayed close to him as many of their waking hours as was possible.

No doubt the other twenty-one aboard the ship had observed this conversational closeness. But since Miles and Chak'ha were together at the bottom of the pecking order, it seemed that none of the others would lower themselves to notice their exception to the normal social pattern aboard the vessel. So for nearly two weeks, undisturbed, Miles had been able to study the others as they moved about the ship and occasionally—without apparent reason—merged in battle or continued to ignore or give way to one another in accordance to their relative positions in the pecking order.

Luhon was the leader—there was no doubt about that. Just below him was Eff, who, oddly enough, turned out to be the rotund, bearlike alien who had seemed so harmless to Miles at first sight. These two seemed satisfied with their relative positions. But below the rank of Eff the members of the pecking order were continually being challenged by the members immediately below them.

"Why do they keep fighting, when the same one always loses and the same one always wins?" Miles had asked Chak'ha.

Chak'ha shook his head.

"I don't know, but," he said, "I think it's because we've got nothing else to do. Fighting is all we've got. And the fight just might turn out differently the next time."

Miles had nodded. He had carefully set himself to learn the rank of each crew member in the pecking order, but his interest had centered on Vouhroi, who was next above Miles himself now that Miles had conquered Chak'ha.

Miles had begun to plan. He could do nothing until he was in control of the others aboard this ship. That meant winning his way to the top of the pecking order. Vouhroi was the first step he must mount. He had studied Vouhroi, therefore, not merely with the desire of someone wanting to improve his rank among his fellows for his own satisfaction, but with the same combination of hunger, fury, and creative desire with which he had attacked his paintings, back on Earth. It was a method of attack that would not consider any result short of success.

Physically, Miles told himself, each of the others aboard must have some point or points at which he was vulnerable. Weak spots. What were the weak spots of Vouhroi?

The one he studied was a lean but powerful-looking, catlike alien. Not heavily catlike as was the tigerish Chak'ha, but with the long-legged, high-haunched feline grace of a Canadian lynx. Vouhroi's chair in the lounge was almost directly opposite that of Miles, and while he had never overtly acknowledged Miles' existence, Miles had come to be expert at reading the small signs in the other aliens that warned him that they were aware of his presence and braced against any sudden unexpected attack by him.

Clearly, of all the others, Vouhroi, who was next in line above Miles, was not about to be taken by surprise by any unexpected attack by Miles. His back was always to the wall, and his eyes—though apparently focused generally on the room—always included Miles within their range of vision. Though apparently relaxed, when Miles was present the lynxlike alien was always in a position from which he could get to his feet in an instant.

Nor was this treatment just for Miles. Everyone in the pecking order, Miles noticed, watched the individual just below him in the same way.

A surprise attack, the jumping of your opponent from behind or in a second of disadvantage, was only one more tactic in the ruleless battles that were fought between members of the crew. No advantage was unfair if it led to winning. Cold-bloodedly Miles made plans to make use of the unfair advantages at his disposal. He gave Chak'ha instructions.

The end result of those instructions was the conversation that they were having now as they sat in the lounge looking across at Vouhroi. The timbre of Miles' voice and that of Chak'ha's were very close—close enough so that practice could make them almost identical. For more than a week now, Miles had been secretly practicing with Chak'ha to imitate the pronunciation Chak'ha gave to Vouhroi's name.

Now he repeated the name after Chak'ha. The tiger-faced alien nodded.

"Right," he said at last. "It sounds right the way you say it now."

"Good," answered Miles. He glanced across at Vouhroi, apparently dozing, with half-closed eyelids, across the lounge. "I'll go forward now. You wait a few minutes and then stroll aft."

Miles got up from his chair in the lounge and wandered toward the front end of the lounge and from there into the corridor leading to the control room in front. He went halfway up the corridor, turned, put his shoulders against the wall, and waited.

With his mind he measured the slow seconds as they flowed by. Ever since the Center Aliens had changed him physically, he had been aware of differences in mind and mental skills as well. One of these was this ability to keep time in his head as well as any watch. So he waited while the minutes passed, and after perhaps three and a half minutes Eff came down the corridor from the control room, gave him the barest glance, and passed on without pausing, his rotund figure disappearing into the lounge. Miles waited another minute and a half. Then, quietly, he walked down the corridor until he was just out of sight of the lounge and the position of Vouhroi's chair in the lounge.

From where he stood flattened against the inside wall of the corridor, he could just see the entrance to the farther corridor leading back to the crew quarters and could see against the inner wall there the blocky outline of Chak'ha waiting.

Then he shouted, in the closest imitation of Chak'ha's voice and accent he could manage.

"Vouhroi!"

"Vouhroi!" It was a shout in Chak'ha's voice from the other corridor. Chak'ha was now running into the lounge, continuing to shout as he came. *"Vouhroi! Vouhroi! Vouhroi . . ."*

Miles launched himself toward the lounge, running at top speed and as noiselessly as he could. He had a moment's glimpse of Chak'ha rushing in from the opposite direction—of Vouhroi with his back turned, staring at Chak'ha. Then Miles hit the lynxlike alien with a hard tackle at waist level.

He slammed the unprepared Vouhroi down against the deck of the lounge—hard enough, Miles would have thought, to knock out a human being. But even as he was thrown to the deck, Vouhroi was attempting to twist around in Miles' grasp, and though his head slammed hard on the uncarpeted surface beneath them, he did not appear to be stunned.

Miles already had Vouhroi in the same full nelson which had worked so well with Chak'ha. At the same time that Miles began to exert pressure against the other's neck, he clamped his own human legs around the legs of Vouhroi and tried to hold them as Vouhroi attempted to kick and scramble loose. But the alien's legs were too powerful. They broke free, and Miles shifted his leg grip to a scissors hold around Vouhroi's narrow waist.

Vouhroi surged about and for one furious moment succeeded in rising to his feet, with Miles riding on his back. Then Miles' weight overbalanced him and he fell backward. Lying underneath the alien, Miles continued to apply pressure to Vouhroi's neck. He half expected the overdrive strength to come to his aid, as it had with Chak'ha. But it did not come, and it was not needed.

Already Vouhroi's neck was starting to give. It did not, indeed, have as much inner stiffness and strength as had Chak'ha's. Miles felt it bend—and almost at once the tranquilizing gray fog, the feeling of weakness and indifference, closed in about him and his opponent, and he drifted dimly off into unconcern, the battle fires of emotion within him damped and extinguished.

When he woke on his bunk after this second battle, however, there was a face looming close above him. It was the face of Chak'ha, and coming from Chak'ha, Miles sensed clearly a strange emotion—something between glee and triumph.

"Awake, Miles?" asked Chak'ha.

"Awake," replied Miles a little thickly.

The face of Chak'ha came closer. He lowered his voice to what, for him, was the equivalent of a whisper.

"We did it, Miles! Didn't we do it?"

"I did it," said Miles. "With your help."

"That's what I mean," whispered Chak'ha savagely. "With my help. You did it with *my* help. The two of us together."

Chak'ha's eyes half-closed. Once more there came from him, to Miles' emotion-sensing capability, a feeling of great relief and joy and friendship.

For the first time, Miles realized that Chak'ha had expected to be disowned by Miles once Miles had moved one more step up the ladder. There was something deeply touching about the emotion that flowed from the tiger-faced individual bent closely above his bunk. Miles reached out to grasp one of the thick, stubby, clawed hands of Chak'ha in his own. Chak'ha looked down at the joined extremities in surprise.

"This is how we do it among my people," said Miles and shook Chak'ha's hand, then let it go. Chak'ha looked for a moment wonderingly at his own released hand, then stared back at Miles, and the feeling of happiness from him increased.

Miles drifted back off into slumber, carrying that feeling of happiness and friendship with him.

In the next few weeks that followed, he fought his way up through the pecking order. In each case, after winning, he tried to make friends with the alien he had just conquered. One or two of those he had beaten became friendly. But none of them became as close to him as Chak'ha, who now followed him about continually. In time, there were left only two crew members aboard who did not acknowledge Miles' presence or answer when he spoke to them. These were Eff and Luhon, the one whom nobody else could beat.

The opposition had grown progressively more difficult as Miles had mounted the ladder of the pecking order. His last fight, with a dark-skinned humanoid named Henaoa, had taken all of Miles' strength and skill to win. Logically, therefore, he could not expect to conquer the two remaining crew members. Even if he did somehow manage to conquer Eff, certainly he would not be able to conquer Luhon.

The secrets of their individual strengths were now quite clear to him. In Eff's case, the rotund body was all muscle—he was not plump, he was a chunk of heavy-bodied power. In Luhon's case, his secret was that speed which Miles had already observed. Certainly there must be strength connected with it. But in any case, Luhon's reflexes were such that it would be necessary for Miles to conquer the gray-skinned alien with his first blow—because the chances were that he would not have a chance to land a second.

But Luhon was in the future. Eff was in the present, and Miles was aware that Eff had been subtly on guard ever since Miles' last victory—for all that the rotund alien appeared to ignore everyone but Luhon.

For a full week, Miles studied Eff. At first it seemed that there was no point of weakness about him. The joints of his body were solid and deeply set in muscle and flesh. His neck was so short as to be almost nonexistent. The full nelson that Miles had used to advantage several times now would not work this time—let alone the fact that Eff had undoubtedly noted its use and was on guard. Miles raked over the dead coals of his younger memories before polio had stricken and made useless his arm. There must have been other wrestling holds or tricks that he must have known or read about or heard about, once upon a time. He needed something unexpected to use against Eff.

In the end, he concentrated his study on Eff's waist and the lower part of his trunk. As far as he could discover, the bearlike alien had a humanlike chest, ribs, and diaphragm. There was just a chance in that fact, if Miles could catch Eff at the right spot in the ship.

He had to wait several days before that chance came. During those days he stayed close to Eff, who only by the merest flicker of an eyelid or twitch of a furry ear acknowledged the fact he was being followed. But Eff's vigilance did not relax. In spite of this, the time came when Miles, following closely behind him, saw Eff less than two arm's lengths away from him, turning from the corridor around a little angle into the lounge.

Miles leaped upon him from behind.

Eff had been on guard against any attack, and he

was turning to face Miles even as Miles hit him. But Miles had waited for just this place to start the fight. The momentum of his charge drove the bearlike alien into the angle where two walls met, so that in falling, Eff was crowded into the corner. He went down on his side, with Miles' leg closing about the thick waist and one furry arm. As they landed on the floor, Miles caught Eff's remaining free arm in both hands and twisted it up behind the stocky body.

Even with his two arms against Eff's one, he found it almost impossible to keep that other arm imprisoned. The arm caught by Miles' legs, however, was held. Eff's shoulder was wedged in the corner, his arm and waist imprisoned by the muscles of Miles' interlocked legs in a scissors grip which Miles proceeded now to tighten around Eff's waist, his left knee driving hard up into the alien's diaphragm area just below the rib cage.

Eff struggled—but they were locked together. Miles could do no more than hold Eff's left arm twisted up behind him while their combined weights and the scissors hold kept the other arm pinned. To the watching crew members that soon gathered in a semicircle around them, it seemed as if nothing were happening. But a great deal was happening of which only Eff and Miles were conscious.

But Miles' left knee was continuing a steady pressure, pushing, grinding in and up against the bottom of Eff's lungs, driving air out of them.

They lay there together in the angle of the wall, seeming barely to move. But the struggle continued—for an intolerably long time, it seemed to Miles. He could feel that the pressure of his legs was gradually shortening the breath available to Eff, but Eff did not seem weakened. Every so often he surged mightily, if without success, against the hold with which Miles was keeping him pinned.

But now Miles felt his own strength leaking away. He had only so much muscle power in his arms and legs, and that power was gradually being exhausted in keeping the heavier and stronger alien beneath him tied up. He felt himself beginning to weaken—and overdrive was not coming to his aid. He almost gave up—and then the old, familiar determination rose in him. Through the bones of his head, he heard his teeth grinding together. He would crush this enemy of his. Crush . . . crush. . . .

But suddenly the gray, tranquilizing mist was rising about him. He felt his grip slackening, he felt his combat fury ebbing away from him. For a second he was dumbfounded, disbelieving. He had not yet lost. Why was the invisible protective device of the ship stopping the battle? It was not fair. . . .

The gray mist rose inexorably around him.

9

For one wild moment he tried to fight mist and Eff at once.

Then, with the last flicker of conscious thought left to him before the tranquilizing effect stole all feeling from him, understanding woke in him. He realized suddenly that it must be the other way around—that he must have brought Eff to the point of suffocation and unconsciousness, where the tranquilizing effect needed to exert itself to save the rotund alien's life. Miles had won.

This time the tranquilizing effect lifted swiftly. It pulled away from both him and his opponent while they were still lying on the floor of the lounge. Miles pushed away the hands that were trying to lift him and got to his feet unaided. Opposite him, he saw Eff also getting to his feet. The bearlike alien's face opened in a grimace that would never have been recognizable as a smile if the outwash of emotion from the other had not confirmed that a smile was intended. The furry chest was heaving for air, and Eff's words came out in short gasps; but there was a cheerfulness to them

that Miles had not yet encountered in any of the aliens
aboard whom he had conquered.

"Better . . . than I am," panted Eff. "Now what? I've
been wanting to know what you've been after . . . ever
since you started fighting your way up to my position on the ship."

Still gasping for air himself, Miles stared at Eff.
With the exception of Chak'ha, he had found no crew
member desirous or capable enough of friendship to
meet him on a level basis after he had conquered him.
Invariably the other had assumed the subordinate
position.

But apparently, with Eff, being conquered physically
did not mean that his soul had been dominated. This
was a good sign for the success of the plan in the back
of Miles' mind.

"I'll tell you what I'm after," Miles replied, "after
I've beaten Luhon."

Around them the other crew members who had
been spectators were drifting off. Only Chak'ha
remained. Eff glanced at the tiger-faced alien for a second, then back to Miles.

"You'll never beat Luhon," Eff said.

"Yes, I will," said Miles. "I have to. So I'll manage
it somehow."

Eff shook his head again, if amiably. His breathing
was slowing to a normal rate.

"You'll never beat Luhon," he repeated, not didac-
tically or stubbornly, but in the calm tone of somebody
who patiently states to a child or someone of simple
intelligence.

"Believe what you like," said Miles. He hesitated,
then took a long chance—a chance he had taken with
no one so far except Chak'ha. "How about helping
me?"

Eff looked him frankly in the face.

"I won't help you fight him," answered Eff. "But outside of that, I'll help you with anything reasonable."

"That's all I ask," said Miles.

Eff grinned more widely. Chak'ha moved in until he stood close to both of them, and the aura of emotion that Miles sensed around all three of them seemed to flow together into one unit of mutual understanding.

From that point on began Miles' first days of anything like comradeship aboard the small vessel.

At first Miles had half expected Chak'ha to resent the sudden inclusion of Eff into what had been a two-way partnership. But he had forgotten that Eff had been high in the pecking order, while Chak'ha had been at the bottom. Chak'ha made no attempt to compete with Eff for Miles' friendship. In fact, as Miles discovered, it would have been hard for anyone to resent Eff.

Once he had opened up to the two of them, the bearlike alien turned out to own a warmth of character closer to human warmth than Miles had found otherwise aboard the ship. Eff was an extrovert. He was frank and—except for his belief that Luhon was unconquerable—apparently daunted by nothing, even including the Center Aliens. Amused by Miles' determination to attempt the apparently hopeless task of fighting Luhon but fascinated by it, he joined happily in helping Miles study Luhon.

"I tell you," Miles kept insisting to him stubbornly, "Luhon has to have a weak spot! Any organism, by its very nature, has to have drawbacks as well as advantages."

"To be sure, he has to have weak spots," replied Eff shrewdly. "But are they weak spots that you have strong spots to correspond with? Luhon's simply too fast for you. He's too fast for any of us aboard here. He's from a heavy world—one where the gravity is much more than any of us is used to."

Miles stared at him.

"You mean," said Miles at last, "he's stronger than he looks, because of that—"

"Stronger? Some, of course." Eff shrugged good-humoredly. "But that's not the point. He's much faster, because of the gravity conditions he's grown up with."

"Faster?" echoed Miles.

Eff laughed.

"You don't understand, Miles?" said the stocky alien. "Stop and think then. The stronger the gravity, the faster an object falls, say from your hand to the ground. Correct?"

"Yes," said Miles slowly.

"Also, the faster *you* fall to the ground, if you get offbalance," said Eff. "Correct?"

"Ah," said Miles, suddenly understanding.

"I see you follow me now," said Eff. "Standing, walking, running—almost everything we bipeds do requires maintaining our balance. And the quicker we fall when our balance is lost, the faster our reflexes have to be to take muscular action to stop us from falling. Luhon is like that—his reflexes are simply that much faster than mine . . . or yours. So I tell you—there's no hope. You will never beat him!"

Miles shook his head. He did not believe that some key could not be found to defeat the slender, quick-moving, gray-skinned alien who continued—out of all those aboard the *Fighting Rowboat*—to ignore him.

In fact, Luhon was isolated now in the old pattern of behavior, for all the rest aboard had begun to associate with and talk to one another, regardless of rank. They did it seldom, and they did it warily, but they were doing it. Miles' friendship with Chak'ha had first broken the ice of the pecking order. Now, slowly but undeniably, a general thaw was setting in.

The exception was Luhon. But if it bothered him to be set aside, separate within the old pattern of behavior aboard the ship, he did not show it. He spent his waking hours working with the ship's controls, and he continued to ignore everyone aboard, Miles included. Nor could Miles notice any increase in the minimal signs that betrayed Luhon's awareness of Miles whenever Miles got within jumping distance of the gray-skinned alien. Moreover, at the end of two weeks of study, with all the help that Eff and Chak'ha could give him, Miles had yet to find any sure counter for that inhuman swiftness of physical reflex Luhon possessed.

The best Miles could do was to plan an attack that would at least give him the advantage of choosing the time and place of battle. He could hope to get in one quick blow—and that would be all. It would need to be a crippling or knockout blow if Miles were to win at all. The best place for it to be landed, Miles thought, was the narrow and apparently soft midsection of Luhon, just above the waist. He planned his blow and rehearsed it in the privacy of the cabin he shared with Chak'ha until it was reflexive, until it was essentially automatic.

Then he stationed himself one day just within the open doorway of his cabin. Eff and Chak'ha took up their posts in the lounge.

Miles waited. It was a long wait, and he ended up sitting rather than standing, until a preliminary signal, which was Chak'ha's own peculiar bark of laughter, alerted him to the fact that Luhon had commenced to move through the lounge headed aft. Miles got swiftly to his feet.

He stepped noiselessly to within half a step of the open doorway and listened, with ears tuned to unnatural acuteness by the tension within him. He heard the footsteps of Luhon approaching down the corridor outside the cabin. A coldness enfolded his forehead, and he knew that he had begun to sweat with anticipation. His heart beat faster. He tensed, poised—

The laugh of Chak'ha rang out again from the lounge.

Miles launched himself forward. He had a glimpse of a gray body before him, swiftly twisting away. His fist grazed a gray side. He felt the shock of a sudden heavy blow at the side of his neck. He caught himself, bounced off a corridor wall, and before he could even try to strike again, another blow somewhere on his head sent him sliding down and away into unconsciousness. . . .

When he opened his eyes, he found he was lying on his bunk. His neck ached with an ache that seemed to penetrate across his chest and down the opposite side of his body. The faces of Eff and Chak'ha floated above him. He opened his mouth to speak, but to his surprise what came out was barely more than a whisper—and even that hurt his neck.

"What happened?" he whispered.

"What I told you would happen," replied the voice of Eff. "He was too fast for you."

The feeling of disillusionment and defeat closed around Miles like quicksand. He slipped back into unconsciousness.

But when he opened his eyes next, it was from sleep, and it was as if his mind had come to its own conclusion and made itself up while he slumbered. Chak'ha was not in the room, but Eff was. Miles struggled to sit up on the edge of the bed. His neck ached, and his head was dizzy. But he made it. Eff looked at him with a tolerant humor.

"Help me up," husked Miles, even those few words sending pain up through his neck and into his head where it spread into a skullcap of headache.

Eff came forward and pulled Miles to his feet.

"There," said Eff. "Now you're up. But what's the use in that? You're just going to have to lie down again."

"No," whispered Miles. In him was something cold and hard as a nugget of meteoric iron flung through light-years of empty space to its destination, death at last in the fires of a sun. "Help me . . . walk."

He headed toward the doorway of the room, with Eff holding one arm and guiding him. As he went, he seemed to draw strength from the very movement. He turned left down the corridor.

"Where's Luhon?" he whispered hoarsely to Eff.

"Where he almost always is," replied Eff, watching him curiously. "Up front by himself, in the control room."

"Good," husked Miles. He continued to totter on down the corridor, with Eff helping to balance him. But his strength was coming back rapidly with that near-magic return of health that was part of the Center Alien science built into the ship. By the time he was halfway across the lounge he was able to shake himself free of Eff's sustaining grip and walk alone.

When he entered the forward corridor leading to the control room, he was striding a little in advance of Eff. The pain was still in his neck and head, but he could bear it. And the action of his muscles was coming more easily to him—which was important.

Eff caught up with him.

"What're you going to do?" asked Eff.

"Wait and see," answered Miles.

He went on, Eff beside him, until he reached the entrance to the control room. There, as usual, sat

Luhon at the controls. But for once his fingers were not playing with them. Instead, his gaze was lifted above them to the control room's main vision screen, which was set now on a view of intergalactic space— looking in that direction from which Miles' implanted inner knowledge told him the Silver Horde was expected to come.

There was something lonely about the way the still, slim, gray-skinned figure sat, with its gaze fixed unmovingly on empty intergalactic space. But Miles had no time for empathy now.

Putting out a hand to stop Eff from following him beyond the open doorway, he walked forward without pausing and, when he was within range, launched himself without any attempt at trickery at the back of Luhon's neck.

This time, when he awoke, he remembered nothing beyond that single jump forward. His neck, surprisingly, was not so painful now. But his head was one single, solid ache, as if Luhon's retaliation this time had been all in that area. He lay awhile, waiting and hoping for the ache to diminish. But if it did so, it did so only slightly.

He turned his head and saw Chak'ha and Eff watching him. Painfully, once more he struggled to sit up on the edge of the bed. Neither of the others came forward to help him.

Rage suddenly flooded through him—not rage at Luhon, but rage at the two who stood watching.

"Come here!" he croaked hoarsely. "Help me!"

It was not a request he was making of them. It was an order. And there was enough of the old pecking order pattern left in them that both came to him and helped him to his feet. For a moment his head reeled, and the room seemed to spin and sway around him. Then his gaze and sense of balance settled.

He turned toward the doorway of the room.

"To Luhon," he said hoarsely. There was a moment's hesitation on the part of the other two aliens. Then, silently, they each took an elbow and guided him out into the corridor and once more toward the front of the vessel.

This time, as he walked through the lounge—which now was filled with silent, watching crewmen in all their various alien shapes and expressions of feature—recovery was slow in coming to him. But come it did. By the time he was halfway down the corridor toward the control room he was once more walking without assistance.

He made it to the entrance of the control room and there paused. Because this time, evidently alerted by the sound of footsteps approaching, Luhon had turned about in his chair and was facing the doorway. His eyes met the eyes of Miles plainly this time, and for the first time without any pretense of avoidance.

Luhon's face, insofar as six weeks had taught Miles to interpret the gray-skinned alien's features, wore a look of puzzlement. He stared searchingly at Miles in the doorway.

Miles launched himself forward in a tottering rush, his hands outstretched to grab the throat of the other.

But before his hands closed around the gray throat, Luhon was no longer before him. Miles found himself seized and swung about. He was pinned, with his back against the slanting face of one of the control consoles. With ease, Luhon held him helpless there, and the gray-skinned face looked down into Miles' from a distance of a few inches.

"What do you want?" asked Luhon.

It was the first time that Miles had heard the voice of the other. It was a soft, low-pitched voice, a strange voice to belong to someone who had outfought everyone else aboard this vessel. And it, together with the emotions that Miles felt emanating from Luhon, was deep-stained with puzzlement

"I want"—Miles' voice was almost too husky to be understandable—"to fight the Silver Horde."

For a long moment Luhon's gray features continued to look down into Miles' face. Then Miles felt the grip that was holding him pinioned against the console released. Luhon stood back from him, a slight, slim figure—not only in contrast with Miles, but also with Eff and Chak'ha, who now filled the control room doorway behind the ship's champion.

"You want to fight the Silver Horde?" echoed Luhon in his soft voice. His eyes traveled up and down Miles. "So do I. But, a great deal better than you, I know how impossible a hope that is."

10

Miles slowly straightened up. He rubbed his aching head with a forefinger and tried to clear the hoarse vocal cords of his painful throat.

"You're wrong," he answered Luhon.

"No," said Luhon evenly.

"Yes," said Miles. His weary legs began to tremble, and he sat down in the control seat Luhon had just vacated. "Do you know what I did the first day I was here? I looked around the ship, and then I looked around the platform. And then I took that small courier ship from its cradle on the platform and went in it up the line toward the big ships where the Center Aliens are."

Luhon's pointed ears suddenly pricked and turned forward toward Miles.

"You went in and saw the Center Aliens?" he asked.

"I didn't get as far as I'd planned to go," said Miles. "All of a sudden I found one of them sitting beside me, and he turned the ship around and brought it back. But he answered my questions. He told me why this ship is never intended to fight the Silver Horde. He told me he only wants us for feedback purposes on the total weapons of the total battle line, if it comes to fighting. He told me that one of them is worth more than all twenty-three of us in this ship put together."

Miles stopped talking. Luhon stared at him for a long moment.

"You took that little boat," said Luhon, almost wonderingly. "And you went in—you tried to get in up to where the Center Aliens are. You did that?"

"None of you ever did anything like that, is that it?" he demanded suddenly of Luhon.

Luhon made the negative gesture of his race. It was only a slight twisting of his upper body, but the aura of emotion around him carried the meaning behind it clearly to Miles' emotional sensitivity.

"But you asked him," said Luhon, staring brilliantly at Miles. "And he gave you the answers."

"Yes," said Miles. He struggled to his feet. "Only, I don't believe him. I don't agree with him. I think we *can* fight the Silver Horde—in this ship, the twenty-three of us, working her alongside all the other ships that go out to fight the Horde when the time comes."

Once more Luhon looked at him for what seemed a long time. Then he made a negative twist of his body again; only this time there was something like a shrug in it.

"So you believe that?" demanded the gray-skinned alien. "And that's why you fought your way up to just below me? You wanted to take over this ship to make it into something that could fight the Silver Horde?"

"That's right," said Miles. He added, brutally. "None of the rest of you seemed to have the guts for it."

He tensed, bracing himself for a sudden attack by Luhon.

But the gray-skinned alien only stared at him for a moment longer, then turned half around so that he had both Eff and Chak'ha in the doorway within his field of vision as well as Miles. Then he took a step backward.

"I didn't believe we could fight the Silver Horde," he said. His eyes fastened brilliantly on Miles. "I still don't. Also, I know that you could never beat me, no matter how many times you try. Do you understand that?"

Miles shook his head.

"No," he said. "You can't kill me. So in the end I'll beat you. No matter how long it takes or how many times I have to try."

Once more, Luhon made that body-twisting movement of negation. But this time it was nearly all shrug.

"You can't beat me, but you'll keep on trying," he said, almost to himself. "You'll keep attacking me until you win, you say. And we all know you can't make this ship into a fighting vessel which the Center Aliens will let go against the Silver Horde when it comes. But you say you'll keep trying until you do."

He took another step back. He looked at Miles, and once more Miles braced himself for a lightning attack. But no attack came.

"All right, then, in that case," said Luhon, "I am defeated."

Miles stared at him. It seemed too sudden, too easy a victory. What had been, dimly but certainly, in the back of his mind was that he would keep on attacking Luhon until he exhausted the other. He had hoped only to be able to bother the gray-skinned alien until Luhon would buy peace at the price of stepping down from the number one position. This sudden admission of defeat made Miles cautious.

"Just like that?" he said, narrowly watching Luhon. "Why?

"Because," answered Luhon softly, "*I* did not take

the little boat and try to talk to the Center Aliens. Because *I* did not plan to fight my way up to the top in this ship for any purpose other than to be on top. Because *I*, even now, don't believe you can make this ship into something that will go out to fight the Silver Horde. But most of all, because I want to fight the Silver Horde as much as you do."

He turned his brilliant gaze toward Eff and Chak'ha.

"All of us aboard here," he said slowly, "have dreamed about fighting when the time comes. Isn't that so, friends?"

For a moment, Eff and Chak'ha stared back at Luhon as if in astonishment at finding themselves directly addressed by him. Then together they made the individual body movements that were the equivalent of a human nod.

"Yes," said Eff. The rough frankness of his usual voice was slowed and more solemn now. "For me— yes. And Chak'ha, here, says yes. If we four feel that way, I'd think the others would feel that way, too."

"They will, I think," said Luhon. "We're a great deal alike, all of us on this ship—more alike than we like to think, considering the differences of body and mind among us. But at least we're alike in being different from those Center Aliens. They don't have feelings, as we do." He turned to Miles. "Isn't that true, friend Miles?"

"They don't feel the way we do, that's certain," said Miles grimly.

"Then it's settled," said Luhon. "I abdicate in favor of you, Miles. For the rest, I think they'll all be glad to join us. If not"—he did not smile (perhaps he could not with the muscles in his gray face), but a touch of humor sped from him like a ripple over the surface of a pond to break against Miles' emotional perceptions—"we'll make them. If there's anything I can do to make it more sure that my people at home survive the Horde, I won't stop at knocking a few heads together here."

"I don't believe it'll be necessary," said Miles. "But let's see."

It was just beginning to sink into him now that Luhon had actually given way, had stepped down and allowed him, Miles, to take top position aboard the *Fighting Rowboat*. The reaction had begun a warm glow that seemed to spread out from the center of his body, soothing all his hurts and aches and clearing his head amazingly. "Let's get them all together in the lounge now and talk to them."

"Yes," said Luhon, "let's go to the lounge."

They went. As they entered the lounge, with Eff and Chak'ha abreast, followed by Luhon beside Miles, and moved to stand together in one corner from which they could survey the rest of the room, the eyes of everyone else there turned to them.

"Get everyone here," said Luhon, raking the room with his eyes. His gaze fastened on Vouhroi, who was closest to the corridor leading back to the crew quarters. "You, Vouhroi, go back and bring everybody else up here."

Vouhroi went. The silence in the lounge continued unbroken. The eyes of those there remained fixed on the four standing in the corner. For the first time a small doubt crawled through the lower level of Miles' mind. They were four combined now—three who were the top three in physical abilities aboard the ship plus Chak'ha, who was least. But with the breakdown of the old pecking order anything was possible. What if, seeing this combination of four, the others of the nineteen remaining moved to combine themselves in an opposing group? Suddenly, he was glad of Luhon's willingness to fight for their plans if necessary.

Five other crew members, followed by Vouhroi, filed into the lounge and filled up the empty chairs, with the exception of those chairs belonging to Miles and his three companions. They sat still, looking at Luhon.

"Miles just conquered me," said Luhon. "So he's on top now aboard this ship. He believes, and we with him here agree, that from now on things are going to be different." He glanced aside at Miles. "Tell them, Miles."

"There isn't going to be any more fighting among ourselves," said Miles, looking around at the different alien faces. "From now on we're going to work together, and we're going to make the *Fighting Rowboat* into a ship that can actually go into battle against the Silver Horde when it comes."

A small sound came murmuring from the rest of the crew members, like the sound of wind through the swaying branches of a grove of trees. It was a combination of sounds, in many verbal ways, of astonishment and disbelief.

"I know!" said Miles swiftly. "The Center Aliens don't think we can do it. But I think we can. Have any of you gotten close to those weapons and felt what they're like with the sensing part of your minds? They're *cold*! We'd have to work with them to warm them up. But who knows what they'd be like if they *were* warmed up?"

He looked around at them.

"We come from fighting races, all of us," he said. "Otherwise we wouldn't have fought among ourselves the way we did. Now, who among you doesn't want to fight the Silver Horde if you get the chance?"

All through the lounge there was silence. No one moved; no one replied.

"None of you!" said Miles. "Of course, if that's the case, what've you got to lose by going along with me? Let's see if this ship and all of us, working together, can't make a fighting unit that the Center Aliens will let join them when the time comes to face the Silver Horde."

He paused. They still looked at him, neither assenting nor dissenting.

"All right," said Miles slowly. "Is there anyone here who won't go along with the rest of us in doing this?"

Beside and behind Miles, Luhon, with Eff and Chak'ha, moved forward a step.

No one spoke. For a moment Miles was tempted to let it go at that. Then some inner instinct warned him that he needed to force his listeners into a positive statement of agreement, rather than just a passive acceptance of his plans.

"Those who're ready to go to work at once," he said, "take a step forward."

There was a pause, a rustle of movement; then Vouhroi stood up. One by one and in groups they all rose from their chairs and stepped toward Miles.

"Good!" said Miles. He kept his voice calm, but triumph sang inside him. "Now let's find out what it takes to operate this ship and her weapons!" he said. "I'll go to the control room. With me will be Luhon as my second-in-command and Eff as my third-in-command. Chak'ha will join the rest of you on the weapons. Scatter around the ship now, find yourselves weapons, and try to warm them up."

Without waiting for any sign of assent from them, Miles turned and strode from the room toward the passageway, the corridor leading to the control room in the vessel's bow. He heard footfalls behind him and knew that Luhon, Eff, and Chak'ha were following, while a general confused sound of voices and movement behind him indicated that at least some of the rest of the crew were obeying. He led the way up into the control room and paused before the central of the three seats that faced the control console under the large vision screen with its view of the blackness of intergalactic space.

"We'll have to practice, too," he muttered, as much to himself as to the three others, who had followed him in.

"Shall I show you how, friend Miles?" murmured the soft voice of Luhon in his ear. Miles turned sharply to face the gray-skinned alien.

"Do you know something about this I don't?" Miles asked. "The information about these controls was evidently put into me by the Center Aliens when they first took me over."

"So it was in me—in all of us," answered Luhon, unperturbed. "But you have to remember I've fought with the ship thousands of times, and you haven't."

Miles stared at him. Another ripple of amusement sped from Luhon to break against Miles' perception.

"What do you think I've been doing up here all alone, all this time?" asked Luhon. "Thousands of times, in my imagination, I've fought this ship against the Silver Horde—never believing it would actually ever happen, that I would really fight her. You know the controls, friend Miles, as well as I do, but I know the *ship* better than you do."

The breath sighed suddenly from Miles' lungs. An empty feeling came to dwell suddenly in the area of his stomach. It had never occurred to him that they would not all be starting out as equals. How was he to keep Luhon as his second-in-command when the gray-skinned alien was not only his physical superior but his superior in experience of controlling the vessel, as well?

"No, friend Miles," said Luhon. Miles turned to see the brilliant eyes regarding him and realized that Luhon had read his emotional reaction with the same

perceptiveness with which Miles and evidently everyone else aboard the ship had been equipped by the
Center Aliens. Luhon's sensing of Miles' emotional
reaction, plus a shrewd guess, could be tantamount to
Luhon's reading Miles' mind. "Remember, you're the
one who believes that we can get good enough to be
allowed to fight the Silver Horde in our own persons.
I still don't believe it, and if the power of this ship is
really psychic rather than physical, that power is going to depend on someone who can *believe*."

Miles nodded. He sat down in the central control
seat. Luhon took the seat to his right, and Eff slid into
the seat at his left, as if at the order of some unspoken command.

"Suppose we lock in together as a single pattern, just
the three of us to start," said Luhon calmly. "And I'll
take the two of you on a computerized version of one
of my imaginary battles."

His fingers flew over the controls of the console
before him, and Miles found his own fingers flying as
well. The consoles were identical—he already knew
that from that information the Center Aliens had
earlier planted in his mind. Each of them could control this ship independently, but there was a triangular
reinforcement of purpose and strength if one individual
and one console led and the other two followed and
reinforced. Now, with Luhon leading but with the
master controls still in off position so that the vessel
did not actually fly or fight, Miles followed Luhon into
the gray-skinned alien's imaginary battle against the
Silver Horde. The ship, Miles realized as his fingers
flashed over the controls, *could* be flown. But the
weapons were dead—and not only because the crew
of the *Fighting Rowboat* had ignored them all this time.
Some master control of the Center Aliens held the
weapons locked and useless.

But the psychic patterns, the emotional reflexes of Miles and his two companions, were joined together now into a single reacting unit. Their thoughts were not joined, but they reached in unison and with an automatic understanding of one another. They were welded into a single purpose and action. It was a strange feeling to Miles, for within Eff's share of that pattern Miles could now sense the direct, open, and vital quality of the bearlike alien, and in Luhon, at his right, he could sense the deep, dark-running feelings beneath the gentle exterior of soft voice and swift, silent movement. Just so, Miles now understood, the other two would be sensing *him* to a greater degree than they ever had previously.

Meanwhile, computer-created before them all, there had appeared on the vision screen before them the shape of a silver crescent in the light of the artificial sun over the battle line. A silver crescent, horns forward, pointing toward them. It was, Miles' Center Alien–implanted knowledge told him, a reconstructed image of what the Silver Horde had looked like attacking this galaxy a million years before.

Their fingers moved automatically on the consoles in response to their wishes. The instruments recorded the *Fighting Rowboat* as lifting from her position—even while in reality she still stayed where she was. In mock action, she was recorded as drifting outward to join the vanguard of other ships from the Battle Line advancing against the invaders.

Now the screen showed that advance. At the far left end of the advancing line was the tiny shape of the *Fighting Rowboat*. Even the ship next to her—the smallest of the great round ships of the Center Aliens—was many hundred times her size and mass.

Together, the galaxy's ships joined in formation, and

faster now—and then faster—they plunged together toward the oncoming silver crescent of the attacking Horde.

The silver crescent shape was pulsing and swelling rapidly on the screen. Now it began to be visible in depth, if not in thickness, like a great flat scimitar swung at them in the same plane as their own battle line's formation. A few moments more, and its front edge began to fuzz, to reveal itself—as the two opposing armadas approached each other in shifts that must be many times the speed of light—as an incredible multitude of individual vessels.

Luhon stepped up the magnification on the screen. The view of the approaching front line of scout vessels of the Silver Horde jumped at them. They were small ships—even smaller than the *Fighting Rowboat* herself, which would have made three of them—but there were literally millions of them in this first line of invaders alone. A feeling of berserk joy leaped from the imagination of Luhon and communicated itself to Miles and Eff. In his imagination the little *Fighting Rowboat* suddenly thrust with extra energy ahead of her huge partners until she alone was drawing away toward the enemy in advance of all the rest of the front line of galaxy ships.

On and on she plunged, faster and faster, now so far in advance of her former linemates that the big ships would not be able to support her during the moment in which she would first make contact with the oncoming scout ships of the Horde.

Their imaginations locked together with the imagination of Luhon, neither Miles nor Eff cared, as Luhon himself did not care. The white fury of battle lust that had flamed within each of them during their fights among themselves aboard the ship was now unified in the locked psychic pattern and was lashing them on against the Horde. To die was nothing. But to cut and slash and kill among the silver vessels—that was everything, no matter what the personal cost.

Now they were almost upon the scout ships. Now they were suddenly among them, striking right and left with their weapons—paralyzing the psychic opposition of the smaller invader vessels long enough to slash open the silver ships with the physical edge of their combined weapons. Like a wolf among a pack of weasels—in the imagination of Luhon—they raged right and left, up and down the oncoming wave of Horde scout ships, snapping, shaking, slashing, and killing.

But now the larger ships of the invaders, their second wave, were almost upon the *Fighting Rowboat*. It would take a miracle to manage their escape. But the imagination of Luhon had programmed the miracle into the exercise. In the nick of time, the *Fighting Rowboat* flung free and raced away—just as the heavy vessels of the Center Aliens came up to engage with the second wave of the Horde.

But the little vessel was not finished. Safe behind her own dreadnoughts, she turned again and hung around the outskirts of the conflict, snapping up those smaller vessels of the enemy that reeled hurt from the battle. She was still among the fury of it all when the Horde's crescent began to break up, began to drift away and reform, moving in a different plane and line away from the galaxy. Mixed with the huge dreadnoughts of the Center Aliens, the *Fighting Rowboat* joined in harrying and driving away the defeated ships of the Silver Horde.

Suddenly Luhon's programmed battle ended. Suddenly the pattern of the three minds broke apart. Miles sat back exhausted in his seat and, looking about, saw Luhon and Eff slumped on either side of him.

For a long moment, even as he sagged exhausted

in his seat before the console, the feeling of the imagined victory continued to glow inside Miles. But slowly that glow dwindled, flickered, and went out.

Of course, it was not true. It would not be like that. It could never be like that except in the self-indulgent imagination of one of them, like Luhon. Only in imagination could pygmies join in battle with giants without being destroyed. The lucky chances that had saved them time and again in Luhon's visualization of the attack in actual fact would not be. The *Fighting Rowboat* would get her chance to fight only at the price of almost certain destruction. That was something they all had to face.

Miles found himself facing it with a cold and settled determination. As the feeling of that determination solidified like some hard and massive diamond within the very core of his being, he felt the minds of Eff and Luhon linking with his in pattern once again, and he felt a comparable hardness of decision and determination in them.

Good. It was settled then. Now the center point of the three-mind pattern, Miles began instinctively to reach out. He reached out and drew into the pattern of three the fourth mind, that of Chak'ha, then that of Vouhroi, and so on down the line of weapons on each side of the ship, as the psychic pattern reached out to enclose all those aboard her.

The skill with which he did this was clearly another of the abilities that the Center Aliens had given him. He had not suspected that he had it until he used it. But now that he had used it, he became suddenly conscious of how little the Center Aliens had expected it to be used in this way before the moment in which the larger pattern of the total battle line should activate them all as part of itself. Now, however, the pattern had set itself up alone in the minds of them all as one unit aboard the ignored and overlooked tiny *Fighting Rowboat.* A fierce and angry pride kindled within the pattern, and Miles was not sure whether he was its kindling point or not. But as the heat of that feeling spread out among them all, it illuminated within each individual the same hard, diamondlike core of decision to fight, even at the cost of dying, that Miles had found in himself, Luhon, and Eff.

They were barbarians in the sight of the Center Aliens. A thousand bloody, primitive battle cries out of their near and savage ancestry clamored in the mind and memory of each one of the twenty-three who was now locked in the pattern. They clamored also in the brain of Miles, at the leading point of that trianglelike pattern. Out of that welter of recalled sound a single phrase he had once read leaped clear and plain into his mind. No proud and noble speech of the battlefield, but the grim and sordid chorus rising from the bloody sand of the arena. The onetime salute of the gladiators of imperial Rome to Rome's Emperor: *Morituri te salutamus!*

"*We who are about to die salute thee!*"

11

The weapons did not warm up quickly. Somewhere in their combined physical and psychic mechanism was some sort of minimum operating level of potency. Until each weapon was warmed by the response of an intelligent mind to a certain value or effectiveness, it would not be capable of working, even if the Center Aliens should unlock the firing mechanism. It was three weeks before they had all the guns on the vessel capable of responding—in theory—when Miles should call upon them for mass fire.

Meanwhile, the actual approaching Silver Horde had been sighted. It was not yet visible on the vision screen in the control room of the *Fighting Rowboat*, but a pale ring of light circled the spot on the screen where it would first become visible. Even this much was like a stimulant to the twenty-three aboard the *Fighting Rowboat*. They worked eagerly now with their weapons and the ship—dry-firing, for the weapons remained locked. But that fact made little difference. As far as the feedback of response from weapon to the one man handling it was concerned, the feeling was the same as if he had actually used it against one of the ships of the Silver Horde.

With Miles now in command, they also practiced actually lifting the ship from its platform, running half a dozen light-years out beyond the Battle Line, and there slashing at the computer-created enemy.

The computer element itself was evidently a smaller version of those large calculative mechanisms which they had been taught to understand were possessed by the Center Aliens in their enormous ships. It would be those larger computers which, calculating up until the last moment before the attack of the Horde, would decide whether opposition would be worthwhile or whether it would not be better for the warships assembled here to break up and run, to hide and try to survive—so that they might protect what few worlds were ignored, from stragglers and small hunting parties of the silver invaders. The small computer aboard the *Fighting Rowboat*, however, would have no hand in this decision. But it could be used like this to program an imaginary attack of the Silver Horde, calling on the crew of the spaceship to repulse it. More than this, it could rate their performance.

In the several weeks that followed that first take-off, with all guns now operating, in dry-fire at least, the computer aboard the *Fighting Rowboat* charted a steady increase in the ability and effectiveness of the ship and crew. However, as the line marking their progress mounted on the chart, it began to level off. Soon it became plain that they were approaching a plateau of skill. Miles, Luhon, and Eff sat down together to figure out what might be the problem that was keeping them from progressing further.

"I don't understand it," said Luhon, as they sat together in the control room of the ship, in conference. The ship lay on its platform, and the rest of the crew had abandoned their weapons for rest after a long session of dry-firing and simulated battle. "We've all handled those weapons at one time or another. You can feel there's no theoretical limit to the psychic energies those weapons can take from us. There couldn't be, because whatever we can feed into them, it's going to be many times multiplied when the full psychic pattern of the total Battle Line locks in and takes over."

"It's plain enough," Eff put in. "It's not the weapons that're at fault. It has to be us. For some reason it looks as if we're reaching the limit of our capabilities. But I don't believe that."

"I don't either," said Miles thoughtfully. "As I understand it, from the information the Center Aliens put in me when they changed me—check me on this, both of you—any individual's psychic power is like the power of any one of his muscles. Continual exercise should increase psychic power, just as it increases muscle power. All right, eventually maybe a limit has to be reached, depending on individual capacity, but it doesn't *feel* to me that we ought to be reaching ours this quickly. Do you two feel the same?"

"It checks," said Luhon briefly. His pointed ears twitched restlessly. "If those Center Aliens were halfway decent, we could get in touch with them and ask them what's wrong. But they wouldn't be interested in helping us."

"Maybe they couldn't," said Miles thoughtfully.

The other two looked at him curiously.

"What we may be having trouble with"—Miles hesitated—"may be outside their experience. Either because it's something they've never run up against. Or because it's something they had so far back in their own history that they've forgotten what it was like. Look—these Center Aliens can get many more times the effectiveness out of one of those weapons than one of us can. The one I talked to told me that he had more power in himself than all of us on this ship put together."

"I can believe it," said Luhon. "But I don't see any help in knowing that."

"It suggests something," said Miles.

"What?" asked Eff.

"Well," said Miles, "obviously, we're different from the Center Aliens. Maybe it's the difference that's tripping us up. Suppose we ask ourselves just how we *are* different."

Eff gave his short bark of a laugh.

"We're barbarians," he said. "They told us that."

"That's right," said Miles. "So maybe it's some barbarian quality of ours that's getting in the way of our doing better with these weapons." He glanced from Eff to Luhon and back again. "What do you think?"

"Well," Luhon began slowly, "we don't have their knowledge obviously. But as I understand it, it isn't knowledge that feeds the psychic force. It's"—again he hesitated—"something like the spirit in the individual."

"Spirit, that's it! The whole emotional pattern we have!" said Miles. He looked closely at Luhon. "You see what I think I see, in that direction?"

Luhon's ears flicked. He stared back without answering.

"I don't see anything at all," put in Eff.

"Wait a minute," said Luhon slowly. "Miles, you mean that something about our emotional pattern is holding us back?" Abruptly he stiffened in his chair. "Of course—they don't react the way we do! They don't lose their tempers. They don't. . . ."

His voice trailed off thoughtfully.

"That's what I mean," said Miles. "We get wound up, self-intoxicated on our own emotion, when we fight. The Center Aliens don't." He paused and glanced at Eff and Luhon again, holding them both in his gaze. "Maybe our trouble's just that—intoxication, this battle fury of ours that keeps us from making better use of the weapons."

"But if that's it—" Luhon broke off sharply. "What're we going to do about it?"

"Practice," answered Miles harshly. "That's what we can do. Practice using the weapons without getting worked up about it. I know it won't be easy to do," he went on as Luhon opened his mouth to speak again, "but we can try—and maybe we can break through what's blocking us this way."

"There's always the possibility," Eff put in, "that the plateau of effectiveness we're on is something temporary. Maybe after staying at a constant level for a little while, we'll break out and start another stretch of improvement."

"The Silver Horde has already been indicated on the far instruments," retorted Miles bluntly. "Do you want to mark time and take the chance?"

Eff hesitated, then slowly shook his head.

"You're right, Miles," said Luhon. "Time's too short. We've got to experiment. When do you want to try this business of operating the weapons without emotional involvement?"

"Right now," said Miles evenly. "And I'll tell you why. Right now we're all dead tired. It should make it that much easier to damp out our emotional reactions."

Eff laughed. Luhon spun about and sounded the signal throughout the ship that summoned all crew members to their battle stations. The gray-skinned alien gave the slight body twitch that was his symptom of amusement.

"They'll enjoy this," he said. He began announcing Miles' plan to the ship.

Meanwhile, Miles was calling on the computer element of the little ship for another simulated attack of the Silver Horde. It was not merely the rest of the crew that was weary. He, Luhon, and Eff were weary as well. As he lifted the ship from the platform and headed out into the interstellar darkness, he deliberately relaxed the tension that searching for an answer to their problem had built within him, and he felt weariness flood through him like a depressant drug.

It was several hours before they brought the ship back to her platform and had a chance to examine the computer's rating of their performance. It was down, of course, from what they had been scoring, but the interesting thing was that it was several points above what the computer calculated it should be with their weariness fed in as part of the performance equation.

Triumph fought with exhaustion within Miles. He heard Luhon's voice beside him and turned.

"Friend Miles," said Luhon, his eyes burning into Miles, "I think you've found the answer!"

Wearily they straggled off to their bunks. And the whole ship rested.

The next emotionless trial run that they held after that was a fiasco. The rested minds of the twenty-three aboard the *Fighting Rowboat* could not contain their emotional reactions, and the results were wildly spotty—highly successful in the case of some individuals, disastrous in the case of some others. But they kept at it until they had once again reached the stage of weariness they had reached on the first occasion.

With weariness, the individual performances evened out. But the total performance was still less than their previous best. Stubbornly Miles clung to the possibility that, with practice, they would be able to hold their emotions down and break free of the plateau after sufficient practice.

So it finally turned out. By the time the Silver Horde was close enough to show as a small bright dot in the midst of the control room vision screen, the general performance of the twenty-three was well above the earlier plateau and still climbing.

By the time the Silver Horde was identifiable as a small crescent shape in the control room screen the ship's computer showed that they had tripled their fighting effectiveness from what it had been at the plateau level.

It was time, thought Miles, for the Center Aliens to be told. Once the Center Aliens saw what the *Fighting Rowboat* could do, they could no longer reasonably withhold permission for the little ship to join the vessels actually engaging the Silver Horde.

He left word with Luhon of what he intended to do, took the small ship that was parked on the platform, and once more headed in toward the center of the Battle Line.

This time he had not made it even to within sight of the first great globe-shaped ship of the Center Aliens before one of them appeared beside him in the other seat of the little craft he was piloting.

"You have been told once," said the Center Alien calmly, but with a cold note in his voice, "that you were not to leave the immediate neighborhood of your ship and its platform. Such incursions must cease—"

He broke off abruptly and gazed steadily at Miles.

"Oh, I see," he went on in the same calm tone. "So you think that this situation now is somehow different?"

"Not only different but entirely new—for you, as well as us!" said Miles.

"No," said the Center Alien. "That is not possible. It is symptomatic of your lack of knowledge that you think that you might have discovered or produced anything outside our knowledge."

"We've become an effective fighting ship," said Miles slowly, unyielding. "We only ask you to come and see for yourselves."

The alien gazed at him for a moment without speaking.

"Suppose this were true," said the Center Alien. "Suppose that you actually had done the impossible and had qualified for a place among the fighting ships. Do you realize that if you joined in the actual battle, there would be no real possibility your ship could survive even the first contact with the Horde?"

"We understand that," said Miles.

"But still you want to throw your lives away in a gesture that can have little or no profit for you, let alone for the rest of the galaxy?" replied the Center Alien. "That in itself is a reasonless, emotion-laden reaction to a situation too large for you to comprehend. Since your basic reaction is flawed by emotion, how can any improvement that has come out of it be superior to that emotion?"

Miles opened his mouth, but there was no answer immediately ready to his tongue.

"You see," said the Center Alien, and under his hands the small boat turned about and began to head back once more toward the end of the line where the *Fighting Rowboat* waited, "you see yourself how you have stated an impossibility. A creature without wings may practice jumping in the air and flapping his limbs to the point where he can jump higher and flap harder—but this is not flying and never will be."

Miles found his voice at last. His voice and his argument.

"I see," he said, "you're never wrong—not even on a statistical basis?"

"Of course—on a statistical basis, we can be wrong," answered the Center Alien.

"Then there has to be a chance you're wrong about us now," said Miles.

"Of course," replied the Center Alien, "there is always a chance—but a chance too small to merit practical consideration."

"Still," said Miles grimly, "no matter how small that chance is, with the galaxy facing a fight for its life, you owe it to yourself and us at least to examine what we've done, to see if even that infinitely small chance may not be fact."

The Center Alien continued to pilot the little ship onward, back toward the end of the line. But he did not seem to Miles to be thinking so much as communicating with some one or ones elsewhere.

Without warning, Miles found himself no longer in the little ship. Instead, he and a Center Alien in human form, who looked like the same one who had just been sitting beside him in the small craft, now stood in an area—it was hard to call it a room—that was walled and floored and ceilinged with shimmering yellow light. Directly before them in one wall a milky blue and white globe seemed either to float or to spin at an incredible speed.

It hurt Miles' eyes to watch the globe. He looked away toward the steadily flowing yellow light of the wall, which was more bearable. Swarming in suddenly upon the heightened perceptivity that the aliens had given him came an impingement, a feeling of being surrounded on all sides by many minds. All at once he realized that he was inside—literally inside—one of the huge ships of the Center Aliens.

"You will look at—" The last word said by the Center Alien had meanings beyond the ability of Miles' mind to grasp. It translated vaguely in his mind as words like "eye" or "window." But he understood that it was the globe to which the Center Alien referred.

He forced his eyes back to the globe, which caught and held his gaze with a strength and intensity that were so great as to be almost painful. He felt himself, his mind, his memories, everything about him, being some way *examined*.

For a long moment the examination continued. Then, abruptly, it was over. He found himself free to look again at the yellow, flowing light of the walls, which he did gratefully.

"It's settled then," said the voice of the Center Alien beside him. "You will be given the observational test for which you've asked."

Abruptly he was back in the small ship. The Center Alien sat beside him again, and they were still headed back toward the end of the line where the *Fighting Rowboat* waited on her platform.

No, *they* were not headed back. Looking sideways at the Center Alien beside him and feeling the emotional response under the illusory appearance of humanity that clothed him, Miles sensed that this was a different individual from the Center Alien who had first picked him up.

Miles opened his mouth to comment on this and then closed it again. They rode in silence back to the platform where the *Fighting Rowboat* waited.

However, when they left the small ship and Miles started up the ladder into the *Fighting Rowboat,* he became conscious of the fact that the Center Alien was not following him. Turning about, halfway up the ladder, he saw the Center Alien standing still on the platform about a dozen steps off.

"Go ahead," said the Center Alien. "I will observe from here."

Miles went on up the ladder and closed the entrance port of the *Fighting Rowboat* behind him. The air of tension and excitement within struck him like a physical blow. He stalked rapidly through the lounge and into the control room, where Eff and Luhon were already in their seats. Their faces looked a question at him, but he did not answer that question to them, alone. Instead, he sat down in his own seat before the central console and, touching a communications control, spoke to everyone aboard the ship.

"Calm down," he said. "All of you, calm yourselves. We can't put on any demonstration, keyed up the way we are now. I'm giving everybody two minutes to damp down his emotions. Remember we're under observation here, and we're going to be judged from the moment we lift off the platform."

He dropped his finger from the control and sat back limply in his chair, trying to relax. He did not look to either right or left at his two underofficers. Before him on the console, a chronometer marked off those secondlike sections of time which made up intervals roughly analogous to Earth minutes.

As he sat there, Miles could feel his own tension lowering like the red line of the spirit level in a thermometer plunged into ice water on a warm day. Not only that, but—he could feel now—the general air of tension in the vessel was also slipping away. At the end of two minutes those aboard the *Fighting Rowboat* were almost calm.

Miles touched the controls, and the ship lifted. For a moment he wondered how the Center Alien was going to observe them when they would be light-years out from the Battle Line in intergalactic darkness. But that was the Center Alien's worry. He dismissed the thought and put his whole mind to handling the craft.

The emotion of the twenty-three aboard the ship had evaporated now. There was left only the hard purpose—the hard, cold purpose—of their intentness on the exercise. The *Fighting Rowboat* was now a good dozen light-years out in front of the rest of the Battle Line. Miles pressed a control on the console before him. The illusory Silver Horde ships that were the first phase of their battle exercise were produced by the computer on the screen before him and on the screens that were the transparent bubbles enclosing the weapons lining the ship's sides.

Miles' hands leaped over the console before him, and the hands of Luhon and Eff followed him on either side as the small ship flung itself against its smaller, imaginary enemies, some fifteen or twenty of the Silver Horde's scout ships backed up by one of the ships of the Horde's second line, which was several times as large and with many times the firepower. As they closed with the imaginary enemy under Miles' direction, the *Fighting Rowboat* altered direction, using her mobility, which was greater than that of the second-line Horde ship, to keep a screen of Horde scout ships always between herself and the superior weapons of the second-line ship. As she did so, the *Fighting Rowboat's* own weapons flashed outward, killing off the enemy scout ships one by one.

Then, when the number of enemy scout ships was down to only four, the *Fighting Rowboat* turned and fled, having done a maximum amount of damage to the ships she was able to kill, and having held up for a number of precious moments a larger ship that she was not able to destroy. In theory, the Horde second-line ship, delayed in this way, should have been a sitting duck for the larger ships on the galactic side that were able to outgun it. The total effect of the exercise had demonstrated, in theory, an effectiveness in the *Fighting Rowboat* that was better than three times what she had possessed originally.

Glowing with inner triumph, Miles turned the small vessel back toward the platform. Inside him was a sort of quiet pride for the other twenty-two aboard. Not one of them had broken emotional discipline. They had remained as cool-headed and objective about their fighting as—Miles thought—any Center Alien would have done.

They headed back to their platform, but as they approached it and hovered ready to land on it, something materialized below them.

It was a Horde scout ship.

This had not been in the programmed exercise. But reflex took over. Miles hit the alarm control, even as the Silver Horde scout ship leaped into the air from the platform. A sudden explosion of emotion from the rest of the twenty-three—all coolness forgotten—struck Miles like a physical blow, even as their weapons opened fire on the scout ship.

But even as they commenced to fire, the scout ship vanished—and hanging there in space before them was the small, unprotected figure of the Center Alien who had been observing them. His eyes met Miles' through the vision screen—and something like a solid blow seemed to strike Miles from within.

It clove through the reflex of white, raging battle fury within him. It froze him, abruptly paralyzed and with a mind suddenly empty of decision. His hand hovered above the controls but did not drop to touch them.

About him, the weapons of the *Fighting Rowboat* were silent. Miles felt his hands moved then, as if by some outside force.

His fingers descended stiffly on the controls, and he brought the *Fighting Rowboat* back down onto her berth on the platform.

Looking out through his screen, once they were down on the platform, Miles saw the Center Alien standing where he had stood before, obviously waiting. Miles rose from his seat before the console, turned, and walked out alone. Around him and behind him as he left it, the other twenty-two who manned the ship were silent, still in their places, locked there by the shock of defeat. Miles walked down the corridor, out the now-open hatch, and down the ladder, which had slid itself out as the hatch was opened. He approached the Center Alien and stopped only a few feet from him. His eyes met the eyes in the apparently human face of the Center Alien.

"So you see," said the Center Alien coldly. "There are stages to the development of a civilized, intelligent race. Once we too were like you. We had the old, savage instincts still in us. But we came to the point where we could deliberately rid ourselves of those instincts—as you would amputate a diseased limb. And then we went on to develop other skills."

He paused, looking at Miles. Miles could think of nothing to say.

"Naturally," said the Center Alien, "you have the barbarian's instinct to fight when you are attacked. But do not confuse that instinct with *ability* to fight—which, by comparison with ourselves, you do not have."

He vanished. Miles stood numbly staring at the blank platform where the other had stood.

12

On the *Fighting Rowboat*, they had come during their weeks of training to believe that they had improved to the point of being at least half equal to the Center Aliens, individual for individual. Now a Center Alien had stopped all twenty-three of them cold, with nothing more than his own personal psychic force. The effect on the twenty-three was crushing.

It did not matter that he had tricked them, with the appearance of a Horde scout ship where no Horde scout ship should be, into letting loose their primitive emotions of battle lust and fury. For if he could make them betray themselves that easily, it was plain that they would betray themselves before the Horde. They had been tricked into proving their own worthlessness by their own instinctive actions, and the knowledge of that worthlessness lay like a bitterness in the pit of the stomach of each.

Their contempt and anger were not turned against the Center Alien who had made them betray themselves. They were turned against themselves—and against Miles. When Miles returned to the ship after

288

his last words with the Center Alien observer, it was as if he had stepped back into a cage of wild beasts, all prowling about with downcast eyes, apparently not looking at him, but waiting only for the smallest movement or sound on his part that could be used as an excuse for an attack.

Grimly, he gave them no excuse. He knew them now, after these weeks of working together, and he knew that the worst thing he could do at this time would be to urge them to go back on their training. Deliberately, except for Chak'ha, who alone had not deserted him, he ignored them and went back to his self-training at the control console, alone. Day after day he worked there, while the dot that was the Silver Horde grew steadily on the control room vision screen.

And slowly, having nothing else to fight, nothing else to do, the rest of the twenty-three began to return. First Luhon, then Eff, then gradually other members of the crew came to join Miles in the control room, standing behind him and silently watching the screen as he watched it. As Miles had gambled they would, those emotions which had betrayed them as barbarians before the Center Alien observer now began to take hold of them once again whether they wished it or not. For this reaction, too, was predictable and instinctive.

The Silver Horde was plainly visible on the screen in all its numbers now—right down to the last line of rearguard vessels. Those in the control room with Miles watched with him as the individual lines of silver ships, the individual squadrons of the Horde's advance, seemed to surge forward individually, then stop, then surge and stop again. In order, like muscles rippling down the many ribs of a moving snake, the Horde came on by shift steps, moving light-years at a shift, through the dark vastness beyond the galaxy's spiral arm. Already its total fleet filled nearly a hundred and twenty degrees of the hundred and eighty degrees of screen. It was a silver mass, thick at the center and thinning out toward the ends with the tips of its line curving forward like horns, ready to encircle any world or solar system or fleet that offered resistance or sustenance to the millions within its silver ships.

Watching it sent a cold feeling, like a chilling draft, across the back of Miles' neck. By this time the Horde was plainly aware of the Battle Line that was waiting for it and, far from avoiding it, its fleet had clearly altered course to meet the Battle Line head on. Early in the fourth week following the *Fighting Rowboat*'s failure before the Center Alien observer, this shift in course became obvious to Miles, and during the rest of the week it began to penetrate the minds of the rest of the crew.

With that penetration, a strange thing began to happen aboard the *Fighting Rowboat*.

Without consultation, in fact almost with a silent, unanimous consent, the twenty-three began to take up their old duties aboard the ship, and, again without consultation, Miles one day found himself with Eff and Luhon seated on either side of him, lifting the *Fighting Rowboat* once more from the platform for a training session.

They ran through a programmed attack without a flaw, and with no trace of that emotion that had betrayed them at the hand of the Center Alien observer. In fact, there was a new air of cold purpose aboard the ship. They all felt it, but Miles most of all. To him, as leader, it felt as if a powerful hand had been laid between his shoulder blades, shoving him irresistibly forward into rehearsal after rehearsal for the attack that was coming.

In fact, there was a new closeness about them all aboard the *Fighting Rowboat*. The approach of the Horde served to gather up the fragments of their collective spirit and weld it back together again into one solid mass—harder now because it had been tempered by what they had been through.

Their efficiency and potency with the weapons climbed sharply. By the time the Horde was less than a week from decision point—that moment in which retreat would be no longer possible for the ships of the Battle Lines—Miles' rating charts showed the *Fighting Rowboat* to have more than doubled her effectiveness since the time the Center Alien had come to observe them.

"But they'll still never agree to let us fight," said Eff, standing beside Miles as he checked the last point of advance on the chart. "We're still only animals to them. Useful because they can drink our blood before the battle to make themselves strong for it. But aside from that, we're just so many cattle to be left behind when the real action comes!"

"Still, anything can happen," answered Luhon softly from Miles' other side. "Maybe the Horde will decide whether we fight them or not. Maybe the decision won't be up to the Center Aliens once the real fighting starts."

Miles said nothing. But he understood the other two, just as he understood the new, welded singleness of decision of all aboard the *Fighting Rowboat*. The other twenty-two had come to the point he himself had reached a long time ago. They had stopped trying to reconcile the powerful, undeniable feelings burning within them with the cold and distant attitude of the Center Aliens. Now they simply disregarded the fact that the Center Aliens had refused them the right to fight when the battle was

13

Three days until Decision Point.

Two days.

One. Miles got up from his seat before the control console and the vision screen. He walked back through the ship, past the rest of the twenty-two. They sat, silently working with their weapons. Miles went alone out onto the platform.

He looked off into the direction in which the Horde was coming.

But here, to the naked eye, there was nothing to see. The silver ships were still buried in intergalactic darkness, light-years distant and invisible still.

Here there was nothing but the shape of the *Fighting Rowboat,* silent under the distant light of the artificial sun overlooking the Battle Line, and the storage shed, motionless on the glinting metal deck of the platform. Miles looked to his right.

Dimly, off there in airlessness, was a little reflection—a faint gleam from the small ship next to the *Fighting Rowboat.* He turned around.

Behind him stretched the long line of misty

whiteness that was the spiral of the galaxy he was here to defend, now shrunk to a spindle shape, so distant that the shape of the Earth he had come from was more than dwindled into invisibility—it had become a part of a whole.

He turned back to look out again into the darkness where the powerful eye of the vision screen had told him that the Horde was rushing down on him at translight speeds. Just hours and minutes away now—and still invisible to the unaided vision.

He chilled at the massiveness of the scene compared to his own smallness as he stood here between the glowing line of the uncounted stars of his galaxy and the uncounted ships of the invisible Horde—part of one single Battle Line of which his ship was the last and least.

Here, as he stood on the platform by the silent ship, it seemed to him suddenly that none of it was real— Horde, galaxy, or Battle Line. Either that or he had been caught in a dispute between things huge and invisible and placed out here to be crushed by the clash of their meeting. . . .

He turned and went slowly back across the platform, up the ladder, and back into the ship. He went back up the corridor to the control room, where Luhon and Eff still sat in their seats before their controls, gazing at the screen, and he took the empty commander's seat between them.

He looked at the screen.

It had been extended now, curved forward through forty-five degrees at each end to encompass the full picture of the Horde as it was now seen from the viewpoint of their ship in the Battle Line. Now, in the directionless blackness of intergalactic space, it no longer seemed to be coming at them horizontally.

It had expanded to fill the expanded screen horizontally and stretch into the screen additions with the hornlike tips of its forward-curving ends, but it had expanded as well in its middle section to fill the center screen from top to bottom. Now it seemed to be not so much ahead of them as above them, hanging over them, rushing down on them like some great voracious amoeba, pulsing with life in the successive shifts of its successive lines of ships, its horntip arms already stretching forward to enclose them and cut off retreat.

"Those armtips must be level with us now, don't you think?" said Luhon, echoing Miles' own unspoken thought. All of the twenty-three aboard the ship had seemed to think with one mind lately. Luhon punched controls on the console before him, requesting a calculation.

After a moment the result flickered on the small console screen. He touched the wipe-out button.

"Yes," he said. "Theoretically, they've got ships behind us now."

"How long to Decision Point?" asked Miles.

"Five hours, some minutes," said Eff.

Time went by. Now it was just four and a half hours to Decision Point. . . .

Four hours to Decision Point. . . .

Three. . . .

Two. . . .

One hour. Thirty minutes. . . .

"What's the matter with them?" snarled Eff. For once his cheerful, bearlike face was all animal fury. "What are they waiting for? What's going to happen that's new in the next few minutes—"

"*Attention!*" The communications speaker above them broke suddenly into life with the flat, passionless voice of a Center Alien. "Attention! Your weapons are now unlocked, ready to be used. You will leave the Battle Line immediately, head back into the galaxy, and attempt to find a hiding place around or on some world of a system that does not possess organic life. I will repeat that. Your ship's weapon controls and weapons are now unlocked. You are to leave the Battle Line immediately, return to the galaxy, and hide yourselves on some lifeless solar system."

The voice ceased as suddenly as it had begun. So quietly had it spoken, so abruptly had it stopped speaking, that it was a few seconds before Miles and the others were able to react. Then a wave of common emotion—felt along that network of emotional sensitivity that enclosed them all—swept throughout the ship like a silent moan of disbelief and new fury.

"They're sending us away," whispered Luhon. His eyes were glittering. "They can't do that to us."

"That's right," said Miles in a voice he hardly recognized as his own. "They can't!"

He was already busy, jabbing at the call button of the communicator in front of him.

"Answer me!" he snapped into the voice grille of the console before him. "Answer me! I'm calling for an answer!"

But there was no answer. Miles continued to call and jab at the button until at last his hand dropped in defeat.

"They won't answer," he muttered. For a moment he sat without moving; then at a sudden thought, his hand leaped out again to punch for a picture of the Battle Line, stretching away to their right.

It took shape on the screen in front of him. He pulled back the focus until he was able to see several dozen of the ships stretching off to the right. As he watched, one of the ships disappeared—it had gone into shift.

A moment later, the ship only two stations up from the *Fighting Rowboat* also blinked out and disappeared.

Miles felt coldness flood through him on a wave of icy shock.

"They can't be," he muttered to himself. "They can't—"

"Can't what?" snapped Luhon.

But Miles' fingers had jumped once more to the communications section of the console in front of him.

"This is the last ship in line!" Miles was snapping into the microphone grille. "This is the last ship in line, calling the ship sixth up from our position. Are you preparing to leave the Battle Line? Answer me! Are you preparing to leave the Battle Line? If so, why? Why? Answer me—"

"We hear you," interrupted the overhead speaker suddenly in the common language of those aboard the *Fighting Rowboat* but in harsh, unfamiliar accents. "Yes, we are leaving. We are retreating with the rest. Why do you ask?"

"Retreating?" echoed Miles. "Retreating—you mean just we little ships are retreating? Or more than just us?"

"Haven't you been informed?" roared the harsh voice above him. "The Center's computational devices have said that all should save themselves. The devices have calculated and found an answer that predicts defeat if we try to stop the Horde. All are leaving. All—"

The voice was cut off suddenly, as Miles jabbed at both voice and sight communication controls. Abruptly, in the screen before them formed a schema of the whole Battle Line. It showed the line from end to end and the ships in all their sizes and varieties, but as if only a few yards were separating them. As Miles, Luhon, and Eff watched, ships were winking out of existence in that line. Even the huge globular dreadnoughts of the Center Aliens were disappearing.

It was true. After everything—after all their work and the work of the Center Aliens and others to set up this Battle Line—now just because of some cold answer given by a lifeless mechanism, the greatest strength the galaxy could gather was not going to face the Horde after all. They all were going to turn tail and run, save themselves, and let the Horde in to feed on the helpless worlds they had been sent out here to protect.

"My people," breathed Luhon.

His hand flashed out with that fantastic speed of reflex he possessed, and without warning, on the screen before them all was the picture of the Horde again, like some evil, glittering silver amoeba, hanging over them all, reaching out as if to swallow not only the former Battle Line but the whole galaxy behind it in one vast and evil embrace.

Before Miles, in that moment, there also rose up a picture of his people and his world—the world as he had seen it during those last days when he had moved like a ghost from spot to spot about its surface and among its many people. He saw it, and at the same time in his mind's eye he saw the picture of the world that the two Center Aliens had shown him—a world that a million years before had been cleaned to the point of barrenness by the Horde.

In his mind's eye now he saw Earth like that. One endless, horizon-wide strength of naked earth and soil, with nothing left. Everything gone—all gone. The cities, the people within them, their history, their music, their paintings, Marie Bourtel. . . .

"I won't!"

It was more than a verbal shout, it was a roar within the very fibers of his being. A roar of no-saying to all

that the Horde represented and to all that retreat
without any attempt to stop the invaders would mean.
It was an answer to the idea that he, Miles, could go
and hide himself while the Horde swept off, possibly
to do to Earth what it had done to that other, unknown
world a million years ago. There was nothing intellectual or sensible about that great roar of negation that
picked him up body, mind, and soul, like a whirlwind.
It was as deep and basic within him as the ancient,
unconquerable savagery that used to reach out and
destroy the intent of his paintings.

And it was echoed around him through the emotional matrix enclosing the twenty-two other savage
beings who shared this ship with him. Like him, they
were reacting without the need for thought, and there
was now not even a need for consultation.

Miles' hands slapped down on the console in front
of him. To his right, Luhon's flashing gray fingers were
already blurring over his controls, and Eff was busy
at his left.

Like a single living creature, with one mind alone,
the *Fighting Rowboat* lifted from her cradle and
flashed into shift—single-handedly and alone into
attack against the uncountable numbers of the Silver
Horde.

14

Alarm bells shrilled. Signal lights on the board before Miles flared in bright silver warning. On the screen the great rippling mass of the Horde seemed unchanged—but the instruments signaled that the invaders had taken note of the little ship's attack and were even now ponderously beginning to swing about to face this one end of the former Battle Line, from which a lone attacker had come.

The massiveness of that shift in itself had something blindly elemental about it, as if the Horde were actually nothing but some vast amoeba reacting blindly to the presence of prey.

But the *Fighting Rowboat* was closing the distance between her and the nearest of the silvery enemy scout ships at a rate beyond mental calculation. Automatic devices aboard the little boat had taken over now. Each shift was shorter than the one before. With each she was zeroing in on that front line of silver, minnowlike attackers. Shortly the last shift would bring her out at almost a matched velocity and direction. She would then be running side by side with the first wave of scout ships, headed back toward the galaxy.

Meanwhile, aboard the *Fighting Rowboat* a new sense of grim unity thrummed through them all. Not only did they feel one another in the common network of sensitivity. It seemed to Miles that they went beyond this, into the unlocked weapons themselves. The weapons seemed like quasi-living things now; Miles felt them against his mind like the touch of the console keys against his fingertips.

He felt more. Beyond the weapons he felt the ship. Now even she seemed alive, driven by the fury of their response to the alien attack. Like a single cornered animal, the *Fighting Rowboat* hurled herself at the invaders.

The shifts were very small now. They had almost ended. . . . They had ended.

Abruptly, the *Fighting Rowboat* found herself in black space, with the light of the artificial sun that the Center Aliens had hung over the Battle Line dwindling to a tiny bright dot behind her. And around the crew, on instruments and on screen, the scout ships of the Silver Horde finally registered—each one no more than a third the size of the *Fighting Rowboat*, but within the *Fighting Rowboat's* vicinity they numbered in the dozens.

In the light of the distant artificial sun Miles could even see the two closest, as gleams of dull silver, seen briefly, like the soft flash of the pale belly of a fish glimmering for a moment up through deep water.

Miles' hands came down on the controls, and the *Fighting Rowboat* flung herself at the nearest pale gleam.

Now the whole crew was aware of the working psychic elements. Now, through their weapons, they could finally feel the alien minds of the weasel-shaped members of the Horde aboard the nearest scout ships. The consciousness of the aliens was like a small, hard fist pushing back at the strength that enclosed and emanated from the *Fighting Rowboat*.

That bubble of strength flowed over and encapsulated the alien consciousness aboard the scout boats within weapon range. Miles, with the others, felt how they had held the scout members of the Horde willless within their bubble of psychic power.

They had done it. The closer scout ships were drifting helplessly, their crews paralyzed. Luhon's quick fingers danced over the firing-control buttons before him, and from the weapons of the *Fighting Rowboat* pale sighting beams reached out to touch the scout ships—and a second later there stabbed down the center of those sighting beams a force which ripped open the enemy vessels.

The *Fighting Rowboat* struck, and moved, and struck again. . . . Suddenly they were in a little open space. They were through the first line of scout ships.

They had won. At least in this first contact.

A furious feeling of triumph rolled through their network of common sensitivity. They had struck the enemy and lived. Their savage souls exulted at the thought.

But now, plainly before them on the screen and swiftly closing down about them, were the second-line scout ships of the Horde, and these were each half again as big as the *Fighting Rowboat*.

The next contact was one they could not win. But their ancient instincts hurled them forward.

Abruptly then, it happened—for a *third* time to Miles.

As it had when his painting had been stolen and he had climbed the cliff, as it had when he was fighting with Chak'ha, so it happened once more now. He went into hysterical strength. Into overdrive.

Suddenly it was on him again—like a motor, relieved of the governor that had artificially limited its potential power, winding itself up tight to full output. He felt all of one piece, and strength raced through him. Now he knew without thinking about it that the two other beings sitting beside him at the controls would be no match for him in any physical encounter. The Horde had evoked it again in him—this final *overdrive* of strength. It seethed within him. He could almost feel it churning and frothing, searching for the needed physical violence that would provide it with a necessary point of escape.

But there was no such point. His physical strength was not needed here—the ship was his muscles. All that was left for him to do here was push buttons, and that he could have done with the ordinary strength that was in him. His arms and legs ached to be in action, but there was no job for them—only the small, easy tasks they were already doing. A feeling of frustration, wild and furious as a storm at sea, began to build to hurricane force inside him.

All the while, the *Fighting Rowboat* was closing with those larger ships of the Horde which must finally destroy her. And here sat Miles, tapping a great reservoir of strength in himself for which there was no use.

The storm mounted in him. It shook his whole body, so that his arms and legs trembled. His vision blurred. He felt as if he were tearing himself apart with a wild urge to greater action.

The overdrive power boiled within him, like a whirlpool of force, like a circular river seeking an outlet and hemmed in by tall mountains. It raced faster, still faster, seeking an outlet—and then, suddenly, he found it.

It was like a pass through the mountains leading to a higher land. It was a release for the explosive, whirling power building within him—but it was something more. It was, at this last moment before his own certain destruction, that which he had always searched for in his painting. An overdrive of the creative spirit, comparable to the overdrive of hysterical strength in the physical body.

In the same moment in which he recognized this, the pent-up force within him went pouring through its newfound outlet. It flashed through and upward, leaving his body at peace but switching his intellectual centers to an almost unbearable certainty and brilliance. Then, without warning, all strain was over.

The motor wound tight in him suddenly shifted to a higher gear, a gear in which its power was more than sufficient and its speed was limitless. He seemed almost to float because of the new power of perception and thought he controlled.

He glanced about him. The control room of the *Fighting Rowboat* seemed both brighter and smaller. The three-dimensional objects within its metal walls seemed to stand out aggressively, with a sort of supersolidity. He looked back at his two companions and found that even the flying fingers of Luhon seemed to have slowed.

To Miles, they had slowed. It was not as if his perception of time had altered, but as if it had *sharpened* to an intense degree. He was able to observe leisurely in one second what it might once have taken him sixty seconds to observe. But he was aware that literal time had not lengthened. Instead, it was as if his perception of it had become microscopic, so that now he could see sixty smaller divisions within the second and make as much use of each of these as he had been able to make the whole second before.

At the same time, his imagination and understanding went soaring. In one great sweeping rush, they integrated him with the rest of the crew aboard the *Fighting Rowboat*, rushing in self-intoxicated fury upon the death that was the multitudinous enemy of the Silver Horde, with the Battle Line that had been, with the Center Aliens who had set it up— with all and everything in time past and time present, from the historic moment in which the Horde had passed through the galaxy once before up through the coming of the aliens to Earth and the present moment.

In that creative moment of understanding he achieved an understanding of it all: overdrive, his fellow crew members, the Center Aliens, everything. It was as if a man might stretch out his arm to encircle a whole universe and lock his fingers together on its farther side. It was an understanding too big for one single concept of explanation. It was a whole network of comprehensions working together.

"Join up!" he shouted into the intercom of the ship. At the same moment, he opened a channel for the overdrive power that was now in him into the network of sensitivity that encompassed them all. It flooded forth.

And the other twenty-two members of the crew felt, recognized, and absorbed it.

Like flame racing along lines of high-octane fuel, the fire of his overdrive power flashed out and kindled overdrive fires in the awarenesses of his crewmates. Like him, they flared with a new, fierce heat, and the fire spread from them to their weapons. Like sun-dried driftwood, the psychic elements of their weapons took flame.

And from those weapons the fire reached forth in the shape of a many-times-multiplied psychic strength to capture and paralyze the new wave of the enemy now closing about them.

Miles felt it through the network of their composite sensitivity aboard the *Fighting Rowboat*—like the sudden tautening of a heavy cable mooring some massive ship to a dock. It tautened and held. Their globe of psychic force was secure. It reached out well beyond the extreme range of the weapons aboard the ships of the Silver Horde that now flocked toward it, holding all the enemy within its perimeter helpless while the physical weapons of the tiny *Fighting Rowboat* tore at and destroyed them, one by one.

A wild joy swept them all. Here, where they should have been destroyed themselves, they were winning. For a moment it seemed to them all that they were invincible, that they could hold off and destroy the whole Silver Horde by themselves. But then the steadily mounting pressure against their psychic hold, as more and more of the silver vessels drove in on them, brought them to a more sober understanding.

As long as they could keep their present strength, they were invincible. As the Center Alien had explained to Miles earlier, the ships of the Battle Line could not be touched by the physical weapons of the enemy as long as their psychic strength endured. But either weariness or too many of the enemy pressing in on them at once could end that strength. For the moment they were winning. But they could not win forever. . . .

"Never mind that!" shouted Miles over the intercom. "We're *winning*! That's what counts! Keep it up. We're stopping the Horde—*we're stopping the Horde!*"

They fought on. The fire of their overdrive burned seemingly unquenchable under the increasing attack, like the unquenchable flame of a welding torch, burning even underwater. But that flame was consuming the reserves of strength in their minds and bodies like a potent chemical stimulant that pushed tiredness away for a while, but only at the expense of exhausting bodily reserves that should not ordinarily be tapped.

Time passed. They fought and slew the Silver Horde. . . .

But the end was in sight now. They were not yet weakening, but the larger scout ships and even some of the light-cruiser-class ships of the Horde were beginning to push against their globe of psychic combination. Aboard the *Fighting Rowboat,* they were still many times more powerful than they should have been. But they were like a giant of a man holding shut a door against the onslaught of an avalanche. At first he holds the door shut easily against the onslaught of the rocks and boulders, but gradually these begin to pile up their weight against his shield. Heavier and heavier—until the whole weight of the mountain begins to lean against him. And against a mountain no flesh and blood can stand.

So Miles and all those aboard the *Fighting Rowboat* felt the breaking point near. Any moment now the final element of pressure would be added, their shield would crumble, and all at once the force of ten thousand weapons of the invaders would tear the little *Fighting Rowboat* to nothingness. But there was no sadness in them. Instead there was a sort of deep-lying, grim joy, like the joy of a wolf who goes down in his last fight with his jaws still locked around the throat of his enemy.

"Hold on," muttered Miles, to himself as much as to the other twenty-two he addressed over the ship's intercom. "Hold on. Keep holding a little longer—"

Sudden and thunderous, roaring without warning at them not only from the speaker in front of Miles, but from every metal strut and metal surface of the ship, unexpectedly came the voice of a Center Alien.

"Get back!" it roared. "Back to your place in the Battle Line! We're taking over the fight now!"

Miles was not conscious of having touched the communication controls before him. But suddenly on the screen there was no longer the image of the many silver ships of the Horde pressing in on them.

Instead, he saw a larger view of the battle. The little pocket of inviolate space that the *Fighting Rowboat* had maintained around herself was now only part of a larger scene in which the front line of the Horde swirled, boiled, and retreated before the advance of a line of different ships. It was the great globular dreadnoughts of the Center Aliens and their allies come at last, after all, into the battle.

15

"Back!" roared the communications speaker. "Back to your place in the Battle Line—"

The great round, planetary shape of the nearest dreadnought was shouldering before the *Fighting Rowboat* now, obscuring three-quarters of the view of the Horde in the screen before Miles. But it was already too late. Even as the voice blared at them through the communications speaker, some mighty blow struck the tiny vessel with irresistible force—and it seemed to Miles that he went flying sideways off into nothingness.

He came back to consciousness gradually, but with a strange determination and effort, like a miner who had been trapped by a rockfall, and picking his way back to freedom, seeing the first small gleam of daylight as the last rock sealing him in tumbled aside.

From that first gleam of mental daylight, Miles swiftly returned to awareness. He found himself seated in his chair before the control console, in a *Fighting Rowboat* that felt strangely still and peaceful. In fact, through the skin of the ship itself, with that sensitivity that had come on him with overdrive during the attack, Miles knew the little ship lay once more on her platform back where it had all started.

With that realization, he switched his attention to observing the silent control room about him. The room and the motionless figures of Eff and Luhon were absolutely still. But, he discovered, so was he. His mind might be awake, but his body was asleep.

Understanding suddenly, a silent chuckle formed in the back of his mind. He recognized his condition now. He was in the grip of that same tranquilizing power which had ended all fights aboard the *Fighting Rowboat* before the Horde appeared. The only difference between the occasions when it had held him before and the present one was the fact that on mental overdrive he was apparently able to keep the sedative effects from the thought centers of his brain.

Examining himself more closely, he observed that the tranquilizing effect rolled like thick fog around the conscious center of his mind but could not enter, because of the fierce flame of his desire to be conscious which tore the fog to tatters. At the touch of that overdrive fire in him the tranquilizing fog was evaporated, so that his consciousness occupied a little clear spot, like the clear spot surrounding a hunter crouched by his morning fire in a mist-choked swamp.

Weighing the situation, Miles suspected that he could even free his physical body and have freedom of movement. And this was interesting—for he had some time since decided that the tranquilizing effect was only another version of the psychic weapon used to paralyze the Horde. Clearly, it was possible that, in overdrive and with some practice and effort, he might even be able to defy the psychic weapon himself.

But there was no point in making the effort to test his powers now. He turned his attention back to the reason for his being under tranquilization.

He freed his neck and eyes enough to be able to look down at his body. He saw that he had been stripped of nearly all his clothing. On the arms, legs, and body now revealed he saw several wounds, already closed. Only two wounds on his leg were still open—and even these were not bleeding. They seemed to be held by some invisible, interior bandage. As he watched, one of them slowly closed from the bottom upward—as if an invisible zipper were being drawn up the length of the slash. A moment later his other cut closed as well. Clearly, some unseen mechanism was at work "repairing" him, but his conscious mind took note that the curious part of it all was that his healing process, while directed from the outside, seemed to be effected by the natural response of his own body.

He looked about the rest of the room. Eff and Luhon were also stripped and in the process of being healed. The room itself was damaged—but in a strange way. There were no holes in the walls—either of the hull or of the partitions within the ship that made up the walls and ceiling of the control room. But here and there these metal inner surfaces had flaked off in jagged shards less than two inches thick at their centers but with knifelike edges.

His brilliantly burning mind jumped immediately to an understanding. Of course—whatever weapon the Horde used would be designed for the end purpose of the Horde. It would want to kill the edible bodies of its enemies, but without rendering them inedible or spilling them out of their ships to be lost in the dark vastness of interstellar space.

Miles looked back at the vision screen before him.

There he saw the full panorama of the battle still in progress. The glittering, new-moon image of the silver invading fleet, and the hornlike tips of its line curving forward and inward, had now changed shape. Those curving arms had now swung further inward, to enclose the attacking ships of the Battle Line.

Once more Miles was reminded of the image of a monstrous amoeba attempting to engulf and absorb some edible morsel. Just so, the silver fleet had gathered into itself the globe-shaped battle formation of the ships of the Battle Line. Around that globe the ships of the Horde were now swarming, enclosing the galaxy's ships completely. What Miles viewed now was a roughly oval shape with a large bulge in the middle.

Miles looked at the battle, which, because of its vastness of scale, both in the number of ships engaged and in the amount of space they occupied, seemed on the screen to be taking place in slow motion. In slow motion and on a microscopic, rather than a telescopic, scale, for all the light-years of distance involved and the thousands-of-miles-per-second velocities of the individual ships. Suddenly there exploded in Miles a fierce hunger to know how it was going—the battle as seen by the Center Aliens and the others within that globe of space, now covered thickly and hidden from him by the swarming silver ships of the Horde.

The hunger gave birth to the means. Immediately the fiercely burning energy of overdrive within him seemed to light up one small corner of his awareness, and he discovered there a tendril of feeling, a connection with the network of sensitivity which was now in existence out there in the midst of the boiling fleet of Silver Horde vessels.

He seized on that trace and followed it. It grew as he

searched along it—and suddenly he found what he hunted. He was locked, emotionally and mentally, into the network of sensitivity which joined together the ships and crews of all those in the Battle Line.

His point of view was central. It seemed to him that he existed at the very center of that vast globe of interior space held by the ships of the galaxy. Here there was no light at all, but in his mind's eye he saw it all as if everything were brightly lit—as if he stood at the center of a sun which illuminated everything.

Around him was space. Beyond this was an invisible globular shell of defensive power, held together by points spaced regularly about its surface—points which were the ships of the Battle Line. Beyond this shell for a depth of several thousand miles were helpless ships of the Horde, in a thick layer—their vessels only a few miles apart, so great was the density. Aboard those invader ships was silence. Their crews were paralyzed and still, held helpless by the psychic force and awaiting the busy scythes of the powerful physical weapons projecting from the Battle Line ships. These weapons were sweeping back and forth like searchlights, to explode—almost to disintegrate— every solid object they touched.

Outside this shell of helpless invader ships was the rest of the Silver Horde, pressing inward, trying desperately to overload the psychic mass potential of the Battle Line fleet. As Miles watched, that pressure grew until it threatened to overload the Battle Line fleet and tear apart not only the buffer-zone layer of helpless Horde ships, but also the formation of Battle Line ships beneath.

But just as overload threatened, an order pulsed outward over the network of sensitivity from whatever vessel or group of vessels among the Center Aliens commanded the rest. Abruptly the shell of defended space shrank. Suddenly the Battle Line ships were that much closer together. The surface they defended was decreased proportionately, and the layer of helpless invader ships standing in the way of the rest of the Horde that had hoped to nose in among them was that much thicker.

With the decrease in size came a proportional increase in power. The nut that the Silver Horde was attempting to crack had become smaller but denser.

The fight went on. . . .

Still the Silver Horde pressed in on the fleet it was attempting to annihilate and absorb. Like endless numbers of grasshoppers smothering a fire with their first hungry approaching waves so that those behind could enter green fields that fire defended, the Horde kept crowding in on the englobed Battle Line fleet. The pressure mounted.

Once more, swiftly, the Battle Line fleet shrank its defended space.

Once more the Battle Line ships acquired new strength. Once more the layer of paralyzed invader ships about them was increased. Still the Horde pressed in on them. . . .

Once again they decreased their defensive area and the area of their perimeter.

Now, to the eyes of Miles' physical body seated before the vision screen of the console back aboard the *Fighting Rowboat,* the shape of the Horde was nothing but one large ball of silver maggotlike shapes completely hiding those they attacked. Anyone who had not known that the Battle Line was trapped within that seething mass, thousands of miles in diameter, must have believed that there was nothing left but the Horde itself. Or that the battle, if there had been one, was already won. Only Miles' linkage with the sensitivity network allowed him to know that the combat still went on.

It had now reached the point of deadlock. The uncountable numbers of the Horde were jammed as tightly as they safely could be about a linked fleet of Battle Line ships that had shrunk to what was its smallest practical diameter of defended space.

Like two massive organisms entangled in a motionless, straining struggle for life or death, the Battle Line and the Silver Horde clung, locked together. It was the sort of straining deadlock which, between human wrestlers, could not have existed for more than a matter of minutes without one opponent or the other giving way in exhaustion. But so massive were the antagonists wrapped in their death struggle beyond the spiral arm of the galaxy that this deadlock continued not for minutes but for hours. And for hours—which seemed like minutes—Miles endured with it, while around him Eff, Luhon, and the others returned to consciousness and began to move around the *Fighting Rowboat*.

They did not speak to Miles. Just as his sensitivity continued linking him with the network of the encompassed Battle Line, so their sensitivity to him had continued. They were aware that he was somehow *with* the battle out there on their screens in a way that they could not be. So they moved about him silently and left him in silence to endure with those who still fought on, hidden by the Horde.

Miles was only peripherally aware of his crewmates. Almost all his awareness was concentrated on the network of sensitivity of the embattled ships. About their globe the Silver Horde was still clustered—and the deadlock continued as if it would never break.

Then, abruptly, it broke.

Suddenly the physical eyes of Miles, watching in the vision screen aboard the *Fighting Rowboat*, saw something that must have begun to happen some moments before but which was now becoming apparent. The Horde swarm enclosing the ships of the Battle Line was no longer globe-shaped. Instead, it was beginning to bulge at one end, becoming faintly pear-shaped. Now, as Miles concentrated his attention on that bulging end, he saw that the bulge was growing, was stretching out—was, in fact, pulling off from the mass surrounding the ships of the Battle Line. Now, as he watched with a perception that speeded up the slow motion imposed on the battle action by the vast units of time and space involved, the bulge began to thin out to a point, stretching away from the fighting ships of the galaxy and away from the galaxy itself.

Slowly the line of fleeing invader ships lengthened and thickened. The awareness of their retreat pulsed through Miles back into the sensitivity network of the still-enclosed Battle Line, and the knowledge was received there like a trumpet call of victory—but the fight went on.

Because, for the englobed ships of the Battle Line, the battle was not yet over. Those silver ships still just without the layer of paralyzed invader vessels continued to fight blindly to move in and overwhelm the defenders. It would be long hours yet—perhaps several days—before the Battle Line dared break its defensive formation.

But outside, as seen on the vision screen of the *Fighting Rowboat*, the shifting shape of the invading fleet continued to lengthen and withdraw, pulling away from its engagement with the Battle Line and forming a new sickle shape headed away from the galaxy.

The invaders had been turned from their feeding ground. The Silver Horde, which no one had been able to stop a million years ago, had now been stopped and averted from its goal. The galaxy, the stars of home, the Earth itself were saved.

16

There was no darkness aboard the egg-shaped craft that was transporting all twenty-three of the *Fighting Rowboat*'s crew to the command ship of the Center Aliens, but Miles had the feeling that if it had been dark, Luhon's eyes would have glowed in the obscurity like the fierce eyes of a cat in the night.

"We shamed them into it!" Luhon said almost in a whisper in Miles' ear. "When we talk to them, friend Miles, remember that! They'd decided to run, but when we attacked, we shamed them into coming back to fight!"

Miles said nothing. Within him was an awareness that both the problem and its resolution had been wider and deeper than Luhon or any of the others understood. But there was no time for him to explain this to them. Luhon's words still echoed in his ear even as the gray ship transporting them seemed to melt away, and they found themselves apparently hanging in space at the midpoint of the interior of one of the huge Center Alien vessels.

They hung or stood there like bodies at a point where gravity balanced in all directions. It was a little like being in a fun house full of distorting mirrors. For looking about casually, Miles could see that they were literally miles in every direction from the interior surface of the globe shape surrounding them. They were too far away to make out the fact of what was abnormally and immediately apparent to them— that the whole interior surface of this globe was filled with individuals of the Center Alien race and their allies. It was as if an auditorium were to be built in the shape of some huge ball, with seats completely covering its inner surface.

When Miles glanced generally at the interior of the globe surrounding him, he saw only a blurred grayness in the far distance, illuminated by a light that seemed to be nowhere in particular but filling all the interior space equally. However, when he looked directly at any one spot on the interior globe face, it was as if some telescopic window had suddenly materialized between him and that point. All at once he was staring into the faces of the aliens seated or standing there, as if no more than ten or a dozen feet separated them from him.

Clearly, this gathering was in honor of the crew of the *Fighting Rowboat*. But, clearly also, the occasion was something more than a mere celebration. Miles felt, with his new sensitivity, a puzzlement reaching out toward them from the surrounding audience. He and his crewmates were being viewed with a strange curiosity and no little lack of understanding.

Suddenly they were joined at their midpoint position by two of the Center Aliens. To Miles' eyes, these still wore human forms. But he was understanding enough now to realize that while he saw them in this fashion, Luhon would be seeing them with the shape and features of Luhon's race—and so on, individually and differently with each one of the rest of the crew.

Miles reached back into his own mind for support, and the now-familiar overdrive reaction abruptly flowed through him, making his vision sharp and clear. Deductions clicked in his mind like totals on an efficient adding machine. The two Center Aliens who had appeared looked no different than all the others he had seen, but the deductive section of his mind told him that they must be different. These two would not have been chosen at random to stand and talk to the crew of the *Fighting Rowboat* before the eyes of the—was it hundreds of thousands or millions?—that occupied the inner surface of the globe, watching them. No, it was more likely—in fact, it was almost a certainty— that these two were as close to being the supreme authorities among the Center Aliens as any of that race available here and now.

A nudge of Luhon's elbow against Miles' ribs reminded him of the other side of the equation. Luhon was waiting for Miles to speak, because Miles was their leader aboard the *Fighting Rowboat*. But Luhon, like the rest, was fiercely expecting that Miles would charge the Center Aliens with cowardice. The gray-skinned alien was waiting for Miles to remind the Center Aliens that they had fled the Battle Line, had run, and that the battle would have been lost if it had not been for the suicidal wild attack of the *Fighting Rowboat*.

Miles, through a mind that was as clear as a perfect lens held up to a powerful light, saw himself caught between the points of view of two groups, neither of which really understood what had happened.

"We have brought you here to do you honor," said the taller of the two Center Aliens. Deductively, for all the lack of variance of feature in this one, as in the others of his race, Miles judged him to be old—probably very old. Once more Luhon's elbow bored sharply into Miles' side.

"Thank you," said Miles. "We appreciate the fact that you want to honor us. But there's a question we want to ask you—all of you."

"Ask anything you wish," replied the Center Alien, and Miles could feel the millions of individual minds all around them, as if the distance at which they were was at once hundreds of miles and only a few feet away, focusing their attention on him and on the question to come.

"Why did you come back?" Miles asked. "You told us that there was no hope of winning the battle. But after we attacked alone, it seems you changed your minds. Of course, we all know the results. The Silver Horde was driven off. But what are we supposed to think about your actions, first running and then returning? Were you wrong in your first judgment of how the battle would go? Or did the sight of us attacking alone make you more aware of your own responsibilities to stand and fight?"

There was no immediate answer to Miles' question. The two Center Aliens stood looking at him as if they were consulting silently with the uncountable numbers that surrounded them, watching. Finally, the taller one spoke again.

"Forgive me," said the Center Alien, "if I seem to insult you by mentioning once more your barbarian condition. But if you were not so primitive and emotion-driven, you would have understood by now why we came back. The fault is ours, of course, being the older and more capable people, for not realizing you had not understood."

"Then perhaps you'll explain it now," said Miles.

"Of course," said the Center Alien. "May I remind

you that it was not an organic decision—our conclusion that our joining battle with the Silver Horde could only result in our defeat? It was a computed decision, the logical result of many factors considered and handled by nonliving devices which are far superior to the aggregate decision-making possibilities of even *our* minds. The factors of the situation were made available continually to these computational devices. At Decision Point, their assessment was plain. The Horde had a tiny but undeniable edge in the total of probability factors needed for victory. We could not logically hope to fight them and win. Therefore, we made the only sensible alternative decision: that all those within the Battle Line should flee and attempt to save themselves as well as possible, in order to have the largest possible number of intelligent, technologically trained individuals with which to rebuild the galaxy after the Horde had passed."

"But you changed your minds," said Miles.

"No," answered the Center Alien. "We are advanced beyond the point where we could, as you say, change our minds—make an emotional judgment at variance with the results of our computations. We came back, not because we 'changed our minds,' but because new computations gave us a different answer."

"New computations?" demanded Miles.

"Of course," replied the Center Alien quietly. "I imagine even you can understand that by attacking as you did, you could introduce a change into the factors on which a judgment of the battle's outcome had been figured. Three matters of sheer chance affected the present situation and altered the future picture built on that situation. First, here was the fact that you had suicidally, and against all reason, chosen to attack alone against the total might of the Horde. Second, there was the fact that your attack came from what had been the farthest end of our Battle Line.

Third, there was the fact that reacting with the instinct of their race, the total fleet of the Silver Horde began to turn to meet your attack instead of ignoring it and allowing it to be absorbed, and yourselves obliterated, by the smallest fraction of its number necessary to deal with you. These things, as I say, altered the factors of the situation. Now I am sure you understand."

Beside Miles, Luhon's elbow no longer urged him on. With his sensitivity, Miles could feel the other crew members, behind him, baffled but equally spellbound.

"Perhaps. But explain it to me anyway," said Miles.

"If you wish. You have earned whatever explanation you desire," said the Center Alien. "As I said, your illogical, suicidal attack altered the factors of the situation—not only to our view, but evidently to the Horde's as well. Your attack, alone, must have been something they could not understand, so that they expected the worst and turned their full strength to crush you. Our devices recomputed and found, as a result, that where before the slight but decisive edge of advantage had been in favor of the Horde, now because of your action there was an equally slight but decisive edge of advantage in our favor."

The Center Alien paused. Miles could feel all the eyes within that huge globe on him and his companions.

"So," the Center Alien went on with the same unvarying tone of voice, as if he were discussing something of no more importance than the time of day, "we came back and engaged the Horde after all."

For a moment, within Miles' brilliantly burning mind, a faint flicker of guilt awoke. With an ability to understand that he would not have had if he had not been in overdrive, he read clearly and sharply some of the meanings behind the Center Alien's words. The individuals of this race, for all their lack of apparent emotion, wanted to live as badly as he did. Also, while their decisions were governed by their computing devices, they had no means of knowing whether that computation was ultimately correct or not. They had only known that the answer they got was the best that could be gotten within their power and the power of their computers. So, just as they had fled without shame—but undoubtedly with as deep an inner pain at the thought of what they were doing in abandoning their worlds to the onslaught of the Horde—they had returned without question. They had returned with as deep an inner courage as was possible to them, to enter a battle which they could not be sure they would win.

Miles felt Luhon stir against him. There was a quality of indecisiveness in that movement that announced that the gray-skinned crewmate was cut adrift from his earlier fierce desire to make the Center Aliens admit to cowardice. Now it was plain they could not be taken to task at all in the sense that Luhon and the others had envisioned. For they had done nothing, after all, but be true to their own different pattern of behavior.

"Thank you," said Miles. "Now we understand."

"We are glad you understand," said the taller Center Alien. "But since this is a moment for understanding, there is something we would like to ask you."

"Ask away," said Miles, already expecting what was to come.

"Of all who joined us in the Battle Line," said the Center Alien, "you twenty-three were the only ones who did not obey our order to retreat and save yourselves. Instead, you did a clearly reasonless thing. You attacked the Silver Horde alone. Yet all of you are thinking beings, though primitive. You must have realized that nothing you could do would make any difference to the question of whether your native worlds and peoples would escape or survive the Horde once it was among the stars of our galaxy. Also, you must have known that by no miracle whatsoever could your one tiny ship so much as slow down the advance of the Horde for a moment. In short, you knew that attacking them could do no good, that it was only a throwing away of your own lives. Older and many times advanced over you as we are, we should understand why you would do such a thing. But we do not. Alone, with no hope, why did you attack the Horde the way you did? Was there some way you could guess that by attacking, you would bring the rest of us back to join you in fighting after all?"

It struck Miles then, with the clarity of his overdrive-sharpened mind, that this was the first time he had ever heard one of the Center Alien race ask a question. Obviously this could mean only one thing. It must have occurred to this advanced race that the only reasonable possibility was that Miles and the others had some means of calculating the battle odds within their own minds and bodies which was superior to the calculating devices the Center Aliens themselves used.

"No," answered Miles. "We didn't expect you back. We knew we were attacking the Horde on our own, and we knew what had to happen if we met them alone."

"Yes," said the Center Alien. There was a second of silence. Then he went on—to Miles' extrasensitive perceptions, it sensed, a little heavily. "We were almost certain that you could not have expected help. But, seeing you did not expect help, the question remains of why you did it."

"We had no choice," said Miles.

"No choice?" The Center Alien stared strangely at him. "You had a clear choice. Your choice was to leave, as you had been ordered to do."

"No," said Miles.

Once more he was conscious of standing between two points of view: the point of view of the Center Aliens and that of his crewmates—neither of whom fully saw and understood the situation and what had taken place in their meeting with the Horde. It was up to Miles now to satisfy them both, even if he could make neither understand what he now understood.

"Maybe it's because, as you say, we're primitive compared to the rest of you in the Battle Line," said Miles slowly. "But our choice wasn't a head choice, it was a heart choice. I don't believe I can explain it to you. I can only tell you that it's that way—with us. You can't take people like myself and those here with me, who care for their own races, and set them out between those races and an enemy who threatens utter destruction—and then expect that we whom you set there will be able to step aside, leaving our people unshielded, simply because logic dictates that we're going to lose if we try to fight the destroyer."

He paused. From the beginning the huge globeful of watchers had been silent, and there was no more silence now than there had been before. Yet Miles felt a certain extra focusing of attention on him, a metaphorical holding of the breath by the hundreds of thousands or millions who were listening. He went on.

"Probably," he said, "there's no way for me to make you understand this. But in running away without fighting the Horde, we were leaving our people—probably to die. And we couldn't do that. We aren't built that way—so that we can cold-bloodedly save ourselves if they're likely to be wiped out. To save ourselves under those conditions would have required a self-control greater than any of us has."

Once more he paused. The globeful of listeners still listened.

"Our peoples," Miles said, slowly, "are part of us, you see—the way our arms and legs are parts of our body. We couldn't any more abandon them just to save ourselves than we could coolly submit to cutting off all our arms and legs so that the useless trunks of our bodies would be left to survive. If our people had to face death, the least we could do—not the most, but the *least*—was to face that death with them. It wasn't any thinking decision we made. I repeat, it was an instinctive decision—to kill as many of the Horde as we could before we were killed. It wasn't any different for us than if we'd come back and found our planets turned to desert, our people dead—and *then* we'd run into the Horde. Then, just as we did here, we'd have tried without thinking to kill as many of the Horde as we could before we were killed ourselves."

Miles stopped talking. The silence that followed his words this time was a long one. But at last it was broken by the taller of the two aliens standing with the crew of the *Fighting Rowboat* at midpoint.

"We were right originally then," said the Center Alien slowly. "It was a part of your primitive nature that caused it—and we could not understand, because it is a part we have long abandoned. You are still on that early road from which we departed a very long time ago. Do not think, though, that we are less grateful to you because of what you have just told us."

He turned a little so that his gaze was directly on Miles. The Center Alien seemed almost to speak directly and privately to Miles.

"No matter from what source it sprang," said the

Center Alien, "from will or mind or instinct, the fact remains that what you did changed the battle picture and resulted in our saving our galaxy. What can we do for you and these others to show our gratitude?"

Miles had been prepared for the question. Now he answered quickly before any of the others from the *Fighting Rowboat* could speak up.

"We want to stay independent," said Miles, "and much of what you could give us might not be good for that independence. But there are a few things. . . . Now that we've been brought together aboard the *Fighting Rowboat,* we'd like our races to stay in touch. So give us ships then, or show us how to build our own ships, so that our twenty-three different races can communicate and travel among our separate worlds."

"The ships and the knowledge you ask for are yours," said the Center Alien. He hesitated. "And if in the future you should want more than this from us, we will arrange a method of communication so that you need only ask."

"Thanks," said Miles. "But I don't think we'll be asking."

17

The summer sun of a later year was sinking toward the hours of late afternoon above the high banks of the Mississippi River by the University of Minnesota campus when the envoy from that race called (by themselves) the *Rahsesh* alighted from a government car at the edge of a road on the west bank of the river. Before the envoy, humans in plain clothes guarded a small section of green lawn that run outward a short distance to the edge of a bluff. Recognized by the guards, in his personal and diplomatic capacities, the alien envoy was admitted through their lines. He went alone across the grass to where a man stood with his back turned, painting on a large canvas set up on a heavy easel. A brown-haired girl sat quietly in a camp chair near him, reading.

The painter was in light slacks and white shirt with sleeves rolled up. Smears of gray, blue, and yellow paint were on his bared forearms, on his hands and fingers, and the canvas before him was heavy with wet paint of many colors. The envoy from the *Rahsesh* went swiftly, smoothly, and quietly up to stand at his elbow.

"Am I interrupting you, friend Miles?" he asked the painter.

"No," Miles shook his head without looking around. "I'm all done, Luhon. I'm just putting a little polish on a last few sections. You've met my wife, Marie?"

She raised her head to smile at Luhon before returning to her book.

"No. I'm honored to meet her," said Luhon. "Continue with your occupation, friend Miles, I can wait."

"No, go ahead. Talk." said Miles, still without turning. "Do you know you're the first one in? None of the rest of our old crew from the *Fighting Rowboat* has got to Earth yet."

"They'll be along shortly, I'd guess," said Luhon. "Did each of the races pick its former representative to be its envoy? It occurred to me that there might be races which might want to send someone else."

"Not for this meeting," said Miles. His brush point placed yellow color lightly on the canvas. "Each of our twenty-three races needs all the understanding it can get about the others, and that sort of understanding is possible only through someone who already knows the rest of us. In fact, I said as much in the message I sent around to the other races. You must have noticed my recommendation to that effect in the letter I sent the *Rahsesh*."

"I noticed," replied Luhon, gazing at the canvas with some small interest and curiosity. "But it occurred to me that perhaps the recommendation was special in my case."

"No," said Miles.

For a few seconds neither one said anything. Miles worked away at his painting.

"You know, friend Miles," said Luhon thoughtfully, "when the Center Aliens asked you, after the battle with the Silver Horde, what we all wanted in the way of reward, you answered him without talking it over with the rest of us first."

"That's right," answered Miles, painting.

"And now," murmured Luhon, "here you've called a meeting of all of us on your world, speaking for all our races—again all on your own. Also, that notice you sent around, friend Miles, didn't say especially what we all were getting together to discuss."

"It said," said Miles, "that what we were going to discuss would at first be understandable only to those who, like we twenty-three, had had experience with the Center Aliens and the Silver Horde."

"True," said Luhon, "and that was enough to satisfy my government—and, I suppose, those who govern the other twenty-one races. But is it going to be satisfactory to the twenty-three of us, when we all come face to face again, I ask you, friend Miles?"

"All right. You've asked me," answered Miles, and paused to squint at the descending sun sending its rays slanting now across university buildings, trees, river bluffs, and river—the entire scene of Miles' painting. "And you've made a point of coming early, to be sure that you'd be the first to ask me."

"I was your second-in-command," Luhon reminded him mildly.

"True," said Miles, straightening up and stepping back from the canvas, brush in hand, to get a longer perspective at what he was doing. "All right, friend Luhon. I'll give you your answer. I've called us all together again here to begin making plans for the day when it'll be our turn, eventually, to take over control of the galaxy from the Center Aliens."

His words sounded calmly on the warm summer air.

But they were received by Luhon in a silence that stretched out and out.

Miles went on, unperturbed, examining his canvas. He stepped forward once more and began to make a few more tiny alterations on it with the yellow-tipped number ten brush he still held. Finally, behind him, Luhon spoke again.

"I have my people to think of," said Luhon slowly. "If you've become mentally unreliable, friend Miles, I'll put off whatever friendship and allegiance I had to you and so inform the rest of the twenty-two—crewmates and races alike."

"That's up to you," said Miles. "Meanwhile, why don't you think a little about what I've just said? I didn't say anything about taking over from the Center Aliens tomorrow, or next year, or even a thousand years from now. I said that we'd be taking over eventually—and we needed to start talking about that eventuality now."

"Have you forgotten"—Luhon's voice was almost a whisper—"the number of Center Alien ships in the Battle Line? Have you forgotten the number of Center Aliens that each of those great ships must have held? And what *one* Center Alien was able to do to our whole ship and crew? Can you imagine how many like him there must be, and the number of worlds they must occupy, in toward the galaxy's center? Can you imagine all that and the thousands of years of technological advantage they must have over us—and still say what you're saying?"

"That's right. I can," said Miles flatly, putting his brush away finally into a jar of muddy turpentine standing on a small table to the left of his easel. "Because it isn't numbers or technology that're the true measure of a race. We found that out when the Horde attacked."

"Did we, friend Miles?" Luhon's eyes narrowed to dark lines in his gray face.

"I'm reminding you," said Miles, "that the Center Aliens failed the rest of the galaxy in the moment of the attack of the Horde. I didn't think you'd forget that."

"Forget? No," replied Luhon slowly. His eyes widened once more.

"Think!" said Miles, turning for the first time to face him. "Nothing shrinks faster with time than the memory of a great struggle. Right now, my race has been completely shaken up, awakened, by its escape from the Horde. But the generation remembering this, the one that shared consciousness with me out there on the Battle Line, isn't going to live forever. How much will its grandchildren remember?"

He paused, staring at Luhon.

"Not—not much," said Luhon, hesitantly. "If your people are like mine, forgetfulness will take the edge off memory, in time. That's true. . . ."

"Of course it's true!" said Miles. "In a hundred years they'll start forgetting that we didn't really conquer the Horde—only caused it enough trouble so that it turned aside to easier feeding grounds. In a thousand years they'll talk about the great victory we won. In two thousand, it'll have been an easy and expected victory. Soon—very soon—as the whole galaxy figures time, another million years'll have gone by and the Horde will be back again. And how ready will we be?"

Luhon hesitated.

"Very well," he said after a second. "But why us? Why not leave the control and the responsibility of remembering to the Center Aliens—or whoever takes their place down in the middle of the galaxy? They kept the records of the Horde's coming once before."

"Kept the records, yes," said Miles. He looked down

from his slightly greater height at the gray-skinned alien. "But that's all they did. Millions of years ago, remember, the Horde wasn't stopped at all. It swept through this galaxy, almost emptying it of life. The Center Aliens must have been one of the few technological races of which individuals survived. But in spite of that, this time the Horde would have done exactly the same thing it did before—if it hadn't been for us. Us! We twenty-three aboard the *Fighting Rowboat!*"

"You have to admit," said Luhon, quietly, "luck had a lot to do with it—with all we did."

"No," said Miles, "I don't have to admit that. Because it wasn't luck. It was something much more important than luck—and that something's to be the topic of this meeting I've called. Because we've got it— a hope and a power that the Center Aliens haven't, and that's why they failed, facing the Horde."

"Failed?" Luhon's voice was almost too quiet.

"They ran. We stayed—and saved the day," said Miles. "Because of our blind instincts, but also because of something I'd found and shared with the rest of you. The ability to go into an overdrive state, to tap hysterical strength of the mind and body. Only 'hysterical strength' is really the wrong term for it. Because what it is, actually, is a breakthrough into a creative ability to draw on all the deepest reservoirs of our minds and bodies at once. Remember how you felt when we attacked the Horde and I reached out to all of you with the strength that was in me?"

"I remember," said Luhon.

"Then you remember that the Center Aliens didn't have anything like that in themselves. If they had, we'd have felt it. More than that, they'd never have needed to run from the Horde in the first place, if their naturally greater psychic strength could be multiplied as ours into overdrive."

"Unmultiplied, their strength was enough—once they did come back and start fighting," said Luhon.

"Yes, once they came back!" said Miles. "But the point is, they didn't come. Not until after we, with no hope, just instinct, had attacked the Horde and changed the battle odds for them. The odds meant everything to them—nothing else did."

"Friend Miles," murmured Luhon, "it seems to me you make too much of one small difference."

"It's not just the difference," replied Miles more quietly. "It's what the difference tells me about the Center Aliens. Don't you remember how they didn't understand—even after I'd explained it—why we aboard the *Fighting Rowboat* felt we'd no choice but to attack the Silver Horde, even though we were left alone? Remember how that was something that the Center Aliens couldn't get?"

"They'd changed, over their longer period of civilization," said Luhon. "They explained that."

"Changed, yes!" said Miles almost fiercely. "*They'd* changed—so that they couldn't any longer understand our reacting the way we did. But it was still *our* reaction that triggered off their own fight to save the galaxy, and that fight succeeded in spite of all their earlier calculations! Don't you see? They'd given up their instincts, years ago, for what they thought were other advantages. But those other advantages couldn't save them—and our instincts, filling in where theirs were missing, did!"

"All this," said Luhon, "I admit, friend Miles. Maybe we do have something the Center Aliens gave up, and maybe their lack of it would have opened the galaxy to the Silver Horde if we hadn't been there. But how can you make this one small, instinctive reaction a basis for some sweeping plan to replace the lords of our island universe?"

Miles smiled a little grimly. He picked up a clean piece of white cloth from the small table, soaked it in kerosene from a container standing nearby, and began to clean the red, the gray, the yellow paint from his hands and lower arms.

"Because it isn't small," he said. "You, I—all of us on the *Fighting Rowboat*—made a wrong guess about the Center Aliens from the start. Seeing how old and powerful they were, we took it for granted that they'd long ago won all their battles with their environment, that they'd evolved beyond the point where they had to prove their right to survive in the universe. But we were wrong."

Luhon looked strangely at Miles.

"I don't understand you," the gray-skinned alien said.

"I'll explain," said Miles. He finished cleaning his hands and, wadding up the now sodden and stained piece of white cloth, threw it into a large coffee can half-filled with other paint-soaked rags.

"Somewhere," he said, "sometime, there may be an end to the physical universe. But only then—only when there are no more frontiers over which something unknown and inimical can come to attack—is any race's struggle for survival going to be over. Up until then, each race is going to have to keep on proving itself. The only differences are going to be that the challenges to survival will come from farther and farther away, as it expands the area it's made safe for itself to live in. We humans, Luhon, are end products of an organism that started as a one-celled animal and that, to date, has won every battle for life that's been forced on it. How is it with your people?"

"The same," murmured Luhon. "But surely the Center Aliens also—"

"No," said Miles. "Somewhere, back thousands of years probably, they made the decision to scrap their instincts for other abilities. And for all those thousands of years it looked like the right decision. Then the Silver Horde came back and proved it was wrong. Oh, the Center Aliens survived the Horde physically, but that doesn't matter, because it was we, not they, who saved them. They were proved vulnerable—and they can't go back to pick up what they've lost. All at once, their road into the future turns out to have been a dead-end route all along."

Miles looked for a long second at Luhon.

"So that's why we'll be taking over the galaxy from them," he went on. "Because from that moment on, they'll have begun to die—somewhere in their race consciousness—just like any prehistoric species that took the wrong evolutionary road and finally came up against something it couldn't handle."

"But, friend Miles," said Luhon, "even if they do die off and we take their place, if we hold on to our instincts, how can we gain what they gained at the price of giving up their instincts? Where can we go—"

"By another route," said Miles, "any other evolutionary road where we hold on to instinct and emotion. They couldn't have given that sort of road much of a try, or they wouldn't have turned away from it so early. They closed a door to themselves that the rest of us, with luck, are going through into a much bigger universe."

"Bigger?" Luhon's tone was doubtful.

"Of course bigger," said Miles. "Take the overdrive— it's from instinct and emotion that you get into over-drive. Can you imagine getting it any other way?"

"But we can't spend all our future fighting off invaders, Miles."

Miles smiled. "Is that all you think overdrive is good for? That's the least of what it can do for you. It's a basically *creative* force—"

Miles broke off and put a friendly hand on the smooth, gray-skinned shoulder beside him.

"You'll see," Miles said. "You'll understand, once I explain it. And I'll be explaining it to all of you from the *Fighting Rowboat*, once everyone's here for the meeting." He checked himself again. "Which reminds me, we'd better be getting back to welcome the rest of them as they get here. Marie?"

She rose from her chair, her finger in her book to mark her place, and walked back toward the road.

But under Miles' hand, Luhon stood still. His attention suddenly caught and arrested, he was leaning forward, staring at the painting. Miles waited and for a moment watched the gray face, in blunt profile, staring at the shapes and colors on the stretched cloth.

Finally, Luhon sighed briefly and relaxed his attention. He turned to Miles, looking sideways and up at the taller human being.

"You've got a lot of sun in it, friend Miles," he said. "Is that—"

Miles' smile widened. He pushed the shoulder he still held, lightly, turning Luhon about, back toward the road, and they started for the car that still waited there.

"That's right," said Miles as they went. "That's overdrive, too. There in my painting, and yes—there *is* a lot of sun in it."

So they went. But in fact, Luhon was correct. For though the scene was the same as the one Miles had painted on the day—years ago, it seemed now—that the sun had turned sullen and red, there was a difference in this canvas.

Once again the painted scene showed the river, the river bluffs, the green lawns and red-brick university buildings—not as they appeared objectively, but grayed and hardened, stained with the marks of old, savage, animal guilts and primitive human failures. Once again

WOLFLING

Chapter 1

The bull would not charge.

James Keil stamped his foot and shouted at the animal, but still it would not charge—and it was programmed to charge. Or rather, it was programmed to still be willing to charge at this point in the bullfight.

There was nothing to be done about it. The finest physical tests available could not measure the probable endurance, or bravery, of a bull. This one was tired. Jim would have to step up the pattern and make the kill, now.

He moved toward the bull, stamped and shouted again, and tempted the weary beast into one more attack. As the near horn swept by, grazing his hip and waist, he sucked his belly in hard, feeling a little streak of internal coldness along the line of the graze. Like the bull, he was programmed; and as long as they both stuck to their programming, he was safe. But he was a bullfighter only by courtesy of six months of intensive training. Also, he had free will, where the bull had not—and free will meant the power to break programming and make mistakes.

If he made a mistake, this bull could still kill him.

Therefore he was careful to make no mistakes, even now. The bull was almost at the end of its strength. He led it carefully through a few more passes, then took his sword and went in over the horns for the kill.

The bull grunted, went to its knees, and rolled over on its side as he withdrew the blade. As he watched its death with an impassive face, a female figure appeared without warning on the sand of the arena beside him, looking down at the fallen bull.

He turned to face her. It was the Princess Afuan, aunt of the All-Emperor and head of the visiting party of High-born who had occupied the official box across the arena, surrounded there by the short, brown-skinned local humans of Alpha Centauri III. Afuan was neither short nor brown—no more than she was, in height or color, in any way similar to an Earth-born Caucasian like Jim himself.

She was dressed—if that was the word—in some sort of white, filmy, cloudstuff. It left her arms bare but covered her otherwise, from the armpits to the ankles, dividing only with the movement of her legs as she walked. Above that cloudstuff, her skin also was white, but not in the sense that Jim's skin was "white."

Afuan's skin was the color of white onyx, and Jim could see the blue veins pulsing dimly within the marble column of her throat. Her face was narrow, and her eyes were large and a startling lemon yellow in color. So that, even though they lacked any epicanthic fold similar to the Oriental, they gave the impression of being slitted and feline below the whitish eyelashes and eyebrows on either side of her long, straight nose. In a sculptured, abstract way, she could have been called beautiful—and she was as tall as Jim himself, who stood six-feet-six.

"Very entertaining," she said now to Jim, speaking

the Empire tongue with a rapid, almost hissing accent. "Yes, we'll certainly take you with us, ah—what's your world name, Wolfling?"

"Earthman, High-born," Jim answered

"Yes, well—come to our ship, Earthman. The Throne World will appreciate seeing you," she said. She glanced past him at the other members of his cuadrilla. "But not these others, these assistants of yours; no point in cluttering up the ship. We can supply you anything you need to perform, once you get to the Throne World."

She started to turn away, but Jim spoke.

"Excuse me, High-born," he said. "You can supply me with new assistants; but you can't supply me with the fighting bulls. They've been genetically selected over generations. I've got half a dozen more in cryogenic storage with me here. I'd like to take those."

She turned back to look at him. Her face was completely unreadable. For a moment Jim was not sure but that in speaking up he had angered her, to the point where she would destroy the work of five years by saying she would not take him along to the Throne World after all. But then she spoke.

"Very well," she said. "Tell whoever takes you aboard our ship that you need these animals shipped too, and that I said they should be."

She turned away again, then, finally, and stood gazing down with interest at the dead bull. As if her movement was a cue, suddenly a dozen or more members of her retinue had also winked into existence on the sand of the arena and were examining the bull and even the suits and equipment of other members of the cuadrilla. The women were none of them more than an inch or two shorter than Afuan; and the tall, slim, onyx-skinned men ranged between six-feet-ten and seven feet in height. Unlike the High-born women, the men wore short kilts and tunics made out of some material more like ordinary cloth. But in almost all cases the color of their clothing was white, except for a single design in some other color, written on either the front or the back of their tunics.

No one offered to examine Jim, as they were examining the others of the cuadrilla. He turned and walked away, sheathing his sword, across the sand and down under the seats of the arena, along a sloping concretelike passageway illuminated by some source of light apparently within the very material of the walls themselves—one of the Empire luxuries which the local humans of Alpha Centauri III seemed to use without making any effort to understand their workings.

He reached the door of his room, opened it, and stepped inside. Within the windowless main dressing room he saw two things in a single glance.

One was Max Holland, the man from the U.N. Special Committee Section. The other was his own two suitcases, already packed in hopes of the trip to the Throne World, which had now become a reality. But now the suitcases were opened and their contents had been strewn about on the furniture of the room.

"What's this?" Jim said, stopping and looking down at the smaller man. Holland's face was dark with anger.

"Don't think—" he began in a choked voice, and then got control of himself. His voice firmed. "Just because Afuan's agreed to take you doesn't mean you're going to take some of these things to the Throne World!"

"So, you know I'm invited?" Jim asked.

"I'm a good lip-reader," answered Max thickly, "and I had binoculars on you from the moment you started your bullfight until you walked away, just now."

"And you came ahead of me down here and decided to have a look at my luggage?" said Jim.

"That's right!" said Max. He turned sharply and

snatched up two items from the couch beside him. One was a Scottish kilt in the Black Watch tartan, with a small knife in a sheath attached to it. The other was a suntan shirt with shoulder tabs, through one of which ran the shoulder belt of a Sam Browne belt, to which was fitted a holster containing a forty-five caliber revolver. Max all but shook these two articles under Jim's nose.

"You're going into the Throne World of a human Empire a hundred thousand years old! A world where they outgrew primitive weapons like this so long ago they probably don't even remember them."

"That's just the point in taking them," said Jim.

He took back the kilt with its small knife and the shirt with its Sam Browne belt from Max's hands so smoothly that the other for a second did not seem to know that they were gone. Jim carried both items of clothing back over to the open suitcases, where he laid them down. He began calmly to repack the luggage.

"*What* point?" Max blazed behind him. "Jim, somehow you seem to have got the idea that you're a loner in this whole project! Just let me remind you—it took a hundred and sixty-two governments, a couple of billion dollars, and the work of thousands of people to train you and bring you here, to the point where you could get yourself invited to play bullfighter on the Throne World!"

Jim, without answering, folded the kilt and placed it back into one of the open suitcases.

"Listen to me, damn you!" snarled Max behind him. The smaller man grabbed Jim's arm and tried to swing him around. Jim turned.

"I'll tell you—*you're not going to take those things!*" said Max.

"Yes, I am," said Jim.

"I say you're not!" shouted Max. "Who do you think

you are, anyway? You're just the man who was picked to go into the Throne World and observe. Got that? *Observe!* Not stick people with knives, or shoot them with guns, or do anything else to draw any more Imperial attention to Earth than there is already. You're an anthropologist, play-acting a bullfighter, not some cloak-and-dagger spy!"

"I'm all three," said Jim quickly and a little coldly.

The color slowly went from Max's face. "God . . ." said the smaller man. His hand fell away from Jim's arm. "Ten years ago we didn't know they existed—a whole empire of human-occupied worlds stretching in from Alpha Centauri here toward the galactic center. Five years ago you were only a name on a list. I could have put a pencil mark through you, and you wouldn't have been here now. Even a year ago I was ready to start questioning whether we'd been training the right man—and you picked just then to put on such a good show nobody'd have listened to me. Now it turns out I was right, after all. An Empire of a thousand worlds, and one little Earth. They forgot us once, and maybe they could forget us again—but not if you're the man who goes in and observes them. I was right a year ago. You've got some ax of your own to grind with these High-born—"

He choked and broke off. He breathed deeply and straightened his back.

"Forget it," he said more calmly. "You're not going. I'm aborting the project—on my own responsibility. Earth can ask me all the questions they want, after that Imperial ship leaves—"

"Max," said Jim almost gently. "It's too late for you to stop me now. I've been invited by the Princess Afuan. Not you, or the whole project, or the whole Earth would be permitted to interfere with her invitation now. Do you think she'd allow that?"

Max stood staring at Jim with dark-circled, blood-shot eyes. He did not answer.

"I'm sorry, Max," said Jim. "But it was bound to come to this sooner or later. From here on out the project can't guide me any longer. From now on I have to follow my own judgment."

He turned back to his packing.

"*Your* judgment!" A little moisture flew with the words, to touch coldly against the side and back of Jim's neck. "You're so sure of your judgment? Compared to those High-born like Afuan, you're just as ignorant, just as primitive, just as savage as all the rest of us back on Earth! You don't know anything! Maybe Earth *is* one of their colonies that they forgot about. . . . Or maybe it's just coincidence that we seem to belong to the same race as them and these people we found here on Alpha Centauri III! Who knows? I don't; no Earthman does. And neither do you! So don't talk about your judgment to me, Jim! Not with the whole future of Earth riding on what you do, once you get there, into the Imperial household!"

Jim shrugged. He turned back to his packing and felt his arm violently seized and wrenched as Max tried to turn him around once more.

Swiftly, this time, Jim turned. He knocked Max's grip loose with the edge of his right hand, and then put that same hand, calmingly, it seemed, upon the smaller man's shoulder. But the thumb reached up from the grip of the other four fingers to lay itself against Max's neck behind the right point of the angle of his jaw-bone; and it pressed in slightly.

Max's face whitened, and he gasped. He drew a quick, short breath and tried to back away. But the grip of Jim's hand held him.

"You—you're a fool!" stammered Max. "You'd *kill* me?"

"If I had to," said Jim calmly. "That's one of the reasons I'm the right man to go."

He released his grip, turned away, closed the open suitcase into which he had put the kilt and the shirt with the Sam Browne belt, and picked up both the heavy suitcases. He turned and went out through the door, turning left and away up the corridor in the opposite direction, which led to the street and the vehicle that was waiting for him outside the arena. As he neared the entrance, he heard Max shouting after him, his words distorted by the long tunnel of the corridor. Glancing back, he saw that the other man had come out of the dressing room to stand staring after him.

"Observe!" Max shouted in English after him up the corridor. "Do anything else, Jim, get Earth into trouble with the High-born, and we'll shoot you for it, like a mad dog, when you get home again!"

Jim did not answer. He stepped out into the bright, yellow sunlight of Alpha Centauri III, and into the open, four-wheeled, jeeplike vehicle that was there waiting for him with its driver at the controls.

Chapter 2

The driver of the vehicle was a staff member of the Earth Trade Delegation, which, with the trade delegations from two other Empire-inhabited solar systems, had combined with the Alpha Centaurans of this planet to put on various local-culture shows for the visiting High-born. It was always the hope of those putting on such shows that the result would be some form of preference by the High-born visitors. Earth had stood the best chance of arousing interest, being, in theory, a newly rediscovered part of the Empire, and now its show of the art of bullfighting was being carried back by the visitors to the Throne World to amuse the Emperor.

The driver took Jim and his luggage through the surrounding city and out to the open spaceport, an endless stretch of brownish, cementlike material. In one area of this, all by itself, sat a huge ovoid that was the ship of the High-born. The driver drove Jim up to this ship and stopped.

"Want me to wait?" asked the driver.

Jim shook his head. He took the two suitcases out of

the vehicle and watched as the driver put it in motion and drove off, dwindling to toy size in the distance across the spaceport area.

Jim set his suitcases down and turned to look at the ship. From the outside it seemed perfectly featureless. There were no ports, no airlocks, no signs of apertures or entrances to the interior. Nor did anyone aboard the huge vessel seem to be aware that Jim was there.

He sat down on one of his suitcases and began to wait.

For a little over an hour nothing happened. Then, abruptly, while he was still sitting on his suitcase, he was no longer on the spaceport concrete, but with both bags in what appeared to be a green-walled, egg-shaped room with some sort of darker green carpet underfoot and cushions of all colors and sizes, from six inches in diameter to something like six feet, furnishing it.

"Were you waiting long, Wolfling?" asked a girl's voice. "I'm sorry. I was busy taking care of the other pets."

He stood up and turned about from his suitcase; and he saw her then. By the standards of the High-born, she was short—probably no more than five feet, ten inches in height. Also her skin, although it approached the onyx-white of the Princess Afuan and the others, had a brownish tinge, like a pale shadow of the brownishness of an American Indian. The brownishness extended to her eyes, which were rather a dark gold, flecked with little sparkles of red highlights—not like the lemon yellow Jim had seen in Afuan. Her face was less long than Afuan's, and more rounded of jaw. She smiled in a way that was very unlike the inscrutability of the High-born princess; and when she smiled, the ghosts of a small cloud of something like freckles appeared across her nose and up her cheeks. Finally, her hair, though she let it hang straight down her back, as had the other High-born females Jim had seen in the arena, was plainly yellow-blond rather than white, and it did not hang as straight as Afuan's, but had a perceptible wave and thickness to it.

Her smile vanished and her face darkened suddenly with an abrupt flood of blood below the skin. It was a literal flush—the last thing Jim had expected to discover upon the face of one of the High-born.

"That's right, stare at me!" she said spiritedly. "I'm not ashamed of it!"

"Ashamed of what?" asked Jim.

"Why—" She broke off suddenly. Her blush fled, and she looked at him contritely. "I'm sorry. Of course— you're a Wolfling. You wouldn't even know the difference, would you?"

"Evidently not," said Jim. "Because I don't seem to understand what you're talking about."

She laughed—but a little sadly, it seemed to him; and patted his arm unexpectedly, with a light, consoling touch.

"You'll learn soon enough," she said, "even if you are a Wolfling. I'm a throwback, you see. Something in my gene pattern was atavistic. Oh, my father and mother were as High-born as anyone outside the Main Royal Line; and Afuan will never dismiss me from her household. But, on the other hand, she can hardly show me off. So I'm left with doing things like taking care of the pets for her. That was why I was the one who brought you on board just now."

She glanced down at his two cases.

"Is that your equipment there?" she asked. "I'll put it away for you."

Instantly the two pieces of luggage vanished.

"Just a minute," said Jim.

She looked up at him, a little puzzled.

"Didn't you want them put away just yet?" she asked. Instantly the bags were back at their feet.

"No," answered Jim. "It's just that there are other things to bring aboard. I told your Princess Afuan that I'd need the bulls—the creatures I work with when I put on my show. I've got six more of them in cryogenic storage back in the city. She said I could bring them along, and to tell whoever brought me aboard the ship that she said it was all right."

"Oh!" said the girl thoughtfully. "No—don't try to tell me. Just think about where they are in the city."

Jim obliged by summoning up a mental picture of the refrigerated warehouse behind the compound housing the Earth Trade Delegation, where his bulls were stored. He felt a curious light touch in his mind—a sort of passing sensation, as if his naked brain had been lightly brushed by a feather. Abruptly he and the girl were standing in the refrigerated warehouse, before the stack of six huge cases, each with the frozen body of a fighting bull in suspended animation within it.

"Yes," said the girl thoughtfully. Abruptly they were someplace else.

This new place was a large, metal-walled chamber with a small assortment of cases and other objects arranged in neat piles at intervals about its floor. The stack of cases containing the frozen bulls was now here also. Jim frowned. The temperature of the room was clearly in the comfortable seventy-degree range.

"These animals are frozen," he told the girl. "And they have to stay frozen—"

"Oh, don't worry about that," she interrupted; and then smiled at him, half in cheerfulness, half, it seemed, in apology for interrupting him. "Nothing about their condition will change. I've left orders with the ship's controls to see to that."

Her smile widened.

"Go ahead," she said. "Put your hand out and feel for yourself."

Jim reached out his hand toward the side of the nearest case. There was no change in temperature until his fingertips came within an inch or two of the surface of the case—then they suddenly encountered bone-chilling atmosphere. The cold, he knew, could not come from the cases, since these were superbly insulated. He withdrew his hand.

"I see," he said. "All right. I won't worry about my bulls."

"Good," she answered.

Instantly they were elsewhere. Not back in the egg-shaped room but in another, a long room, one side of which appeared to be glass looking out on a strip of beach and the surf of an ocean shore—the shore of an ocean aboard a spaceship was no less startling than the other things to be seen within the rectangular, glass-walled room itself.

These were a variety of creatures, running from something like a small, purple-furred squirrel to a creature farther down the room who was tall and covered with black fur—more than apelike, but still less than human.

"These are my other pets," he heard the girl saying at his elbow, and looked down into her smiling face. "I mean—they're really Afuan's pets. The ones I take care of for her. This one—"

She stopped to pet the small, purple-furred squirrel, which arched itself like a satisfied cat under her hand. Neither it nor any of the others seemed to be chained or restrained in any way. Yet they all stayed some little distance from one another.

"This one," the girl repeated, "is Ifny—"

She stopped suddenly, jumping to her feet.

"I'm sorry, Wolfling," she said. "You must have a name too. What is it?"

"James Keil," he answered her. "Call me Jim."

"*Jim,*" she echoed, trying it out, with her head cocked on one side. In her Empire accent, the '*m*' sound was prolonged, so that the short, familiar form of James came out sounding more musical than it might have in English.

"And your name?" Jim asked her.

She started, and looked at him almost in shock.

"But you should call me High-born!" she said a little stiffly. But the next moment the stiffness had melted, as if her interior warmth of character would not endure it. "But I do have a name, of course. I have several dozens of them, in fact. But you know we all go by one name familiarly. My normally used name is Ro."

Jim inclined his head.

"Thank you, High-born," he said.

"Oh, call me Ro—" she broke off, as if a little frightened at what she was saying. "When we're alone, anyway. After all, you are human, even if you are a Wolfling, Jim."

"That's something else you can tell me, then, Ro," said Jim. "What is this 'Wolfling' that everyone calls me?"

She stared at him for a moment, almost blankly.

"But you—no, of course, you'd be the very one who wouldn't know!" she said. Once more she blushed in that remarkable fashion he had noticed earlier. Plainly it was the lightness of her skin, for all its brown tint, that caused the sudden rush of blood to her features to be seen. But it was unusual to Jim to see such a marked reaction in any adult woman. "It's . . . not a very nice name for you, I'm afraid. It means—it means something like . . . you're a human being, all right, but one who's been lost in the woods and brought up by animals, so that you don't have any idea of what it's really like to be a human."

Her blush flared again.

"I'm sorry . . ." she said, looking down. "I shouldn't have called you that myself. But I didn't think. I'll always call you Jim, from now on."

Jim smiled. "It doesn't matter," he said.

"Yes, it does!" she said fiercely, looking up at him abruptly. "I know what it's like to be called names. I never let anybody call any of my—Afuan's—pets names. And I'm not going to let anybody call you names if I can help it."

"Well, thank you, then," said Jim gently. She patted his arm again soothingly.

"Come meet my other pets," she said, moving down the line.

He went with her. The creatures in the room seemed free to wander about the room, but at the same time enclosed and protected by an invisible barrier that kept them from coming any closer than four or five feet to one of the other creatures. They were plainly all animals. Curiously, also, they all appeared to resemble, at least to some extent, an animal type that either was on Earth or had been at some period in its geologic history. This, in itself, was interesting. It seemed to substantiate the Empire's assumption that the people of Earth were part of its own basic stock—lost, only to be found again when they ventured by their own scientific powers back in as far as Alpha Centauri. The alternative was to assume that human-habitable planets had evolutionary parallels to an extremely remarkable degree.

Still, even this could be; a parallelism among fauna on various worlds did not absolutely prove a common ancestry for its dominant species.

Jim noticed something also that was very interesting about Ro herself. Most of the animals responded happily when she spoke to them or petted them. Even those who did not—and she handled even the fiercest of them without hesitation—showed absolutely no hostility. The farthest they got from expressions of happiness at her attention was something like a lazy indifference.

Such as in the case of one large catlike creature— easily as big as a South American jaguar and somewhat resembling the jaguar in its spotted coat, although a heavy, horselike head spoiled the general picture. This catlike creature yawned and allowed itself to be petted but made no great effort to respond to Ro's caresses. The apelike creature in the black hair, in contrast, sadly clung to her hand and gazed into her face as she spoke to it and stroked its head; but it made no other response

Letting go of its hand at last—pulling away, in fact— Ro turned finally to Jim.

"Now you've seen them," she said. "Maybe you'll help me take care of them sometimes. They really should have more attention than I give them alone. Afuan forgets she has them for months on end. . . . Oh, that won't happen to you—" She interrupted herself suddenly. "You understand? You're to perform for the Emperor when we get back to the Throne World. And as I say, you're not an animal."

"Thank you," said Jim gravely.

She looked surprised, then laughed. She patted his arm in the gesture he was beginning to find customary on her part.

"Now," she said, "you'll want to get to your own quarters."

Instantly they were in a room that they had not been in before. Like the room containing the pets, it had a glass wall window looking out on the beach and the ocean beyond, which, whether illusion or reality, rolled its surf within thirty feet of the glass wall itself.

"These will be your quarters," said Ro. Jim looked around him. There was no sign of a door in any of the walls.

"Don't you suppose," he said, "you'd better tell this Wolfling how to get around from one room to the next?"

"To the next?" she echoed with a puzzled frown, and suddenly he realized that she had taken him literally. His mind seized on the implications of that.

"I'm sorry," he said, "I simply meant from this room to any other room. But—just for the fun of it—what is the room that's just beyond that wall there?"

He pointed to the blank wall of the room opposite the one of glass overlooking the beach and the ocean.

She stared at the wall, frowned again, and finally shook her head.

"Why . . . I don't know," she said. "But what difference does it make? You go to all rooms the same way. So there's really no difference. It doesn't matter where in the ship they are."

Jim filed this information mentally for future reference. "I should know how to get myself from room to room, though, shouldn't I?" he asked.

"Oh," she said, "I'm sorry. Of course, you don't know. The ship runs everything. You have to tune in to the ship; then it'll do anything you want."

She lit up suddenly.

"Would you like to see what the rest of the ship looks like?" she asked. "I'll take you around. Why don't you get yourself settled in here, or unpack, or whatever you want to do; and I'll come back in a little while. How soon should I come back?"

Jim mentioned a time in Empire units that was roughly the equivalent of fifteen minutes.

"Fine," Ro said, smiling at him. "I'll be right back when the time's up."

She vanished.

Left alone, Jim examined the room, which was furnished with hassocks and pillows of all size—much as the first room he had seen aboard ship, where he had met Ro. The one very large hassock, some four feet thick and eight feet in diameter, at one end of the room, he took to be the bed. At first there seemed nothing in the shape of a bathroom. But the moment this thought occurred to him a section of the wall obediently slid aside, and he found himself looking into a smaller room fitted out with a complete assortment of recognizable lavatory facilities, up to and including a swimming pool—and with several other articles of plumbing which seemed to make little sense. For example, there was one shallow, completely dry basin large enough for him to stretch out in.

He turned back to his main room and with a corner of his eye saw the door to the bathroom slide shut behind him. He picked up his two suitcases, put them on the bedlike hassock, and opened them. No sooner had he done so than another section of the wall opened, and he found himself looking into what might have been the closet if there had been any pole or clothes hangers in it.

Experimentally—he was beginning to get the hang of things aboard ship now—he tried to imagine his clothes as being hung up in the closet.

Obligingly, they were suddenly there—the only unusual part of their appearance and situation being that they hung as he had imagined them, but without any visible means of support, suspended vertically in midair as if held by invisible hangers from an invisible rod.

Jim nodded. He was about to think the closet closed

again, when a second thought made him take the
Scottish costume, complete with kilt and knife, from
where it hung unsupported in midair, and change into
it, placing his suit of lights in the closet in its place,
where it hung invisibly supported with the rest of his
clothes.

The closet closed, and Jim was just turning away
from it when a visitor materialized in the center of his
room. But it was not Ro. Instead, it was one of the
male High-born—a man with onyx-white skin, at least
seven feet tall.

"There you are, Wolfling," the High-born said.
"Come along. Mekon wants to see you."

They were suddenly in a room which Jim had not
been in before. It was rectangular and long, and they
stood in about the middle of it. There were no other
humans in the room. But at the far end, on a sort
of pillow-strewn dais, there lay curled a feline similar in every respect to the one among Ro's pets. It
lifted its horse's head at the sight of them in the
room, and its eyes fastened upon Jim.

"Wait here," said the High-born who had brought
him. "Mekon will be with you in just a moment."

The tall man vanished. Jim found himself left alone
with the feline beast, which was now lazily rising to
its feet, staring down the room at him.

Jim stood still, staring back.

The animal made a curious, whining sound—a sound
almost ridiculously small to come from something
obviously so physically powerful. Its short stub of a
tufted tail began to jerk vertically up and down, stiffly.
Its heavy head lowered until its lower jaw almost
touched the floor of the dais, and its mouth gradually
opened to reveal heavy, carnivorous teeth.

Still whining, it began slowly to move. Softly, almost
delicately, it put one front paw down from the dais;

and then the other. Slowly it began to move toward him, crouching and whining as it did. Its teeth were fully visible now, and as it approached, its whine grew in volume, until it was a sort of singing threat.

Jim waited, moving neither backward nor forward.

The animal came on. About a dozen yards from him it stopped and gradually crouched. Its tail was jerking like a metronome now, and the singing whine that came from its throat was filling the whole room.

For what seemed a long time, it crouched there, jaw hung open, whining. Then, without warning, the whining stopped, and it launched itself through the air at Jim's throat.

Chapter 3

The feline creature flashed forward and upward into Jim's face—and vanished.

Jim had not moved. For a moment he was alone in the long, rectangular room; and then suddenly there were three of the High-born males around him, one of them with the dragonlike insignia upon his shirt, or tunic, front. That one had brought Jim here. Of the other two, one was almost short by High-born standards—barely three inches taller than Jim. The third was the tallest of the three—a slim, rather graceful-looking man with the first expression resembling a smile Jim had ever seen on purely onyx-colored features; and this last of the three High-born wore a red insignia which looked somewhat like the horns and head of a stag.

"I told you they were brave, these Wolflings," drawled this last member of the group. "Your trick didn't work, Mekon."

"*Courage!*" said the one addressed as Mekon angrily. "That was too good to be true. He didn't even move a muscle! You'd think he'd been—"

Mekon bit off the words abruptly, glancing hastily at the tall Slothiel, who stiffened.

"Go on. Go on, Mekon," drawled the tall High-born, but there was an edge to his drawl now. "You were going to say something like . . . 'warned'?"

"Of course Mekon didn't mean to say anything like that." It was Trahey, almost literally pushing himself between the other two men, whose eyes were now fixedly fastened on each other.

"I'd like to hear Mekon tell me that," murmured Slothiel.

Mekon's eyes dropped. "I—of course, I didn't mean anything of the sort. I don't remember what I was going to say," he said.

"Then I take it," said Slothiel, "that I've won. One Lifetime Point, to me?"

"One—" The admission clearly stuck in Mekon's throat. His face had darkened with a rush of blood similar to the flush that Jim had noticed come too easily to the face of Ro. "One Lifetime Point to you."

Slothiel laughed. "Don't take it so hard, man," he said. "You can have a chance to win it back anytime you've got a decent wager to propose."

But Mekon's temper had flared again. "All right," he snapped, and swung to face Jim. "I've given up the point—but I'd still like to know why this Wolfling didn't even twitch when the beast went for him. There's something unnatural here."

"Why don't you ask him?" drawled Slothiel.

"I *am* asking him!" said Mekon, his eyes burning upon Jim. "Speak up, Wolfling. Why didn't you show any sign of a reaction?"

"The Princess Afuan is taking me to the Throne World to show me off to the Emperor," Jim answered quietly. "I could hardly be shown off if I were badly torn up or killed by an animal like that one. Therefore, whoever was responsible for the cat coming at me was certain to make sure that I wouldn't be hurt by it."

Slothiel threw back his head and laughed loudly. Mekon's face, which had paled back to its normal color, now flushed again with a dark rush of angry blood.

"So!" snapped Mekon. "You think you can't be touched, is that it, Wolfling? I'll show you—"

He broke off, for Ro had suddenly appeared in the room beside them; and now she literally shoved herself between Jim and the angry High-born.

"What're you doing to him?" she cried. "He's supposed to be left with me! He's not for the rest of you to play with—"

"Why, you little mud-skinned throwback!" snapped Mekon. His hand darted out to the small black stick running through the two loops of the ropelike material that acted as a belt to her white dress. "Give me that rod!"

As his hand closed upon it, she snatched at it herself; and for a moment there was a tug-of-war in which the rod had come loose from the belt and they both had hold of it.

"Let go, you little—" Mekon raised one hand, clenching his fingers into a fist as though to strike down at Ro; and, at that moment, Jim stepped suddenly up to him.

The High-born yelled suddenly—it was almost a bass scream—and let go of the rod, falling back and holding his right arm with his left hand. All down along his forearm a line dripped red, and Jim was putting the little knife back into its scabbard.

There was a sudden, utter, frozen silence in the room. Trahey, the heretofore self-possessed Slothiel, and even Ro were utterly still, staring at the blood running down Mekon's forearm. If the walls of the ship had begun to crumble about them, they could not have looked more overwhelmed and stupefied.

"He—the Wolfling damaged me," stuttered Mekon, staring wildly at his bleeding arm. "Did you see what he did?"

Slowly Mekon raised his eyes to his two companions.

"Did you see what he did?" Mekon screamed. "Get me a rod! Don't just stand there! Get me a rod!"

Trahey made a slow move as if to step toward Ro, but Slothiel, with suddenly narrowed eyes, caught Trahey's arm.

"No, no," murmured Slothiel. "Our little game isn't a game anymore. If he wants rods, let him get them himself."

Trahey stood still. Ro abruptly disappeared.

"Blind you, Trahey!" shouted Mekon. "I'll collect from you for this! Get me a rod, I say!"

Trahey slowly shook his head, though his lips were almost bloodless.

"A rod—no. No, Mekon," he said. "Slothiel's right. You'll have to do that for yourself."

"Then I will!" screamed Mekon—and disappeared.

"I still say you're a brave man, Wolfling," said Slothiel to Jim. "Let me give you a piece of advice. If Mekon offers you a rod, don't take it."

Trahey made an odd little sound, like a man who has started to speak and then suddenly thought better of it. Slothiel turned his eyes upon the other Highborn.

"You were going to say something, Trahey?" he asked. "Perhaps you were going to object to my advising the Wolfling?"

Trahey shook his head. But the glance he threw at Jim was baleful.

Mekon suddenly reappeared, his arm still bleeding,

but the hand at the end of it clutching two short black rods like the one Ro had worn in the loops of her belt. He held one of these in his good hand, and stepping forward, thrust it at Jim.

"Take this, Wolfling!" he snapped.

Jim shook his head and drew the small knife from his kilt.

"No thanks," he said. "I think I'll stick to this."

Mekon's face lit up savagely.

"Suit yourself!" he said, and threw the rod he had offered across the room. "It makes no difference to me—"

"But it does to me!" cut in a new voice. It was a woman's voice, behind Jim. Jim turned quickly and backed off a step so as to keep everyone in the room in front of him. Ro had reappeared, he saw; and with her was a tall female High-born whom Jim believed he recognized as Afuan. Behind both women towered a slim High-born male, possibly even an inch or two taller than Slothiel.

"Well?" went on Afuan, if it was indeed she. "Has something happened to alter the tables of precedence, so that you think you can take it on yourself to rod one of my pets, Mekon?"

Mekon had frozen. Even the expression on his face, caught halfway between rage and astonishment, seemed fixed there by a sort of paralysis.

Behind the two women the unusually tall male High-born smiled slowly. It was a smile something like the lazy smile of Slothiel, but there was more of a feeling of power—and perhaps more of cruelty—in it.

"I'm afraid you've offended Her Majesty, Mekon," he said. "That could cost you more than a few Lifetime Points. Men have been banished to the Colony Worlds for less."

Surprisingly, it was Slothiel who came to the defense of the paralyzed Mekon.

"Not perhaps in just such a case as this," said Slothiel. "The Wolfling assaulted Mekon first. Certainly someone like Galyan would understand how a man could react to something like that."

The eyes of the tall High-born addressed as Galyan went out to meet with Slothiel's. They looked at each other with a mutual amusement that seemed to hang upon the very lip of animosity. *Someday,* those looks seemed to say, *we will clash, but not now.* The Princess Afuan noticed the exchange, and instantly her own manner changed to one of brisk reasonableness.

"Nonsense!" she said. "He's only a Wolfling, after all! Do you enjoy looking disgusting, man?" This last phrase was addressed to Mekon. "Heal yourself!"

Mekon woke abruptly from his trance and looked down at his wounded arm. Jim looked at it also; and before his eyes he saw the long shallow cut slowly begin to close and firm over—without any of the ordinary signs of scabbing or healing. Within perhaps a second and a half the wound had disappeared, leaving only white-onyx skin that looked as if it had never been cut. The dried blood on the arm remained, but after a second Mekon passed his other hand along it, and this too vanished. He was left with an arm not only whole but clean. Jim put the knife back into its scabbard at his belt.

"That's better," said Afuan. She turned to the tall man beside her. "I'll leave it to you now, Galyan. See that Mekon pays some kind of a fine."

She vanished.

"You can go too, girl," Galyan said, looking down at Ro. "I didn't have a chance to watch this Wolfling putting on his act on the planet. After I deal with Mekon, I'd like to examine the wild man myself."

Ro hesitated. Her face was unhappy.

"Go along," said Galyan softly but sharply. "I'm not going to hurt your Wolfling! You'll have him back in perfect shape before you know it."

Ro hesitated a second longer, then vanished, in her turn, casting a strangely appealing glance at Jim just before she went, as if to caution him against any act that might lead to further trouble.

"Come with me, Wolfling," said Galyan. He disappeared. After a second, he reappeared, smiling quizzically at Jim.

"So you don't know how to move around in the ship, do you?" he said. "Very well, Wolfling. I'll provide your motive power."

At once Jim found himself in a large, oval, low-ceilinged room with yellow walls, which more resembled an office or a place of work than any of the rooms he had so far visited aboard the vessel. At hard-surfaced slabs of what looked like stone floating in mid-air and plainly in use as desktops, three men were at work—none of them High-born.

Two were brown, squat men—about the color of a white-skinned human from Earth with a good heavy suntan. They were no more than five and a half feet tall. The third, who was looking at what appeared to be a map, was possibly six inches taller and a hundred pounds heavier than the other two. His greater weight was not in body fat, but plainly in a very heavy, even massive skeleton and corresponding musculature. Unlike the two shorter men, who had long, straight brown hair hanging down their backs almost in the fashion in which the white hair of the High-born women was allowed to hang, the third man was completely bald. His round, hairless skull, with its grayish skin stretched tightly over the bone beneath, was the most prominent feature about him, so that it made his eyes, his nose, his mouth, and even his fairly good-sized ears seem small by comparison. This third man got up on seeing Galyan and Jim appear in the room.

"No, no. It's all right, Reas," said Galyan. "Back to your work."

The powerful-looking man sat down again without a word and returned to his map study.

"Reas," said Galyan, waving a hand at him, and looking down at Jim, "is what you might call my bodyguard. Although I don't need a bodyguard—no more than any of the High-born do. Does that surprise you?"

"I don't know enough about it to be either surprised or not surprised," answered Jim.

Galyan nodded, surprisingly, as if in approval.

"No, of course you don't," he said. He sat down on a handy cushion and reached out a long arm.

"Let me see that tool of yours," he said. "The one you used to hurt Mekon."

Jim drew the knife and passed it over, hilt first. Galyan accepted it gingerly, holding it between a thumb and two opposing fingers. He held it up in the air before his eyes and tenderly touched its point and edges with the long forefinger of his left hand. Then he handed it back to Jim.

"I suppose you could kill an ordinary man with something like that," he said.

"Yes," said Jim.

"Very interesting," said Galyan. He sat for a moment, as if caught up in his own thoughts. Then his eyes focused on Jim once more. "You realize, I suppose, that you aren't allowed to go around damaging the High-born with tools like that?"

Jim said nothing. In the face of his silence, Galyan smiled, almost as he had smiled at Slothiel—a little enigmatically, a little cruelly.

"You're very interesting, Wolfling," he said slowly. "Very interesting indeed. You don't seem to realize that you exist like an insect in the palm of any one of us who are High-born. Now, someone like Mekon would have closed his hand and crushed the life out of you long before this. In fact, that is just what he was about to do when Afuan and I stopped him. But I'm not the sort of High-born that Mekon is. In fact, I am like no other High-born you will meet—except the Emperor; and, since we're first cousins, that's not surprising. So I'm not going to close my hand on you, Wolfling. I'm going to reason with you—as if you were High-born yourself."

"Thank you," said Jim.

"You do not thank me, Wolfling," said Galyan softly. "You do not thank me, or curse me, or plead with me, or praise me. You do nothing where I am concerned— but listen. And answer when you are questioned. Now, to begin with. How did you get into that room with Mekon, Trahey, and Slothiel?"

Jim told him briefly and emotionlessly.

"I see," said Galyan. He clasped his long hands around one knee and leaned back a little on his cushion, looking at a slight slant up into Jim's face. "So you trusted to the fact that the Princess intended to show you off to the Emperor, and that for that reason no one else would dare harm you. Even if such a faith were justified, Wolfling, you showed a rather remarkable control of your nerves to stand absolutely still while that beast jumped at your face."

He paused, as if to give Jim a chance to say something. When Jim did not, he murmured, almost deprecatingly, "You have my leave to speak."

"What would you like me to speak about?" asked Jim.

Galyan's lemon-yellow eyes glowed almost like a cat's eyes in the dark.

"Yes," he murmured, drawing the *s* sound out slowly, "you are most unusual—even for a Wolfling. Though I haven't actually met that many Wolflings, so that I don't consider myself much of a judge. You're fairly good-sized for someone not High-born. Tell me, the rest of your people aren't as big as you, are they?"

"On the average, no," said Jim.

"Then there're bigger males among you?"

"Yes," said Jim, without expanding on the subject.

"As large as the High-born?" asked Galyan. "Are there any as tall as myself?"

"Yes," said Jim.

"But not many," said Galyan, his eyes glowing. "In fact, they're rare. Isn't that so?"

"That's right," said Jim.

"In fact," said Galyan, nursing his knee, "to be truthful about it, you might say that they are practically in the case of freaks—aren't they?"

"You might say that," said Jim.

"Yes, I thought we'd get at the truth," said Galyan. "You see, Wolfling, we of the High-born are not freaks. We're a true aristocracy—an aristocracy of not merely inherited power superior to anything else owned by the various races of man. We're superior physically, mentally, and emotionally. This is a fact that you will not have grasped yet; and normally the practice would have been to let you discover it the hard way on your own. However, I've taken an interest in you. . . ."

He turned to Reas.

"Bring me a couple of rods," he said.

The heavy-boned bodyguard got up from his map, went across the room, and came back holding a pair of short black rods like the one Jim had seen at Ro's belt and like the two which Mekon had produced after Jim had used the knife on him. Another black rod, just

like the two in Reas' hands, Jim noticed, was stuck
through loops in the ropelike belt that encircled Reas'
thick waist.

"Thank you, Reas," said Galyan, accepting the two
rods. He turned to Jim. "I told you that you won't find
other High-born like me. I'm remarkably free of prejudice toward the lesser races of man—not out of any
sentimentality, but out of practicality. But I would like
to show you something."

He turned his head and beckoned to one of the
small, brown-skinned men with the brown hair hanging straight down his back. The man got up and came
over to stand beside Reas, and Galyan handed him one
of the two black rods. The man stuck it through the
belt around his own waist.

"Reas, as I said," said Galyan to Jim, "is not only
trained but actually bred to be a bodyguard. Now,
observe how he handles his rod, compared to his
opponent here."

Galyan turned to Reas and the other man, who
were now facing each other at a distance of about
four feet.

"I will clap my hands twice," said Galyan to them.
"The first clap commences the draw—only, Reas will
not be allowed to draw until the second clap. Observe,
Wolfling!"

Galyan lifted his hands and clapped them softly
together twice, the second clap following about a half-
second behind the first. At the sound of the first clap,
the small brown man snatched the rod from his belt
and was just bringing its far end up to point at Reas
when the second clap sounded and Reas drew his own
rod swiftly and smoothly.

Just then, something in appearance like a cross
between the flame of a welding torch and the arc of
a static-electricity charge crackled from the end of the

rod held by the smaller man. It was aimed directly at the chest of Reas, but it never reached its target. Even as it burst from the end of the rod, Reas' rod was already in position, and a counterdischarge met and deflected the discharge from the smaller man's rod, so that both charges went upward.

"Very good," said Galyan. The discharge from both rods ceased, and both men lowered their rods and turned to face the High-born. Galyan reached out and took the rod from the small brown man and dismissed him with a wave back to his work.

"Now, watch closely, Wolfling," said Galyan. He slid the black rod he held into a pair of loops on his own belt; and as if in response to an unseen signal, the bodyguard, Reas, did the same with his rod.

"Now, as I say—observe, Wolfling," said Galyan softly. "Reas can draw at any time he wishes."

Reas stepped forward until he was less than an arm's length from the seated High-born. For a moment he stood completely motionless; then he looked off into a corner of the room; and at the same moment his hand flashed toward his belt.

There was a sudden sharp *click!* Galyan's arm was extended, and the rod in his hand was holding Reas' rod in half-drawn position from its belt loops. Galyan chuckled softly and released the pressure he was putting against the other rod. He handed his rod back to Reas, who took them away across the room.

"You see?" said Galyan, turning to Jim. "Any High-born has faster reflexes than any single human of any of the other races of man. Let alone wild men like yourselves. That was why in going after rods as Mekon did, he was intending to force you into a duel that you had no chance whatsoever of winning. As I say, we are true aristocracy. Not only are my reflexes faster than those of Reas, but my memory is better, my intelligence is greater, my discernment and perceptions are sharper than those of any other human beings—yes, even among the High-born themselves. But, in spite of that, I employ more of the low-born than any of my fellow High-born. I have many things for them to do, and I keep them busy at it. Do you wonder why I do this, when I myself could do any of these things better, by and for myself?"

"I'd assume," said Jim, "for the simple reason that you can't be in two places at once."

Galyan's eyes glowed with a new intensity.

"What a brilliant Wolfling it is!" he said. "Yes, other men are useful to me, even though they are inferior. And it strikes me, just now, that maybe you and the little tool of yours with which you damaged Mekon might one day be useful to me, too. Are you surprised to hear that?"

"Not after you spent this much time on me," said Jim.

Galyan rocked himself softly on his cushion, holding to his knee.

"Better and better," he murmured. "This Wolfling has a brain—raw gray matter, of course. But a brain, nonetheless. I wasn't wrong. Yes, I may have a use for you, Wolfling—and do you know why you'll be useful to me when the time comes?"

"You must plan to pay me, some way or another," said Jim.

"Exactly," said Galyan. "We High-born do not show our age, so I'll tell you right now, Wolfling, that while I'm by no means into middle age, as we know lifetimes, still, I'm not a raw youngster anymore. And I've learned how to get members of the lesser human races to work for me. I give them whatever they most want by way of reward and payment."

He paused. Jim waited.

"Well, Wolfling," said Galyan after a minute, "what is it you want most? If you were not a wild man, I wouldn't have to ask you. But I don't know Wolflings well enough to know what they want. What do they want most?"

"Freedom," said Jim.

Galyan smiled.

"Of course," he said. "What all wild beasts want— or think they want. Freedom. And in your case, freedom means the right to come and go, doesn't it?"

"That's the base of it," said Jim.

"Particularly the right to go, I should think," murmured Galyan. "No doubt you never stopped to think of it, Wolfling, but it is simple fact that once you have been taken in by us to the Throne World, you would have no way of ever going back to the place where we first found you. Did you realize that? That, once you joined us on this trip to the Throne World, you would never be able to go home again?"

Jim stared down at him.

"No," he said, "I hadn't planned never to go home again."

"Well, that's your situation," said Galyan. He lifted a slim forefinger. "*Unless* you turn out to be useful to me. I might see to it that you got home again."

He let go of his knee and rose suddenly to his feet, towering over Jim.

"I'll send you back to Ro now," he said. "Carry that thought I've just given you away with you. Your only hope of ever seeing the world from which you came again is if in some way you please me."

The High-born made no further movement, but abruptly Jim found himself back in the glass-walled room with the other pets. Ro was crouched at one end, weeping over the body of one of the feline creatures. It was not the one who had been among the pets, because this one now stood, whining anxiously, just out of reach of the tearful girl. It was another one that lay dead—and it looked rather as if it had been cut almost in half by a thunderbolt.

Chapter 4

Jim went to the girl. She was not aware of his presence until he had reached down and put his arms around her. She looked up, startled and suddenly stiff; but then, when she saw who it was, she clung to him.

"You're all right. At least, you're all right . . ." she managed to get out.

"Where did this come from?" asked Jim, pointing down at the dead feline.

The question triggered off a new burst of emotion. But gradually the story began to come out. She had raised this feline, as she had raised the other one that was one of the pets. This feline had been given to Mekon by Afuan some time back, and Mekon had taught it to attack on command.

"But it was all right when I saw it last," said Jim. "How did this happen to it?"

She drew back a little from him and stared at him, shakily and with surprise.

"Didn't you hear?" she asked. "Afuan left it up to Galyan to fine Mekon for what he'd done. And Galyan decided that the fine would be . . ." She choked and could not go on, pointing at the animal.

"It's a strange sort of fine," he said slowly.

"Strange?" She looked up at him puzzledly. "But it's just the sort of fine that Galyan would exact. He's a demon, Jim. Where somebody else, operating on the Princess' orders, might have fined Mekon one of his favorite servants, or something else he valued, Galyan chose this poor animal instead—because along with losing it, of course, Mekon's going to lose a point. Oh, not a Lifetime Point. Galyan's too clever to be that hard on someone like Mekon. But it'll be at least a One-Year Point. And Mekon has enough points against him already, Lifetime and otherwise, so that he can seriously worry from time to time about some kind of an accident that might bring him up to the level of banishment."

"Banishment?" asked Jim.

"Why, of course. Banishment from the Throne World—" Ro caught herself suddenly, and wiped her eyes. She stood up straight and looked down at the body of the dead animal at her feet. Immediately it vanished.

"I keep forgetting you don't understand things," she said, turning to Jim. "There's so much I'm going to have to teach you. All the High-born play points. It's one game that even the Emperor can't overrule; and too many points means you have to leave the Throne World forever. But I'll explain it all to you a little later. Right now I'd better begin teaching you how to move from room to room—"

But Ro's words had woken a new train of thought in Jim's mind.

"Just a second," he said. "Tell me something, Ro. If I wanted to step back into the city right now on an errand before the ship leaves, could I do it?"

"Oh!" she shook her head sadly at him. "I thought you at least knew that. The ship left that outworld world we were on some time ago. We'll be at the Throne World in three ship's-days."

"I see," said Jim grimly.

Her face paled abruptly, and she caught his arms with her hands, as if to keep him from stepping backward from her.

"Don't look like that!" she said. "Whatever it is, you shouldn't look like that!"

Jim forced his face to smooth out. He put away the sudden fury that had exploded inside him. He forced himself to smile down at Ro.

"All right," he said. "I promise you I won't look like that."

Ro still held him by the arms.

"You're so strange," she said, looking up at him. "So strange, in every way. What made you look like that?"

"Something Galyan said to me," he answered. "Something to the effect that I could never go back home again."

"But—you aren't going to want to go back home!" said Ro, a little wonderingly. "You've never seen the Throne World, so of course you don't know. But no one ever wants to leave it. And the only ones who can stay are the High-born who can keep their point levels down in the Game, and their servants and their possessions. Not even the Governors of the Colony Worlds can do more than visit the Throne World for short periods of time. When their time is up, they have to leave. But the High-born and people like you and me— we can stay."

"I see," he said.

She frowned down at his arms, which she still held. Her fingers were feeling them through the sleeves of his jacket.

"You're as hard-muscled as a Starkien," she said puzzledly. "And you're so tall for someone who's not High-born. Was it natural for you to be this tall back on that wild world you came from?"

Jim laughed a little shortly.

"I was this tall when I was ten years old," he said. The look of slight incomprehension on her face made him add, "That's halfway through my normal growing period."

"And you stopped growing then?" Ro asked.

"I was stopped," he said a little grimly. "Some of our medical practitioners ran a lot of tests on me because I was so big for my age. They couldn't find anything wrong, but they put me on an extract of the pituitary gland to curb my growing. And it worked. I stopped growing—physically. But I went on growing otherwise."

Jim interrupted himself abruptly. "Never mind that," he said. "You were going to show me how to move around the ship, from room to room."

"That—and other things!" Suddenly she seemed to grow several inches in front of him, and something came into her that was like the cold imperiousness of Princess Afuan. "They can take my animals and give them away or kill them. But they're not going to hurt you. When I get through with you, you'll know more than enough to survive. I may be a throwback, but I'm as High-born as any of them. The Emperor himself can't dismiss me, without cause, from the Throne World; and everything that is High-born's, by right is mine! Come along, and I'll begin to show you what it's like to live among the High-born and be a citizen of the society of the Throne World!"

She took him first to a section of the ship he had not yet visited. It consisted of a large, high-ceilinged, metal-walled room, with one wall covered with the rays of blinking lights of various colors. Tending this wall was one of the short brown men with long hair down his back. He was, Jim discovered, all that the ship possessed in the way of a crew—in fact, he was not even that. In actuality, he was nothing more than a standby engineer, on hand in case of the unlikely chance that some small repair or adjustment needed to be made to the ship's mechanism.

The ship, in fact, ran itself. It not only ran itself, it supplied the motive power for all the transfers of people between rooms, and everything else in the way of visible and invisible equipment aboard. Like some huge robot dog, it responded immediately to the mental whims of the Princess Afuan; and, to a lesser extent, it stood ready to accommodate the whims of everyone else aboard.

"Now," Ro instructed Jim, "simply stand here and relax. Let it make contact with you."

"Make contact with me?" Jim echoed. He assumed that she was talking about something like telepathy, and tried to say so—but found he had no word for it in the Empire language. Ro, however, understood him, and to his considerable surprise, launched into a complete and highly technical explanation of how the ship worked. In brief, it was simply that the ship studied the electrical activity of an individual brain and from this drew up what amounted to an individual electrical code for whatever the person was thinking or doing. Thoughts which were visualized clearly enough, Ro explained, triggered off motor subactivity in the body—in short, the body physically responded at a very low level to the scene it was imagining, as if that scene were real. The ship then matched these responses with the proper scene, and shifted the person to the scene by literally disassembling him at his present position and reassembling him at the location of the imagined scene.

The process by which the ship crossed light-years of empty space was the same method of disassembly and reassembly, only on a larger scale. That is, the whole ship and its contents were disassembled and reassembled farther along its line of passage. There was a certain limitation to the distance over which one of these shifts could take place, but since each shift took place at computer speeds, the effect was exactly like that of trans-light velocities, without effort.

" . . . Actually," wound up Ro, "the ship really never moves at all. It simply changes the coordinates of its position. . . ." And she went off into an explanation too technical for Jim to follow.

Nonetheless, after a little practice at visualization, Jim felt that same sensation—like that of a feather tickling the surface of his mind—that he had felt when Ro had asked him to visualize the warehouse in which his frozen bulls were stored. The first time it happened, he moved from one end of the room he was in to the other. But within minutes after that, he had mastered the knack and was easily shifting from room to room about the ship, although he was restricted to those rooms that he had once seen.

Ro took him back to her quarters, and the social aspects of his education began. The achievements of the few days before they landed on the Throne World surprised both of them. Jim was startled to discover that Ro, like all of the High-born, possessed vast stores of education covering both the scientific and the social aspects of every facet of her ordinary life. It was like her knowledge about the ship. Never in her life would she be called upon to do so much as pay attention to the pattern of winking lights on a ship's control board. But if necessary, she could have built the vessel from scratch, given the necessary tools and materials. Ro, on the other hand, was amazed to discover that she had to tell Jim things only once.

" . . . But are you sure you remember that?" she kept interrupting herself to ask Jim. "I never heard of anybody but a High-born who didn't have to work to remember things."

Jim would respond by quoting the last few paragraphs she had said word for word. Reassured, but not really convinced, she would plunge into further detail; and Jim would continue to soak up knowledge about the Throne World, the society of the High-born, and the Empire which Throne World and High-born together ruled.

The picture of it all was beginning to click together for him, as a coherent shape finally emerges after a certain critical number of the pieces of a jigsaw puzzle have been put together. Curiously, the High-born were not direct descendants of those natives of the Throne World who had gone out to colonize the other inhabited worlds of the Empire. They, who were now not merely in theory but in fact rulers of the Empire, had actually come into that position of authority by being weak rather than strong.

It was true that in the beginning the Throne World had tried to keep control of the other worlds it had colonized. But this attempt was soon defeated by the time and space intervening between it and them. Very quickly the newer worlds became autonomous; and by the time, several thousand years later, that the Empire had pushed outward in all directions, until it came to areas where there were no stars with habitable planets within any further reasonable distance, the Throne World had been all but forgotten, except as a birthplace of the human expansion among the stars.

However, even before that expansion had reached its limits, the older colonized worlds had begun to see the advantage of some general organization, some nominal authority and center point which could act as a clearing house for scientific and other developments achieved on other worlds than their own. The Throne World had therefore been revived by common consent and set up as a sort of worldwide combination library and information center. That—though no one knew it at the time—was the beginning of the High-born.

To the Throne World, in its new role, drifted inevitably the better academic and inventive minds of the Colony Worlds. Here was the intellectual hub of the human universe. Here, therefore, it was most profitable to live—not only in terms of practical reward for intellectual labors, but in the matter of intellectual companionship and access to new information in one field as well.

During the next few thousand years this immigration reached the point that it had to be restricted by the Throne World itself. Meanwhile, the Throne World, by virtue of being the source of supply for most technological advances, had become both rich and powerful in comparison to the Colony Worlds. Its intellectual population was already developing into an elite, added to only sparingly by the best minds of the Colony Worlds and eagerly served by inhabitants of the Colony Worlds who were not qualified to join the elite but greatly desired to live among the mighty.

Eventually, during the last ten thousand years or so, during which the Empire not only had remained static but had indeed shrunk its borders slightly, the Throne World elite had indeed become High-born—with special breeding controls which gave them the physical marks of their aristocracy. The onyx-white skin, the lemon-yellow eyes, the white hair and eyebrows and eyelashes—all these, Jim learned, were not developed out of any other necessity than to place the badge of superiority upon those who ruled the Empire from the Throne World. Instead of badges or escutcheons to mark their aristocracy, they had given themselves outsize bodies and minds, at the same time ensuring that none who did not belong to their elite could compete with them as individuals. They still gleaned the geniuses and the unusually capable from among what they called the lesser races of man, but that gleaning was highly selective now, and those gleaned did not so much enter the elite themselves as acquire the chance that through inbreeding their great-grand-children would be one of the tall, white-haired, onyx-skinned masters of the Empire.

" . . . You see," Ro said at last to Jim, when they had finally reached the Throne World and were preparing to leave the ship, "there's a chance—even for a Wolfling like you. Oh, they'll try to tear you down, all of the High-born, once they begin to suspect that you want to become one of them. But if you're educated and ready, they won't be able to do it. And with my help, we'll see they won't!"

Her eyes gleamed with triumph. Jim smiled at her and turned the topic of conversation to what he might expect next, once they had left the ship.

She looked suddenly sober.

"I don't know," she said. "Afuan doesn't tell me. Of course, she'll want to show you off to the Emperor as soon as possible."

With this answer in mind, he was consequently at least partly prepared when, an hour or so after the ship had landed on the Throne World, his own room aboard it suddenly vanished around him and he found himself standing in an arena. His luggage was at his feet, and facing him was a complete cuadrilla—banderilleros and picadors, with costumes and horses and all—an exact duplicate of the cuadrilla he had used back on Alpha Centauri III, with the exception that the men in the costumes were all of the breed of short brown men with long, straight hair down their backs.

"These beasts are artificial," said a voice beside him. He turned and saw Afuan standing a few feet from him. "That will include the bull with which you'll be practicing. Both the artificial beast and the men have been set to repeat exactly what you did the time we watched you once before. Simply keep them doing it until they learn how."

The Princess vanished. Apparently she considered that she had said all that needed to be said.

Left alone with his imitation cuadrilla and their mechanical horses, Jim looked around him. The arena was an exact duplicate of the huge arena in which he had fought the two bulls on Alpha Centauri III— except that it had been cleaned up to an almost ridiculous degree.

The stands of the arena, which on Alpha Centauri III had been of some brown, concretelike material, seemed here to be made of white marble. Everything was white, everywhere—even the sand on the floor of the arena was as white as snow.

Jim bent down, opened one of his luggage cases, and took out the large cape, the small cape, and the sword. He did not bother to take out his costume. He closed the luggage cases and put them behind one of the barreras. Music suddenly began, emanating from some unknown source. It was the right music, and moving with it, Jim lined up before his cuadrilla and began the slow walk across the ring toward a section of seats outlined in red that was plainly the Imperial box.

From Jim's standpoint, it was almost eerie. The longhaired little brown men moved through their motions, not only with professional certainty but also in exact imitation of the men he had left behind on Alpha Centauri III. Even small, useless, personal actions were copied. Evidently all these had been remembered by either Afuan or someone else of the High-born and faithfully fed into whatever programming was controlling the men who were now playing their parts with the bull. Where a man had leaned upon a barrera during an inactive moment, his duplicate here on the Throne World copied the pose exactly, on the equivalent barrera, and to an inch of the spot equivalent to where the original had placed his elbows. But the eeriness of duplication grew even stronger when Jim went out to work the bull himself with the large cape. For the duplication was doubled. There was even a sort of wry humor to it, thought Jim. The High-born had produced an imitation bull, programmed to follow exactly the motions of a live bull they had watched, but which they did not know had also been programmed by the biological sciences of Earth to go through exactly those same motions.

They carried through the whole business to the moment of the kill. When Jim's sword went in, the mechanical creature obediently collapsed, exactly as the real one had done back on Alpha Centauri III. Jim looked around at his pupils, wondering if it was time to stop; but they seemed quite rested and evidently were expecting to continue.

It was the second time through the whole pantomime that Jim began to spare attention from his own work with the imitation animal to study the actions of the men he was training. For the first time, he noticed that although they moved with a great deal of sureness, there was a certain amount of clumsiness in their efforts. It was not a clumsiness of the mind as much as the muscles. These men were doing what they had been programmed or instructed to do—doing it promptly and well. But the instinctive responses of their bodies were not yet there.

Jim ran through the complete performance two more times before calling it a day. By that time, although his own responses to the artificial animal had become automatic and without tension, he himself was thoroughly tired. Still, on the succeeding four days he continued to run through the bullfight as it had happened on Alpha Centauri III, until the responses of the small men with the long hair began to be not so much a matter of programming as of experience and natural reflex.

It was somewhere along in this period that he discovered that he could vary the actions of the bull by the same sort of deliberate mental imagery that Ro had taught him to use aboard the ship. Somewhere aboard the Throne World there was a master power source performing the same function for him with regard to the bullring that its counterpart had provided aboard the ship. Therefore, on the sixth day, he introduced his new cuadrilla to a different version of a bullfight.

The truth of the matter was, each of the bulls in cryogenic storage that he had brought with him had been programmed differently—just in case it should be suspected that they had been programmed at all. Jim himself had rehearsed each set of programming. Now he put his new assistants to work in the pattern they would encounter with the last bull in cryogenic storage. He used the last bull advisedly, hoping either that he would never have to use it in actuality or that his makeshift cuadrilla would have forgotten its specific and unvarying actions if he did have to use it.

During all these days he had discovered that he had what appeared to be a suite of rooms in some endless, one-story structure. Unlike the rooms aboard ship, the rooms here on the Throne World had doors and corridors; moreover, he seemed free to wander about at will, which he did. But though he explored outward from his rooms through a number of other parts of the building, across an open courtyard and through gardens, he encountered no High-born and only a few other men and women of what were clearly the lesser races—obviously servants here on the Throne World.

Ro had not come near him. On the other hand, Afuan had appeared several times, inquired briefly as to how the training sessions were coming along, and disappeared again. She showed neither pleasure nor impatience with the time he was taking; but when the day finally came that he told her he judged his trainees were ready, her reaction was prompt.

"Excellent!" she said. "You'll put on a show for the Emperor, then—within the next day or two."

She disappeared, to return briefly the following morning and announce that the bullfight would take place in the arena within a certain span of the Imperial time scale roughly equivalent to about forty minutes.

"I can't get one of my bulls thawed and revived that quickly," Jim said.

"That's already been taken care of," Afuan answered, and disappeared again. Jim began rather hastily to get into his suit of lights. Theoretically, he should have had an assistant help him to dress; but there was no chance for it. He had managed to struggle into about half the costume when the humor of it struck him. He laughed out loud.

"Where are you when I need you, Ro?" he asked the bare white walls of his room humorously. To his utter astonishment, Ro suddenly materialized before him as if she had been a genie summoned from a bottle.

"What do you want me to do?" she demanded.

He stared at her for a second, then laughed again.

"Don't tell me you heard what I said?" he asked her.

"Why, yes," she answered, looking a little surprised. "I set up a notice to let me know if you ever called for me. But you never did."

He laughed again. "I'd have called you before this," he said, "if I knew that was all I had to do to get hold of you."

He was treated to the sight of one of her astonishing blushes.

"But I want to help you!" she said. "Only—you didn't seem to be needing any help."

At that he sobered.

"I'm afraid I'm not in the habit of asking for it, usually," he said.

"Well, never mind now!" she said energetically. "What do you want me to do?"

"Help me into these clothes," he said. Unexpectedly, she giggled; and he stared at her in puzzlement.

"No, no. It's all right," she said. "It's just that that's the sort of thing a servant, a human of one of the lesser races, is supposed to do for a High-born. Not the other way around."

She picked up his hat.

"Where does this go?" she asked.

"It doesn't go—not yet. That's the last item," he told her. Obediently she put it down, and under his instructions began to help him into the rest of the costume.

When he was fully dressed, she looked at him with interest.

"You look strange—but good," she said.

"Didn't you see me in the arena at Alpha Centauri III?" he asked.

She shook her head.

"I was busy on the ship—and I really didn't

expect it to be too interesting." She stared at him with interest as he took his two capes and sword from the larger luggage case. "What're those for?"

"The pieces of cloth," he said, "are to attract the attention of the bull. The sword"—he pulled it a little way out of its scabbard to show her its blade—"is to kill him, at the end."

Her hand flew to her mouth. She paled and stepped backward. Her eyes were enormous.

"What's the matter?" he asked.

She tried to say something, but the only sound that came from her throat was more of a little cry than an understandable word. He frowned sharply.

"What is it?" he demanded. "What's wrong?"

"You didn't tell me . . ." The words came out of her, finally, in a sort of wail. "You didn't tell me you were going to *kill* him!"

She choked, whirled about, and disappeared. He stood staring at the space where she had been. Behind him a woman's voice spoke unexpectedly.

"Yes," it said. It was the voice of Princess Afuan, and he himself turned sharply, to find her standing there looking at him. "It seems that even a Wolfling like you can make mistakes. I'd have thought you'd have learned by this time that Ro has a soft spot in her for all animals."

He looked at her coldly.

"You're right," he said flatly, "I should've remembered that."

"Unless," she said, then paused, watching him with her lemon-yellow eyes, "that is, you had some reason for deliberately wanting to upset her. You've made quite a marked impression for a Wolfling, in such a short time. You not only made a friend of little Ro, but you made an enemy of Mekon, and interested not only Slothiel, but Galyan himself."

She considered him for a second with a close gaze
that seemed to have something hidden in it.

"Do you see me?"

"Of course," he said. And then he stiffened internally, although he was careful to keep his face and body
noncommittal.

For, before his eyes Afuan suddenly changed. It was
a strange changing, because no single thing about her
that he could see altered in any way. Even the expression on her face was the same. But suddenly she was
entirely different.

Suddenly, tall, onyx-skinned, yellow-eyed, white-
haired as she was, she became attractive. No—not
merely attractive—voluptuous to an almost overwhelming degree. It was more than merely a sensual attrac-
tion she projected. Her demand upon his capability of
desire was almost hypnotic.

Only the long, solitary years of internal isolation and
growth allowed him to resist the fascination Afuan was
now exerting upon him. Only the fact that he realized
the lust she was trying to awaken in him meant an
abandonment of all that he had searched for and won
by lonely journeys of the mind and soul, where the
mind and soul of man had never searched before—only
this allowed him to stand still, relaxed and calm,
unresponsive.

Abruptly, again without any physical sign of change,
Afuan was back as she had always been. Cold and
remote in appearance, striking, but not necessarily
attractive by the human standards of Earth.

"Amazing," she said a little softly, gazing at him
through eyes which—though they were not slitted—gave
the impression of being slitted. "Totally amazing, particularly for a Wolfling. But I think I understand you now,
wild man. Something in you, at some time, has made you
ambitious with an ambition larger than the universe."

After a second Jim performed the mental exercise that transferred him to the arena.

When he appeared there, the stands were already full of the white-clothed High-born. Not only that, but within the red-bordered area that was plainly the Imperial box was a party of six men and four women. The music had already begun, and Jim formed up with his cuadrilla for the walk across the white sand toward the Imperial box. As he got close, he saw that Afuan was one of the people in the box, seated to the left of someone who seemed to be Galyan, who was occupying the center seat, with an unusually broad-bodied, older-looking High-born man to his right, who had slightly yellowed eyebrows.

When Jim got close to the box, however, he saw that the man who resembled Galyan was not Galyan. Still, the resemblance was striking, and Jim suddenly remembered Galyan's comment about the Emperor being his first cousin. This, plainly, was the Emperor.

If anything, he was taller than Galyan himself. He lounged in his seat more casually than the other High-born seated around him, and there was something—for a High-born—unusually frank and open and intelligent about his gaze. He smiled down at Jim as he gave permission for the bullfight to commence. Afuan's eyes looked coldly down at Jim meanwhile.

Jim had eliminated the procedure of dedicating the bull to someone in the audience, and he did not revive the practice now. He returned with his cuadrilla across the ring and went directly into the bullfight. His men did well with the different behavior of the bull, which Afuan or someone else among the High-born had apparently chosen to revive at random from among the six in cryogenic storage. Luckily, each bull was a little different, and Jim recognized the differences, so that he was able to adjust himself to the bull's pattern of behavior the minute he saw it come charging into the ring.

Still, he had his hands full with it, as he had had his hands full in the arena on Alpha Centauri III. Moreover, what little space for thought he had was taken up with Afuan's comment about his ambition. Clearly the Princess possessed a sense of perception that was very nearly deadly.

The bullfight continued, and drew eventually to its closing moments. This bull, unlike the one on Alpha Centauri III, remained strong right up to the predicted point in its programming. Jim finally went in over the horns with his sword for the kill, almost directly in front of the Imperial box. Then, withdrawing his sword, he turned and took a few steps to confront the Emperor— as much from his own sense of interest in how the Emperor would respond to the spectacle as for the reason that on the ship Ro had told him that approaching the Emperor afterward would be expected of him. He walked up to the barrier itself and looked upward at a slant into the face of the Emperor, less than a dozen feet away. The Emperor smiled down. His eyes seemed to shine with an unusual brightness— although suddenly Jim noticed there was something almost unfocused about them.

The Emperor's smile broadened. A small trickle of saliva ran down from one corner of his mouth. He opened his lips and spoke to Jim.

"Waw," he said, smiling all the while and staring directly through Jim. "Waw. . . ."

Chapter 5

Jim stood still. There was nothing to give him a clue as to how he should react. The rest of the High-born in the Imperial box—in fact, all the High-born within view—seemed deliberately to be paying no attention at all to whatever fit or stroke had suddenly taken the Emperor. Plainly, Jim judged that he would be expected to ignore it also. Afuan and all the others in the royal box merely sat as if the Emperor was in fact engaged in a private conversation with Jim. In fact, so persuasive and so massive was the reaction, which was *no* reaction, that it had something of the same hypnotic compulsion that Afuan had used earlier, except that in this case it seemed determined to convince not only Jim but also themselves that what was happening to the Emperor was not happening.

Then, suddenly, it was all over.

The saliva vanished from the Emperor's jaw as if an invisible hand had wiped it away. His smile firmed, his eyes focused.

" . . . Moreover, we are exceedingly interested to know

more about you," the Emperor was suddenly saying, as if continuing a conversation that had been going on for some time. "You are the first Wolfling we have seen in many years here at our court. After you have rested, you must come to see us, and we'll have a talk."

The Emperor's smile was open, frank, and charming. His voice was friendly, his eyes intelligent.

"Thank you, Oran," replied Jim. He had been instructed by Ro that the Emperor was always referred to as "the Emperor" in every way except direct address; when one was speaking to him directly, one always called him simply by his first name—Oran.

"You're entirely welcome," said the Emperor, smiling cheerfully. He vanished, and a second later all the seats in the stands were empty of High-born.

Jim visualized his own quarters and was instantly back in them. Thoughtfully, he began to remove his costume. He was struggling out of the tight jacket when he suddenly felt himself assisted from behind, and looking around, saw Ro helping him.

"Thank you," he said, and smiled over his shoulder at her as the jacket came off. She went on helping him, her eyes fixed on the floor; but a dark flush stained her downcast features.

"I still think it's terrible!" she muttered to the floor. "But I didn't realize—" Suddenly she lifted her face to him, paling again. "I really didn't realize, Jim. That animal was trying to kill *you*."

"Yes," said Jim, feeling once more the secret, internal touch of shame that came to him whenever he remembered how his bullfighting was rigged, rather than honest. "That's the way it is."

"Anyway," said Ro in very nearly a grim tone of voice, "if we're lucky, you won't ever have to do it again. It's a stroke of luck, to start off with, the Emperor being interested in you. And—guess what?"

She stopped assisting him, and he stood there, half-undressed, staring quizzically down at her.

"What?" he asked.

"I've found a sponsor for you!" she burst out excitedly. "Slothiel! He liked you when you didn't flinch—that first time he saw you. And he's willing to have you numbered among his acquaintances. Do you know what that means?"

She stopped and waited for his answer. He shook his head. What she was talking about now was something she had not gone into aboard the ship.

"It means you're not really in the servant class from now on!" she burst out. "I'd hoped to get someone to sponsor you—but not this soon. And I didn't want to raise your hopes by mentioning it. But Slothiel actually came to me!"

"He did?" Jim frowned internally, although he was careful to keep his physical brow smooth for Ro's benefit. He wondered if Slothiel had anything to do with Afuan's visit to him earlier—or what Galyan had said to him aboard the ship. He found himself on the verge of asking Ro this, and then he changed his mind. Afuan's visit, and the reaction she had tried to provoke in him, he found, was not something he wanted to tell Ro about—at least, not just yet.

He came out of his thoughts abruptly, to realize that Ro was still busily undressing him, with no apparent self-consciousness about the matter. He had no great self-consciousness about it himself. But Ro's attitude struck him just then as being a little too zealously proprietary, like that of an owner lovingly grooming a pet horse or dog for show purposes. Besides, Jim had needed assistance, not complete care and handling.

"That's fine," he said, moving out of her grasp. "I can handle the rest of it myself."

He picked up his Black Watch kilt from the hassock

on which he had dropped it when he had hastily started to dress for the bullring. He put it on, together with a short-sleeved green shirt. Ro watched him with fond pride.

"Tell me more about this sponsorship business," said Jim, "sponsorship for what?"

"Why," said Ro, opening her eyes wide, "for adoption by the Throne World, of course! Don't you remember? I told you that still, occasionally, a few rare people of unusual abilities or talents are allowed to move from one of the Colony Worlds to the Throne World and join the High-born. Though, of course, they aren't really High-born themselves; the best they can hope for is that their great-grandchildren will become true High-born. Well, that whole process is called adoption by the Throne World. And adoption proceedings start by someone among the High-born being willing to act as sponsor to whomever wants to be adopted."

"You're thinking of getting me adopted as a High-born?" asked Jim, smiling a little.

"Of course not!" Ro literally hugged herself with glee. "But, once you've been sponsored, the adoption proceedings have been started. And you're protected by the Emperor's authority as a provisional High-born, until he gets around to either accepting you or refusing you. And the thing is, nobody ever gets refused, once he's been sponsored, unless he's done something so bad that there's no alternative but to get him off the Throne World. Once Slothiel sponsors you, none of the High-born can do anything to you the way they can to a servant. I mean, your life's protected. None of the High-born—not even Afuan or Galyan—can simply act against you. They have to complain about you to the Emperor."

"I see," said Jim thoughtfully. "Should I mention that Slothiel is going to do this when I talk to the Emperor?"

"Talk to the Emperor?" Ro stared at him and then burst out laughing. But she stopped quickly and put an apologetic hand on his arm. "I'm sorry. I shouldn't have laughed. But the chances are you'll spend your whole life here and never talk to the Emperor."

"The chances are wrong, then," said Jim, "because after the bullfight the Emperor asked me to come and see him as soon as I'd had a chance to rest a bit."

Ro stared at him. Then slowly she shook her head.

"You don't understand, Jim," she said sympathetically. "He just said that. Nobody *goes* to see the Emperor. The only time they see him is when he has them brought to him. If you're going to see the Emperor, you'll suddenly find yourself brought into his presence. Until then, you just have to wait."

Jim frowned.

"I'm sorry, Jim," she said. "You didn't know it, but the Emperor often says things like that. But then, something else comes up and he forgets all about it. Or else he just says it without meaning it, just because it's something to say. Like paying a compliment."

Jim smiled slowly, and Ro's face paled again.

"Don't look like that!" she said, catching hold of his arm again. "No one should look savage like that."

"Don't worry," said Jim. He erased the grin. "But I'm afraid you're wrong. I'm going to see the Emperor. Where would he be?"

"Why, in Vhotan's office, this time of day—" She broke off suddenly, staring at him. "Jim, you mean it! Don't you understand? You can't go there—"

"Just show me the way," said Jim.

"I won't!" she said. "He'd order his Starkiens to kill you! Maybe they'd even kill you without waiting to be ordered."

"Oh? And why would the Starkiens want to kill our wild man?" broke in Slothiel's voice unexpectedly. They turned to discover that the tall High-born had just materialized in the room with them. Ro wheeled upon him as if he were the cause of her argument with Jim.

"After the bullfight the Emperor told Jim to rest awhile, then come and see him!" said Ro. "Now Jim wants me to tell him how to get to the Emperor! I told him I won't do it!"

Slothiel broke out laughing.

"*Go* to the Emperor!" he echoed. "Well, why don't you tell him? If you won't, I will."

"You!" flared Ro. "And you were the one who said you'd sponsor him!"

"True," drawled Slothiel, "and I will—because I admire the man and because I'll enjoy the look on Galyan's face when he hears about it. But if—what did you say his name is—Jim is bound and determined to get himself killed before the sponsorship can be arranged, who am I to interfere with his fate?"

He looked at Jim over the head of Ro, who had pushed herself between them.

"You really want to go?" Slothiel said.

Jim smiled again, grimly.

"I'm a Wolfling," he said. "I don't know any better."

"Right," said Slothiel, ignoring Ro's frantic attempts to silence him by her voice and her hand over his mouth. "Hang on. I'll send you there. For all the Emperor and Vhotan will know, you found the way yourself."

Immediately, Jim was in a different room. It was a very large circular room with some sort of transparent ceiling showing a cloud-flecked sky above—or was the sky with its clouds merely an illusion overhead? Jim had no time to decide which, because his attention was all taken up by the reaction of the half-dozen people already in the room, who had just caught sight of him.

Of the half-dozen men in the room, one was the Emperor. He had checked himself in mid-sentence on seeing Jim appear; and he stood half-turned from the older, powerfully bodied High-born who had sat at his right during the bullfight. Standing back a little way from these two, with his back to Jim, and just now turning to see what had interrupted the Emperor, was a male High-born whom Jim did not recognize. The other three men in the room were heavily muscled, gray-skinned, bald-headed individuals like the one Galyan had referred to as his bodyguard. These wore leather loin straps, with a black rod thrust through loops in the belt around their waist, and about the rest of their body and limbs were metallic-looking bands, which, however, seemed to fit and cling to position on them more like bands of thick elastic cloth than metal. At the sight of Jim, they had immediately drawn their rods and were aiming them at him when a sharp, single word from the Emperor stopped them.

"No!" said the Emperor. "It's—" He seemed to peer at Jim without recognition for a second; then a broad smile spread across his face. "Why, it's the Wolfling!"

"Exactly!" snapped the older High-born. "And what's he doing here? Nephew, you'd better—"

"Why," interrupted the Emperor, striding toward Jim, still smiling broadly at him, "I invited him here. Don't you remember, Vhotan? I issued the invitation after the bullfight."

Already the Emperor's tall body was between Jim and the three thick-bodied, armed bodyguards. He stopped one of his own long paces away from Jim and stood smiling down at him.

"Naturally," the Emperor said, "you came as soon as you could, didn't you, Wolfling? So as not to offend us by keeping us waiting?"

"Yes, Oran," answered Jim.

But now the older man, called Vhotan, who was apparently the Emperor's uncle, had come up to stand beside his nephew. His lemon-yellow eyes under their yellowish tufts of eyebrows glared down at Jim.

"Nephew," he said, "you can't possibly let this wild man get away with something like this. Break protocol once, and you set a precedent for a thousand repetitions of the same thing!"

"Now, now, Vhotan," said the Emperor, turning his smile appeasingly on the older High-born. "How many Wolflings have we on our Throne World who don't yet know the palace rules? No, I invited him here. If I remember, I even said I might find him interesting to talk to; and now, I believe I might."

He stepped aside, and folded himself up, sitting down on one of the large hassocklike pillows that played the role of furniture for the High-born.

"Sit down, Wolfling," he said. "You too, Uncle—and you, Lorava—" He glanced aside at the third High-born, a slim, younger male who had just come up. "Let's all sit down here together and have a chat with the Wolfling. Where do you come from, Wolfling? Out toward galaxy's-edge of our Empire, isn't it?"

"Yes, Oran," Jim answered. He had already seated himself; and reluctantly Vhotan was lowering himself to a hassock beside the Emperor. The young High-born called Lorava took two hasty strides up to them and also sat down on a nearby pillow.

"A lost colony. A lost world," mused the Emperor, almost to himself, "filled with wild men—and no doubt wilder beasts?"

He looked at Jim for an answer.

"Yes," said Jim, "we still have a good number of wild beasts—although that number's been reduced, in the last few hundred years particularly. Man has a tendency to crowd out the wild animals."

"Man has a tendency to crowd out even man, sometimes," said the Emperor. For a moment a little shadow seemed to pass behind his eyes, as if he remembered some private sadness of his own. Jim watched him with careful interest. It was hard to believe that this man before him was the same one he had seen drooling and making incoherent sounds in the arena.

"But the men there—and the women. Are they all like you?" the Emperor said, returning the focus of his eyes to Jim.

"Each one of us is different, Oran," said Jim.

The Emperor laughed.

"Of course!" he said. "And no doubt, being healthy wild men, you prize the difference, instead of trying to fit yourselves all into one common mold. Like we superior beings, we High-born of the Throne World!" His humor calmed slightly. "How did we happen to find your world, after having lost it so many centuries—or thousands of years—ago?"

"The Empire didn't find us," said Jim. "We found an outlying world of the Empire."

There was a second's silence in the room, broken by a sudden half-snort, half-bray of laughter from the youngster Lorava.

"He's lying!" Lorava sputtered. "They found us? If they could find us, how did they ever get lost in the first place?"

"Quiet!" snapped Vhotan at Lorava. He turned back to Jim. His face and the face of the Emperor were serious. "Are you telling us that your people, after forgetting about the Empire, and the falling back into complete savagery, turned around and developed civilization all over again—including a means of space travel?"

"Yes," said Jim economically.

Vhotan stared hard into Jim's eyes for a long second, and then turned to the Emperor.

"It might be worth checking, Nephew," he said.

"Worth checking. Yes . . ." murmured the Emperor. But his thoughts seemed to have wandered. He was no longer gazing at Jim, but off across the room at nothing in particular; and a look of gentle melancholy had taken possession of his face. Vhotan glanced at him and then got to his feet. The older High-born stepped over to Jim, tapped him on the shoulder with a long forefinger, and beckoned for him to rise.

Jim got to his feet. Behind the still-seated, still abstractedly gazing Emperor, Lorava also rose to his feet. Vhotan led them both quietly to a far end of the room, then turned to Lorava.

"I'll call you back later, Lorava," he said brusquely.

Lorava nodded and disappeared. Vhotan turned back to Jim.

"We've had an application from Slothiel to sponsor you for adoption," Vhotan said quickly. "Also, you were brought here by the Princess Afuan; and I understand you had some contact with Galyan. Are all of those things correct?"

"They are," said Jim.

"I see. . . ." Vhotan stood for a second, his eyes hooded thoughtfully. Then his gaze sharpened once more upon Jim. "Did any of those three suggest that you come here just now?"

"No," answered Jim. He smiled slightly at the tall, wide-shouldered old man towering massively over him. "Coming here was my own idea—in response to the Emperor's invitation. I only mentioned it to two other people. Slothiel and Ro."

"Ro?" Vhotan frowned. "Oh, that little girl, the throwback in Afuan's household. You're sure *she* didn't suggest your coming here?"

"Perfectly sure. She tried to stop me," said Jim. "And as for Slothiel—when I told him I was coming, he laughed."

"Laughed?" Vhotan echoed the word, then grunted. "Look at my eyes, Wolfling!"

Jim fastened his own gaze on the two lemon-yellow eyes under the slightly yellowish tufts of eyebrows. As he gazed, the eyes seemed to increase in brilliance and swim before him in the old man's face, until they threatened to merge.

"How many eyes do I have?" he heard Vhotan's voice rumbling.

Two eyes swam together, like two yellowish-green suns, burning before him. They tried to become one. Jim felt a pressure upon him like that of the hypnotic influence Afuan had tried to bring to bear on him before the bullfight. He stiffened internally, and the eyes separated.

"Two," he said.

"You're wrong, Wolfling," said Vhotan. "I have one eye. One eye only!"

"No," said Jim. The two eyes remained separate. "I see two."

Vhotan grunted again. Abruptly his gaze ceased burning down upon Jim, and the hypnotic pressure relaxed.

"Well, I see I'm not going to find out that way," said Vhotan, almost to himself. His gaze sharpened upon Jim again, but in an ordinary rather than a hypnotic fashion. "But I suppose you understand that I can easily find out if you've been telling the truth or not."

"I assumed you could," said Jim.

"Yes. . . ." Vhotan became thoughtful again. "There's

a good deal more here than surface indication implies. . . . Let's see, the Emperor can act on Slothiel's application for sponsorship, of course. But I think you'll need more than that. Let's see. . . ."

Vhotan turned his head abruptly to the right and spoke to empty air.

"Lorava!"

The thin young High-born appeared.

"The Emperor is appointing this Wolfling to an Award Commission as unit officer in the Starkiens. See to the details and his assignment to a section of the palace guard . . . And send Melness to me."

Lorava disappeared again. About three seconds later another, smaller man materialized where he had stood.

He was a slim, wiry man in typical white tunic and kilt with close-cropped reddish hair and a skin that would almost have matched the color of Jim's own if there had not been a sort of sallow, yellowish tinge to it. His face was small and sharp-featured, and the pupils of his eyes were literally black. He was clearly not one of the High-born but there was an air of assurance and authority about him which transcended that even of the armed bodyguards called Starkiens.

"Melness," said Vhotan, "this man is a Wolfling—the one that just put on the spectacle in the arena a few hours ago."

Melness nodded. His black eyes flickered from Vhotan to Jim, and back to the tall old High-born once more.

"The Emperor is appointing him to an Award Commission in the Starkiens of the palace guard. I've told Lorava to take care of the assignment but I'd like you to see to it that his duties are made as nominal as possible."

"Yes, Vhotan," answered Melness. His voice was a hard-edged, masculine tenor. "I'll take care of it—and him."

He vanished, in his turn. Vhotan looked once more at Jim.

"Melness is majordomo of the palace," Vhotan said. "In fact, he's in charge, at least in theory, of all those not High-born on the Throne World. If you have any difficulties, see him. Now, you can return to your own quarters. And don't come here again unless you're sent for!"

Jim visualized the room where he had left Ro and Slothiel. He felt the slight feather touch on his mind, and at once he was back there.

Both of them, he saw, were still there. Ro rushed at him the minute she saw him and threw her arms around him. Slothiel laughed.

"So you came back," said the languid High-born. "I had a hunch you would. In fact, I offered to bet on the point with Ro here—but she's not the betting kind. What happened to you?"

"I've been given an Award Commission in the Starkiens," said Jim calmly. His eyes met Slothiel's. "And Vhotan tells me that the Emperor will act promptly upon your offer to sponsor me."

Ro let go of him and stepped backward, staring up at him in astonishment. Slothiel condescended to raise his eyebrows in surprise.

"Jim!" said Ro in a wondering tone. "What—what *did* happen?"

Briefly Jim told them. When he was done, Slothiel whistled admiringly and cheerfully.

"Excuse me," he said. "This looks like a good chance to clean up on a few small bets before the rest of the Throne World hears about your promotions."

He disappeared. Ro, however, had not moved.

Looking down at her, Jim saw that her face was tightened by lines of worry.

"Jim," she said hesitantly, "Vhotan did ask exactly that about me, did he? . . . About whether I might've suggested that you go to the Emperor that way? And he asked that after he remembered that I was in Afuan's household?"

"That's right," said Jim. He smiled a little bleakly. "Interesting, isn't it?"

Ro shivered suddenly.

"No, it isn't!" she said tensely but in a low voice. "It's frightening! I knew I could teach you things and help you survive here in the ordinary way. But if things are going on in which others of the High-born want to use you. . . ." Her voice trailed off. Her eyes were dark with unhappiness.

Jim considered her in silence for a moment. Then he spoke.

"Ro," he said, slowly, "tell me. Is the Emperor ill?"

She looked up at him in astonishment.

"Ill? . . . You mean, sick?" she said. Then, suddenly, she laughed. "Jim, none of the High-born are ever sick—least of all the Emperor."

"There's something wrong with him," said Jim. "And it can't be much of a secret if it happens the way it happened in the arena after the bullfight. Did you see how he changed when he started to speak to me after the bull was dead?"

"Changed?" She literally stared at him. "Changed? In what way?"

Jim told her.

" . . . You didn't see how he looked, or hear the sounds he made?" asked Jim. "Of course not—come to think of it, you probably weren't sitting that close."

"But, Jim!" She put her hand on his arm in that familiar, persuasive gesture of hers. "Every seat in the arena there has its own focusing equipment. Why, when you were fighting with that animal"—she shuddered briefly, in passing, then hurried on—"I could see you from as closely as I wanted, as if I were standing as close to you as I am now. When you turned toward the Imperial box, I was still focused right in on you. I saw the Emperor speak to you, and if he'd done anything out of the ordinary, I'd have noticed it too!"

He stared at her.

"You didn't see what I saw?" he said after a second.

She continued to meet his eyes in a pattern of honesty; but with a sudden sensitivity inside himself, he seemed to feel that, within, she was somehow refusing to meet his eye—without being really aware of this herself.

"No," she said. "I saw him speak to you and heard him invite you to visit him after you'd had a chance to rest. Nothing more than that."

She continued to stand, gazing up into his eyes in that pattern of exterior honesty, with the inner aversion of her gaze unknown to her but evident to him. The seconds stretched out, and he suddenly realized that she was fixed. She was incapable of breaking the near-trance of this moment. He would have to be the one to interrupt it.

He turned his head away from her and was just in time to see the gray-skinned, bald-headed figure of a Starkien appear in the room about five feet away from them.

Jim stiffened, staring at him.

"Who are you?" Jim demanded.

"My name is Adok I," responded the newcomer. "But I am you."

Chapter 6

Jim frowned sharply at the man, who, however, showed no reaction to his frown at all.

"You're me?" Jim echoed. "I don't understand."

"Why, Jim!" broke in Ro. "He's your substitute, of course. You can't actually be a Starkien yourself. Any more than a—" She fumbled for a parallel and gave it up. "Well, look at him. And look at yourself!" she finished.

"The High-born is quite right," said Adok I. He had a deep, flat, emotionless voice. "Award Commissions are usually given to those who are not Starkien by birth and training. In such cases a substitute is always provided."

"A substitute is, is he?" said Jim. "In that case, what do they call you officially, in the records?"

"Officially, as I said, I'm you," answered Adok I. "Officially, my name is James Keil. I am a Wolfling from a world that calls itself"—the Starkien's tongue stumbled a little with the pronunciation of the unknown word—"Earth."

"I thought you told me that you were Adok I," Jim

said. The extreme seriousness of the Starkien was tempting him to smile, but an instinct kept the smile hidden within him and off his face.

"Unofficially, to you, Jim," said the other man, "I am Adok I. Your intimates, like the High-born lady here, may call me either Adok I or Jim Keil—it makes no difference."

"I'll call you Adok I," said Ro. "And you can call me Ro."

"I'll do that, Ro," said Adok I in a tone of voice as if he were repeating an order he had just been given, and affirming his willingness and ability to execute it.

Jim shook his head, amused and intrigued by the combination of characteristics the Starkien was exhibiting. The man seemed humorless to the point of woodenness, obedient to the point of servility, and in conjunction with these things, evidently considered it the best possible manners to address Jim by the familiar short form of Jim's first name. Moreover, beyond this, Adok I seemed to assume a strange mixture of superiority and inferiority toward Jim at the same time. Clearly the Starkien did not for a moment appear to consider that Jim had the capabilities to perform the tasks that Adok I was himself fitted to perform. On the other hand, plainly he considered himself completely a creature of Jim's will—at Jim's beck and call. However, thought Jim abruptly, investigation of Adok's character could come later. There was a more immediate question.

"Well," Jim said, "now that I've got you, what am I supposed to do with you?"

"We should begin with my doing things with you, Jim," said Adok I. He looked over at Ro. "If Ro will excuse us, I should immediately begin instructing you in the necessities and duties of being a unit officer—over and above those in which I can substitute for you."

"I've got to get back to my pets anyway," said Ro. "I'll come and find you later, Jim."

She touched him lightly on the arm and disappeared.

"All right, Adok," said Jim, turning back to the Starkien, "what do we do first?"

"We should begin with a visit to the quarters of your unit," Adok said. "If you will allow me to show you the way, Jim—"

"Go ahead," said Jim, and immediately found himself with Adok in what seemed to be an enormous, windowless, high-ceilinged room. In spite of all that space, however, something within Jim felt the sensation of closeness, an oppression as of confinement.

"Where are we?" he asked Adok, for the polished floor stretching away from them was empty in all directions for large distances, except for a few distant moving figures almost lost in the dimness and distance.

"We're at the parade ground." Adok's head came around to gaze at Jim with the first faint sign of emotion the Starkien had yet shown. After a second Jim realized Adok was registering surprise. "We are also below ground." Adok gave their depth in Empire terms, which translated to something like half a mile down from the surface of the planet. "Does it disturb you? It disturbs the High-born, but only a few of the servants are disturbed by it."

"No, I'm not disturbed," Jim said. "I felt something, though."

"If you are disturbed, you should admit it to me," said Adok. "If you are ever afraid or disturbed, you should tell me, even if you tell no one else. No one else but I need to know. But it is necessary for me to know when you are emotionally weakened, so that I can take measures to protect you from such weakness and hide the fact from others."

Jim chuckled, and the sound echoed eerily away into

the distances around them. It was an odd moment and place for humor, but Jim was finding Adok I strangely likeable.

"Don't worry," he told the Starkien. "I don't usually feel emotionally weakened. But if I ever do, I promise to let you know."

"Good," said Adok seriously. "Now I brought you first to this point on the parade ground because one of the things I cannot do for you is stand certain parades with the unit. At some parades we both must be present. Now that you have been brought to this spot, you can instantly return to it on your own in case something may have made you a little late in showing up for the parade. Now, let's go to the armory, and we'll draw your weapons and accouterments while you memorize that destination also."

The next room they appeared in was more brightly lit and a very great deal smaller than the parade ground. It was a long narrow room, both long walls of which seemed to be divided into compartments holding the leather straps and the bands of silver stuff such as those which encircled the legs, arms, and body of Adok, as well as those of the Starkiens in the room with the Emperor and Vhotan. Adok led Jim directly to several of the compartments and collected an assortment of the straps and silver bands. He did not, however, suggest that Jim put them on at this time. Instead, Adok himself carried them, while he transported Jim in quick succession to the barracks, or living quarters, of the Starkiens in Jim's unit—these were suites of rooms not unlike those that Jim himself had been given, except that they were smaller and in this below-ground location; a gymnasium; a dining hall; a sort of underground park, with grass and trees flourishing under an artificial sun; and finally to a sort of amusement and shopping center, where many Starkiens mingled with many times more their own number of other servants of the lesser races.

Finally Adok concluded the quick shift about these various locations by bringing Jim to a large room fitted out somewhat like the room in which Jim had encountered the Emperor and Vhotan. Not only was it large and well furnished, but Jim instantly felt a lightening of the sensation within him that had warned him before that he was below ground. Apparently this room, whatever it was, was above ground.

"Who—" he began to Adok, and then found his question answered before he could enunciate it. The olive-skinned man called Melness materialized in front of them and looked, not at Jim, but at Adok.

"I have taken him around the places concerned with his unit," Adok said to the Master Servant of the Throne World, "and brought him here finally to you, as you asked, Melness."

"Good," said Melness in his sharp tenor. His black eyes flicked to Jim's face. "The sponsorship for your adoption has been accepted by the Emperor."

"Thanks for telling me," said Jim.

"I'm not telling you for your benefit," said Melness, "but because it's necessary for me to make your situation clear to you. As a candidate for adoption, you are in theory a probationary High-born, who is superior to me, as to all servants. On the other hand, as an officer of the Starkiens below the rank of a Ten-unit Commander, as well as because you were born among one of the lesser races of man, you are under my orders."

Jim nodded.

"I see," he said.

"I hope you do!" said Melness sharply. "We have a contradiction; and the way such contradictions are

414 Gordon R. Dickson

resolved is to accord you with two official personalities. That is, any activity, occupation, or duty which you deal with in your capacity as a candidate for adoption invokes your personality as a probationary High-born, and my personal superior. On the other hand, any activity which deals with your duties as an officer of the Starkiens invokes your servant personality; and you are my inferior in everything connected with that. In any activities that deal with neither personality officially, you can choose which position you want to occupy—High-born or servant. I don't imagine you'll want to choose the servant often."

"I don't suppose so," said Jim, watching the smaller man calmly. The black eyes flickered upon him like dark flashes of lightning.

"Because of the conflict of personalities," said Melness, "I have no physical authority over you. But if necessary, I can suspend you from duty with your Starkien unit and enter a formal complaint to the Emperor about you. Don't let yourself be misled by any foolish notion that the Emperor will not act upon any complaint I make to him."

"I won't," said Jim softly. Melness looked at him for a moment more, then disappeared.

"Now, Jim," Adok said at his elbow, "if you like, we can return to your quarters; and I will show you the use of your weapons and accouterments."

"Fine," said Jim.

They transported themselves back to Jim's quarters. There Adok fitted Jim out with the straps and belts he had brought from the armory.

"There are two classes of weaponry," said Adok, once Jim was outfitted. "This"—he tapped the small black rod he had inserted in the loops of the belt attached to Jim's loin strap—"is independently powered and is all that is normally used for duty upon the Throne World."

He paused and then reached out softly to touch a silver band encircling the biceps of Jim's upper left arm.

"These, however," said Adok, "are part of the weaponry of the second class. They are completely useless at the moment, because they must be energized by a broadcast power source. Each of them is both a weapon and an enabler at the same time."

"Enabler?" Jim asked.

"Yes," said Adok. "They increase your reflex time, by causing you to react physically at a certain set speed—which in the case of anyone not High-born is considerably above his natural speed of reflex. Later on, we'll be working out with the enabler function of the second-class weaponry. And eventually, perhaps you can get permission to go to the testing area, which is at a good distance below the surface of the Throne World, and gain some actual experience with the weapons themselves."

"I see," said Jim, examining the silver bands. "I take it, then, that they're fairly powerful?"

"A trained Starkien," said Adok, "under full control of effective second-class weaponry, should be the equivalent of two to six units of fully armed men from the Colony Worlds."

"The Colony Worlds don't have Starkiens of their own, then?" asked Jim.

For a second time Adok managed to register a mildly visible emotion. This time the emotion seemed to be shock.

"The Starkiens serve the Emperor—and only the Emperor!" he said.

"Oh?" said Jim. "On the ship that brought me to the Throne World, I had a talk with a High-born named Galyan. And Galyan had a Starkien—or somebody who looked exactly like a Starkien—bodyguarding him."

"There's nothing strange in that, Jim," said Adok. "The Emperor lends his Starkiens to the other High-born when the other High-born need them. But they are only lent. They still remain servants of the Emperor, and in the final essential their commands come only from the Emperor."

Jim nodded. Adok's words rang an echo off the remembered words of Melness a short time before. Jim's thoughts ran on ahead with the connection.

"The underground area on the Throne World is occupied only by the servants, is that right, Adok?" he asked.

"That's right, Jim," said Adok.

"As long as I'm going to be going down there as a matter of duty from now on," said Jim, "I think I'd like to see some more of it. How large an area is it?"

"There are as many rooms below grounds," said Adok, "as there are above. In fact, there may be more, because I don't know them all."

"Who does?" asked Jim.

Adok looked for a second as though he would have shrugged. But the gesture was evidently too marked a one for him to make.

"I don't know, Jim," he said. "Perhaps . . . Melness."

"Yes," said Jim thoughtfully. "Of course, if anyone would know, it would be Melness."

During the next few weeks Jim found himself involved in several parades down on the parade grounds. He discovered that his duties on these occasions were nothing more than to get dressed and to stand before his unit, which consisted of seventy-eight Starkiens, a noncommissioned Starkien officer, Adok, and himself.

But the first parade he witnessed, it came as a shock to him to see that vast space underground completely filled with rank upon rank of the impassive,

bald-headed, short, and massive-boned men who were
the Starkiens. Jim had assumed that the Throne World
was a full-sized planetary body, that there would be
a large number of servants and all types, and that the
Starkiens should be a fair proportion of these. But
he had not realized, until he saw it with his own eyes,
how many Starkiens there were. A little calculation
afterward based upon what Adok could tell him of
the floor space of the parade ground area led him
to estimate that he must have seen at least twenty
thousand men under arms in that space.

If it was indeed true, what Adok said, that each
Starkien was the equivalent of four to five times a unit
of eighty soldiers from the Colony Worlds, then what
he had seen gathered there had been the equivalent
of between half and three-quarters of a million men.
And Adok had told him that this parade ground was
only one of fifty spaced about the Throne World,
underground.

Perhaps it was not so surprising that the High-born
of the Throne World considered themselves above any
threat that could be posed by any Colony World or
combination of Colony Worlds.

Outside the parades, Jim found that his only duties
during the first few weeks consisted of a session in the
gymnasium every other day with Adok, wearing the
second-class weaponry.

The silver bands that represented the second-class
weaponry were still not energized as weapons, but within
the confines of the gymnasium they became active in
their capacity as enablers. The exercises that Jim was put
through by Adok, therefore, consisted merely of running,
jumping, and climbing over various obstacles, with the
enablers assisting. After the first session of this exercise,
which Adok permitted to go on only for some twelve
minutes, the Starkien took Jim almost tenderly back to

his own quarters and had Jim lie down on the oversized hassock that served as a bed there, while Adok gently removed the class-two weaponry bands.

"Now," said Adok, "you must rest for at least three hours."

"Why?" Jim asked, curiously gazing up at the stocky figure standing over him.

"Because the first effects of wearing the enablers is not appreciated by the body immediately," said Adok. "Remember, your muscles have been forced to move faster than your nature intended them to. You may think that you feel stiff and sore now. But what you feel now is nothing to what you will feel in about three hours' time. The best way of minimizing the stiffness and soreness when you first begin to use the enablers is to remain as still as possible for the three hours immediately following exercise. As you become hardened to their use, your body will actually adapt to being pushed at faster than its normal speed of reflex. Eventually you won't become stiff unless you really overextend yourself, and you won't need to rest after each exercise."

Jim kept his face impassive, and Adok vanished, considerately dimming the lights of the room before he went. In the dimness Jim looked thoughtfully at the white ceiling overhead.

He felt no stiffness or soreness of his muscles whatever. But, as Adok had said, possibly the maximum effect would not be appreciated until about three hours from now. Conscientiously, therefore, he waited those three hours without moving from the bed.

But at the end of that time, he found no difference in himself. He was not sore, and he was not stiff. He filed that piece of information with the gradually accumulating store of knowledge about the Throne World and its inhabitants in the back of his mind.

It did not immediately fit with the other pieces of

the jigsaw puzzle that was forming in his mind. But one of the things that had helped him, from that day when as a boy he had at last faced the fact that he had no choice but to bear the loneliness of his life in silence, was the capacity in him for an almost infinite patience. The picture forming in his mind was not yet readable. But it would be. Until then . . . Adok had assumed that at the end of three hours the stiffness and soreness of Jim's body would have effectively immobilized him. Since he had never been able to discover if he might be under surveillance—and to this he had added lately the possibility of surveillance not only by High-born, for their own reasons, but also by servants, for *their* own reasons—he resigned himself to staying as he was.

Stretched out on his hassocklike bed, he willed himself to sleep.

When he woke up, it was because Ro was shaking him gently. She stood in the dimness of the room beside his bed.

"There's someone Galyan wants you to meet," she said. "He sent word through Afuan. It's the Governor of the Colony Worlds of Alpha Centauri."

He blinked at her for a moment sleepily. Then wakefulness sprang upon him, as the implications of what she had said woke inside him.

"Why would I want to meet the Governor of the worlds of Alpha Centauri?" he asked, sitting abruptly upon the hassock-bed.

"But he's *your* Governor!" Ro said. "Didn't anyone ever tell you, Jim? Any new Colony World is first assigned to the nearest Governor."

"No," said Jim, swinging his legs over the edge of the bed and getting to his feet. "No one ever did tell me. Does this mean I have some sort of obligation to this Governor?"

"Well . . ." Ro hesitated. "In theory, he can take you away from the Throne World right now, since you're under his authority. But, on the other hand, the sponsorship for your adoption has been entered. In practice, he would find this out and would know better than to try to do anything that might interfere with any possible future High-born. Remember, his worlds will gain a lot of prestige if anyone under their authority becomes at least a probationary High-born. In other words, he can't really do you any harm; but you can hardly, politely, turn down the chance to visit with him, now that he's here."

"I see," said Jim grimly. "They sent you to bring me?"

Ro nodded. He reached out his hand, and she took it in one of hers. It was an easy, shorthand way of taking somebody else where they had never been before. It required a certain mental effort, Jim had been told, to transport someone to a place unknown to him but known to his guide, without this physical contact. Adok, of course, as with Ro earlier, had done it the polite way. But now Ro customarily reached out and took hold of him when she wished to take him anyplace.

Immediately they were in a relatively small room— a room, however, which in the number of writing surfaces standing flatly suspended in midair, and the relative scarcity of sitting hassocks, bespoke the utilitarian kind of office-type room that Galyan had brought Jim to aboard the ship.

Present in the room were the usual workers and the single Starkien bodyguard. Present also was Galyan, and with him a man with the American Indian-like coloring of the Alpha Centaurans. But this man was almost five-ten, a good three or four inches taller than most of the Alpha Centaurans Jim had met when he had been on Alpha Centauri III.

"There you are, Jim—and you too, Ro," said Galyan, turning softly to face them as they appeared. "Jim, I thought you might like to meet your regional overlord—Wyk Ben of Alpha Centauri III. Wyk Ben, this is Jim Keil, sponsorship of whom has been offered here on the Throne World."

"Yeth," agreed Wyk Ben, turning quickly to face Jim and smiling. In contrast to the hissing accent of the High-born, which had come to sound almost natural to Jim by this time, the Governor of Alpha Centauri lisped slightly in his speech.

"I just wanted to see you for a moment, Jim, to wish you luck. Here, your world's just come under our Governorship . . . and, well, I'm very proud!"

Wyk Ben smiled happily at Jim, apparently unaware that of the three other people concerned in the conversation, there was a slight frown of foreboding on the face of Ro, a touch of sardonic humor in the lemon-yellow eyes of Galyan, and a detachment and reserve about Jim.

"Well . . . I just wanted to tell you. I won't take up any more of your time," said Wyk Ben eagerly.

Jim stared down at him. He was absurdly like a puppy wagging its tail in eagerness and pride, coupled with a sort of innocence about the Throne World in general. Jim could not understand why Galyan should have wanted him to meet this man. But he filed the fact that Galyan *had* wanted him to meet the Alpha Centauran Governor, for future reference.

"Thank you again," Jim said. "Yes, as a matter of fact, I'm due for an exercise session with the Starkien who's my substitute." He looked over at Ro. "Ro?"

"Good to have seen you again, Jim," said Galyan slowly in a tone of voice almost matching the amused drawl of Slothiel. Clearly, whatever he had hoped to gain from bringing Jim and Wyk Ben face to face, he had gained. But there was no point in trying to pursue the matter, here and now, any further. Jim turned to Ro and held out his hand. She took it, and immediately they were back in his room.

"What was all that about?" asked Jim.

Ro shook her head puzzledly.

"I don't know," she said not happily. "And when anything happens on the Throne World that you don't understand, it's a danger signal. I'll try to find out, Jim—I'll see you later."

Hastily she disappeared.

Left by himself, Jim ran over the meeting with Wyk Ben in his mind. It struck him that things were in danger of happening so fast that they might get ahead of him. He spoke out loud to the empty room.

"Adok!"

It took possibly three seconds—no more—and then the figure of the Starkien appeared before him.

"How are you feeling?" asked Adok. "Do you need—"

"Nothing," said Jim brusquely. "Adok, are there any library facilities down in the servant's area, underground?"

"Library? . . ." For a moment Adok's face squeezed faintly, in what Jim was beginning to understand was an expression of extreme puzzlement. Then it cleared. "Oh, of course, you mean a learning center. Yes, I'll take you to one, Jim. I've never been there myself, but I know about where it is."

Adok ventured to touch Jim on the arm, and they were in the underground park Jim had passed through with Adok before. Adok hesitated, then turned left and began to walk off toward a side street.

"This way, I think," he said. Jim followed him, and they left the park, going down the street until they came to a flight of what looked like wide stone steps leading up to a tall open portal in a wall of polished brown stone.

There were a few people coming and going through the portal, up and down the steps—all of them servants rather than Starkiens. Jim watched these, as he had watched all the servants they had passed on the way here, with a close attention. Now, going up the steps, his concentration was rewarded. Coming out of the portal as he and Adok started up the steps was a yellowish-skinned, black-eyed man like Melness. As he started down the steps, his eyes went to one of the servants entering—one of the short brown men with long, straight hair. The brown man ran the heel of his hand, in apparently an idle gesture, across his waist just at belt level. In response, without breaking stride, the yellow-skinned man who looked like Melness reached casually across with his right hand to lay two fingers momentarily against the biceps of his left arm, before dropping the arm once more to his side.

Without another gesture—in fact, without looking at each other after that—the two passed, going opposite ways on the steps.

"Did you see that?" Jim asked in a low voice to Adok as they entered the portal. "Those gestures? What were they all about?"

For an unusually long moment Adok did not answer, so that Jim turned to glance at him as they walked. Adok's face, insofar as Jim could read it, was serious.

"It's strange," said the Starkien, almost to himself. "There *has* been more of it lately."

He lifted his eyes to Jim.

"It's their Silent Language."

"What did they say, then?" asked Jim. Adok shook his head.

"I don't know," he answered. "It's an old language—

the High-born first learned of it after the first Servant's Revolt, thousands of years ago. The servants have always used it. But we Starkiens are shut out from it. That's because we're always loyal to the Emperor."

"I see," said Jim. He became thoughtful.

They passed down a wide hallway of the same polished brown stone and into a large interior room which seemed to be filled with rank on rank of whirling, glowing globes of light—like small suns. They spun—if that indeed was what they were doing—too fast for the eye to follow their rotation. But they were obviously in constant movement.

Adok halted. He gestured at the miniature suns.

"This is one of the Files," he said. "Which one, I don't know, because they're designed to feed not to us here but to the learning centers for the young High-born above ground. But off to the right here there're carrels, where you can tap the information stored, not only here, but in Files all over the Throne World."

He led Jim off to the right and out of the room with the miniature suns into a long, narrow corridor with a series of open doorways running down its right side. Adok led him down the corridor and into one of the doorways.

Within was a small room—the first unoccupied one they had passed—fitted with a chair and a sort of desk or table, with a raised surface, sloping upward at an angle of about forty-five degrees to the horizontal.

Jim sat down in front of the raised surface, which seemed perfectly blank except for a pair of small black studs, or buttons, near the bottom. Adok reached over and touched one of the buttons, however, and immediately the sloping surface resolved itself into a white screen, with one word, in the sort of shorthand figures that were the Imperial language, glowing blackly in the center of it. The word was "ready."

"Speak to it," said Adok.

"I'd like to examine whatever records there are of Empire expeditions," said Jim slowly to the screen, "with a view to finding any that went out past—" and he gave the Imperial name for Alpha Centauri.

The squiggles that stood for the Imperial word "ready" vanished from the screen. Its place was taken by a line of writing moving from left to right at a slow pace.

Jim sat, reading. It appeared that the retrieval system of the File was not equipped to hunt down the information he wanted directly. It could only supply him with a vast quantity of information about past expeditions in general out in the direction in which Alpha Centauri lay from the Throne World. Apparently Jim's task would require his searching all the relevant records of expeditions in that general direction in order to find the one which had gone on to Earth—if indeed any expedition ever had. It was not a task to be done at one sitting, Jim saw. It would take hours, days, perhaps even weeks.

"Is there any way to speed this up?" he asked, looking up at Adok. Adok reached over to the second stud and turned it. The line of type moving across the screen began to move more rapidly. Adok's hand fell away, and Jim raised his own. He continued to increase the speed of the line until the stud stopped, evidently having reached its highest rate. Adok made a small sound, like a badly stifled grunt of surprise.

"What?" demanded Jim, not lifting his eyes from the swiftly sliding line of information.

"You read," said Adok, "almost like a High-born."

Jim did not bother to answer that. He remained

fixed before the screen, hardly conscious that time was sliding by, until, with the ending of one set of records and the beginning of the next, there was a momentary interruption in which he became conscious of the fact that he had very nearly stiffened in position, after sitting without moving for so long.

He straightened up, shut off the machine for a moment, and looked about him. Abruptly, he saw Adok, still standing beside him. Evidently the Starkien had not moved either.

"Have you been waiting there all this time?" asked Jim. "How long have I been reading?"

"Some little time," said Adok without apparent emotion. He gave Jim a period in Empire time units that was the equivalent of a little over four hours.

Jim shook his head and got to his feet. Then, remembering, he sat down before the screen again and turned it on. He asked for information on the Silent Language.

The screen responded—not with one Silent Language, but with fifty-two of them. Apparently there had been fifty-two recorded "revolts" by the servants of the Throne World. Jim made a mental note to look up these revolts next time he was here. Apparently, after each revolt the High-born had investigated and translated the secrets of the current Silent Language; but by the time the next revolt took place, some hundreds or thousands of years later, an entirely new language had grown up.

They were not so much languages, in fact, as sets of signals—like the signals passed back and forth between the pitcher and the catcher in a baseball game, or between the players in the game and the coaches on the sideline. Rubbing one's fingers together, or scratching one's chin, was clearly and visibly a signal—or a part of the current Silent Language. The question lay not in seeing the signal but in interpreting it. The question was what it meant this particular time.

Jim skimmed the information of the Silent Languages, shut off the machine, and got to his feet. He and Adok left the Files, and with Jim leading, they walked out of the place, down the steps, and back into the community area near the park.

They strolled about its streets, shops, and places of entertainment for nearly an hour, while Jim kept his eyes quietly alert for any more signals in the current Silent Language.

He saw many, none of which made sense according to any of the earlier fifty-two versions of the language. Nonetheless, he carefully stored up in his memory each signal as he saw it, and the conditions under which it was used. After a certain time of this, he left Adok and returned to his own room.

He had hardly been back five minutes when Ro appeared, accompanied by Slothiel. Jim made a mental note to ask Ro what kind of warning system alerted her that he was back in his quarters, and also how such a warning system could be screened out or turned off.

But as he rose to face the two of them now, he mentally filed that thought also, at the sight of the faint worry on the face of Ro and the look of rather grim humor on Slothiel's face.

"I take it something's happened?" Jim asked.

"You take it correctly," answered Slothiel. "Your adoption is being approved, and Galyan has just now suggested to me that I give a large party for you to celebrate. I didn't realize he was that much a friend of yours. Now, why do you suppose he'd do something like that?"

"If you give such a party," said Jim, "will the Emperor attend?"

"The Emperor and Vhotan," answered Slothiel. "Yes, almost certainly they'll both be there. Why?"

"Because," said Jim, "that's why Galyan suggested you give the party."

Slothiel frowned. It was a slightly haughty frown, with the faint implication that a member of the lesser races should not make statements to a High-born that a High-born could not fully understand.

"Why do you say that?" asked Slothiel.

"Because Melness is a very clever man," said Jim.

Chapter 7

Slothiel's tall body stiffened.

"All right, Wolfling!" he snapped. "We've had enough question-and-answer games!"

"Jim—" began Ro warningly.

"I'm sorry," said Jim, looking steadily at the taller man. "The explanation doesn't concern me—it concerns the Emperor. So I'm not going to give it to you. And you're not going to force me to give it. In the first place, you can't. And in the second place, it would be impolitic of you to try, since you're the one who's sponsoring me for adoption."

Slothiel stood perfectly still.

"Believe me," said Jim, this time persuasively, "if I was free to answer you, I would. Let me make you a promise. If by the time the party is over you haven't had an assurance either from the Emperor or from Vhotan that I had good reason not to tell you, then I'll answer any question you have about the whole thing. All right?"

For a long second longer Slothiel remained rigid, his eyes burning down at Jim. Then, abruptly, the tension leaked out of him, and he smiled his old, lazy smile.

"You know, you have me there, Jim," he drawled. "I can hardly forcibly question the very lesser human I'm sponsoring for adoption, can I? Particularly since it would be impossible to keep the fact quiet. You'll make a good man at wagering for points, if by some freak chance you ever should happen to get adopted, Jim. All right, keep your secret—for now."

He disappeared.

"Jim," said Ro, "I worry about you."

For some reason, the words rang with unusual importance in his mind. He looked about at her sharply and saw why they had. She was looking at him with concern, but it was a different sort of concern from that which she lavished on all her pets and which she had heretofore lavished on him. And the tone of her voice had conveyed a difference to match.

He was suddenly, unexpectedly, and deeply touched. No one, man or woman, had worried about him for a very very long time.

"Can't you at least tell *me* why you say Galyan's suggesting the party because Melness is a very clever man?" Ro asked. "It sounds as if you're saying that there's some connection between Galyan and Melness. But that can't be between a High-born and one of the lesser races."

"How about you and me," said Jim, remembering that new note in her voice.

She blushed, but this, as he had come to learn, did not mean as much with her as it might have with another woman.

"I'm different!" she said. "But Galyan isn't. He's one of the highest of High-born. Not just by birth—by attitude, too."

"But he's always made it a point to make a good deal of use of men of the lesser races."

"That's true. . . ." She became thoughtful. Then she

looked back up at him. "But you still haven't explained. . . ."

"There's nothing much to explain," said Jim, "except for that part that I say is really a matter belonging to the Emperor rather than to me. I said what I did about Melness being a clever man because men can make mistakes out of their own cleverness, as well as out of foolishness. They can try too hard to cover something up. In Melness' case, when Adok first took me to meet him, Melness went to a great deal of trouble to make it look as if he resented my being placed under his responsibility."

Ro frowned.

"But why should he resent . . ."

"There could be a number of reasons, of course," said Jim. "For one—and the easiest answer—the fact that he resented a Wolfling like myself being sponsored for adoption when a man like him stands no chance of such sponsorship, just because he is so useful in his capacity as a servant. But, by the same token, Melness should have been too clever to let me know that resentment, particularly when there was a possibility that I might end up as a High-born myself, in a position to resent him in return."

"Then why did he do it?" asked Ro.

"Possibly because he thought I might be a spy sent by the High-born to investigate the world of servants," said Jim, "and he wanted to set up a reason for harassing or observing me while I was underground that would not lead me to suspect that he suspected I was a spy."

"But what would you be spying on him for?" asked Ro.

"That, I don't know yet," said Jim.

"But you think it has something to do with the Emperor and with Galyan. Why?" Ro said.

Jim smiled down at her.

"You want to know too much too quickly," he said. "In fact, you want to know more than I know yet. You see why I didn't want to get into questions and answers on this with Slothiel?"

Slowly she nodded. Then she gazed at him with concern again.

"Jim—" she said unexpectedly. "What did you do? I mean, besides bullfighting, when you were back on your own world among your own people?"

"I was an anthropologist," he told her. "Bullfighting was—a late avocation with me."

She frowned puzzledly. For to his knowledge, the word did not exist in the Empire tongue, and so he had simply translated it literally from the Latin root—"man-science."

"I studied the primitive background of man," said Jim. "Particularly the roots of culture—all cultures—in the basic nature of humankind."

He could almost see the lightning search she was making through that massive High-born memory of hers. Her face lit up.

"Oh, you mean—*anthropology!*" She gave him the Empire word he had needed. Then her face softened, and she touched his arm. "Jim! Poor Jim—no wonder!"

Once again—as he so often found it necessary to do—he had to restrain the impulse to smile at her. He had thought of himself in many terms during his lifetime so far. But to date he had never had occasion to think of himself as "poor"—in any sense of the word.

"No wonder?" he echoed.

"I mean, no wonder you always seem so cold and distant to anyone High-born," she said. "Oh, I don't mean me! I mean the others. But, no wonder you're that way. Finding out about us and the Empire put an end to everything you'd studied, didn't it? You had to face the fact that you weren't evolved from the ape-men and prehumans of your own world. It meant all the work you'd ever done had to be thrown out."

"Not exactly," said Jim.

"Jim, let me tell you something," she said, "the same thing happened to us, you know. I mean us—the High-born. Some thousands of years ago the early High-born used to think that they were evolved from the pre-humans on this one Throne World. But finally they had to admit that not even that was true. The animal forms were too much the same on all the worlds like this one that our people settled. Finally, even we had to face the fact that all these worlds had evidently been stocked with the common ancestors of their present flora and fauna by some intelligent race that existed even long before our time. And the evidence is pretty overwhelming that the ancestors with which this world was stocked were probably a strain pointing toward a superior type of premen who then were planted else-where. So, you see, we had to face the fact that we weren't the first thinking beings in the universe, too."

This time Jim let himself smile.

"Don't worry," he told her. "Whatever shock there was to me on learning the Empire existed has evapo-rated by this time."

She was, he thought, reassured.

The party celebrating Slothiel's sponsorship of him for adoption, it turned out, was to be held in just under three weeks. Jim spent the time learning Starkien ways and warfare from Adok, putting in the few nominal appearances that duty required of him with that military caste and studying in the Files section to which Adok had introduced him underground.

In between times, he moved about the servants' areas underground, observing any hand signal that was made and committing it to memory. In his spare time he tried to catalog and arrange these signals into some kind of coherent form that would allow him to begin to interpret them.

Two things were in his favor. In the first place, as an anthropologist, he was aware that any sign language derived from primitive, common basics in human nature. As one of the early explorers had said about his experiences in that regard while living with the North American Eskimo, you did not need anyone to teach you the basic signs of communication. You already knew them. The threatening gesture; the come-here gesture; the I-am-hungry gestures, such as pointing to the mouth and then rubbing the stomach—all these, and a large handful more, came instinctively to the mind of any man trying to communicate by hand or body movements.

In the second place, a language mainly of hand signals was necessarily limited. The messages conveyed by such a language necessarily had to depend a great deal upon the context in which the gestures were made. Therefore, the same signal was bound to reappear frequently before any observer watching over a period of time.

Jim therefore assumed success. And, in fact, it was only a little more than two weeks before he identified the recognition signal—that hand movement that was equivalent to a greeting and a recognition signal among users of the Silent Language. It consisted of nothing more than the tapping of the right thumbtip against the side of the adjacent forefinger. From that point on, the various signals began to reveal their meaning to him rapidly.

His search in the Files to discover whether an expedition from the Throne World—or, for that matter, from one of the then-existing Colony Worlds—had set out in the direction of the solar system containing Earth was meeting with no similar success. Perhaps records of such an expedition were there in the Files. Perhaps they were not. The point was, the records that Jim himself had to examine to eliminate all the possibilities were too multitudinous. The job was equivalent, in fact, to his reading through the entire contents of a small public library.

"And besides," said Adok when Jim finally one day mentioned this problem to the Starkien, "you have to remember that you could go all through the records you're permitted to see and still not know of such an expedition, even if record of it was there."

They had been strolling through the underground park. Jim stopped suddenly and turned to face Adok, who automatically stopped also and turned to face Jim.

"What's this?" demanded Jim. "You said something about my being permitted to see only part of the records?"

"Forgive me, Jim," said Adok. "I don't know, of course, if any of the records of such trips are secret. But the point is, how can you be sure some are not? And further, how can you be sure that if some are secret, the one you're looking for is not among them?"

"I can't. Naturally," said Jim. "What bothers me is that I never stopped to think that any of the history of this planet might not be fully available." He thought for a second. "Who gets to see secret information in the Files, anyway?"

"Why," answered Adok with the faint note of surprise in his voice that was the ultimate in his reaction that way, "all the High-born see all the information, of course. In fact, since you are as free to move around above ground as below, all you need to do is to go to one of the learning centers for the High-born children—"

He broke off suddenly.

"No," he said in a lower tone of voice. "I was forgetting. You can go to one of the learning centers, of course. But it won't do you any good."

"You mean the High-born won't let me use the learning center?" asked Jim. He was watching Adok closely. Nothing on the Throne World could be taken for granted, even the transparent honesty in someone like Adok. If Adok was going to tell him that there was some kind of a rule against his using the learning center, it would be only the second outright prohibition he had encountered above ground on this singularly prohibitionless planet. The first, of course, being the rule against anyone approaching the Emperor without being directly summoned. But Adok was shaking his head.

"No," Adok said. "I don't think anyone would stop you. It's just that you wouldn't be able to use the reading machines above ground. You see, they're set for use by the young High-born, and they read too fast for the ordinary men to follow."

"You've seen me read," said Jim. "They read faster than that?"

"Much faster," said Adok. He shook his head again. "Much, much faster."

"That's all right," said Jim. "Take me to one of these learning centers."

Adok did not shrug—in fact, it was a question whether his shoulders were not too heavily muscled for such a gesture, even if his nature permitted it. Instantly they were above ground in a large structure like an enormous loggia—or rather, like one of the Grecian temples, consisting of roof and pillars and floor, but without any obvious outside walls. Through the nearby pillars green lawn and blue sky showed. About on the floor, scattered at intervals, seated or curled up on hassocks, were children obviously of the High-born,

and of all ages. Each of them was gazing at a screen
that floated at an angle in the air before them, and
moved about to stay before them as they altered
position on the hassock, always maintaining roughly
the same forty-five-degree reading angle Jim had found
in the carrels of the Files below ground.

None of the children, even the few who paused to
glance at Jim and Adok, paid more than a second's
attention to the newcomers. Clearly, Jim decided, the
fact that neither he nor Adok was a High-born ren-
dered them for practical purposes invisible, unless
needed, by these High-born children.

Jim moved over to stand closely behind one of
them—a boy as tall as Jim himself, though extremely
thin of limb and with the face of a ten- or twelve-year-
old. The same running line of symbols to which Jim had
grown accustomed below ground was running in front
of the youngster. Jim looked at that line.

It was blurring by at a tremendous rate. Jim
frowned, staring at it, trying to match his perception
to its movement, to change it from a streak of spiky,
wavy blackness to readable symbols.

Astonishingly, he could not.

He felt a sudden shock through him internally of
something very like anger. He had never yet found
anything that anyone else could do that he was not
capable of matching within the limits of his own
physical resources. Moreover, he was perfectly sure
that the problem was not with his vision. His eyes
should be as capable of resolving the blurred line
into symbols as any High-born eye. The problem was
in his brain, which was refusing to accept the readable information at the rate at which it was being
offered.

He made a grim internal effort. Around him, glimpses
of sunlight and lawn, pillars, ceiling, floor—even the boy

himself, unheedingly reading—were blanked out. Jim's concentration focused down upon the line of reading—the line alone. The pressure of his efforts to resolve it was like a cord twisted tight around the temples of his head. Tighter, and tighter. . . .

Almost, for a second, he made it. For a second it seemed as if the line was beginning to break apart into readable symbols, and he gathered that the text had something to do with the organization of the Starkiens themselves. Then his efforts broke—out of sheer physical inability of his body to sustain it any longer. He swayed a little, and vision of the rest of the universe, including pillars, walls, and ceiling, opened out about him once more.

He was suddenly aware that the boy on the hassock had noticed him finally. The High-born child had stopped reading and was staring at Jim himself with a plain expression of astonishment.

"Who are you—?" the boy began in a reedy voice. But Jim, without answering, touched Adok on the arm and translated them both back to Jim's quarters before the question could be completed.

Back in the familiar room, Jim breathed deeply for a second and then sat down on one of the hassocks. He motioned Adok to sit down likewise, and the Starkien obeyed. After a moment Jim's deep breathing slowed, and he smiled slightly. He looked across at Adok.

"You don't say, 'I told you so!'" said Jim.

Adok shook his head in a gesture that clearly conveyed that it was not his place to say such things.

"Well, you were right," said Jim. He became thoughtful. "But not for the reasons you think. What stopped me just then was the fact that I hadn't been born to this language of yours. If that writing had been in my own native tongue, I could've read it."

He turned his head abruptly away from Adok and spoke to the empty air.

"Ro?" he asked.

He and Adok both waited. But there was no answer, and Ro did not materialize. This was not surprising. Ro was a High-born and had her own occupations and duties, unlike Adok, whose single duty was to await, and wait upon, Jim's call.

Jim shifted himself to Ro's apartment, found it empty, and left a note asking her to contact him as soon as she came in. It was about two and a half hours later that she suddenly appeared beside Adok and him in the main room of Jim's quarters.

"It's going to be a big party," she said without preamble. "Everybody's going to be there. They'll have to use the Great Gathering Room. The word must've gotten out somehow that there's something special about this celebration—" She broke off suddenly. "I'm forgetting. You wanted to see me about something, Jim?"

"Oh," said Jim, "could you get one of those reading screens from the learning centers set up in your apartment?"

"Why—of course!" said Ro. "Do you want to use one, Jim? Why don't I just have one set up for you here?"

Jim shook his head.

"I'd rather not have it generally known that I was using it," Jim said. "I take it that it isn't too unusual a thing for someone like you to want one where she lives?"

"Not unusual. No. . . ." said Ro. "And of course if you want it that way, that's the way I can do it. But what's this all about?"

Jim told her about his attempt to try to read at the same speed as that of the young High-born he had stood behind in the learning center.

"You think study will speed up your reading comprehension?" asked Ro. She frowned. "Maybe you shouldn't get your hopes too high—"

"I won't," said Jim.

Within a few hours the screen was set up, floating in a corner of one of the less-used rooms of Ro's apartment. From then on, Jim spent the time he had spent in the Files underground in Ro's apartment room instead.

He had made only slight progress, however, within the next week. He gave it up entirely and spent the last few days before the party lounging around the underground servants' area with Adok, observing the Silent Language in use about him. He had become fluent in understanding it now, but, wearyingly, most of what he absorbed was the hand-signaled equivalent of gossip. Nonetheless, gossip could be useful if properly sifted and interpreted.

Jim returned from the last of these expeditions just an hour or so before the party, to find Lorava waiting for him in the main room of his quarters.

"Vhotan wants to see you," said Lorava abruptly as Jim appeared.

No more notice than that. Jim found himself standing beside Lorava in a room he had not been in before. Adok was on the other side of him, so evidently the invitation had included the Starkien as well.

Vhotan was seated on a hassock before a flat surface suspended in midair with its top covered with what looked like several different studs of various shapes and colors. He was turning or depressing these studs in what appeared to be a random pattern, but with a seriousness and intensity that suggested his actions were far from unimportant. Nonetheless, he broke off at the sight of them, rose from his hassock, and came over to face Jim.

"I'll call for you a little later, Lorava!" he said.

The thin young High-born vanished.

"Wolfling," said Vhotan to Jim, his yellowish brows drawing together, "the Emperor is going to attend this party of yours."

"I don't believe it's my party," answered Jim. "I think it's Slothiel's party."

Vhotan brushed the objection aside with a short wave of one long hand.

"You're the reason for it," he said. "And you're the reason for the Emperor being at it. He wants to talk to you again."

"Naturally," said Jim. "I can come anytime the Emperor wants to summon me. It needn't be at the party."

"He's at his best in public!" said Vhotan sharply. "Never mind that. The point is, at the party the Emperor will want to talk to you. He'll take you off to one side and undoubtedly ask you a lot of questions."

Vhotan hesitated.

"I'll be glad to answer any of the Emperor's questions," said Jim.

"Yes . . . you do exactly that," said Vhotan gruffly. "Whatever questions he asks you, answer them fully. You understand? He's the Emperor, and even if he doesn't seem to be paying you complete attention, I want you to go right on answering until he asks you another question or tells you to stop. Do you understand?"

"Fully," said Jim. His eyes met the lemon-yellow eyes of the older, High-born man.

"Yes. Well," said Vhotan, turning abruptly, walking back to his console of studs, and sitting down before it once again.

"That's all. You can go back to your quarters now."

His fingers began to move over the studs. Jim touched Adok on the arm and shifted back to the main room of his own apartment.

"What do you make of that?" he asked Adok.

"Make of it?" Adok repeated slowly.

"Yes," said Jim. He eyed the Starkien keenly. "Didn't you think that some of what he said was a little strange?"

Adok's face was completely without expression.

"Nothing dealing with the Emperor can be strange," he said. His voice was strangely remote. "The High-born Vhotan told you to answer fully to the questions of the Emperor. That is all. There could not be any more than that."

"Yes," said Jim. "Adok, you've been lent to me to be my substitute. But you still belong to the Emperor, don't you?"

"As I told you, Jim," said Adok, still in the same expressionless, remote voice. "All Starkiens always belong to the Emperor, no matter where they are or what they're doing."

"I remember," said Jim.

He turned away and went to get out of the Starkien straps and belts he had been wearing, into the white costume like that of all the male High-born, but without insignia, which he had chosen to wear for the occasion.

He was barely dressed when Ro appeared. In fact, she materialized so suspiciously close upon the end of his dressing that once more he wondered whether he was not under surveillance—by others as well as Ro—more than he thought. But he had no chance to speculate upon this now.

"Here," she said a little breathlessly, "put this on."

He saw she was holding out to him what seemed to be something like a narrow band of white satin. When he hesitated, she picked up his left arm and wrapped it around his wrist, without waiting for his approval.

"Now," she said, "touch mine." She held up her own left wrist, around which was already wrapped—and clinging as if through some inner life of its own—a similar piece of white cloth. It was the only piece of clothlike material that she was wearing. Otherwise, she was clothed from shoulders to ankles in that same filmy, cloudlike stuff that he had seen Afuan and the other High-born women wearing at the bullfight on Alpha Centauri III.

She picked Jim's wrist up and touched his band to hers.

"What's this?" asked Jim.

"Oh—of course you don't know," she said. "At a party, particularly a big one like this, people move around so much that you can't keep track of where someone is if you want to find them. But now that we've checked our sensors with each other, all you have to do is visualize me, and you'll automatically come to whatever part of the Great Gathering Room I'm in. You'll see." She laughed a little. To his surprise, she was more than a little bright-eyed and excited. "Everything's always very mixed up on occasions like this!"

When they, with Adok, moved to the Great Gathering Room forty minutes or so later, Jim immediately saw what she had meant. The Great Gathering Room was a wall-less, pillared, and roofed area like the learning center he had visited, only much larger. Clearly its polished floor of utter black, upon which the white pillars seemed to float, was at least several square miles in area. On that floor groups of male and female High-born, in their usual white costume, stood talking, while servants moved among them carrying trays of various edibles and drinkables.

At first sight, except for the appearance of the High-born and the size of it all, the gathering looked ordinary enough. But as he gazed, Jim became aware that not only High-born individuals themselves, but the servants, were appearing and disappearing continuously all over the place. For a moment, even to Jim, the size and movement of the crowd was slightly dizzying.

Then he did what he had always done when faced with a situation that threatened a temporary mental or emotional overload. He filed what he could not handle in the back of his mind and concentrated on what he could.

"Adok," he said, turning to the Starkien, "I want you to circulate. Try to locate for me a particular servant. I don't know what he'll look like, but he'll be a little different from all the rest, in that he will, first, have a fixed position in the room someplace; second, it will be a fairly secluded position, from which only one other servant in the hall at any time will be able to see him. He may be watched by any number of other servants in succession, but there will never be more than one watching him at a time, and he will always be under surveillance by the other servant observing him at the time. Will you get busy about that right away?"

"Yes, Jim," said Adok. He vanished.

"Why did you ask him to do that?" asked Ro in a low, puzzled voice, pressing close to him.

"I'll tell you later," said Jim.

He saw by her attitude that she would like to ask him more questions, in spite of this answer of his. She might indeed have done so, but at that moment Vhotan and the Emperor appeared beside them.

"There he is—my Wolfling!" said the Emperor cheerfully. "Come and talk to me, Wolfling!"

Instantly, with his words, Ro vanished. Also, all the other High-born nearby began to disappear, until Jim, Vhotan, and the Emperor were surrounded by an open space perhaps fifty feet in diameter, within which they could talk in casual tones without anyone else being near enough to overhear. The Emperor turned his gaze on the older High-born.

"Go on," he said, "enjoy yourself for once, Vhotan. I'll be all right."

Vhotan hesitated a moment, then winked out of sight.

The Emperor turned back to Jim.

"I like you—what is your name, Wolfling?" he asked.

"Jim, Oran," answered Jim.

"I like you, Jim." The Emperor leaned down, stooping a little from his more than seven feet of height, and laid a long hand on Jim's shoulder, resting part of his weight on Jim like a tired man. Slowly he began to pace idly up and down. Jim kept level with him, held by the shoulder.

"It's a wild world you come from, Jim?" Oran asked.

"Up until about half a century ago," said Jim. "Very wild."

They had gone perhaps half a dozen steps in one direction. The Emperor turned them about, and they began to pace back again. All the while they talked, they continued this movement—half a dozen paces one way, half a dozen paces back again, turn and return.

"You mean, in only fifty years you people tamed this world of yours?" asked the Emperor.

"No, Oran," said Jim. "We tamed the world sometime before that. It's just that fifty years ago we finally succeeded in taming ourselves."

Oran nodded, his gaze not on Jim, but fixed on the floor a little ahead of them as they moved.

"Yes, that's the human part of it. The self-taming is always the hardest," he said, almost as if to himself. "You know, my cousin Galyan, looking at you, would think immediately, what marvelous servants these people would make. And perhaps he's right. Perhaps he's right . . . but"—they turned about at the end of one of their short distances of pacing, and the Emperor for a moment looked from the floor up and over at Jim with a friendly smile—"I don't think so. We've had too many servants."

The smile faded. For a moment they paced in silence.

"You have your own language?" murmured the Emperor in Jim's ear, once more gazing at the floor as they went. "Your own art and music and history and legend?"

"Yes, Oran," said Jim.

"Then you deserve better than to be servants. At least"—once more the Emperor flashed one of his quick, brief, friendly smiles at Jim before returning his eyes to the floor ahead of them—"I know that you, at least, deserve better. You know, I shouldn't be surprised if someday I really do approve your adoption, so that you become technically one of us."

Jim said nothing. After a second, and after they had completed another turn, the Emperor looked sideways at him.

"Would you like that, Jim?" Oran said.

"I don't know yet, Oran," said Jim.

"An honest answer . . ." murmured the Emperor. "An honest answer . . . You know how they tell us, Jim, in probability, all events must sooner or later occur?"

"In probability?" Jim asked. But the Emperor went on as if he had not heard.

"Somewhere," said the Emperor, "there must be a probability in which you, Jim, were the Emperor, and all the people of your world were High-born. And I was a Wolfling, who was brought there to show off some barbaric skill to you and your court. . . ."

The grip on Jim's shoulder had tightened. Glancing

up and sideways, Jim saw that the Emperor's eyes had become abstracted and seemingly out of focus. Though he continued to push Jim forward with his grip on Jim's shoulder, it was now as if he were blind and letting Jim find the path for him, so that he followed Jim, instead of leading him, as he had at the beginning of their pacing.

"Have you ever heard of a Blue Beast, Jim?" he murmured.

"No, Oran," said Jim.

"No. . . ." muttered the Emperor. "No, and neither have I. Also, I looked through all our records of all the human legends on all the worlds—and nowhere was there a Blue Beast. If there never was such a thing as a Blue Beast, why should I see one, Jim?"

The grip on Jim's shoulder was like a vise now. Still, the Emperor's voice was murmurous and soft, almost idle, as if he were daydreaming out loud. To any of the High-born watching from the edges of the circle surrounding them, it must look as if the two of them were in perfectly sensible, though low-voiced conversation.

"I don't know, Oran," answered Jim.

"Neither do I, Jim," said the Emperor. "That's what makes it so strange. Three times I've seen it now, and always in a doorway ahead of me, as if it was barring my path. You know, Jim . . . sometimes I'm just like all the rest of the High-born. But there are other times in which my mind becomes very clear . . . and I see things, and understand them, much better than any of these around us. That's why I know you're different, Jim. When I first saw you after the bullfight, I was looking at you . . . and all of a sudden it was as if you were at the other end of the telescope—very small, but very sharp. And I saw many very small, very sharp details about you that none of the rest of us had seen.

You can be a High-born or not, Jim. Just as you like. Because it doesn't matter . . . I saw that in you. It doesn't matter."

The Emperor's voice stopped. But he continued to urge Jim on, pacing blindly alongside him.

"That's the way it is with me, Jim . . ." he began again after a moment. "Sometimes I see things small and clear. Then I realize that I'm half a step beyond the rest of the High-born. And it's strange—I'm what we've been working for down all these generations—that one step further on. But it's a step that we aren't built to take, Jim . . . do you understand me?"

"I think so, Oran," answered Jim.

" . . . But at other times," went on the Emperor. Jim could not tell whether Oran had noted his answer or not. " . . . But at other times, things only start to get sharp and clear—and when I try to look more closely, they go very fuzzy, and out of focus, and large. And I lose that sense of extra, inner sharp sight that I had to begin with. Then I have bad dreams for a while— dreams, awake and asleep. It's in dreams like that, that I've seen the Blue Beast, three times now. . . ."

The Emperor's voice trailed off again, and Jim thought that they had come merely to another temporary pause in the conversation. But abruptly the Emperor's hand fell from his shoulder.

Jim stopped and turned. He found Oran looking down at him, smiling, clear-eyed and cheerful.

"Well, I mustn't keep you, Jim," said Oran in a thoroughly normal, conversational voice. "This will be your first party—and after all, you're practically the guest of honor. Why don't you circulate and meet people. I've got to go find Vhotan. He worries too much when I'm away from him."

The Emperor vanished. Jim stood still, and the cleared circle of floor began to fill in around him, as

those on the outskirts drifted inward, and new arrivals
began to appear. He looked about for Ro but could
not see her.

"Adok!" he said in a low voice.

The Starkien appeared beside him.

"Forgive me, Jim," said Adok. "I didn't know that the
Emperor was through talking to you. I found the servant you sent me to find."

"Take me where I can see him but he can't see me,"
said Jim.

Abruptly they were in a narrow, shadowy place
between two pillars, looking toward a further area
where a cluster of close pillars enclosed a small open
space, where a large number of trays loaded with food
and drink stood neatly racked in the empty air, one
above another. Standing amidst these trays was a servant, one of the short brown men with the long hair.
Jim and Adok stood behind him, and looking past him,
they could see out to where another servant was circu-
lating within view with a tray of food.

"Good," said Jim.

He memorized the location and shifted both himself and Adok back to where he had been standing
when the Emperor had left him.

"Adok," he said softly, "I'm going to try to stay continuously within sight of the Emperor. I'd like you to
stay within sight of me, but not exactly with me. Keep
your eyes on me, and when I disappear, I want you to
go to Vhotan, who'll be with the Emperor, and tell him
I want him to be a witness to something. Then bring
him to the place where that servant is. You understand?"

"Yes, Jim," said Adok unemotionally.

"Now," said Jim. "How do I find the Emperor?"

"I can take you to him," said Adok. "All Starkiens
can always find the Emperor, at any time. It's in case
one of us should be needed."

They were suddenly elsewhere in the Great Gathering Room. Jim looked about and from a distance of a couple of dozen feet saw the Emperor—this time without a circle of privacy around him, talking and laughing with several other High-born. Vhotan, his yellowish brows knitted, was at the younger man's elbow.

Jim looked around him again and discovered Adok looking at him from perhaps twenty feet away. Jim nodded and drifted off at an angle that would keep him moving through the crowd, but at about always the same distance from the Emperor.

Twice the Emperor shifted position suddenly. Twice Jim found himself shifted by Adok to a new position within sight of the High-born ruler. Surprisingly, through all this, none of the High-born around Jim paid particular attention to him. They seemed to have no eagerness to see the Wolfling in whose honor the party was being given, and if their eyes rested on him unknowingly, they evidently took him for simply one more of the servants.

Time stretched out. Nearly an hour had gone by, and Jim was almost beginning to doubt his earlier certainties, when abruptly he saw what he had been waiting for.

At first glance, it was nothing much. The Emperor was half-turned away from Jim, and all that betrayed his change in condition was a slight stiffening of his tall figure. He had become somewhat immobile, somewhat rigid.

Jim hastily took two steps to the left so that he could catch sight of the man's face. Oran was staring through and past the other High-born man he had been talking to. His gaze was fixed; his smile was fixed; and as at the bullfight, there was a little trickle of moisture shining at the corner of his mouth.

None of those around him appeared to be in the least aware of this. But Jim wasted no time watching them. Instead, he turned to look about for servants. He had made less than a half-turn before he saw the first man, a thin black-haired member of the lesser races, carrying a silver tray of what looked like small cakes.

The man was not moving. He was stopped, still, as frozen in position as the Emperor.

Jim hastily completed his turn. He saw three more servants, all of them rigid, all of them unmoving as statues. Even as he looked, the High-born around them began to take notice of this strange lack of activity in their midst. But Jim did not wait to see how their reaction would develop. Instantly he transferred himself to the shadowy area behind the servant with the trays— to that place where Adok had earlier taken him.

The man with the trays was standing, looking. But he was not rigid—as was the servant who could be seen a couple of dozen yards beyond him, surrounded by High-born.

Jim bent nearly double and ran forward swiftly and silently behind the trays until he came up with the servant who was looking out. At once he caught the man from behind with both hands. One hand taking him at the top and back of the neck just under the overhang of the skull, the other hand caught hold of the left armpit from behind, with the thumb resting over a pressure point just to the left of the shoulderblade.

"Move," whispered Jim swiftly, "and I'll break your neck."

The man stiffened. But he made no sound, and he did not move.

"Now," whispered Jim again. "Do exactly as I tell you—"

He paused to glance around behind him. There, in

the shadows, he saw the stocky form of Adok, and with Adok a towering High-born shape that would be Vhotan. Jim turned back to the servant.

"Put the two first fingers of your right hand across the biceps of your left arm," Jim whispered to the man.

The other did not move. Still keeping himself crouched low and hidden behind the servant's form, Jim pushed his thumb in again against the pressure point.

For a long moment the man resisted. Then, jerkily, almost like a robot, he moved his right hand up, up, and laid the forefingers of it, extended in V form, across the biceps of his left arm.

Outside, the immobile servant in sight suddenly began to move, as if nothing had happened, trailed by a small cloud of puzzled and interested High-born. Jim quickly clapped a hand over the mouth of the man he was holding, and half-lifted, half-dragged him back into the shadows.

Vhotan and Adok came forward to face down at the man.

"Now—" began Vhotan grimly. But at that moment the servant made an odd, small noise and suddenly slumped, heavy in Jim's grasp.

"Yes," said Vhotan, as if Jim's laying the man down had been a comment in words, "whoever planned this wouldn't have taken any chances on leaving him alive for us to question. Even the brain structure will be destroyed, no doubt."

He raised his eyes and looked across the dead body to Jim. His High-born mind had plainly already deduced much of what Jim had brought him here to see. But Vhotan's eyes retained a bit of their chill, nonetheless.

"Do you know who's behind all this?" he asked Jim. Jim shook his head.

"But you clearly expected it to happen," said Vhotan. "You expected it enough to send your Starkien to bring me here. Why me?"

Jim looked unstaringly at him.

"Because I decided you were the one man among the High-born who had to admit to yourself, consciously, that the Emperor's mind is not all it should be—or perhaps," said Jim, for a second remembering their talk, his and the Emperor's, as they walked up and down the polished floor, "his mind is a little too much more than it should be."

A faint click seemed to come from the throat of Vhotan. It was several long seconds before he said anything; and when he did speak, it was on another topic.

"How did you find out about this—this, that the servants had planned?" Vhotan asked.

"I didn't find out, to the point where I was absolutely sure it would happen," said Jim. "But I taught myself the Silent Language of the servants underground and learned that something was in the wind. Putting that together with this party, and the Emperor's known frailty, gave me an idea of what to look for. So when I got here, I sent Adok around to look for it; and when he found it, I acted as you've just seen."

Vhotan had stiffened again at the coupling of the words "Emperor" and "frailty." But he relaxed as Jim finished talking, and nodded.

"You've done a good job, Wolfling," he said; and the words were plain enough, even though the tone was grudging. "From this point on, I'll handle it. But we'd better get you off the Throne World for a while, sponsored for adoption or not sponsored for adoption."

He stood and thought for a second.

"I think the Emperor will promote you," he said

finally. "As a rank more commensurate with your effective High-born status as someone sponsored for adoption, he'll promote you to a Starkien Commander of Ten-units and send you off on some military-police job on one of the Colony Worlds."

He turned away from Jim, Adok, and the dead servant, as if about to disappear. Then, apparently changing his mind, he swung back to look at Jim again.

"What's your name?" he said sharply.

"Jim," answered Jim.

"Jim. Well, you did a good job, Jim," said Vhotan grimly. "The Emperor appreciates it. And—so do I."

With that, he did disappear.

Chapter 8

The planet Athiya to which Jim was sent with his Ten-units of Starkien, Adok, and Harn II—who was the Ten-units' original commander but now acting-adjutant to Jim—was one of the many worlds populated by the small brown men with long, straight hair hanging down their backs. The Governor, a burly little chestnut of a man, avoided all references to the uprising, to put down which he had asked the High-born to send him Starkien help. He insisted that they go through a large and formal welcoming ceremony, during which he avoided all references to the uprising and any questions about it made to him by Jim.

However, explanations could not be put off forever. Jim, Harn II, Adok, and the Governor all ended up at last in the Governor's private office of the capital city of Athiya. The Governor attempted to fuss around getting them hassocks and refreshments, but Jim cut him short.

"Never mind that," said Jim. "We don't want food and drink. We want to know about this uprising—

where is it, how many people are involved, and what kind of weapons have they?"

The Governor sat down on one of the Hassocks and abruptly burst into tears.

For a moment Jim was dumbfounded. Then knowledge that had its roots not in what he had learned on the Throne World as much as what he had learned back in his anthropological studies on Earth reassured him with the obvious deduction that the Governor belonged to a culture in which it was not unusual for the males to cry—even as publicly and noisily as the Governor was doing now.

Jim waited, therefore, until the Governor had gotten rid of his first explosion of emotion, and then put his question again.

Snuffling, the Governor wiped tears from his eyes and tried to answer. "I never thought they wouldn't send me a High-born in command of the Starkiens!" he said thickly to Jim. "I was going to throw myself on his mercy . . . but you're not a High-born—"

His tears threatened to flood his explanations once again. Jim spoke sharply to him, to bring him out of it.

"Stand up!" Jim snapped. Reflexively, the Governor obeyed. "As a matter of fact, I've been sponsored for adoption into the High-born. But that's beside the point. Whatever the Emperor sent you is what your situation deserves."

"But it isn't!" choked the Governor. "I—I lied. It isn't just an uprising. It's a revolution! All the other families on the planet have joined together—even my cousin Cluth is with them. In fact, he's the head of it all. They've all banded together to kill me and put Cluth here in my place!"

"What's this?" demanded Jim. He was aware that the Colony Worlds of the empire had their miniature courts, modeled on the Throne World's. These courts consisted of the noble families of the Colony World, headed up by the family and person of the Governor, who was a small Emperor locally, in his own right.

"Why did you let it get this far?" put in Harn II. "Why didn't you use your colonial troops earlier to put it down?"

"I—I—" The Governor wrung his hands, obviously incapable of speech.

Watching him, Jim had no doubt what had happened. His studies of the past few weeks, both underground and at the learning-center screen in Ro's apartment, once he had trained himself to read at the rapid High-born rate, had given him a good insight not merely into Throne World society but into the society of these Colony Worlds. Undoubtedly the Governor had let things get this far out of hand because he had been confident of his own ability until recently to bargain with the dissident elements of his world. Evidently he had underrated his opposition.

Then, having let things get out of hand, he had been afraid to admit the fact to the Throne World and had put in a request for much less in the way of Starkien troops than he needed to control the situation, possibly imagining he could use the Starkiens coming as a threat and still make a deal with the rebels.

However, understanding this was no help now. The Throne World was committed to backing up the Governors, who were allowed to hold power on the Colony Worlds.

"Sir," said Harn II, tapping Jim on the elbow. He beckoned to Jim, and they walked aside, where they could talk privately at the far end of the room. Adok followed them, leaving the Governor standing, a lonely little brown figure surrounded by hassocks and floating table surfaces.

"Sir," said Harn II in a low voice, once they had stopped at the far end of the room, "I strongly suggest that we stay put here and send a message back to the Throne World for additional Starkiens. If half what that man there says is true, those who are against him will already have control of most of the colonial armed forces. A Ten-unit of Starkiens can do a lot, but they can't be expected to defeat armies. There's no reason we should lose men just because of *his* blunder."

"No," said Jim. "Of course not. On the other hand, I think I'd like to look into the situation a little further and see for ourselves what we're up against before shouting for help. So far the only account of things is what we've gotten from the Governor. Things may be a great deal different from what he thinks, even if everything he's afraid of is true."

"Sir," said Harn II, "I have to protest. Every Starkien is an expensive and valuable man in terms of his training and equipment. They shouldn't be risked in a hopeless cause; and as their former commander, I have to tell you I think it isn't fair to them to risk them that way."

"Sir," said Adok—since they had left the Throne World, Adok also had been addressing him with military respectfulness—"the Adjutant-Commander is right."

Jim looked at both of the Starkiens in turn. They were subtly reminding him of the fact that while Jim was in nominal command of the expedition, the only one with real experience as a commander of Starkien Ten-units in that room was Harn himself.

"I appreciate your objections, Adjutant," said Jim slowly to Harn II now. "But I'd still like to look the situation over."

"Yes, sir," said Harn II. There was not the slightest

flicker of emotion visible in him at being overruled. How much of this was normal Starkien self-control, and how much of it was Harn's own resignation to the situation, was something Jim could not tell. But Jim turned now and led the way back across the room to the Governor, who looked up hopelessly as they came to him.

"There are a good many things I want to know," said Jim. "But you can start out by telling me what it was your cousin—or whoever it was who's behind this insurrection—used in order to get the others to join him."

The Governor started to wring his hands and cloud up toward tears again, but on meeting Jim's eye, evidently thought better of it.

"I don't know . . . I don't know!" he said. "There was some talk about their having protection. Protection . . ." He trailed off timorously.

"Go on," said Jim. "Finish what you were going to say."

"Protection . . . from someone on the Throne World," said the Governor fearfully.

"Protection by one of the High-born?" demanded Jim bluntly.

"I—I never exactly heard them say so, now!" chattered the Governor, paling. "I didn't ever really hear that said in so many words!"

"Don't worry about it," said Jim. "Now, listen to me. Your cousin and his allies undoubtedly have armed forces. Where are they, and how many of them are there?"

With the topic off the High-born and back on his own people, the Governor revived like a wilted flower. His burly little shoulders twitched, and his voice deepened, as he turned and pointed off through the walls of his office.

"North of here." He gave a distance in Imperial units that amounted to something under sixty miles. "They're camped on a plain with a ring of hills around it. They've got sentry posts up on the hill, and the posts are manned by the best men in our colonial armed forces."

"How many of those are with them?"

"Three—three—" the Governor stuttered with new apprehension, "—three-quarters, maybe."

"More likely ninety-eight percent of them, sir," put in Harn II, gazing at the Governor, "if he estimates them as high as three-quarters."

"Why haven't they moved into your capital city here before now?" asked Jim.

"I . . . I told them you were coming," said the Governor miserably. "In fact I . . . offered to send you away if they'd make terms."

"The only terms to be made," said Harn II to the little man, "will be by us. How many men does ninety-eight percent of your colonial armed forces amount to?"

"Three divisions," stammered the Governor, "about forty thousand trained and armed men."

"Sixty to seventy thousand," amended Harn II, looking at Jim.

Jim nodded.

"Very well," he said. He looked out a long, low window in one side of the office. "It's almost sunset locally. Do you have a moon?" he added, turning to the Governor.

"Two of them—" the Governor was beginning, when Jim cut him short.

"One would be enough, if it gives us enough moonlight," he said. He turned to Harn and Adok. "As soon as it's dark, we'll go up and have a look at that camp of theirs."

He looked back at the Governor, who bobbed his head, smiling.

"And we'll take you with us," said Jim.

The Governor's smile vanished as suddenly as the smile of a cartoon figure wiped from the drawing by the cartoonist's eraser. Four hours later, with the earlier of the two moons just beginning to show a small orange rim over the low hills of the horizon surrounding the capital city, Jim, with Harn and Adok up front and the Governor in the rear of a small, completely enclosed combat reconnaissance craft, lifted out of the capital city, rose into the darkness of the night sky just below the black belly of some overhanging clouds, and slid silently northward in the direction the Governor indicated. Some fifteen minutes later they descended close to the ground and approached the hills ringing the plain they sought, with the underside of the reconnaissance vessel brushing the heads of the three-foot-tall grass as it dodged in and out of clumps of elmlike trees.

When the terrain began to tilt upward toward the encircling hills themselves, they hid the reconnaissance vessel in a clump of brush and young trees and continued the rest of the way on foot. The two Starkiens, together, went first, spread out about fifteen yards apart. They moved with an amazing silence, which Jim was able to match only because of his hunting experience back on Earth. But most surprising of them all was the little Governor, who turned out to be quite at home stealing quietly through the patches of alternate moonlight and shadow. Once he was sure the small man could keep up and would make no noise, Jim spread out from him to approximately the same distance existing between Adok and Harn.

They were nearly to the top of the slope that would at last allow them to overlook the plain beyond when the two Starkiens dropped suddenly out of sight on their stomachs in the grass. Jim and the Governor immediately did the same.

Some minutes went by. Then Adok suddenly rose from the grass immediately before Jim.

"It's all right, sir. Come on. You can walk the rest of the way," he said. "The sentry was asleep."

Jim and the Governor got to their feet and followed the Starkien up the slope and into a little enclosure perhaps a dozen feet across, fenced in with what looked like a silver-wire mesh perhaps a yard high. In the center of the enclosure was an instrument resembling a beach umbrella with the fabric removed from the ribs supporting it. The sentry Adok had mentioned was nowhere in sight.

"There's the camp," said Harn, pointing over the far rim of the wire mesh and down a further slope. "It's all right. You can speak up inside the fence, sir. We can't be seen or heard now."

Jim walked over to stand beside Harn and look down. What he saw looked not so much like an armed camp as a circular small town or city of dome-shaped buildings divided by streets into pie-shaped sections.

"Come here," he said, looking back at the Governor. The Governor came obediently up to the wire mesh. "Look down there. Tell me. Do you see anything unusual about that camp down there?"

The Governor gazed and finally shook his head.

"Sir," said Harn, "the camp is laid out according to one of the customary military patterns, with different groups or units in each section, and a guard of men from each section to complete the perimeter circuit."

"Except they've set up a council building!" said the Governor self-pityingly. "Look at that! Just as if I was there with them!"

"Where?" asked Jim.

The Governor pointed out a larger dome-shaped building just to the right of the geometric center of the camp.

"Only a Governor is supposed to call a council among the troops!" he said. "But they've been going ahead, anyway. As if I were deposed already—or even dead!" He snuffled.

"What are you suspicious of, sir?" asked Harn. Adok had moved up close behind them. Jim could now see him out of the corner of his eye.

"I'm not exactly sure," said Jim. "Adjutant, what kind of weapons do our Starkiens have that these colonial soldiers wouldn't have?"

"We have vastly better individual defensive screens," answered Harn. "Also, each of our men represents fire power equal to that of one of their heavy companies."

"Then it's just a case of having the same sort of weapons, only better ones?" said Jim. "Is that it?"

"Sir," answered Harn, "the greatest weapon of the Starkiens is the trained individual Starkien himself. He—"

"Yes, I know that," interrupted Jim a little sharply. "What about"—he fumbled in his mind for means of translating the Earth terms there into the Empire language—"what about large fixed weapons? Unusually powerful explosives—nuclear fusion or fission weapons?"

"These colonials aren't allowed the technological machinery to make large fixed weapons," said Harn. "It's possible that they might secretly have built some sort of fission device—but unlikely. As for any antimatter weapon, that's completely impossible—"

"Just a minute," Jim interrupted him. "Do the Starkiens have all these things available back on the Throne World? The—what was it you called it? Antimatter devices?"

"Of course. But they haven't been required for use off the Throne World for some thousands of years," said Harn. "Are you aware of what an antimatter device is, sir?"

"Only," said Jim grimly, "to the extent of knowing that a little bit of antimatter coming in contact with a little bit of matter can cause a good deal of destruction."

He stood for a second without saying anything. Then he spoke abruptly.

"Well, Adjutant," he said to Harn, "now that you've seen how things look down there, do you still want to send back to the Throne World for help?"

"No, sir," answered Harn promptly. "If the sentry we surprised in his post is at all representative, their armed forces are incredibly poor. Also, their camp seems set up more for the convenience of those dwelling in it than with any eye to overall defense. The pattern is there, but there are no street patrols, no perimeter patrols that I can see, and—most amazing— no overhead warning system whatsoever. Those people down there are just going through the motions of being an army."

Harn stopped, as if giving Jim a chance to comment.

"Go on, Adjutant," said Jim.

"Sir," acknowledged Harn, "what with what I've mentioned, the fact that we've just now discovered that their leaders are all concentrated in that one building, makes the military solution to this situation extremely simple. I'd suggest we send Adok back for the rest of the men right now, and as soon as they get here we mount a raid on that one building, coming down on it from directly overhead so as to avoid triggering their perimeter defenses, and either kill or capture the ringleaders. Then they can be returned to the capital city for trial."

"And what," asked Jim, "if the rumor the Governor heard was correct—that these rebels have a friend among the High-born on the Throne World?"

"Sir?" said Harn. Insofar as a Starkien could, he sounded puzzled. "It's impossible, of course, for a High-born to have any dealings with colonial revolutionists like those down there. But even assuming that they down there had such a friend, there's nothing he could do to stop us. And, moreover, we Starkiens are responsible only to the Emperor."

"Yes," said Jim. "All the same, Adjutant, I'm not going to follow your advice here, any more than I followed it when you suggested earlier that we send back to the Throne World for reinforcements."

He turned away from Harn to confront the little Governor.

"Your noble families are always fighting with each other, aren't they?" he asked.

"Why—they're nearly always intriguing against me, all of them!" said the little Governor. Then he giggled unexpectedly. "Oh, I see what you mean, Commander. Yes, they do fight among one another a lot. In fact, if they didn't, I might have some trouble handling them. Oh, yes, their main sport is intriguing and accusing one another of everything you can think of."

"Naturally," said Jim, half to himself. "They're *noyaux*."

"Sir?" said Harn beside him. The little Governor was also looking puzzled. The scientific term in the language of Earth meant nothing to them.

"Never mind," said Jim. He went on to the Governor, "Would there be anyone among these other leaders down there that your cousin generally doesn't get along with?"

"Someone who Cluth doesn't—" The little Governor stopped thoughtfully. He stood a second, gazing at the moonlit grass at his feet. "Notral! Yes, if there's anyone he isn't likely to get along with, it would be Notral."

He turned and pointed down at the encampment.

"See?" he said. "Cluth's people will be in that slice there of the encampment. And Notral's will be way over there, almost directly opposite. The farther they are away from each other usually, the better they like it!"

"Adjutant. Adok," said Jim, turning to the two Starkiens. "I've got a special job for you. Do you suppose that you could go down there quietly and bring back to me, alive and in good shape, a perimeter guard from the section just outside Notral's area of the encampment?"

"Of course, sir," answered Harn.

"Fine," said Jim. "Be sure to blindfold him when you take him from the perimeter. And you'll have to blindfold him again when you take him back. Now"— he turned to the Governor—"point them out Notral's area of the encampment again."

The Governor did so. The two Starkiens let themselves out of the sentry post and effectually disappeared—as effectually as if they had translated themselves from there to some other spot, in the fashion of the Throne World. It was a little over half an hour, by earthly standards, before they returned, and Jim saw the section of the mesh fence of the sentry post swing open. He had been sitting on the ground, crosslegged, with the little Governor sitting to one side of him. But now Jim got to his feet, and the Governor scrambled up, as ordered, to stand alongside him, his extreme shortness emphasizing Jim's six-foot-four.

Adok crawled into the sentry post and stood up, to be followed a second later by a small brown youngster in a straplike harness somewhat like that of the Starkiens. The young colonial soldier was so frightened that he shook visibly. Harn followed closely behind him and shut the mesh gate once he was inside.

"Bring him here," said Jim, imitating the breathy, hissing accents of the Throne World High-born. He was standing so that his back was to the rising moon, which had finally been joined by its smaller partner of the skies. Their combined light flooded over his shoulder and showed him clearly the face of the small long-haired soldier but left his own face in the darkness of deep shadow.

"Do you know who it is I have chosen to be your final leader?" Jim asked in a hard, deep-voiced tone when the young soldier was almost literally carried by the two Starkiens to stand before him.

The colonial soldier's teeth chattered so badly he could not make a coherent answer. But he shook his head violently. Jim made a short sound of anger and contempt, deep in his throat.

"Never mind," he said harshly. "You know who controls the area behind your section of the perimeter?"

"Yes. . . ." The young soldier nodded his head eagerly.

"Go to him," said Jim. "Tell him I've changed my plans. He's to take over command of your people now, without waiting."

Jim waited. The young soldier trembled.

"Do you understand me?" Jim shot at him.

The prisoner went into a violent convulsion of nodding.

"Good," said Jim. "Adok, take him outside. I want a word with my adjutant before you go."

Adok shepherded the prisoner out beyond the mesh fence. Jim turned and beckoned both Harn and the Governor to him. He pointed down at the camp.

"Now," he said to the Governor, "point out to the adjutant the part of the perimeter lying outside the area that your cousin Cluth will be occupying."

The Governor shrank a little from Jim, apparently infected by the fear of the prisoner, and stretched out a trembling forefinger to indicate to Harn the section Jim had mentioned. Harn asked a few questions to make certain of the location and then turned to Jim.

"You want me to take the prisoner back there?" he asked Jim.

"That's right, Adjutant," said Jim.

"Yes, sir," said Harn, and went out through the mesh fence.

This time the trip took them nearer an hour of earthly time. The moment they returned, with word that they had set the prisoner to walking forward and heard him challenged and picked up by the soldiers of Cluth's perimeter, Jim ordered them all out of the sentry post and back down the slope toward their vessel.

They went swiftly, at Jim's orders. It was not until they were fully airborne that Jim relaxed. Then he ordered Adok, who was at the controls, to take the ship up and out to the farthest possible distance from which their night-vision screens could keep view on the camp. Adok obeyed. Some six or eight minutes later they settled into a circling patrol some fifteen thousand feet up and ten miles' ground distance from the camp. As silently as a cloud itself, the reconnaissance vessel swung like a huge toy at the end of an invisible string better than ten miles long about the drowsy armed camp below.

Jim sat unmoving, gazing at the night-vision screen in the control area beyond Adok, up in the front of the ship. With him sat Harn, the Governor, and, for that matter, Adok himself, all gazing at the screen, but, with the exception of Jim, with no idea of what they were watching for.

For quite a while it seemed that their watch would produce nothing out of the ordinary. Reaching out, Jim worked the telescopic controls of the night screen, from time to time zooming in for a view of the streets and buildings. The night patrols were going their rounds without incident. Most of the buildings were dark. And so it continued.

Then, without warning, there was a little wink of light, hardly brighter than the blink of a flashlight, in what seemed the center of the Governor's council-quarters building.

"I think that's—" Jim was beginning, when Harn threw himself past him, literally tore the control out of Adok's hands, and sent the small craft twisting away, fleeing at top speed from the scene they had just been watching.

Adok, trained soldier that he was, did not fight his superior officer except for a first instinctive grab at the controls as they were taken from him. He slipped out of the control seat and let Harn take his place.

Jim leaned forward and spoke in Harn's ear.

"Antimatter?" Jim asked.

Harn nodded. A moment later the shock wave hit, and the little vessel went tumbling end over end through the night sky, like some insignificant insect swatted by the paw of some monster.

Harn, clinging to the controls, finally got the ship back on an even keel. Within, they were all of them battered to a certain extent. The little Governor was only half-conscious, and his nose was bleeding. Jim helped Adok to prop the little man up on his feet and buckle his seat harness around him. Ironically, not one of them had his harness buckled at the moment they had been struck by the shock wave.

"Is there any point in our going back?" Jim asked Harn. The adjutant shook his head. "There'll be nothing to see," he said. "Only a crater."

"How much antimatter would you judge was involved in that?" Jim asked.

Harn shook his head.

"I'm no expert in amounts, sir," he said. "The total *unit* is about as big as you can hold comfortably in one hand. But that's for convenience. The effective element inside it may be no larger than a grain of sand, for all I know. . . . Sir?"

"Yes?" said Jim.

"If I may ask, sir," said Harn evenly, "what made you believe that there was antimatter down in that camp?"

"It was a guess, Adjutant," said Jim somberly. "Based on a lot of factors—here and back on the Throne World."

"It was a trap, then," said Harn, without perceptible emotion in his voice. "A trap for me and my—I beg your pardon, sir—your Starkiens. We were meant to go in through the door they left open—that unguarded direct descent upon the main building. The whole Ten-unit would have been wiped out."

He was silent.

"But, sir," said Adok, looking first at him, then turning to Jim, "these colonials must've known that they'd be wiped out too?"

"What makes you think they'd know, Starkien?" said Harn. "There was no reason that whoever supplied them with that antimatter should have wanted them to know what they were handling."

Adok subsided. After a few moments Harn spoke again to Jim.

"Sir?" he said. "Could I ask the commander what *noyaux* are?"

"Social groups, Adjutant," said Jim. "Family groups whose chief occupation is badgering, insulting, and struggling with other family groups in every way short of actual fighting."

"These"—Harn glanced for a moment at the Governor—"form *noyaux*?"

"Their chief families do," said Jim. "Ordinarily their bickering just gives them something to do, because subconsciously they don't intend to harm each other, no matter how much they may believe consciously that they're ready to fight at the drop of a hat. But the point is, the *noyaux* never trust each other. When that soldier of Notral's perimeter guard was brought in and questioned, Cluth leaped at the conclusion that he had been betrayed by whomever from the Throne World gave him the antimatter. He made an effort to take it back from wherever it was being guarded, and some accident set it off. I hadn't hoped for that so much as for a splitting up of the encampment, which would give us a chance to swoop down on Cluth's party and take the antimatter back from him."

"I see, sir," said Harn. He said nothing for a second. "And now, sir?"

"Now," said Jim grimly, "we head back to the Throne World as quickly as possible."

"Sir!" acknowledged Harn.

He said no more after that, and both Jim and Adok sat without speaking. In the little vessel there was silence, until the Governor, recovering full consciousness, began to mourn his dead cousin, with mutterings of Cluth's name, and stifled, low-voiced sobs.

Chapter 9

The ship that had brought Jim and the Starkiens to this world was a smaller version of the space-going vessel that had brought Jim back from Alpha Centauri III. It was just big enough to hold the Ten-units of men, and required only one individual on duty watch in the ship's Power Room. It was directed by the same economical method according to which most things owned by the High-born were run. Whoever was in command of the ship merely visualized his destination and left it to the ship to pick up that visualization, resolve it, match it with the destination itself, and bring the ship to it. On their outward-bound voyage from the Throne World, it had been Harn II who had directed the ship, since Jim had no mental picture of their destination. Now, headed back to the Throne World, Jim needed no help. He needed only to visualize any spot on the surface of the Throne World—his own quarters, if need be—and the ship would take over from there. He did so, and the ship obeyed.

As they were about to land, however, he took Harn II and Adok aside.

"Adjutant," he said to Harn, "I want you to keep the men aboard ship here after we land. Don't go directly to your quarters to report back. Wait here in the ship until I send for you."

Harn stood still without saying anything for a long second.

"This is against usual practice," he said at last. "I assume it's an order?"

"It's an order," said Jim.

"In that case . . ." said Harn, "the only thing that can override it would be either orders from the Emperor or reason for us to believe that our staying aboard would be contrary to the Emperor's wishes. After what we've been through, I'm inclined not to think that these orders of yours can be contrary to the Emperor's wishes."

"You can believe me, Adjutant," said Jim slowly. "It's the Emperor's welfare I'm concerned about. And that welfare may be better served if you men stay out of sight aboard this ship instead of going back to your quarters."

"Sir!" said Harn II acknowledgingly. "You're returning to your own quarters, Sir?"

"I am," said Jim, "and I'm taking Adok with me."

He touched Adok on the arm and shifted them both back into his own quarters. They were empty. He shifted to Ro's apartment.

Ro was there, in the room with all her pets—hers and Afuan's—cutting the nails of the apelike creature. But she dropped her tools and practically tackled him in her enthusiasm at seeing him again.

"Jim!" she said. *"Jim! . . ."*

He let her squeeze him for a moment, and hugged her back briefly. Then, patting her head gently, he reached behind him and unlocked the grip of her hands so as to put her arms away from him.

"I'm sorry," he said gently. "But the situation's rather urgent."

She giggled, almost wickedly, ignoring the fact that he held her hands. Her eyes ran over him.

"Is that your Starkien uniform?" she asked. "How big you look in it! . . . Are those bands you're wearing still powered?"

"Yes," said Jim, not knowing quite what to make of this sudden, mad humor of hers, and hoping that a calm answer would calm her as well.

"They are?" she giggled again. "Show me! Smash that wall there down for me—"

She broke off suddenly and did sober up.

"No, no. What am I saying?" Abruptly the ridiculous humor was gone from her. She looked up at him gravely. "What is it Jim? You look worried!"

"Worried?" He let go of her wrists. "Not exactly— but there may be something going on to be worried about. Tell me, Ro. What on the Throne World here is blue?"

"Blue? You mean the color blue?" she asked. He nodded his head. "Why . . . white is the color we usually use. You know that. Occasionally, a little red. I don't think there is much blue on the Throne World nowadays, except a stray object or two that one of the High-born might've brought back from one of the Colonial Worlds."

"Think," said Jim, staring steadily at her. "Think hard."

"But, there really isn't any—oh," Ro interrupted herself, "unless you want to count the usual things. The sky here is blue. And the water is blue. Oh, and"— she paused to smile again—"there's the Emperor's Blue Beast still hidden somewhere in the palace someplace, if you want to count that."

"Blue Beast?" His question was so sharp and abrupt that she paled.

"Why, yes, Jim," she said, staring at him, "but it's nothing. It's just a toy that he used to have when he was a baby. Only he started to have nightmares about it, and they hid it from him. I don't know who hid it, or where it was hidden, and I don't think anybody knows nowadays. But it got so bad that anything blue-colored was likely to—upset him. That's why there's never anything blue left lying around where the Emperor might see it. Why is it so important to you?"

He heard the question at the end of her speech, but it was like hearing an unimportant noise far off. His mind was whirring, and he did not bother to answer her.

"I've got to see Vhotan right away," he said. "How do I find him, Ro?"

"Jim, what is it?" She was really alarmed now. "Vhotan's with the Emperor. You can't just go charging in on the Emperor. Oh, I know you did it once and got away with it. But you can't do it now. Particularly now."

"Why, particularly now?" Jim asked.

She took a small step back from him.

"Jim . . ." she said, uncertainly. "Don't . . ."

Jim made an effort to return his face to calmness.

"All right," he said. "Now tell me. Why is now so particular?"

"It's just that right now there's all this trouble going on, on the Colony Worlds," said Ro. "Vhotan's been sending out Starkiens to help the Governors of the lesser races put down the trouble, until there aren't any left here on the Throne World. He doesn't have a moment to spare to talk to anyone—"

She broke off, staring at him again. *"Jim, will you tell me what it is!"*

But again he hardly heard her. His thoughts were galloping far ahead under the impetus of this new piece of information. For a moment he gazed unseeingly out the transparent window of the pets' room at the ocean shore. An ocean shore, here too? The idea that Ro must carry a sandy beach and a piece of ocean around with her to provide a view for Afuan's pets was so ridiculous that it jolted his thoughts back into effectiveness.

"I want to get in touch with Slothiel," he said, looking back at Ro. "Then, the four of us—you, I, Slothiel, and Adok—must go and find Vhotan, whether he's with the Emperor or not."

"Are you crazy, Jim?" she said. "You can't go into the Emperor's presence wearing power bands like that! No one's allowed in his presence with anything more than a rod. His Starkiens would kill you out of reflex the minute you appeared. If you have to do this wild thing, at least take those power bands off! You too, Adok!"

She glanced past him at the Starkien. Her own fingers were already busy stripping the power bands off Jim's left arm. The wisdom of what she said was undeniable, and after a second he began to assist her. A moment later he had no weapon left but the rod in its loops at his belt. Looking around, he saw that Adok had similarly rid himself of power bands.

"Now," he said to Ro. "To Slothiel's. You'll have to find him for us. I don't even know where his quarters are."

She touched his arm, and they were abruptly in a different suite of rooms.

"Slothiel!" called Jim. But no answer came back through any of the three doorways leading off from the room in which they had appeared.

"He's not here," said Ro. "And it's no use our moving all over the Throne World looking for him. He could be one jump ahead of us, and we'd never catch up with him that way. The best thing is just to wait here for him, Jim."

"Wait?" said Jim. "Waiting is the one thing we can't afford to do. Can't we—"

He broke off. For Slothiel had just appeared before them.

"Welcome home, Jim," said Slothiel. "You're the first of our conquering heroes to get back. I heard you'd landed ship, but when I went to your quarters just now, you weren't there. I tried Ro's—and all I found was a batch of discarded power bands. So I came back here to look for messages—and, here you are!"

He smiled and waved Ro and Jim graciously to hassocks. Adok he ignored.

"Sit down," Slothiel said. "How about something to eat and drink? I can get you—"

"Nothing!" interrupted Jim. "Slothiel, are you loyal to the Emperor?"

Slothiel raised his eyebrows.

"My dear ex-Wolfling," he drawled, "*all* High-born are loyal to the Emperor. Otherwise how could we be loyal to ourselves?"

"There's loyalty and loyalty," said Jim bluntly. "I didn't ask you if you were loyal, in the academic sense. I asked you if you were loyal in the—say—Starkien sense?"

Slothiel stiffened slightly. His white eyebrows drew together.

"What sort of catechism is this, Jim?" he asked. But the tone of his voice was no longer one of completely idle banter. Under a surface of indifference there was a note of hard interest.

"You haven't answered me, Slothiel," said Jim.

"Should I answer, then?" murmured Slothiel in the tone of voice of a man choosing between two canapes on a serving tray. But his eyes remained unmoving on Jim. "After all, I am a High-born, and this is only an ex-Wolfling, a being of the lesser races . . . yes, I will answer. I'm loyal, Jim." His voice had suddenly become hard, with none of the soft nonsense left about it. "Now, what is this? And I want a straight, direct answer!"

"My Ten-units of Starkiens on Athiya," said Jim evenly, "were baited into a military trap that would have been no trap at all, if it hadn't been equipped with an antimatter weapon."

"Antimatter?" Slothiel's face stiffened for a second in astonishment, then quickly relaxed again as his Highborn mind accepted the incredible statement and ran quickly on to examine the implications of it. Within a few seconds he looked at Jim again. "Yes, you're right, Jim. We should see Vhotan about this."

"That's what I've intended to do, all along," said Jim. "I was only waiting to find you and take you along with the rest of us."

"Rest of us?" Slothiel glanced at Ro and Adok. "You and I are sufficient."

"No," said Jim. "I need Adok with me as a witness to what happened. And Ro stays with us because it's safest for her."

"Safest?" Slothiel shot a glance at Ro, who was watching both men and looking puzzled. "Oh—yes, I see what you mean. She could be taken and used as a hostage against you by whoever's behind this if we left her unprotected. All right, Starkien!"

He beckoned Adok in close, and the four of them shifted as a group to their destination.

They appeared in a room that was not the same room in which Jim had encountered Vhotan and the Emperor before. This was a larger room, something like a ballroom with a lounge area at one end. All the other walls of the ballroom except that which opened upon the lounge area were covered to the high, white ceiling with light-green draperies. In the center of the ballroom floor sat a peculiar instrument with a basketball-shaped head that was slowly rotating. In time with its rotation, various patterns in many colors other than blue flickered and played and swam around the ceiling. The Emperor was seated—almost sprawled—on the large hassock at the edge of the ballroom floor, staring raptly up at those patterns.

Nearby were three Starkiens, carrying rods and wearing power bands. Vhotan was some twenty feet away from the Emperor, standing over a table surface patterned with studs.

Except that he was not seated, his position and actions were very much like those Jim had seen in him once before.

With the appearance of the four people, the three Starkiens had automatically drawn their rods. Vhotan looked sharply up, caught sight of Slothiel, and waved the rods back into their belt loops. He turned from the table surface to face the group, scowling a little at Jim.

"I wasn't notified your Ten-units had returned to quarters," he said to Jim. "I can use those men right now."

"That's why I ordered them not to return to quarters," answered Jim.

Vhotan frowned sharply.

"What do you mean?" he said sharply. "And who gave you the authority to—"

He was interrupted by the sudden appearance of a servant—a man of the same appearance of Melness, carrying a small white box.

"This has just been delivered for you, Vhotan," the servant said. "It was sent through the Princess Afuan from the Governor of—" The servant gave the imperial name for Alpha Centauri.

"All right," scowled Vhotan. The servant disappeared. Vhotan carried the box over to his table service, felt about it for a second, and then lifted off a cover. His scowl deepened.

"What is this?" he asked. He started to swing back to face them, but at that moment a new voice interrupted him.

"Why, it's Oran," said the voice. It was the Emperor, woken from his gazing at the refulgent patterns of the ceiling, and now walking over to peer interestedly into the box. His hand went down and came up holding what looked like a chunk of granite, rough-cut, perhaps three inches in diameter. "And there's a note with it."

He picked up a card from the box and looked at it.

"It says, '*At the request of my good friend, Jim Keil,*'" said the Emperor, turning to face Vhotan and the group as he read, "'*this specimen of rock from his homeland, the planet Earth, as a souvenir for the High-born, Vhotan.*'"

The Emperor, smiling delightedly, lifted his eyes to Vhotan.

"It's a present for you, Vhotan," he said cheerfully, "from our ex-Wolfling, here! Here, you'd better take it!"

The Emperor tossed the rock to the older Highborn, whose long hands went up automatically to catch it in midair.

Vhotan's right hand closed about the flying object, and instantly he was covered with a brilliant blue light—an eye-baffling light in which his outlines were distorted and altered from the human into something unclear, but heavy and thick-bodied, bestial.

The Emperor screamed, stumbling backward and throwing up both long-fingered hands to shield his face from the sight.

"Nephew—" It was the voice of Vhotan, but somehow distorted and mangled into a growling bass. He raised blue-dazzling, thick, pawlike arms of light and took a step toward the Emperor, protectively.

The Emperor screamed again and stumbled backward, almost falling over a hassock, but keeping to his feet. His heels rang on the bare floor beyond the lounge area. He flung up a long arm with finger pointing.

"The Blue Beast!" he screamed to his Starkiens. "Kill it! *Kill it!*"

If there was a hesitation on the part of the Starkiens, it was for less than a fraction of a second. At once the three rods were drawn and came up, and the blue-haloed figure of Vhotan, still stepping toward the Emperor with arms outstretched, was laced with white fire.

The figure slumped. The blue light went out. A small piece of reddish rock rolled unheeded across the carpeted floor of the lounge section. Silent and still, sprawled upon that same carpet, lay Vhotan, his face untouched, but his body and limbs almost dismembered by incredible burn-lines.

There was no more sound or movement in the room. The Emperor stood staring at Vhotan. He stared for a long moment before his face and eyes began to change.

"Uncle?" he said in a quavering, uncertain voice. *"Uncle?"*

Slowly he began to move toward Vhotan. As he got closer, his shoulders bowed, and his face twisted like a man undergoing some process of torture. Slowly he came up to Vhotan and stood over him. He gazed down into Vhotan's untouched face. For such a violent death, Vhotan's face was strangely serene. His eyes and mouth were closed; the muscles of his features were relaxed. From the neck up he looked like someone engaged in a moment's silent meditation or thought.

"Vhotan . . ." began the Emperor on a note of anguish. But then his voice died in him, like the voice of a talking doll which had run down. He froze, unmoving, in the position in which he was, leaning over Vhotan, his arms half-reaching down toward the body of the older man. For a moment, to Jim, it seemed impossible that such a pose could be maintained. But the Emperor stayed as he was, as unmoving as a statue cast in plaster of paris.

Behind Jim, Slothiel stirred. He stepped forward toward the Emperor.

"Oran!" Slothiel said.

There was sudden amused laughter at the far end of the ballroom floor. Out of the corner of his eye, Jim caught sight of the three Starkiens spinning about swiftly, their rods coming up.

Then there were three odd, coughing sounds; and as Jim finished raising his head, he saw the three Starkiens stumble and fall. On the polished ballroom floor, they lay as still as Vhotan lay.

Jim turned to look toward the far end of the polished floor. There, just in front of one of the green curtains, stood Galyan, holding a black rod in his right hand, and a strange, handgun sort of device, with a long, twisted barrel, in his left. Behind Galyan were Melness and Afuan. As Jim caught sight of them, Galyan tossed the handgun contemptuously away from him. It skidded across the polished floor until its further progress was blocked by a leg of one of the dead Starkiens.

Followed by Melness and Afuan, Galyan walked toward the lounge end of the room. His heels rapped with a strange loudness on the polished surface of the floor. He laughed again at the small group still standing there, as he came.

"You're quite a problem, Wolfling," he said to Jim. "Not only do you come back alive, but, having come back, you force me into taking action ahead of schedule. But it's all come out all right."

He reached the end of the polished floor and stepped onto the carpet. He stopped and transferred his gaze from Jim to Slothiel.

"No, Slothiel," he said mockingly. "Not 'Oran.'—'Galyan.' We will have to teach you to say 'Galyan.'"

Chapter 10

Galyan's words seemed to echo all about them. Looking at Slothiel, Jim saw the other High-born begin to stiffen and straighten. Galyan was the tallest of the High-born that Jim had seen, with the exception of the Emperor himself. But Slothiel was almost as tall. And now that he abandoned his carefully indifferent slouch, it could be seen how tall he was. The two men, both well over seven feet, faced each other across a distance of perhaps a dozen feet of carpeting.

"You've never been able to teach me anything, Galyan," said Slothiel in a dry, hard voice. "If I were you, I wouldn't expect to begin now."

"Slothiel, don't be an idiot!" Afuan spoke up. But Galyan cut her short.

"Never mind!" he said sharply, his lemon-yellow eyes still glittering unmovingly on Slothiel. "Who are we to tell Slothiel what to do? As he said—we've never been able to teach him anything."

" '*We?*' " Slothiel smiled bitterly. "Are you into the Emperor's second person plural already, Galyan?"

"Did I say—*we*?" responded Galyan. "A slip of the tongue, Slothiel."

"Then you don't intend to kill him?" said Slothiel, indicating the frozen figure of the Emperor with a slight movement of his head.

"Kill him?" said Galyan. "Of course not. Care for him—that's what I'm going to do. Vhotan never did take the best care of him. He's not well, you know."

"Are you?" asked Jim.

Galyan's eyes flickered for a moment to Jim.

"Be patient, little Wolfling," Galyan purred. "Your time is coming. Right now I'm amusing myself with Slothiel."

"Amusing yourself?" said Slothiel with a grim irony that matched the cruel humor in Galyan's voice. "You'd better be thinking up explanations for how Vhotan died."

"I?" chuckled Galyan. "The Emperor's Starkiens killed Vhotan, at the Emperor's order. You saw that."

"And who killed the Starkiens?" said Slothiel.

"You, of course," said Galyan. "You went out of your head at the sight of Vhotan ordered killed for no reason—"

"No reason?" echoed Slothiel. "What about that disguised blue distortion light? Jim never had the Alpha Centauran Governor send it to Vhotan. That was your doing."

Galyan twitched a finger. Melness scuttled forward and sideways, to pick up the small granitic-looking shape from the carpet and tuck it into a pocket in his kilt. He retreated hastily behind Galyan again.

"What distortion light?" asked Galyan.

"I see," said Slothiel. He took a deep breath. "But of course I didn't kill the Starkiens."

"I wouldn't go around telling the other High-born that, if I were you," said Galyan. "The Emperor will need someone to look after him; now that Vhotan's dead, I'll be taking our uncle's place. If you go around telling a wild story like that, the Emperor may well decide that you need treatment and isolation for your own good."

"Oh? But even if I say nothing," drawled Slothiel, "those three Starkiens were killed by a heavy-duty intersperser. The other Starkiens, when they get back, will wonder how three of their number could have been killed by a rod while those three were wearing full power bands. I can prove that I haven't been near the heavy-duty weapon armory for years."

"No doubt," said Galyan. "But you said, 'when the other Starkiens get back.' You see, they won't be back."

Slothiel looked about suddenly at Jim. Jim nodded.

"So the Wolfling brought back word of our little traps on the colony planets, did he?" said the voice of Galyan. Both Jim and Slothiel looked back at the tall High-born. "You know then, Slothiel. The Starkiens won't be back. I've got it in mind to create some new Starkiens—some responsible to me rather than to the Emperor. At any rate, you see your own choice. Be silent—or be removed from the social scene."

Slothiel laughed, and reaching over, drew the rod from the loops in Adok's belt.

Galyan laughed also, but with a half-incredulous note of contempt in his voice.

"Have you really lost your senses, Slothiel?" he said. "We've fenced as boys. You've got fast reflexes, but you know that no one's faster than I am. Except—" He nodded at the still-paralyzed figure of the Emperor.

"But we haven't tried it as men," said Slothiel. "Besides, I'm a little tired of all our play-acting here on the Throne World. I think I'd like to kill you."

He took a step forward. Galyan stepped hastily back onto the polished surface of the ballroom floor and slowly drew the rod from the loops in his own belt.

"Shall we bet on it?" he said. "Let's bet a banishment amount of Lifetime Points, Slothiel. How about fifty Lifetime Points? That ought to put either one of us over the limit."

"Don't talk to me of toys," said Slothiel, slowly advancing foot after foot, as Galyan equally slowly backed and circled away from him. "I think I've lost my taste for gambling. I want something a little more exciting."

They were almost in the center of the polished floor area now. There was still a dozen feet between them, but tall and bent over as they were, their wide shoulders hunched forward, the rods held low before them, it seemed as if scarcely one of their own long arm lengths separated the two of them.

Abruptly the rod in Slothiel's hand spouted the white lightning of its charge. At the same time, he leaned back and to one side in an attempt to outflank Galyan.

Galyan, however, crouched under the white bolt, which crackled where his head had been a moment before, and spun on his heels, still in crouched position, to come up facing Slothiel and with his own rod shooting white fire.

A little faster, and Galyan would have been able to drive the fire of his own rod under the line of fire from Slothiel's rod. However, the moment of Galyan's turning was enough time to allow Slothiel to lower the aim of his own weapon, so that the discharge from Galyan's rod met the discharge from Slothiel's head-on, and the two lines of white fire splashed harmlessly into an aurora of sparks. From that first moment, the lines of fire from the two rods were never disengaged.

Following the first wild gambles by both men (and Jim had practiced at the rods enough with Adok to understand what gambles they had been)—Slothiel's attack and Galyan's counter—both of the High-born fought defensively and warily for more than a dozen fairly routine engages. As Jim had discovered with Adok, fighting with the rods was very similar to fencing with sabers, provided they were sabers that changed lengths frequently and unexpectedly. The focal point of the fire put forth by the rods—that point at which the discharge was most destructive—was at the tip of an inner cone of pure white light, and this cone could be extended by the man holding the rod, at will, from a length of six inches to ten feet. This was the point at which the utmost power of the rod was exerted. Directly in counter, the point of the cone of fire in one rod could be blocked only by the point of the cone of fire in another. However, if the cone tip should miss its target and the opposing rod could project its cone tip into the stream of fire behind the other tip, the penetrative cone could be bent aside, so that the attacking cone could go on to strike its target.

It was not just a matter of deflecting the stream of fire from the opponent's rod, therefore, but of deflecting it with a portion of your own flame, which was stronger than that part of the opponent's flame it encountered.

Slothiel and Galyan moved about the polished floor, each careful to avoid being backed against one of the green-draperied walls. From the encounters of their weapons came a steady succession of spark showers—exploding suddenly into near-fountains of light when the two cone points were the parts of the flames to make contact. Galyan was smiling grimly, thin-lipped and narrow-nostriled. Slothiel, on the other hand, after his first savage attack, fought with a sort of dreamy grace and a relaxed face, as if this were not a duel to the death but some minor sporting engagement in which he had perhaps backed himself with a small bet. But Slothiel's apparent indifference was no true clue to the way in which the duel was progressing. Hardly more than a few weeks ago, it would have looked to Jim more like some smoothly expert dance by two large men with some sort of Roman candles in their hands— a dance intended to demonstrate the rhythm of the man and the beauty of the fireworks rather than anything else. Now he knew better. Moreover, because he knew better, he was able to see that the duel could have only one ending. As graceful and swift as Slothiel was, half a dozen times already Galyan had almost caught him on the disengage from an encounter of the cone tips of their weapons. Sooner or later Slothiel's luck and skill would not prevent him from being a little bit too slow in deflecting the other man's fire.

Galyan was, indeed, the quicker of the two. And in this sort of duel, that meant everything.

In fact, as they all watched, the end came. Galyan leaped to his left suddenly, struck high with his flame, dropped down under the line of Slothiel's countering discharge, and flicked up again inside to slash across Slothiel's left thigh and left upper arm, which held the rod.

Slothiel went down on the polished floor on his right knee, his left arm dangling. His rod dropped and skidded a little way across the floor.

He laughed up into the face of Galyan.

"You find it funny, do you?" panted Galyan. "I'll wipe that smile off your face!"

Galyan lifted his rod to bring it down across Slothiel's features.

"*Galyan!*" shouted Jim, running forward.

The sound of his voice did not stop Galyan, but the rapid beating of Jim's shoes upon the polished floor did. Galyan whirled like a cat.

Jim had drawn the rod from his own belt as he ran. He had just time to get it up and send the flame lancing from it, ahead of him, before Galyan's rod joined its discharge with his in a shower of sparks.

Jim broke the flames of both rods high, disengaged, and stepped back. Galyan laughed.

"Wolfling, Wolfling . . ." he said, shaking his head. "You never really have learned what High-born means, have you? It seems I'll have to give you a lesson?"

"Jim!" called Slothiel from the floor behind Galyan. "Don't do it! You haven't got a chance! Run!"

"You're both wrong," said Jim. Now that he was actually engaged with Galyan, his mind was as cold as ice, and the remote coldness of his voice echoed that iciness within him.

He engaged with Galyan, and they fought through at least a dozen engage-and-disengage actions. Galyan's eyebrows rose.

"Not bad at all," he said. "In fact, very good for any-one not a High-born—and unthinkably good for a wild man. I do hate to waste you, Wolfling."

Jim did not answer. He continued to fight on, warily and conservatively, concerned only with keeping the cone tip of the discharge from Galyan's weapon always out beyond the cone tip of his own flame and mak-ing sure he would not be backed against one of the walls. If he had not had experience fencing with foil, épée, and saber back on Earth, he would never have been able to pick up enough of the technique of han-dling the rods in the few short weeks in which he had trained with Adok. But that experience, combined with his own native ability, was now paying off. Little by little, as the duel went on, he found himself making his moves more surely.

"In fact, why should I waste you?" panted Galyan during one of the engages in which their faces came within a few feet of each other. The white skin of the High-born's features gleamed with perspiration.

"Be sensible, Wolfling, and don't make me kill you. Slothiel has to die anyway—now. But I had large plans for you, as head of my own, new Starkiens."

Jim maintained his silence. But he stepped up the pressure of his attack. Off to one side, without warning, he heard the sound of running feet on the bare floor, and Ro's voice shouting.

"Keep back!"

Jim dared not look up at the moment, but a few seconds later he found himself facing toward the lounge end of the room, and he caught a quick glimpse of Ro, standing beside the fallen Slothiel, holding the rod Slothiel had dropped, and covering Afuan with it. Melness lay sprawled at Adok's feet, and it looked as if the master servant's neck had been broken. Only the unmoving figure of the Emperor, standing over the dead Vhotan, was unchanged.

"Who do you think you are?" snarled Galyan suddenly. "When I speak to you, I want an answer, Wolfling!"

Jim countered a high thrust from the taller figure and stepped to the left in a disengage, without a word.

"All right!" said Galyan, showing his teeth in an almost mechanical smile. "I've had enough of this! I've been playing with you, hoping you'd come to your senses. Now I'm through with that. I'm going to kill you, Wolfling!"

The High-born attacked suddenly, in a shower of sparks, and Jim found himself fighting for his life. Galyan had a tremendous advantage in reach over him, and the taller man was using that reach, as well as the spring in his long legs, to the upmost advantage. Parrying swiftly and continuously, Jim was still forced to give ground. He backed away, and Galyan crowded close upon him, driving him still further backward. Jim attempted to circle to the right, but found that way cut off by the blazing white lightning of Galyan's weapon. He tried to break to the left, but Galyan outreached him. Out of the corners of his eyes he could see the other walls of the room, and from their distances he knew that the fourth wall must be close behind him. If Galyan could pin him against the wall, the restriction of Jim's movements would give the Highborn an advantage that would end the duel quickly.

Galyan's teeth were bared fixedly now, and sweat dripped from his chin. His great advantage in reach cut off any escape to right or left. Shortly, also, there would be no possible retreat straight backward for Jim.

There was only one way out of this prison of flame with which Galyan was fencing him about. That was to outdo Galyan at the High-born's strongest point. Jim must counter Galyan's attack with an attack of his own, which would force Galyan first to halt, then to retreat in his turn. And in such an attack, there could be only one counter to Galyan's advantage in reach—and that was speed. Jim would have to be quicker than the High-born.

There was no point in further hesitation. Jim came out of a disengage and attacked savagely. At the first fury of Jim's onslaught, Galyan gave ground along three steps out of sheer, reflexive surprise. But then he stood his ground.

He laughed hoarsely, pantingly, and briefly. He seemed about to say something, but evidently decided against wasting his breath, of which neither he nor Jim had any to spare. For better than a dozen engages and disengages they stood essentially toe to toe on the gleaming floor, neither one giving an inch.

It was a murderous pace, one that neither man could keep up for another minute without dropping from exhaustion and breathlessness. But Jim did not slacken off, and slowly Galyan's eyes began to widen. He stared at Jim across the twin, clashing streams of fire, through the showers of white sparks.

"You—can't—do—" he gasped.

"I am—" panted Jim.

Galyan's face unexpectedly contorted into a staring mask of fury. He disengaged from Jim's current attack and went immediately into a sweeping circle with the fire from his instrument—almost the type of maneuver that singlestick fighters call a *moulinet*.

It was a simple, raw bid to outspeed the cone tip of flame from Jim's weapon. If Galyan could get ahead of that guarding cone tip, he would have a fraction of a second in which to go back in over Jim's guard and destroy him. Galyan's flame whipped over and down, and Jim's blurred along with it. For a full arc, the desperate race held, without Galyan's weapon gaining—and then, it was Jim whose cone tip moved ahead.

He gained, coming up on the second arc, broke in over the line of Galyan's weapon, and shot the full force of his flame into the taller man's unprotected chest.

Galyan tottered and fell, his own weapon coming around and down, to tap its rod end against Jim's right side just below the ribs before falling from his hand to the floor. Jim felt a sudden coldness and hollowness inside him. Then Galyan was slumped at his feet.

Jim lifted his head slowly, his lungs pumping heavily to restore oxygen to his exhausted body.

He saw, through sweat-blurred eyes, that Slothiel now held the rod that Ro had held earlier, covering Afuan. Not only that, but Slothiel was, amazingly, back on his feet, although he leaned heavily on Ro. As soon as he had breath left to spare for walking, Jim moved slowly from Galyan's dead body over toward Ro and Slothiel.

"Jim . . ." said Slothiel wonderingly, looking at him and slowly putting the rod he held back into his belt. Now he ignored Afuan, as Jim came up, "what are you?"

"A Wolfling," said Jim. "What're you doing back on your feet?"

Slothiel laughed, not entirely cheerfully.

"We heal fast, with the help of our power sources, we High-born," he said. "How about you?"

"I'll do," said Jim. He kept his right elbow pressed close against his side. "But I've left another body for you to clean up. I think it's time for me to go home."

"Home?" Slothiel echoed.

"Back to Earth—the world I came from," said Jim. "The more thoroughly this is hushed up, the better for the Emperor. Nobody will miss me if I disappear, and you can tell the other High-born that Galyan killed Vhotan and the Starkiens in a fit of madness, and you had to kill him in return to protect the Emperor."

He glanced over at Afuan, who stood like a tall, white statue.

"That is," Jim said, "if you can persuade the Princess to keep quiet."

Slothiel looked at her only briefly.

"Afuan won't disagree with me," Slothiel said. "Galyan suggested that if I didn't agree with him, the Emperor might decide I needed isolation and treatment. The same can apply to her."

He turned, letting go of Ro, and walked, a little limpingly but completely under his own power, off the polished floor onto the carpet and up to the unmoving figure of the Emperor. Jim and Ro followed him.

Slothiel touched the Emperor lightly on the arm.

"Oran . . ." he said gently.

For a moment the Emperor did not move. Then, slowly, he straightened and turned about, breaking into a warm smile as he did so.

"Slothiel!" he said. "Good of you to come so quickly. Did you know that I can't find Vhotan anywhere? He was here just a few minutes ago, and I could swear he hadn't left the room, but he's vanished completely."

The Emperor looked down the long length of the polished floor, around the draperied walls, back up and around the lounge, at the carpet, and at the ceiling, over which the colored shapes still played. He looked everywhere but at the still shape down at his feet.

"You know, I had a dream, Slothiel," the Emperor went on, wistfully looking back at the other Highborn. "It was just last night—or at least, it was some time recently. I dreamed that Vhotan was dead, Galyan was dead, and all my Starkiens were dead. And when I went looking around the palace and the Throne World to find the other High-born to tell them about this, there was no one—not in the palace, not on the whole world. I was all alone. You don't think I would ever be left alone like that, do you, Slothiel?"

"Not while I'm alive, Oran," said Slothiel.

"Thank you, Slothiel," said the Emperor. He looked around the room again, however, and his voice became a little fretful. "But I wish I knew what happened to Vhotan. Why isn't he here?"

"He had to go away for a while, Oran," said Slothiel. "He told me to stay with you until he gets back."

The Emperor's face lit up once more with his warm smile.

"Well, then, everything's all right!" he said happily. He threw an arm around Slothiel's shoulders and looked around the room. "Why, there's Afuan—and little Ro and our little Wolfling. Ex-Wolfling, I should say."

He gazed at Jim, and his smile slowly faded into a solemn, rather sad expression.

"You're going away, aren't you—Jim?" he said, plainly dredging up the name from some hidden corner of his memory. "I thought I heard you say something about that just now."

"Yes, Oran," said Jim. "I have to go now."

The Emperor nodded, his face still sadly solemn.

"Yes, I heard it, all right," he said, half to himself. His eyes fastened on Jim. "I hear things sometimes, you know, even when I'm not really listening. And I understand things, too; sometimes I understand them better than any of the other High-born. It's a good thing you're going back to your own world, Jim."

The Emperor's hand slipped from Slothiel's shoulder. He took a step forward and stood looking down at Jim.

"You're full of young energy out there, Jim," he said. "And we're tired here. Very tired, sometimes. It's going to be all right for you and your Wolflings, Jim. I can see it, you know—very often I see things like that, quite clearly. . . ."

His lemon-yellow eyes seemed to cloud, going a little out of focus, so that he stared through Jim rather than at him.

"I've seen you doing well, Jim," he said. "You and the other Wolflings. And what's well for you is well for all—all of us." His eyes unclouded, and once more he was focused on Jim again. "Something tells me you've done me a signal service, Jim. I think before you go, I'd like to finish your adoption. Yes, from now on I declare you to be a High-born, Jim Keil." He laughed, a little, suddenly. " . . . I'm not giving you anything you don't already have."

He straightened up and turned back to Slothiel.

"What should I do now?" he asked Slothiel.

"I think you should send Afuan back to her quarters now," said Slothiel, "and tell her that she's to stay there until she hears something more from you."

"Yes." The Emperor's glance swung around to fasten on Afuan, but she met it for only a moment, before turning furiously upon Jim and Ro, who stood beside him.

"Mud-face! Wild man!" she spat. "Crawl off into the bushes and mate!"

Jim stiffened, but Ro caught hold of his left arm.

"No!" she said, almost proudly. "You don't need to. Don't you see—she's jealous! Jealous of *me!*"

Still holding strongly to his arm, she looked up into his face.

"I'm going with you, Jim," she said. "Back to this world of yours."

"Yes," said the Emperor unexpectedly but thoughtfully, "that's right. I saw it that way. Yes, little Ro should go with him. . . ."

"Afuan!" said Slothiel sharply.

The Princess threw him a glance as full of hatred as the one she had directed at Ro and Jim. She disappeared.

Jim's head swam suddenly. He took a strong grip on himself internally, and the room steadied about him.

"We have to go quickly, then," he said. "I'll send you those Starkiens from my ship, Slothiel. You can keep them close to the Emperor until you're able to get back as many as possible of the other units who've been sent out to the Colony Worlds. If you order them back quickly, you shouldn't lose too many of them to Galyan's antimatter traps."

"I'll do that. Good-bye, Jim," said Slothiel. "And thank you."

"Good-bye, Jim," said the Emperor. He stepped

forward, offering his hand. Jim freed his left arm from Ro's grasp and took the long fingers awkwardly with his own left hand.

"Adok," said the Emperor, without letting go of Jim's hand, but glancing over at the Starkien, "do you have a family?"

"No more, Oran," answered Adok in his usual flat tone. "My son is grown, and my wife has gone back to the women's compound."

"Would you like to go with Jim?" asked the Emperor.

"I—" For the first time since Jim had known him, the Starkien seemed at a loss for words. "I am not experienced in liking or not liking, Oran."

"If I order you to go with Jim and Ro, and stay with them for the rest of your life," said the Emperor, "will you go willingly?"

"Yes, Oran. Willingly," said Adok.

The Emperor let go of Jim's hand.

"You'll need Adok," he said to Jim.

"Thank you, Oran," said Jim.

Ro's grip tightened on his arm once more.

"Good-bye, Oran. Good-bye, Slothiel," said Ro. And at once they were no longer in the palace room, but at the docking berth where Jim had left the ship containing his Ten-units of Starkiens.

Harn was standing just outside the ship, like a man on watch, when they appeared. He turned quickly to face Jim.

"It's good to see you, sir," he said.

Jim unexpectedly felt ship and berthing dock waver and slip around him once more. He pulled himself back to clearheadedness again just in time to hear Adok speaking to Harn.

"The High-born Vhotan and the Prince Galyan are dead," Adok was saying quickly, "and three Starkiens have been killed. The High-born Slothiel has taken

Vhotan's place. You and your men are to go to the Emperor."

"Yes," Jim managed to say.

"Sir!" acknowledged Harn, and vanished.

Abruptly they were inside the ship, Jim, Ro, and Adok. Another wave of disorientation passed through Jim, and he felt Ro helping him down gently onto the level surface of a hassocklike bed.

"What is it—Adok!" He heard her voice, but distantly, as if at the far end of a tilted corridor, down which he was sliding, ever faster, ever farther away from her. He made a great effort, and visualized in his mind, first, the spaceport at Alpha Centauri III, and then, from there, the spaceport back on Earth from which he had taken off. It was his last effort—from now on it would be up to the ship. But from what he had read out of the Files of the Throne World's learning centers, he had no doubt the ship would be able to locate Earth from the directions he had just given it.

He let go, and went back to sliding away down the tilted corridor. But there was one thing more yet he had to do. He fought his way back to consciousness and Ro for a second.

"Galyan burned my side as he died," he muttered to her. "Now I'm dying. So you'll have to tell them for me, Ro. On Earth. Tell them . . . everything. . . ."

"But you won't die!" Ro was crying, holding him fiercely with both her arms about him. "You won't die . . . you *won't*. . . ."

But even as she held him, he slipped out of her grasp and went sliding—this time with no further check or hope of return—down that long tilted corridor into the utter darkness.

Chapter 11

When Jim opened his eyes at last to light after that long slide into darkness, it took him a long time with the help of the light to recognize the shapes of things around him. He felt as if he had been dead for years. Gradually, however, vision sharpened. Perception returned. He became aware that he lay on his back on a surface harder than any hassock; and the ceiling he stared up at was white, but oddly grainy and close above him.

With a great effort he managed to turn his head, and saw shapes that he gradually made out to be a small bedside table, several chairs, and a white screen of the sort used in hospitals. In all, a single room, with a window at the far end that let in a yellow, summer sunlight he had not seen for quite a while. Through the window he could see only sky, blue sky, with a few isolated puffs of white clouds scattered about it. He lay staring at the sky, slowly trying to put things together.

Obviously he was on Earth. That meant that at least five days must have passed while he was unconscious.

But if he was on Earth, what was he doing here? Where was here? And where were Ro and Adok, to say nothing of the ship? All this, leaving aside the fact that he seemed to be alive, when he had certainly seemed to have had no right to be so.

He lay still, thinking. After a little while, absently, he felt the side where the flame of Galyan's torch had penetrated as the High-born had died. But his side felt smooth and well. Interested, he pulled down the covers, pulled up the blue pajama top he seemed to be wearing, and examined that side. As far as he could see, it looked as if he had never been wounded at all.

He pulled the covers up again and lay back. He felt well, if a little heavy-bodied, as if the lassitude of a long sleep were still clinging to him. He turned his head and looked at the small table by his bedside. It held an insulating plastic pitcher, a glass with some remnants of ice floating at the top of the water within it, and a small box of paper handkerchiefs. The signs were overwhelming that he was in a hospital. This would not be surprising if he still had the deep wound in his side that Galyan's rod had made. But there was no wound.

He investigated further. Below the top level of the table by his bed was a vertical surface with a telephone handset clinging magnetically to it. He picked up the handset and listened, but there was no dial tone. Experimentally he tried dialing some numbers on the dial set in the center of the inner face of the handset. But the phone remained dead. He put it back, and in the process of doing so, discovered a button on the vertical surface.

He pressed the button.

Nothing happened. After about five minutes of waiting, he pressed it again.

This time, it was only a matter of seconds before the door swung open. A man entered—a heavy-bodied young man not much shorter than himself, with a thick, powerful-looking body dressed in white slacks and white jacket. He came up to the bed, looked down at Jim without a word, and reached to the bed to take Jim's left wrist. Lifting the wrist, he counted the pulse, gazing at his wristwatch as he did so.

"Yes, I'm alive," Jim told him. "What hospital is this?"

The male nurse, as he seemed to be, made a non-committal sound in his throat. Finished counting, he dropped Jim's wrist back onto the bed and turned toward the door.

"Hold on!" said Jim, sitting up suddenly.

"Just lie there!" said the man in a deep, gruff voice. Hastily he opened the door and went out, slamming it slightly behind him.

Jim threw back the covers and jumped out of bed in the same quick motion. He took three steps to the door and grasped its handle. But his fingers slipped around the smooth, immovable metal as he tried to turn it. It was locked.

He shook the handle once and then stepped back. His first impulse—quenched almost as soon as it was born by the immediate caution of his now thoroughly awakened mind—was to pound on the door until someone came. Now, instead, he stood gazing at it thoughtfully.

This place was beginning to look less like a hospital and more like a place of care for the violently insane. He spun about quickly and went to the window. What he saw confirmed the growing suspicion in him of his surroundings. Invisible from his bed, a mesh of fine wire covered the window opening completely, some four inches beyond the window itself. The wire looked relatively thin, but it was undoubtedly strong enough to be escape-proof for anyone lacking tools.

Jim looked out the window and down, but what he saw gave him little information—merely a width of green lawn bordered on all sides by tall pine trees. The trees were tall enough to cut off the view of whatever lay beyond them.

Jim turned around and thoughtfully went back to sit down on the edge of his bed. After a moment he lay down and pulled the covers up over him again.

With the patience that was so much an innate part of him, he waited.

At least a couple of hours must have gone by before anything more happened. Then, without any advance notice, the door to his room opened and the male nurse came back in, followed by a slight man in his late forties or early fifties with a balding head and narrow face, wearing a white physician's coat. They came up to the head of the bed together, and the slight man in the white physician's coat met Jim's eyes.

"Well, all right," he said, turning his head slightly toward the male nurse. "I won't need you."

The male nurse went out, clicking the door shut behind him. The physician, for such he certainly must be, reached out for Jim's wrist and took his pulse as the other man had done earlier.

"Yes," he said, as if to himself, after a moment. He dropped the wrist, pulled back the covers, lifted the pajama coat, and examined Jim's side—the one that had been wounded. His fingers probed here and there. Abruptly Jim stiffened.

"Sore?" the physician asked.

"Yes," said Jim flatly.

"Well, that's interesting," said the doctor. "—if true."

"Doctor," said Jim quietly. "Is there something wrong with you? Or with me?"

"No, there's nothing wrong with you," said the physician, yanking Jim's pajama top down and tossing the covers up on him again. "As for me—I don't believe it. The only thing I believe is what I saw when you came in here—and that was a small perforation in your right side."

"What is it you don't believe, then?" asked Jim.

"I don't believe that you had a burned area where that perforation was, a burned area at least two inches wide and six inches deep, six days ago," said the physician. "Yes, I've seen the pictures of your ship on television, and I know what that tall girl told me, but I don't believe it. In the first place, with that kind of damage done to you internally, you'd be dead long before you got here. Now, I can believe in a small perforation that heals without a visible scar. But I can't swallow the larger story."

"Is there any reason you should?" asked Jim gently.

"No, there isn't," said the physician. "So I'm not going to worry about it. As far as I'm concerned, you're well and ready for anything—and I'll so advise them."

"Who's them?" asked Jim.

The physician stared down at him.

"Doctor," said Jim quietly, "for some reason you seem to have a bad opinion of me. That's your privilege. But I don't think it's your privilege to keep a patient in the dark—not only about where he is, but about who it is who are evidently concerned with him. You mentioned a tall girl who told you about me. Is she outside right now?"

"No, she isn't," said the physician. "As for answering your question, the people who are concerned with you are officials of the world government. And I've been told that it's my duty not to talk to you except as required in your treatment. You don't require any more treatment, and so I've got no more excuse to talk to you."

He turned and headed for the door. With his hand on the knob, he seemed to experience a twinge of conscience, for he paused and turned back to Jim.

"They'll be sending someone in to see you shortly after I tell them you're well," he said. "You'll be able to ask him all the questions you like."

He turned away from Jim once more, tried the door, and found it locked. He pounded on it with his fist and shouted through it to someone who was evidently on the far side. After a moment the door was cautiously unlocked, and he was allowed to slip out through the least possible opening. The door slammed and clicked shut once more.

The wait was considerably shorter this time. It was no more than fifteen or twenty minutes before the door opened again—and immediately clicked shut once more—behind a man about ten years younger than the physician, with a brown, tanned face and a gray business suit. He came in, nodded unsmilingly at Jim, and briskly drew one of the chairs up to the bed. Jim sat up on the edge of the bed.

"I'm Daniel Wylcoxin," the man said. "Call me Dan, if you like. There's going to be a Government Committee Inquiry, and I've been assigned as your counsel."

"What if I don't want you?" asked Jim mildly.

"Then, of course, you don't have to have me," said Wylcoxin. "Actually, the Inquiry has nothing to do with a court trial. That's to come later, if the Inquiry decides to take that course of action. Actually, you don't legally need counsel, and if you don't want me, I'm not going to be forced on you. On the other hand, it's not likely the Committee would recognize someone else as counsel for you, since—as I say—counsel really isn't supposed to be necessary for you."

"I see," said Jim. "I'd like to ask a few questions."

"Fire away," said Wylcoxin, leaning back in his chair and laying his arms flat on the armrests of it.

"Where am I?" asked Jim bluntly.

"That, I'm afraid, I can't tell you," said Wylcoxin. "This is a government hospital for special people and situations where secrecy is required. I was brought here in a closed car myself. *I* don't know where we are, except that we're no more than twenty minutes' ride from Government Center, where my own office is."

"Where's my spaceship? And where are the woman and the man who came with me?"

"Your ship is at Government Center spaceport," said Wylcoxin, "surrounded by security guards that keep everyone at a quarter-mile distance. Your two companions are still aboard the ship—for which you can thank the Governor of Alpha Centauri III. He's here on Earth, and when government people wanted to move your two friends out and put their own men aboard the ship, the Governor evidently talked them out of it. It seems the woman you have with you is what they call a High-born, and the Governor is evidently scared silly of anyone in that classification. I suppose I can't blame him—"

Wylcoxin broke off to look curiously at Jim.

"I understand the High-born run the Empire?" he wound up.

"They do," said Jim flatly. "What am I doing here?"

"This lady, this High-born—"

"Her name is Ro," interrupted Jim grimly.

"Ro, then," said Wylcoxin, "met the first government people to come aboard your spaceship after it landed. There was quite a well-known group, I understand, because the Alpha Centauri Governor, who's visiting Government Center here, recognized the ship as being one belonging to these High-born. Anyway, Ro let them aboard and told them quite a story, including how you got wounded fighting some kind of duel with a Prince of the Empire. She said you were a lot better, but she didn't object when the government offered to take you to one of our own hospitals for care. Evidently they convinced her that whatever she could do, the kind of medicine you were used to might do you more good in the long run."

"Yes," murmured Jim. "She's not the suspicious kind."

"Evidently," said Wylcoxin. "At any rate, she let them take you. And here you are. And the Committee's scheduled to start its Inquiry as soon as you're well enough to appear before it. I understand the doctor's already certified you in that respect, so the proceedings will probably start tomorrow morning."

"What are they inquiring about?" asked Jim.

"Well . . ." Wylcoxin leaned forward in his chair. "That's the point. As I say, the Inquiry has no relation to any court procedure. Theoretically it's called simply to supply the government with information, so that it will know how to act about you, your friends, and your ship. Actually, and I imagine you expected something like this, it's merely a get-together to determine if there's any reason why they shouldn't set the wheels in motion to bring you to trial for treason."

The final words of Wylcoxin's sentence fell softly on the still air of the hospital room. Jim looked at him for a second.

"You said I 'expected' it?" Jim echoed quietly. "What makes you think I expected something like this when I got back here?"

"Why"—Wylcoxin paused and shot him a keen glance—"Maxwell Holland came back after you left Alpha Centauri III for the Throne World with those other High-born, and evidently he reported you as saying then that you meant to pay no attention to your orders, but to raise any kind of hell you felt like raising at the Imperial Court. Certainly Holland is going to testify to that effect tomorrow before the Committee. Didn't you say what he says you said?"

"No," said Jim. "I said I'd have to follow my own judgment from there on."

"That might sound like the same thing to the Committee," said Wylcoxin.

"It sounds," said Jim, "like this Committee has already made up its mind to consider me guilty of— what was it—treason?"

"I'd say they have," said Wylcoxin. "But then, I'm automatically on your side of it. And your side of it doesn't look too good from where I sit. You were carefully selected to be the man sent in to the Throne World, and trained at a great deal of trouble and expense, so that you could go among these High-born and observe them. Then you were to report back to Earth with your observations, so government could make up its mind whether we were really a lost bit of this Empire, and bound to consider ourselves a part of it, or whether there was a chance we'd evolved on Earth here entirely separately—and really were a different race entirely from the so-called human beings of the Empire. Right?"

"Yes, that's right," said Jim.

"Good, so far," said Wylcoxin. "But now, according to this Ro, instead of merely observing, you started out by getting into a fight with one of the High-born and knifing him aboard the ship going to the Throne World, then followed that up by joining some military bodyguard belonging to the Emperor when you got there, winding it all up by involving yourself in some kind of intrigue in which the Emperor's uncle and cousin were killed, as well as several bodyguards. Is *that* right?"

"It covers the physical facts of what happened," said Jim evenly, "but it distorts them, and the situations that gave rise to them, completely out of recognition."

"You're saying that this girl Ro is a liar?" Wylcoxin demanded.

"I'm saying that she didn't tell it that way," said Jim. "Tell me, did you get the story direct from her, or secondhand from somebody else who heard it from her?"

Wylcoxin sank thoughtfully back in his chair and rubbed his chin.

"I got it secondhand," he admitted. "But if the man who reported what she said to me can make it sound the way I made it sound just now to you, then that's the way government witnesses will be making it sound to the Committee tomorrow morning."

"It sounds more than ever like a hanging Committee," said Jim.

"Maybe. . . ." Wylcoxin rubbed his chin thoughtfully again. Suddenly he jumped to his feet and began to walk up and down the room.

"I'll tell you," he said, stopping in front of Jim. "I wasn't too happy about being assigned as your counsel. Maybe I'd been brainwashed a little myself."

He checked himself.

"I don't say that because so far you've said anything to make me alter my own feelings about you and the situation," he said hastily. "I say that simply because you've opened my eyes to the fact that there might— I say *might*—be a certain amount of prejudice on the other side."

He sat down again in his chair before Jim.

"Well," he said, "let's hear your side of it. What happened from the time you left Alpha Centauri III until you landed back here?"

"I got myself taken to the Throne World," said Jim, looking straight at the other man, "to find out, as you say, whether the Empire was populated by humans we were related to, or whether we were a separate stock from them entirely. Everything else happened after that as necessity dictated."

Wylcoxin sat for several seconds after Jim had stopped talking, almost as if he expected Jim to continue.

"Is that all you've got to say?" he demanded then.

"That's all for now," said Jim. "I'll tell a more complete story to that Committee tomorrow if they care to listen."

"You're deliberately not telling me anything you know that might help you, then," said Wylcoxin. "Don't you understand, I can't be of any use to you unless you're as open with me as you possibly can be?"

"I understand it," said Jim. "Quite frankly, I don't trust you. I trust your goodwill and honesty toward me, but I don't trust your capability to understand what I tell you, any more than I'd trust the capability of anyone else who hadn't been to the Throne World himself."

"Why, man," said Wylcoxin, "that takes in everyone on Earth!"

"That's right," said Jim. "I don't think anyone from Earth could help me much. Not if Max Holland, as you say, is there to testify against me, and the Committee seems determined to find grounds for bringing me to trial for treason."

"Then I can't be any good to you!"

Wylcoxin jumped to his feet out of the chair and headed toward the door.

"Wait a minute," said Jim. "Perhaps you can't help me by defending me, any more than any other Earth-born human can. But you can help me in other ways."

"How?" Wylcoxin turned almost belligerently, with one hand on the doorknob.

"To start off with," said Jim quietly, "by considering me innocent until I'm proven guilty."

Wylcoxin stood for a second with his hand on the doorknob; then his hand dropped free. He came slowly back and sat down in the chair once more.

"My apologies," he said, looking up to Jim. "All right. You tell me what I can do."

"Well," said Jim, "for one thing, you can go to that Committee meeting with me tomorrow as my counsel. For another thing, you can answer a few questions. First—why should the Committee and the government and people in general be so eager to find me guilty of treason when all I've done is come back safe, with a valuable spaceship and a couple of people from the Throne World? I don't see how either of those things could suggest that I had treason in my heart when I was on the Throne World. Of course, there's Max Holland wanting to nail me. But if it was just him, it doesn't seem to me that I'd have too much to worry about."

"Why, don't you understand?" Wylcoxin frowned up at him. "All this talk of treason—all this is because they're afraid that you did things on the Throne World that will make the Empire want to take it out on Earth, in payment or revenge."

"Why?" asked Jim.

"Why . . ." Wylcoxin did not quite sputter, but he

came close to it. "Maybe it's because of you that an uncle and a cousin of the Emperor are dead. Isn't it possible that this Emperor would want to make somebody pay for those deaths?"

Jim chuckled. Wylcoxin's eyebrows rose in astonishment and bafflement.

"You think that's funny?" the other man demanded.

"No," said Jim. "It's just that I suddenly see where it all came from, this fear that has me threatened with a charge of treason. Treason carries the death penalty, doesn't it?"

"Sometimes . . ." said Wylcoxin, grudgingly. "But what're you talking about?"

"I'm afraid I couldn't explain it to you," said Jim. "Tell me, can you go and see Ro aboard the spaceship?"

Wylcoxin shook his head.

"I tried that earlier," he said. "The authorities wouldn't let me go out to the ship."

"Can you send her a message?" asked Jim.

"I think I can do that." Wylcoxin frowned. "I don't know if I can get an answer for you, though."

"An answer won't be necessary," said Jim. "Ro gave me up to Earth's doctors without any protest. So she must be trusting them, where I'm concerned. That leads me to believe that she doesn't know what this Committee is aiming at with me tomorrow. Could you get word to her of what they're after, and what their attitude toward me is likely to be?"

"I think so," said Wylcoxin. More energetically he added, "Yes, I know I can! If nothing else, I can get word to her when she comes in tomorrow morning. They'll be calling her to repeat her story to the Committee. She'll be there tomorrow too, undoubtedly."

"If you can get word to her this evening on the ship, I'd appreciate that more," said Jim.

"I should be able to." Wylcoxin looked at him oddly. "But what do you expect from her? She can't very well change her story from what it was earlier."

"I don't expect her to," said Jim.

"But you said no one from Earth could help you. That leaves only Ro and that other passenger you brought back from the Throne World," said Wylcoxin. "Let me warn you that these are almost in the position of being prosecution star witnesses. In short, you don't have anyone to testify for you."

"I might have." Jim smiled slightly. "There's the Governor of Alpha Centauri III."

"Him!" Wylcoxin's eyes lit up. "I'd never thought of him! That's right—he did put in a good word for your Ro when she wanted to stay aboard the spaceship. Maybe he would speak up in your defense tomorrow. . . . Want me to get in touch with him?"

Jim shook his head.

"No," he said. "Leave that to me."

Wylcoxin shook his head.

"I don't know," he said helplessly. "I just don't know. But I guess I'm along for the ride. Anything else?"

He looked up at Jim.

"No," said Jim. "Just get that message to Ro if you can."

"All right." Wylcoxin got to his feet. "I'll be around about half an hour before it's time for you to be taken into Government Center, and I'll ride in with you."

He went over to the door, rattled the doorknob, and pounded on the door panel.

"It's Wylcoxin!" he shouted through the door. "Let me out!"

After a second the door opened gingerly. Wylcoxin looked over at Jim.

"Well, good night," he said. "And good luck."

"Thank you," said Jim.

Wylcoxin went out, and the door was shut and locked behind him.

Jim lay down on the bed and closed his eyes. For a moment the rush of thoughts that came immediately upon him threatened to overwhelm him. But he stemmed and silenced them with a grim self-control. After a little while, like a soldier in the field and under arms, he slept.

Chapter 12

Daniel Wylcoxin came for him at eight-fifteen the following morning and rode along as Jim was transferred by closed car to the Committee room in one of the government buildings at Government Center. The Inquiry, Wylcoxin told him, was to start at nine.

Jim asked the other man only whether he had been able to get in touch with Ro. Wylcoxin nodded.

"They wouldn't let me out to the ship to see her," Wylcoxin said, "but I was able to talk into the ship from the guard line outside it, on a field phone they've rigged in order to keep in touch with her and that other fellow aboard. I asked her a lot of general questions, ostensibly for answers I needed in acting as your counsel, and slipped the information you wanted given her in between the lines, so to speak."

"Good," said Jim.

However, after that, and during the half-hour ride into Government Center in the closed car, Jim withdrew into himself and ignored the questions Wylcoxin put him, to the point where the other man finally got exasperated and forced himself on Jim's attention by joggling Jim's elbow.

"Look. Give me some answers, will you?" demanded Wylcoxin. "In half an hour I'm going to have to be up there, theoretically aiding and representing you as your counsel. You *owe* me some answers! Don't forget, I got through to Ro for you, and that wasn't easy. There was absolutely no line of communication open to her except that field telephone from the spaceport outside into your ship."

Jim looked at him.

"Government Center is less than ten miles from Government Center spaceport," he said, "isn't that right?"

"Why . . . yes," said Wylcoxin, wondering.

"If I'd been in a building in Government Center, I wouldn't have needed you to get in touch with Ro," said Jim. "At that distance, I could've talked directly to the ship myself."

Wylcoxin looked at him with a mixture of disbelief and puzzlement.

"I'm only pointing out," said Jim quietly, "that there's no point in my wasting valuable thinking time giving you answers you're not going to be able to understand, even if you could believe them. As far as the Committee members, Max Holland, and the other witnesses are concerned—it doesn't matter what they say, or what they ask me. All I'm asking from you, now that you've got word to Ro, is to sit by my side and do whatever seems necessary as things come up."

Jim went back to his thoughts. This time Wylcoxin left him alone with them.

They reached Government Center and the building where the Inquiry was to take place. Jim was kept in a small side room until just before the Committee members were due to appear. Then he and Wylcoxin were taken to their seats in an already filled Committee room.

Jim and Wylcoxin were installed at one of the several tables directly in front of the raised platform with its long table at which the six Committee members would sit. As he came in, he saw, seated separately in the crowd a few rows back from the front row tables, Max Holland and Styrk Jacobsen—the executive heads of the program that had trained him to go to the Throne World—and Ro, as well as a handful of other, minor figures out of his past from the time when he had been selected to be trained and sent.

Ro caught his eye, looking a little pale and anxious, as he came in. She was dressed in a plain white clothlike tunic and skirt, not too remarkably different from the lightweight, summer-colored clothes of the Earth women seated in the same room. But some general effect of her total appearance made her stand out in the crowd, as if spotlighted. Jim's eyes had adjusted to the height and cleanliness of feature of the High-born on the Throne World. Now, in spite of himself, the people of his own world, thronging this courtroom, seemed shrunken and small and drab by comparison. Ro, ignoring all the rest, was looking at him anxiously. Jim smiled to reassure her, as he took his seat, necessarily turning his back on her and the rest of those in seats behind him. The six Committee members came in, representatives of their various area sectors on Earth. The audience rose on order, to wait for the members to take their seats; and at the same time, a buzz of excitement ran through them, as there came in with the other members a small, reddish-brown man, who took his seat to the right of Alvin Heinman, representative from the powerful Central European sector. Jim looked at the small man and smiled faintly. But the other only looked back with extreme solemnity. The members seated themselves, and the audience was told they could regain their seats as the Committee went on to open proceedings.

" . . . And let the records show," said Heinman a little nasally into the recording sensors built in the table before him, "that the Governor of Alpha Centauri III has consented to sit with this board unofficially, in order to give it the benefit of his experience and knowledge in the matter under Inquiry."

Heinman rapped on the table with the gavel and called for the government's Investigating Officer to describe the matter under Inquiry.

The Investigating Officer did so. The word "treason" was carefully avoided, but the Investigating Officer talked a clever circle around it, until there was no doubt left in the minds of those listening to him that this Inquiry had been brought to determine not whether the government should commence treason proceedings against Jim, but whether there was the slightest doubt that the government should not do so. The Investigating Officer sat down again, and Styrk Jacobsen was brought up to answer the questions of the Committee.

These questions had to do mainly with Jim's background and the procedure which had chosen him from several hundred candidates preselected on a worldwide basis to be the man trained to go to the Throne World.

" . . . James Keil," Jacobsen said, "was unusually qualified in many respects. His physical condition was superb—as it needed to be, since we planned to train the man we would send to be a bullfighter. Also, at the time Jim came to our attention, he not only had degrees in history and chemistry, as well as anthropology, but he had established himself as a respectable authority in the field of social and cultural studies."

"Would you say," broke in Heinman, "in character he was markedly different from the other candidates?"

"He was a strong individualist. But then, they all were," said Jacobsen dryly. He was a spare, erect man with silver hair, in his mid-sixties, originally from Odense, Denmark. Jim remembered that Jacobsen, from the first, had taken what seemed to be an instinctive liking to him, as opposed to Max Holland's immediate, instinctive dislike.

" . . . That was one of the requirements for the job," Jacobsen was saying. He went on to list, in order, those requirements as they had originally been laid out. Roughly, they covered unusual physical and mental capacity, emotional stability, and a broad educational background.

"But about this matter of emotional stability," Heinman pounced again. "Didn't you find him unusually—say—unsocial? To the point of being noncommunicative and withdrawn from the people around him? What I mean is, wasn't he from the start pretty much of a loner?"

"Yes. Again," said Jacobsen, "we wanted someone with exactly those traits. Our man would be plunged into an unfamiliar culture—much more unfamiliar than anything he could encounter here on Earth. We wanted him to be as self-sufficient as possible."

Jacobsen had not backed up a step. Though Heinman picked up the questioning for some little time, the silver-haired man refused to give ground. His testimony amounted to the fact that Jim was no more and no less than the man the Project had been set up to find, train, and send out.

With Max Holland, who followed Jacobsen before the Committee, the response was entirely different.

" . . . The other members of the team engaged in the Project," Holland said, leaning forward over the table, a cigarette burning between his fingers, "weren't equipped to consider the risk involved in it—the risk to the Earth as a whole, I mean. In resources and population, our world, to the Empire, is like a baby chick to an elephant. The chick's so small that it's likely to be safe through being ignored, unless by accident or mistake it gets under one of the elephant's feet. Then there's no hope for it. It seemed to me the whole Project ran a serious danger of bringing us under one of the elephant feet of the Empire, either accidentally or by error on the part of the man we were sending in to look at their Throne World. And my uneasiness was increased by the character and attitudes of James Keil himself. . . ."

Holland, like Jacobsen, was closely questioned by Heinman and a couple of the other Committee members. Unlike Jacobsen, Holland was ready and willing to paint a dangerous picture of Jim. Jim, he testified, had struck him as being socially withdrawn to the point of near-paranoia, self-confident and arrogant to the point of near-megalomania. Then, coldly, he reported the conversation he had had with Jim underneath the stands of the arena on Alpha Centauri III, in which Jim had told him that from then on he would have to make his own decisions.

"Then, in your opinion," said Heinman, "this man, even before he reached the Throne World, was already determined to ignore the directives given him and do whatever he chose, regardless of whatever consequences to the rest of the people of Earth that might entail?"

"I do," said Holland as fervently as any bridegroom. That ended his appearance before the Committee.

Ro was called up next. But her appearance consisted only of sitting and listening to a recording that had been made of her own account of what had happened to Jim from the time she had first met him aboard the Princess Afuan's spaceship until the time in which she had brought him back to the spaceport outside Government Center, Earth.

As the recording ended, Heinman cleared his throat and leaned forward as if to speak to her. But the Governor of Alpha Centauri III, beside him, hastily leaned over in his turn and whispered in the Committee chairman's ear. Heinman listened and then sank back in his seat. Ro was released from her interview with the Committee without any further questions.

Beside Jim, through all this, Wylcoxin had been fidgeting in his chair. Now he leaned over and spoke urgently, low-voiced to Jim.

"Look!" he said. "At least let me take advantage of your right to cross-question her. That Alpha Centauran Governor made a mistake when he stopped Heinman from asking her questions. It may have been a kindness to her, but it wasn't any help to you. She *wants* to testify in your favor. If we get her up there, I'm sure we can make a good impression with her!"

Jim shook his head. In any case, there was no more time to argue, because now he was being called upon to answer the questions of the Committee himself. Heinman began, mildly enough, by reviewing Jim's qualifications for being sent as an observer to the Throne World. But he drifted from these almost imperceptibly into sensitive territory.

" . . . Did you at any time have doubts about the wisdom of this Project?" he asked Jim.

"No," said Jim.

"But at some time between your selection as the man to go and when you arrived at the Throne World, you seemed to have developed such doubts." Heinman plowed among the notes before him on the table and finally located what it was he sought. "Mr. Holland reports you as saying on Alpha Centauri III—and I quote—'. . . Max, it's too late for you to interfere now. I've been invited. From now on I make my own decisions.' Is that correct?"

"No," said Jim.

"No?" Heinman frowned at him over the notes he still held in his hand.

"The wording isn't correct," said Jim. "What I actually said was, 'I'm sorry, Max. But it was bound to come to this sooner or later. From here on out the Project can't guide me any longer. From now on I have to follow my own judgment.'"

Heinman's frown deepened.

"I don't see any essential difference," he said.

"Neither did Max Holland, evidently," said Jim. "But I did—or else I wouldn't have phrased it that way."

Jim felt his left sleeve below the tabletop being plucked frantically.

"Easy!" hissed the whispering voice of Wylcoxin in his ear. "For God's sake, take it easy!"

"You didn't?" said Heinman with a faint note of triumph in his voice. He sat back and looked right and left along the table at the other members of the Committee. "And do you deny taking a knife and a revolver in your luggage to the Throne World, over Mr. Holland's objections?"

"No," said Jim.

Heinman coughed dryly, took out a white handkerchief and patted his lips, then tucked the handkerchief away again and sat back in his chair.

"Well," he said. "That seems to cover that."

He reached for a fresh sheet of paper and wrote something on it in pencil.

"Now"—he began leaning forward over the table once more—"you've heard the account of your actions from the time you left Alpha Centauri III until you returned to Earth that's been given us by Miss—the High-born Ro. Have you any exception to take with that account?"

"No," said Jim.

Once more he was aware of Wylcoxin's fingers plucking at his sleeve. But he paid no attention.

"No exception," said Heinman, leaning back once more. "Then I take it you've no explanation at all for these extraordinary actions of yours, completely at odds with your original purpose in being sent to the Throne World?"

"I didn't say that," said Jim. "The account you got is correct. The interpretation of it you've made is wrong. Just as wrong as your assumption that my intentions or actions were at variance with the reason for which I was originally sent to the Throne World from Earth."

"Then you'd better explain those intentions, don't you think, Mr. Keil?" said Heinman.

"I intend to," said Jim.

The response brought a little color to Heinman's somewhat gray cheeks. But the chairman of the Committee evidently decided in favor of letting the implied challenge pass. He waved to Jim to continue.

"The explanation's simple enough," said Jim. "The High-born of the Empire's Throne World"—he glanced at the Governor—"I'm sure the Governor of Alpha Centauri III will agree with me—are quite literally superior beings, not only to what they call the lesser races on their own Colony Worlds, men like the Governor himself"—Jim glanced at the Governor, but this time the small man avoided his eye—"but to our kind of human on Earth, as well. Accordingly, any preplanning of my actions, no matter how thoroughly or capably done here on Earth, could not guide me in an unfamiliar culture of a race whose least member was more capable than our best here on Earth. So I had to face the fact early in my training that I'd have to react to situations as I found them on the Throne World, following my own best judgment and paying no attention to how I knew people back on Earth would have decided."

"You didn't tell your superiors during the training period about this decision, I take it," asked Heinman, still leaning back in his chair.

"No," answered Jim. "If I'd told them early enough in my training to be replaced, undoubtedly I'd have been replaced."

Jim heard a little explosion of breath to his left, a gusty exhalation of despair from Wylcoxin.

"Of course, of course," said Heinman pleasantly. "Go on, Mr. Keil."

"Accordingly," said Jim evenly, "when I got to the Throne World, I discovered that the best interests of Earth would be served there by involving myself in the situation about the Emperor rather than just staying an observer. The Emperor was mad, and his cousin Galyan had been conspiring for a long time to gain control over the Emperor, by eliminating the man who really ran the Empire, Vhotan—the Emperor's uncle and Galyan's also. Galyan's plan called for him to eliminate Vhotan and the Starkiens, who were unswervingly loyal to the Emperor. Then Galyan would assume Vhotan's place, take over control of the Throne World and the Empire, and develop a new corps of Starkiens, loyal not to the Emperor but to himself. The Starkiens were literally a special breed of men, created originally by gene control and controlled breeding over several generations. But Galyan knew he could produce a new breed within two or three generations, given the means and the raw material. And the raw material was to come from us—from Earth."

He stopped and looked at the Committee members behind their long table.

Chapter 13

It was a second or two after Jim had stopped talking before his last few quiet words exploded with their proper implication upon the minds of his Earth-born audience. Then the effect was, in a small way, dramatic. Heinman sat straight up. The other members of the Committee, all up and down the table, reacted with an equal and sudden alertness.

"What was that, Mr. Keil?" demanded Heinman. "You're accusing this Prince Galyan—he was one of the ones killed, wasn't he—of wanting to alter us genetically to some sort of single-minded bodyguards for his own purposes?"

"I'm not accusing him," said Jim evenly. "I'm stating a fact—the acknowledged fact of Galyan's intentions. The fact he acknowledged to me. He planned to do exactly what I say. I don't think you understand"—for the first time a little touch of irony swept into Jim's voice—"that his doing that, by itself, wouldn't have seemed so terrible to the rest of the High-born on the Throne World. After all, the lesser breeds of humans on their Colony Worlds were available material

526

for the High-borns' using. And we weren't even that important. We were Wolflings—wild men and women living out beyond the fringe of the civilized Empire."

Heinman leaned back and turned to whisper to the Governor of Alpha Centauri beside him. Jim sat without speaking until the whispered conversation came to an end. Heinman turned back to Jim and leaned forward. His face was slightly flushed.

"A little while earlier," Heinman said, "you told us that the High-born on the Throne World were superior beings. How can you reconcile the fact they were superior beings with such inhuman plans on the part of this Prince Galyan? Let alone the fact that, according to you, he planned to murder his uncle and dominate his Emperor? If the High-born are what you say they are—and the Governor of Alpha Centauri III, here, agrees with you, at least in that—the Prince Galyan would've been far too civilized to entertain such savage and murderous intentions."

Jim laughed.

"I still don't think you, or the other members of this Committee, understand the cultural situation between the High-born and the humans on the Colony Worlds—or us," he said. "Galyan's plan against the Emperor was an ultimate in crimes, from the viewpoint of any decent High-born, like Slothiel. But his plans about us weren't inhuman at all, as any High-born would see it. In fact, most High-born would consider us lucky to have the benefit of Galyan's attention. In making us into Starkiens, they'd have pointed out, he'd have rid us of disease and made us a much more healthy, happy, and uniform race. Just as the Emperor's Starkiens are disease-free, happy, and uniform."

Once more Heinman held a whispered consultation with the Governor. This time when it broke off, however, both men looked annoyed and a little dissatisfied.

"Are you trying to tell us, Mr. Keil," said Heinman, and it was more of an honest, open demand for information than any of the questions the Committee chairman had asked Jim earlier, "that all the actions you took on the Throne World were justified, not merely for the good of the Emperor there, but for the good of the people of Earth back here?"

"Yes," said Jim.

"I'd like to believe you," said Heinman, and at the moment it sounded as if he actually would have liked to believe Jim. "But you're asking us to take a great deal on faith. Not the least of which is how you could come to know the plans of this Prince Galyan, when they necessarily must have been kept extremely secret."

"They were kept secret," said Jim. "Certain of the Governors and Nobles on the Colony Worlds"—his eyes lingered for a second on the Alpha Centauran Governor—"had to know about his plan to get rid of the Starkiens. The Princess Afuan and Melness, the master servant in the Throne World palace, had to know other parts. But as much as possible, Galyan told nobody but himself."

"Then how could you find out?" demanded another member of the Committee—a short-bodied, fat man in high middle age whom Jim did not recognize.

"I'm an anthropologist," said Jim dryly. "My main field of interest is human culture, in all its types and variations. And there's a certain limit to the variations that can take place in human culture, given concentrated population, no matter how advanced the culture may be. The social arrangement of the High-born on the Throne World, and the social arrangements of the Nobles on the Colony Worlds, which mirrored the Throne World arrangement, were at odds with the cultural level which the High-born themselves believed they had achieved. The High-born—and the colonial

Nobles in imitation—were split into small artificial cliques or groups which operated essentially like *noyaux*."

Jim paused and waited for them to ask him what *noyaux* were. Heinman did.

"The French ethnologist Jean-Jacques Petter coined the term *noyau* as a label for a society of inward antagonism," Jim answered. "Robert Ardrey, writing some years later, identified it as a 'neighborhood of territorial proprietors bound together by a dear-enemy relationship.' The Callicebus monkey is an example of the *noyau* in nature. Each Callicebus family spends its time, apart from eating and sleeping, in going to the borders of that territory which they had marked out for their own among the general treetops and engaging in screaming and threatening with the adjoining family of Callicebus, who have also come to their boundary so that the display of antagonism can take place. This, except for the fact that physical territory was replaced by 'position' and screaming and threats were replaced by intrigue to make the next person or group lose status among his fellows, exemplifies the *noyau*-like situation existing among the High-born on the Throne World. The only ones exempt from it were those like the High-born Ro, because she was an atavism—a throwback to a time when the High-born specialized physical and mental type was not yet fully developed—and therefore the others considered her not able to compete. . . . Although, she was."

Jim paused again. For a moment no one on the Committee said anything. Then Heinman spoke again.

"A little earlier," he said, "you were likening these High-born to superior beings, compared to us here on Earth. Now you're comparing them to a society of monkeys. They can't be both."

"Oh, yes, they can," said Jim. "Ardrey also made the statement that 'nations produce heroes, *noyaux* geniuses.' In the case of the Throne World, which set the pattern for the colonial Governors and Nobles, the process was reversed. Geniuses made *noyaux*. The Callicebus monkey lives in what is essentially a utopia. Food and drink are right at hand for him on the trees. Just so, the High-born on the Throne World also lived in a utopia where their technology took care of every possible physical need or want they could have. Normally, under utopian conditions, they should have grown soft and become easy prey to the members of the human race on the Colony Worlds who did not have it quite so soft. That's the historical turnover of society, in which an aristocracy weakens and becomes supplanted by those from below."

"Why didn't it happen with the High-born?" asked Heinman.

"Because they succeeded in achieving something unique—a practical, self-perpetuating aristocracy," said Jim. "The Empire began by pooling all its best minds on the planet that was later to become the Throne World. When it became the Throne World, it still drew to it anyone of unusual talent who appeared on any of the other worlds. This gave it a small trickle, a small but continuous supply, of new blood. In addition to this, the aristocracy that developed on the Throne World and became the High-born did something earlier aristocracies never were able to do. It required each member of the aristocracy to know everything there was to know about the technology that made the Empire work. In other words, the High-born were not merely pan-geniuses, they were pan-authorities. The High-born Ro, behind me now, given time, materials, and labor, could turn the Earth into a complete small duplicate of the Empire in every technological respect."

Heinman frowned.

"I don't see the connection between this, and their being *noyaux*," the chairman said.

"An indefinitely self-perpetuating aristocracy," said Jim, "runs counter to the instinctive process of human evolution. In effect, it creates an artificial situation in which social, and therefore individual, evolution can't take place. Such an aristocracy, while it can't be destroyed from the outside, therefore has to end up destroying itself. In short—the High-born after certain lengths of time had no alternative than to begin to become decadent. And they are decadent."

The Governor leaned over urgently to whisper in Heinman's ear. But Heinman shrugged him off almost angrily.

" . . . As soon as I realized they were decadent," said Jim, keeping his eye not only on Heinman, but on the Governor, "I realized that the seeds of the destruction of their Empire were already sown. The *noyaux* into which their social patterns had degenerated were evidence of that decadence. In other words, within a few centuries at most, the Empire would start to break up, and no one there would have any time to bother with us back here on Earth. Unfortunately, at the same time, I discovered Galyan's plan to seize power for himself. Not all the High-born were ideally satisfied by the outlet the *noyaux* gave their emotions and hungers. A few individuals—like Galyan, and Slothiel, and Vhotan—wanted and needed the real thing in the matter of conflict and victory, rather than the shadow of its substance, which the bickering between the *noyaux* and the Game of Points offered them. Also, Galyan was dangerous. Like the Emperor, he was mad—but he was *effectively* mad, the kind of man who could put his madness to practical use, in contrast to his cousin. And Galyan had plans for Earth. He would have sucked us into the decadence of the Empire, before the Empire had time to collapse of its own weight."

Jim paused. He felt a sudden longing to look around at Ro, to see how she was taking this revelation. But he dared not turn.

"So," he said, "I set out to stop and destroy Galyan—and I did."

He stopped speaking. The Committee members at the table, the Governor, even the people sitting silent in the room behind him, continued to stay noiseless and unmoving for several seconds, as if they expected him to continue talking. Finally a slow stir along the line of the Committee members signaled their recognition of the fact that he was through.

"And so that's your explanation," said Heinman, slowly leaning forward and peering directly at Jim. "You did what you did to save Earth from a decadent madman. But, how do you know you were right?"

"I'll tell you," said Jim. He smiled a little grimly. "Because I found enough evidence in the records on the Throne World to satisfy me that Earth was, in fact, originally colonized by the Empire—by a party including several High-born, as they were just beginning to be called. And"—he hesitated, then said the words very slowly but clearly—"*I myself am a throwback to those High-born colonists, just as Ro is a throwback. I am a High-born. Otherwise I couldn't have done what I did, in competition with Galyan and the other High-born. I was a throwback to an earlier, healthier version of their aristocracy, and I'd look it even more than I do now if it hadn't been for the treatments that were given me here on Earth to stop my growth when I was ten years old!*"

In the silence following this remark, Jim turned and looked squarely at the Governor. The Governor sat as if frozen, his mouth a little open, his brown eyes staring fixedly at Jim. In one sweep, Jim felt the audience's sympathy and belief in himself, that had been building all during his explanation—even among the Committee members, even in Heinman himself—swept away by a cooling reaction of incredulity and distrust.

"High-born? You?" said Heinman in a low voice, staring at him.

It was almost as if the chairman questioned himself. For a long moment he continued to stare at Jim; then he shook himself back into self-control. Clearly he remembered who he was and where he was.

"That's hard to believe," he said, and his voice had the same note of faint underlying sarcasm that had been in it at the beginning of his questioning of Jim. "What kind of proof have you got to back up such a claim?"

Jim nodded quietly at the Governor of Alpha Centauri III.

"The Governor knows the High-born," said Jim, his eyes fixed on the small man. "Not only that, but he saw me on the Throne World in the midst of the native High-born there. He should be able to tell you whether I am one or not. . . . That is, provided you'll accept his evidence?"

"Oh," said Heinman, not only leaning back, but tilting back a little in his chair. "I think we can accept the Governor's opinion." He turned to the small figure beside him and asked, loudly enough for the room to hear, "Mr. Keil claims to be one of the High-born. What do you think, Governor?"

The Governor's eyes stared fixedly at Jim. He opened his mouth, hesitated, and spoke, thickly accenting the Earth-born words.

"No, no," he said. "He is not a High-born. He could never be a High-born. No . . . *No!*"

A sort of low gasp, a groan of reaction, trembled through the audience behind Jim. Jim rose slowly to his feet and folded his arms.

"Sit down, Mr. Keil!" snapped Heinman. But Jim ignored him.

"Adok!" he said, addressing the empty air.

Suddenly Adok was with them, standing in front of Jim's table, in the little clear space between it and the raised platform on which stood the table of the Committee members. He stood silent, his powerful body darkly gleaming a little under the lights, white power bands stark on his arms, body, and legs.

There was a new, shuddering gasp from the rest of the room. Then silence.

Jim turned and pointed at one long wall of the room.

"Adok," he said. "That's an outside wall. I want you to open it up. I don't want any falling debris or undue heat. I just want it opened."

Adok turned a little toward the wall Jim indicated. The Starkien did not seem to move, otherwise, but there was a wink of light that seemed brilliant enough to blind them all, if it had not been for the extremely short duration of its existence; and something like an unbearable sound, equally cut short.

Where the wall had been there was an irregular opening ten feet in height, fifty feet in length, and with edges smoothly rounded, as if the stone of the wall had been melted.

Through the opening they could see, over the rooftops of a few adjoining buildings, blue sky in which half a dozen cloud masses floated. Jim pointed at the sky.

"Those clouds, Adok," he said, softly. "Take them away."

There were five or six short, whistling noises—again like mighty sounds cut so short that the human ear did not suffer from hearing them.

The sky was clear.

Jim turned back to face the table on the raised platform. Slowly he raised his arm and pointed at the Governor of Alpha Centauri III.

"Adok—" he began. The squat brown figure came hurdling over the table before him, down off the platform, and across the table to Jim himself, reaching out his hands supplicatingly.

"No, no, High-born!" cried the Governor in the language of the Empire. Then, desperately, he switched to English.

"No!" he shouted, twisting his head sideways to look back over his shoulder at the members of the Committee. His voice in its thickly accented speech rang wildly against the silence of the room. "I was wrong! Wrong! He *is* High-born. I tell you, he is!"

The Governor's voice rose frantically, for Heinman and the other Committee members were staring at him with expressions of mixed horror and disbelief. He twisted around on the tabletop to confront them.

"No, no!" he cried thickly. "I don't say that because he pointed at me. No! It's because of the Starkien! You don't understand! The Starkiens obey nobody but the Emperor and those other High-born the Emperor tells the Starkiens to obey. The Starkien couldn't obey like that for anybody but a High-born! It's true! He *is* High-born, and I was wrong! I was wrong! You have to treat him like a High-born! Because he *is*!"

The Governor collapsed into a fit of hysterical weeping, huddled up on the tabletop. Jim felt a hand slide into his own, and looking down, saw that Ro had come from her seat to stand at his side.

"Yes, indeed," Ro said slowly in careful but

unpracticed English, to Heinman. "I am a High-born, and I tell you that Jim is one too. The Emperor adopted him as one, but even the Emperor said that he was giving Jim nothing Jim did not already have. Jim risked his life for all of you, and he brought me and Adok back to make you a people who will some-day inherit the Empire."

She stopped and turned to point to the sobbing Gov-ernor.

"This man," she said, "must have been one of the colonials in Galyan's plot. He sent a stone from Earth in Jim's name. Only it was not a stone, but a device to project a blue, distorting light over Vhotan; and when it did this, the poor Emperor thought he saw the Blue Beast of his nightmares, and was so afraid that he ordered Vhotan killed, just as Galyan had planned. Wasn't it this man who suggested you should try Jim for treason?"

"I lied. I told them the Princess Afuan would shortly remove the High-born Slothiel, and then she would seek payment from Earth for what Jim had done," moaned the Governor, swaying on the table with his face hid in his hands. "But I was wrong—*wrong!* He *is* High-born. Not just by adoption, but by birth. I was wrong, wrong. . . ."

On Heinman's face there was a war of expressions, but gradually dominating them all came the look of a man who had just emerged from many miles of dark tunnels to find a daylight so much brighter than he had expected that it was almost too painful to bear.

Jim looked at him, then nodded down at the weep-ing Governor before returning his eyes grimly to Heinman once more.

"Yes," Jim said. "So now you understand. . . . And you can also understand why the Empire was something to be kept from Earth, at any cost."